Jessica Prince Mysteries
Book One

Jessica Prince and the Crimson Caper

Dana Gricken

JESSICA PRINCE AND THE CRIMSON CAPER

ISBN: 979-8-88653-478-8

Fire & Ice Young Adult Books
An Imprint of Melange Books, LLC
White Bear Lake, MN 55110
www.fireandiceya.com

Published in the United States of America.

Cover Design by Ashley Redbird Designs

Contents

Dedicated to Nancy Drew, both the books and the video games, for being the inspiration for these Jessica Prince novels

One

A TRIP TO MILAN

When the bell rang at Blackwood Academy, I pushed through the chattering crowd of students to reach my locker. We had a whole week off for March Break, and it couldn't come fast enough.

Uncle Henry promised me a trip but refused to say where he was taking me. He was good at keeping secrets, but cracking a mystery was my favorite pastime.

I ran into my best friends, Madison Carter and Tiffany Hampton, near the front doors.

"Hey, girls. What are your plans for March Break?" I asked as we entered the courtyard. "Anything exciting?"

Madison rolled her eyes. "My parents are taking me back to Louisiana. They don't want me to forget where I come from, they said. Oh God, it's going to be awkward seeing my old friends again."

Madison was your typical goth girl—black hair, dark makeup, and knee-high boots. Her family won the lottery a year ago, moved to Willowbrook, and enrolled Madison at Blackwood Academy. We've been best friends ever since.

"And my family's having a reunion this week. Can you

believe that? During March break!" Tiffany cried, crossing her arms. "I don't want to spend time with my cousins. They're so, ugh, what's the word I'm looking for...?"

I've known Tiffany much longer, almost my whole life. Her parents work for my uncle at Prince Enterprises. That was my family's tech company that had made us billionaires. She dressed a lot like me—pink skirts, white heels, and the latest purse—except her hair was as red as fire and her eyes emerald green.

"Careful, Tiffany," Holly Blackwood said, walking up behind us. She had the terrible twins, Lorraine and Kelsey Hartford, by her side like always. "Wouldn't want your parents to find out you're trash-talking your cousins, would you?"

Holly, Lorraine, and Kelsey were the meanest girls at Blackwood Academy—but Holly was by far the worst. Her parents owned our very expensive, very fancy Academy, so she got away with a lot of terrible things. And the twins, Lorraine and Kelsey—who were almost identical to Tiffany with their red hair and green eyes—were her partners in crime. I felt bad for Tiffany that she had to see them more often than Madison and I did.

"See you soon, cousin," Kelsey said to Tiffany, smirking.

"This family reunion is going to be *so* fun," Lorraine added sarcastically.

They pushed past us, knocking into our shoulders. We watched as the three girls hopped into Holly's pink convertible. Holly cut off several cars as she backed up. The drivers honked at her, but she didn't care or pay attention.

"Later, losers!" Holly called out as they sped away, making the twins laugh like hyenas in the back seat.

"God, I hate them," Madison muttered.

"At least you're not related to two of them," Tiffany said,

sighing. "They're going to make this reunion a nightmare for me...."

That was when I spotted him. Eric Worthington. He was dreamy, like a teen heartthrob on a popular Netflix show. He was the quarterback of our football team, and the coach thought he was so good that he might play professionally one day. With his blond hair, ocean-blue eyes, and muscles, he was the boyfriend of my dreams.

He waved at me and smiled as he got into his truck and drove off. I had no idea if I waved back or not. My brain turned to mush whenever he was around.

"Jess? Hello?" Madison snapped her fingers in my face.

"Huh? Oh, sorry. I was distracted."

By a boy I'll never have. Rumors floated around that Holly and Eric were dating, although the two had never admitted it. And besides, his parents—the wealthy Worthingtons—were business rivals of my uncle. That doomed us from the start. Talk about a modern day Romeo and Juliet.

"We asked what you were doing for March break," Madison said as we walked through the courtyard. "You never told us."

"Not sure yet, but I hope Uncle Henry has something good planned. If not, I'll be *so* bored this week without the two of you."

"Same, girl. Same."

After we hugged goodbye, I walked toward the black limousine that waited for me. Larry Kibbler, a kind, graying man in his early sixties with a thick mustache, opened my door. He smiled at me through the rearview mirror as he jumped in the driver's seat.

"Hi, Larry. How's your family doing?"

"Very good, Miss Prince. My eldest daughter gave birth

to a baby girl last night. My wife and I are thrilled," he replied with a smile. "How was school today?"

I sighed. "Filled with too much homework. And mean girls."

"Both terrible things. I trust you'll handle them both with dignity. Now, can I take you somewhere or are you heading home?"

"Home, please. Uncle Henry said he has a surprise for me."

I looked down the sidewalk for my best friend, Ben, but didn't see him anywhere. Had he *really* left without saying goodbye? And especially before March break?

As we drove through the busy streets, Larry turned on the radio. I liked to listen to the world news, especially about the latest crimes and mysteries. True crime was *so* hot right now.

"Fashion enthusiasts are going to love this next story," the radio host said. "The Fashion Palace in Milan is all decked out for Carla Valentine's debut fashion show tomorrow morning. It's said to have been months in the making. This is big for her, as it could make or break her entire career."

I sat up straighter. Carla Valentine was the latest up-and-coming fashion designer from Milan. She had sold her clothes online for years with moderate success, but this was her first fashion show. Everyone all over the world was talking about her. I would've given anything to see her fashion in person.

A few miles from the school, I spotted someone familiar walking down the road. His curly brown hair, Star Trek backpack, and thick laptop were hard to miss. He looked so sad walking by himself in the rain.

I smiled. "Larry, can you pull over? Right beside that boy, if you can."

"Sure thing, Miss Prince."

As the limo stopped beside the boy, I rolled down my tinted window. "Hey, stranger. Need a lift?"

Ben turned, startled before he realized it was me and laughed. "Jess, you almost gave me a heart attack! Thought you were a kidnapper or something."

"No kidnapper today. Better luck next time. Come on, get in," I replied, opening the door.

He jumped into the limo, and his wet hair splashed a little on my lap. He shut the door, and Larry pulled into the flow of traffic.

"Hey, why didn't you say goodbye to me, you big jerk?"

"Sorry, Jess. Just wanted to get out of there as soon as possible. There's only so much of Blackwood I can take."

"Understandable. Where are you heading?"

He shrugged. "Home, I guess. Dad's working late tonight. He probably won't be back until morning. Now I *really* hope there aren't any kidnappers hanging around."

I frowned. "Why don't you stay at my house tonight? I'm sure Uncle Henry won't mind. You can take the guest room. It has to be safer than being home alone at night, right?"

He smiled. "You're a lifesaver, Jess. I owe you one."

"What are best friends for?"

He grinned in response and I slid over to give him some more room.

Benjamin Clark was my closest friend. He was totally out of place at Blackwood Academy as his family wasn't rich like everybody else's. His father was our local sheriff, Norman Clark. I never found out how Ben could afford to go to our school. Madison and Tiffany wondered why I was friends with him, but he was my sense of normalcy—the only thing that kept me grounded.

I couldn't imagine my life without him.

Larry inputted the code at the black gate to Prince Manor, then I waved goodbye to him and hopped out. Ben and I walked through the long field before we approached the chamber doors.

"You know, I've been here a million times and I still can't believe how big your house is," Ben said, glancing around with wide eyes. "Makes mine look uber small."

I laughed. "Your house isn't *that* small, Ben. It's... cozy."

"See, Jess? This is why we're best friends. No one else would've lied to spare my feelings like that."

I laughed and opened the doors, and as I stepped inside, I nodded politely to the housekeepers. Several of my suitcases—pink and frilly, of course—waited in the foyer. I was about to ask one of the housekeepers why they were there but then I noticed Uncle Henry walking down the spiral staircase.

Uncle Henry was never home before dinner. Being the CEO of Prince Enterprises took a lot of time and effort, and I was usually left to my own devices after school. He was dressed in a fancy blue suit, which wasn't too unusual. But the giant grin across his face was.

"Jessica! Glad you got off school early." He walked over to us. "Hello, Mister Clark. A pleasure to see you."

Ben stood straighter and cleared his throat. "You too, sir."

Uncle Henry looked back at me. "Remember that surprise I told you about?"

I nodded. "Of course. How could I forget?"

"Get ready to give the uncle-of-the-year award to me," he said. "I got us front row seats to Carla Valentine's debut fashion show in Milan!"

I squealed and hugged him. "You have no idea how much I love you right now! But how did you do it?"

"Carla's... an old friend of mine. A really old friend."

"Why did you never tell me this before? You know I've been following her career for a little while now. Me and fashion go together like peanut butter and jelly."

"Well, I...just didn't want to talk about it before." He checked his watch. "Anyway, come on, we have to hurry. Our jet's waiting and the show starts tomorrow morning."

I looked back at Ben, who seemed a little disappointed. "Have fun, Jess. I know how much you love fashion. And don't worry about me—I'll be fine at home tonight."

I shook my head. "Why don't you come with us, Ben? He *can* come with us, right, Uncle Henry?"

Uncle Henry nodded. "Of course! All your friends can, if you'd like."

"Oh, Tiff and Mads can't come. They've already got plans. But Ben, you don't have anything planned for March break, right?"

"You're right, and I appreciate it, but... I can't. I really don't have the money to go."

Uncle Henry placed a hand on Ben's shoulder. "Don't worry about that, kid. Consider it a gift for being such a good friend to my niece."

"Oh, I don't know, sir," Ben replied. "I don't want to take advantage of you or anything."

"Stop it, Ben. You deserve this trip—and you know the Princes don't take no for an answer."

He looked at Uncle Henry and then back at me again before he nodded. "All right, you've convinced me. Now I just have to convince one other person. My dad."

"Uh-oh." I watched him pull out his old cell phone and search for his dad's contact. "Good luck."

He nodded just as his dad picked up. "Hey, Dad? Yeah, I

know you're busy with work but I need to ask you something. Jess and her uncle Henry want to take me to Milan for Carla Valentine's fashion show. Yeah, I know you don't like them."

I glanced at Uncle Henry, an awkward silence spreading over us. I wished Sheriff Clark could play nice and get along with us. But pigs had a better chance of flying than that.

"Okay, okay. I'll tell them." Ben hung up, looking at us with a sigh. "Dad said I can go. But that I'll be grounded when I get back."

I shook my head. "Ben, I'm sorry."

"Yeah, but I'm not. Getting grounded for a few weeks is nothing compared to seeing Milan. Freaking Italy! I've never been there before. Really, thank you for this, Mister Prince."

Uncle Henry grinned. "My pleasure."

"I haven't been there either," I said, placing my arm around him, "but I have a feeling this trip is going to be amazing."

Uncle Henry called Larry, then he drove us to Ben's house so he could pack his bags. But not before I could grab a few mystery novels off my bookshelf for the journey. After Ben had his things, we sped to the airport. Ben and I boarded Uncle Henry's private jet called *Lady Luck*. He painted it pink just for me. I smiled at the pilot and stewardess as we took our seats.

"Wow, a private jet. I've never been on one before," Ben said, looking around. "Man, I've only seen this stuff in movies."

Uncle Henry and Larry boarded after us and shut the door. "You kids should sleep on the flight. When we get to Milan, we won't have time."

"Larry, glad you're coming with us," I said. "I didn't know."

Larry smiled. "Your uncle managed to convince me. I would've declined, but my wife told me it was a once-in-a-lifetime opportunity. Can't say no to her—so here I am!"

After about ten minutes, we were ready for take-off. The flight attendant handed us a few snacks before we took off. It was a long flight—a little over twelve hours—so I read the mystery books I brought and chatted with Ben about school and Italy. Uncle Henry did some business work on his laptop to pass the time, Larry solved crossword puzzles, and Ben looked a little bored as he played with the Nintendo Switch he had brought. He paused his video game to glance over at me.

He snorted. "Julia Joy again? You're addicted, Jess."

I nodded. "Emily Pratt knows how to write the perfect mystery, and Julia Joy Steel is the best detective. They take place in the future, actually. Robots, time travel, spaceships. A sci-fi mystery series."

"That's cool. They seem like good books." He was silent for a few minutes before he sighed. "Look, Jess... can I talk to you for a second?"

I placed the book down. "Of course. What's up?"

Before he could tell me what was on his mind, the airplane jolted. My heart raced as I grabbed Ben's hand, fearing we were going down. But then the airplane recovered, and we were, thankfully, still alive.

"Nothing to worry about, folks," the pilot said through the intercom. "Just a little turbulence. Rain likes to make things difficult."

Uncle Henry nodded, looking up from his laptop. "Happens all the time, kids."

Ben exhaled, his face white with fear. "Good. I don't want to die on my first plane ride."

When my heart stopped pounding, I turned to Ben. "What were you going to say?"

"It's nothing," he muttered. "Forget about it."

For the next twelve hours, I went back to reading, sleeping, and snacking. I woke up to someone shaking me, and when my eyes opened, I realized it was Uncle Henry. He smiled at me as Ben and Larry collected their things behind us.

"Good morning, sleepy head. We made it."

Disappointment washed over me that I had missed the view of Milan from overhead, but there would be plenty of time to sight-see. I squealed in delight when I noticed the rain had cleared and dawn was over the horizon.

This fashion show was going to be incredible. I could feel it.

"And now, for my second surprise," Uncle Henry began, opening a suitcase, "I've brought better outfits for us all. I mean no offense, but what you're wearing now isn't fashion show approved."

Ben shook his head. "Mister Prince, I really can't—"

"Oh, but I insist, Ben. Try it on and tell me what you think."

Uncle Henry was already dressed up, so Ben, Larry, and I alternated in the small bathroom. The outfit Uncle Henry picked for me was a strapless pink gown with silver embroidery. I put on some lipstick and eyeshadow to match. Ben looked handsome in his black tux, but I'd never tell him that. It would go straight to his head.

Ben smiled at me. "You look nice, Jess. You should be the one modeling."

I blushed. "Aw, thanks. You don't look too bad yourself."

We grabbed our suitcases and then hopped into a limo my uncle had rented. Uncle Henry gave Larry the address and he assured us he could drive in a foreign country. Soon, we wove in and out of the traffic in Milan. I still couldn't believe we were here.

When the limo pulled up to a large coliseum, I unbuckled my seatbelt. This was it. It was time to see Carla Valentine's creations in the flesh. I only wished Madison and Tiffany could be here, but I settled for talking Ben's ear off instead.

After the limo had sped off, Ben gasped. "Wait—we didn't get our suitcases!"

Uncle Henry laughed. "Don't worry about it, Ben. Larry will take our stuff back to the hotel. But now, for my last surprise. Jess, I've arranged for us to meet Carla Valentine right before the show."

"What? How?" I asked. "Isn't she busy making last-minute adjustments and directing the models?"

"She is, but after prodding for a while, I got her to agree to meet you. We'll have to be quick though—she only said we could pop in and say hello. It's starting soon, so we'd better move it."

Joy flooded my veins. We were in Italy, meeting a fashion designer. It felt like a dream.

"Jess? Are you okay?" Ben asked, looking at me with concern.

All I could do was nod. Uncle Henry laughed. "She's just excited. Come on, you two."

We pushed through the crowd and entered the tall coliseum, known as the Fashion Palace—or *Palazzo della Moda* in Italian. It was here that many fashion designers had gotten their start, and Carla was lucky to have booked it for her first big event. Those trade shows and online sales she had done years before this paled in comparison, but they had helped to establish herself and her brand a bit.

People swarmed like bees inside the Palace as we walked

in. We passed through the foyer and into the stadium where hundreds of seats were set up. Everyone—from regular citizens to fashion designers—was here for Carla. I spotted some very famous celebrities, all wearing their finest clothes. I looked down at my dress and hoped I fit in.

At the very front sat a large runway with flashing strobe lights. Men and women in headsets walked around, preparing for the show. It was loud in the Palace, but I heard someone close by say the show was starting soon.

"This way, kids," Uncle Henry gestured near the back of the stadium. "Hope it isn't too late to meet Carla."

He walked up to a burly bodyguard who stood in front of a door. Uncle Henry pulled out his I.D. and showed it to him. "We're here to meet Carla Valentine. She knows us and authorized it."

The bodyguard nodded. "*Buongiorno, Signore* Prince." His Italian accent made me grin. "*Signora* Valentine is excited to see you again. Her dressing room's through this door. Head on in and take the first left—"

The door burst open, and a woman walked out. But it wasn't Carla. This woman was younger, most likely in her twenties, and was pale-faced and wore glasses. She carried a headset with a clipboard and looked frantic.

"This can't be happening. Not now." She was on the verge of tears and talking to herself more than anyone else. "What am I going to do?"

"Excuse me, miss?" Uncle Henry stepped toward her. "What's going on?"

"I can handle this," the bodyguard interrupted. "*Signora* Arias, what's wrong? You look troubled."

But the young woman paused, unsure of whether to say what was going on in front of us. "Oh, it's nothing to worry about, sir. Please take your seats before the show starts."

"Look, if something's wrong, I want to know," Uncle

Henry urged. "Carla's a good friend of mine. Or, she was at one point. Maybe I can help."

The woman sighed. "No, I don't think you can help. Unless you're a cop."

"*Signora* Arias?" the bodyguard asked again.

"Someone needs to call the police. And quickly." She took a deep breath. "Because Carla Valentine is missing."

Two

A FLASH OF RED

The bodyguard pulled out his cell phone and dialed 112, the number in Italy for the police. Uncle Henry ran his fingers through his blond hair, something he always did when he was stressed. I still didn't know *how* he knew Carla Valentine, but he seemed shaken up by her disappearance.

Signora Arias paced back and forth, while I pulled out a notepad and a pen from my purse. I always brought them with me.

"What are you doing?" Ben whispered.

"Julia Joy always carries a notepad in case she finds a mystery. Even though the books are set in the future, she's pretty old-fashioned."

I scribbled down Carla Valentine's name, the time of her disappearance, and where it occurred, while the crowd seemed to get louder behind me. They had no idea Carla was missing.

"This is the worst thing that could've happened," *Signora* Arias muttered. "The fashion designer's missing, and the show's starting in a few minutes. What are we going to do?"

The bodyguard hung up the phone and nodded at us.

"The *polizia* will be here soon. The inspector will find her, *Signora* Arias. No need to worry."

But *Signora* Arias still looked worried. Out of the corner of my eye, I saw a flash of red. I turned to see a person wearing a crimson trench coat, cape, and fedora, with matching red gloves. Their bright red color immediately stood out.

It seemed out of place with the tone of the fashion show, especially when everyone else was wearing fancy dresses and tuxes. I wouldn't have thought anything of it until I realized they were leaving. And in a hurry. Who would leave a fashion show before it began?

"Stay here," I said to Uncle Henry and Ben. "I need to check something out."

"Absolutely not," Uncle Henry said. "There's been a kidnapping. Only God knows what's going on. I want you to stay close to me, Jess. You and Ben. Just in case something else happens."

I sighed. When Uncle Henry turned to chat with the bodyguard, I winked at Ben, then pushed through the crowd while trying to hurry in my heels. Ben only shook his head as I got away.

The person in crimson turned their head to scan their surroundings. A large red scarf covered their face, and a pair of dark sunglasses shielded their eyes. I couldn't tell if they were young or old, male or female, or any other defining features.

But when they noticed I was following them, they ran toward the exit door.

"Hey! Someone stop that person in red!" I cried as I ran. "Help!"

The people in the crowd glanced at me, but they didn't do anything. Typical celebrities. The person in crimson must've heard my yelling because they sprinted faster than before.

I reached the exit door a few seconds too late. The strange person had already escaped. The exit led into a back alley, and as I glanced around, I saw no one. The sounds of horns honking and tires squealing filled my ears.

But as I walked out, my heel stepped on something soft and squishy. When I bent down, I noticed it was a crimson glove—the same one the person wore. I picked it up and studied it. The fabric was genuine leather. Shoes were more my area of expertise, but this glove seemed designer to me—probably worth a lot of money.

My mind spun with questions. Was this glove left here on purpose for me to find? Was the person in crimson related to Carla's disappearance? And why, if someone was going to commit a crime, would they dress in something so bright and noticeable?

I scribbled down the clue in my notepad and raced back to Uncle Henry and Ben. They waited by the door with the young woman pacing in front of them. I saw no sign of the police yet.

"Where'd you go?" Ben asked.

"And without my permission?" Uncle Henry's cheeks were red, his lips in a tight line. "I told you to stay where I could see you. I turn my back for one second, and you're gone!"

"Sorry, Uncle Henry. But look at this." I showed the glove to everyone. "I found it near the back alley. Someone in a crimson trench coat ran out the door when they saw me following them. Don't you think that's weird?"

"Not really," *Signora* Arias replied. "This is a fashion show. Maybe the trench coat was designer?"

"Then why did they run?" I asked. "That's suspicious."

"Is it really?" *Signora* Arias asked. "Maybe they ran because you were chasing them? I would've run, too."

"I didn't see anyone, *Signorina*," the bodyguard said as he turned to me. "Security's tight around here. But people wear strange costumes to fashion shows all the time. I'm sure no one thought twice about it."

I tapped my finger against my chin. The security guard had a point.

"Are you sure Carla's missing?" Uncle Henry asked. "I know Carla. If someone kidnapped her, she wouldn't go down without a fight —or without leaving a clue."

The woman huffed. "You don't believe me? Fine. I'll take you to her dressing room—well, it's more like a small backstage area—and you'll see she's gone."

"I'll wait here for the *polizia*," the guard said. "I'll let them know what's going on."

Ben, Uncle Henry, and I followed *Signora* Arias through the door. It led into a long corridor with many different rooms, and *Signora* Arias led us down to the last one. I could hear talking and laughing down the hallway. Several tall women with slim, flawless bodies walked past us. I rolled my eyes as Ben stared at them in their revealing dresses and swimsuits.

"Stop staring," I whispered.

Ben blushed. "Oh, no—I wasn't looking at them. I was looking at... okay, you caught me. Sorry. Can't help it."

"The models are getting ready for the show," *Signora* Arias said. "Everything should be ready in a few minutes. The only thing we're missing is Carla!"

"What's your name?" I asked, getting my notepad ready.

"Josephine Arias. I'm Carla's personal assistant."

"And you're American, right? I noticed you don't have an Italian accent like everyone else."

"Very good, Sherlock," she replied, rolling her eyes. "I'm

from New York City. When I found out Carla Valentine was looking for an assistant in Milan, I applied. I've heard of her online merchandise and like a lot of her pieces. A friend and I even went to a trade show she was at a while ago, and she's got something special. I've worked with a few fashion designers back in New York and I guess she liked my resume. I don't regret coming out here for this, but...."

"But what?"

She paused, sighing. "Carla Valentine isn't a nice woman. She can be bossy and demanding, and she's a total know-it-all. If she wasn't a brilliant fashion designer, I would've told her where she can stick her clothes by now. Sometimes, I really regret taking this thankless job."

"Carla? Bossy and demanding?" Uncle Henry shook his head. "That's impossible. She wasn't like that when I knew her."

"Then you must've gotten her good side. Lucky you. But people change," Josephine said. "Still, I hope nothing bad happened to her. I want to design my own clothes one day, and I need this job to get my name out there. You know, schmooze with the right people in the industry? Carla's a powerful friend to have. She's really building a name for herself now that she got this place booked for a fashion show."

"What about surveillance? Does the Palace have video cameras?"

"No, none. Carla deactivated them for her show," Josephine replied. "She's really private. Comes with being in the public eye, I guess. When the owners tried to fight it, she paid them off. Handsomely. I hear she comes from a wealthy family. Half American, half Italian."

"Hmm. Did Carla have any enemies? Anyone who'd want to hurt her or her career?"

Josephine didn't even answer that. "Forgive me for

saying this, but I think you're a little too young to be playing detective. Leave the investigation to the pros, all right? That's what I plan to do. Seems to be the safest option."

Uncle Henry stared at me. "Good idea."

I ignored that—both Uncle Henry and Josephine. People tended to underestimate me. "You didn't answer my question, though."

She sighed. "Yeah, Carla probably has enemies. As I said before, she's not a nice person. I can't name one friend of hers."

"We used to be friends," Uncle Henry mumbled. "Has Carla ever mentioned me? Henry Prince?"

Josephine shook her head, turning the handle on the nearby door. "Nope, not at all. Sorry."

Uncle Henry looked disappointed as we entered a small dressing room. It was really just a part of the backstage area that it looked like the stagehands had thrown together quickly. They put up black sheets to block off the room for privacy, then added racks of clothes, a mirror, and a lot of makeup products on a small table. A beautiful, petite blonde woman stared at her reflection in the bright lights of the mirror. A young stagehand stood behind her, and the woman turned around to snarl at her.

"This dress doesn't look good on me at all!" she cried. "I can't believe Carla would make me wear something this ugly."

I had no idea what she was talking about. I thought the purple gown she wore was stunning. But the more I stared at the blonde, the more she looked familiar.

"I'm sorry, *Signora* Simpson. Is there anything I can do to help?" the stagehand asked. "Anything at all?"

"Yeah. Get out!"

The stagehand sighed and slipped past us, leaving the makeshift dressing room with her head down. The blonde turned to us and sighed. "Great, more people. What do you want?"

"Sasha, Carla's missing. And please, drop the attitude. This is a stressful time for us all," Josephine replied. "Do you know where she went?"

Now I knew who she was—Sasha Simpson. She was a big model in the United States, and her timeless beauty was the reason why. Carla Valentine must've booked Sasha for her debut fashion show. Her online fashion store and trade show history had given her some power, plus she had the money, like Josephine had said, to book Sasha. Carla was going to be *so* much more famous after this show.

Ben looked starstruck as he stared at her. I was afraid he'd drool any second. I elbowed him, and it seemed to bring him back to reality. He blushed and looked away when he realized I'd noticed.

Sasha spritzed some perfume on her neck and shook her head. "No, I have no idea. I'd like to tell her what I think of this dress!"

Josephine sighed, turning to us. "See? I've asked all the models if they've seen Carla, but the answer's always no. You'd think she'd be coordinating with the models right before the show starts. Odd."

"And another thing," Sasha began, "I came out here to Milan because I thought this fashion show would be about *me*. But Carla told me there are other models walking, too! Can you believe that? I deserve better than to be treated like a second-rate model!"

"When did you see Carla last?" I asked, clutching my notepad.

Sasha scoffed. "I don't know. An hour ago? I passed her in the hallway, but she wouldn't talk to me. Looked like she was in a hurry."

"An hour ago? Yes, that's probably around the time she

disappeared," Josephine said. "Strange. Thanks for telling me this now, Sasha."

She sighed. "I'm not her keeper! Why do I care where she went?"

Sasha's attitude was starting to get on my nerves. She was beautiful but needed to work on her kindness. I wrote down her testimony, wanting the questioning to be over with quickly.

"Did she say where she was going? Or why she was hurrying?" I asked. "Anything at all?"

"No. Look, I know nothing about her disappearance," Sasha replied, looking at me in her mirror's reflection. "The fashion show's still on, right? I didn't come all this way for nothing?"

Josephine nodded, checking her watch. "Yes, everything's on schedule. You'd better get to the stage. It'll start in a few minutes."

Sasha pulled a black shawl over her shoulders. "When you find Carla, let me know. I'm demanding a raise for putting up with this. And I deserve a better dressing room. Or, you know, an actual room!" She pushed past everyone, flung aside the sheet flap functioning as a door, then stormed out.

As the material fluttered closed, Josephine glanced around. "Sorry about that, everyone. Sasha has a reputation for being hard to work with. I tried to warn Carla not to hire her, but she never listens to me."

Something was poking out of the vanity table dresser drawer, and it caught my attention. I walked over and pulled on it. It slipped out of the drawer. When I pulled on it, I realized it was a red scarf. It looked identical to the one the person in crimson wore.

It couldn't have been Sasha I chased, could it? But how did she have time to run outside and get back in? It didn't seem likely, though I couldn't afford to rule anyone out right now.

"Do you know how this got here, Josephine?" I asked, holding up the scarf.

Josephine shrugged. "No, not at all. There aren't any red scarves in Carla's collection, come to think of it. Maybe Sasha brought it from home and left it behind or something?"

"Maybe. Could anyone have left this here? Is this a public dressing room for all the models?"

Josephine laughed. "Are you kidding? No, it belongs to Sasha. She demanded a private dressing room like a major diva. The other models were perfectly fine changing in the backstage area. You know, the way it's supposed to be during a fashion show. If someone left this here, I'm sure Sasha would've known about it. And definitely had something to say."

"Either that or someone planted it in advance," I muttered. "Like someone planned this for a while. And Sasha hadn't noticed, too busy getting ready."

"We're getting off track," Uncle Henry said. "Who cares about a red scarf? Carla's missing!"

"You're right. We should split up," I said, noticing Uncle Henry's frown. "Before you say no, Uncle Henry, this is the quickest way to find Carla. So get mad at me later about it and let's search this Palace from top to bottom. We'd better hurry before the show starts."

"I'll come with you, Jess. This person in crimson could be dangerous," Ben said. "And I like being your sidekick."

Uncle Henry nodded. "Fine, but stick together. I'll talk to the celebrities in the crowd and see if they know anything. But I want you to stay safe, Jess. Keep your phone on you at all times, and don't chase anyone else without me."

"Got it, Uncle Henry. I'll be fine inside the Palace."

"I wish I could help you, but we need an emcee," Josephine said. "And if Carla's M.I.A, it'll have to be me. I guess it *will* look pretty good on a resume, though. Silver linings, huh?"

I heard a knock on the door. A second later, the bodyguard walked in. "*Signorina* Arias? The police have arrived."

Josephine sighed. "They better be quick. This fashion show's happening, with or without Carla Valentine!"

As Josephine left the room, I frowned. She seemed so concerned about Carla's disappearance before—until she realized it put her in charge.

And that seemed like a good motive to me.

Uncle Henry vanished into the crowd, and he blended in like he belonged. As he spoke to some of the audience, not wanting to spook them, I retraced Carla's steps. Sasha said Carla walked down the hallway in a hurry. But where did she go next?

"Jess, this is hopeless," Ben said. "We're not going to find any clues. It's like she vanished without a trace!"

"Shh!" I said. "Don't interrupt me when I'm sleuthing!"

As I explored the backstage area, I found Josephine talking with the police near the door. A tall Italian man with a black mustache and gelled hair looked to be the inspector. Josephine kept looking over her shoulder, glancing at the stage. The lights and music would go off any second now.

"Look, Inspector," Josephine began, "I have to go. The show must go on, as they say! Talk to me later, okay? I'd be happy to answer all your questions when it's over."

But the inspector didn't approve of that. "Look, *Signora*, a woman is missing. And a rising celebrity at that. I really must insist—"

But she rushed off, fading into the crowd. Ben and I walked over to the inspector. He nodded at us and reached for his own notepad. "*Ciao*. Who are you?"

"Jessica Prince and Benjamin Clark," I replied. "We know Carla's missing, but we don't know anything about it."

"Yeah, we just got here," Ben said. "But we're worried about her. Are you the inspector?"

He nodded and showed us his badge. "*Sì*, I'm Inspector Luca Esposito."

The Italian police weren't messing around if they sent an inspector instead of a rookie officer right off the bat. Given Carla's fame, it made sense they'd assign a high-ranking officer to find her.

"Well, take a look at this," I said, holding up the scarf and glove. "A person dressed in red was wearing these items. They ran from me when I chased them."

As the inspector took the accessories from me, he shrugged. "I fail to see what's so special about it, *Signorina*. We're at a fashion show, *sì*?"

I couldn't believe no one would take the evidence seriously, especially an inspector. I was about to explain why it was important, but the lights in the room dimmed. The inspector stepped away, whispering to his police officers. I really needed to brush up on my Italian so I could eavesdrop better while I was here.

The crowd hushed as Josephine approached the stage and stood on the runway. She tapped her microphone to ensure it was working. I noticed the models standing off to the side, waiting for their cue. Sasha had her arms crossed and looked impatient but was always picture-perfect.

"Hello, everyone. I hope you can understand me in English," Josephine said. "Welcome to Carla Valentine's debut fashion show—the first of many, I hope. We've all seen her online store and know how incredible her work is. Let's give a round of applause for a wonderful woman and her wonderful designs!"

A wonderful woman? Josephine had told us otherwise.

The crowd clapped and cheered as Uncle Henry pushed his way over to us. I rushed over to him immediately. "Find anything?"

Uncle Henry shook his head. "No, nothing on Carla. I spoke to some high-profile people in the audience, but they claim they haven't seen her."

"That's weird," Ben whispered. "How come no one's seen her? Is she Houdini or what?"

When the crowd quieted, Josephine cleared her throat and continued. "Well, I guess you're wondering why I'm up here instead of Carla. There's a good reason for that. You see... um...."

But she didn't have to make up an excuse. The entire crowd murmured as the front door slammed open, then a shadowy figure walked into the room.

When I turned around, it was Carla Valentine.

Three

SIGNS OF SABOTAGE

Carla Valentine was as beautiful as her pictures—dark curly hair, the clearest olive skin, perfect makeup. And, of course, she dressed fashionably in a long skirt, scarf, and red blazer. Red was definitely her color. But as I looked at her, I saw no signs of distress or pain.

"Is that her?" Ben whispered to me.

I nodded. "Yeah. She doesn't look like she's been kidnapped."

The crowd buzzed with excitement as Carla Valentine pushed through, approaching the stage. Josephine looked pale. It seemed like she wasn't expecting Carla to be back so soon.

"Miss Valentine, there you are," Josephine stammered. "Didn't think you'd make it in time."

Carla scoffed. "And miss the beginning of *my* fashion show? Absurd. Where else would I be at a time like this?"

"We received a call that you were missing, *Signora* Valentine." Inspector Esposito stepped forward. "Your assistant was very worried about you. She even suspected you'd been kidnapped."

The crowd murmured. Some even looked afraid.

Carla laughed. "Missing? That's absurd! As you can see, I was clearly *not* kidnapped." She turned and glared at Josephine. "My assistant can be overdramatic. You'll learn to ignore her, Inspector."

Josephine looked down, her cheeks red.

"Then where were you?" Uncle Henry asked. "We looked everywhere."

"Henry Prince. It's been a long time," Carla's eyes filled with sadness. Then she cleared her throat and composed herself. "If you all must know, I suffer from anxiety. I had a panic attack an hour ago and needed some fresh air. Went out into the back alley to calm myself down."

"That can't be right," I said. "I was out in the alley and didn't see you there."

"Well, I was. We must've passed each other without realizing it. I don't remember seeing you out there, either." Carla turned to the crowd. "Without further ado, after many years of selling my clothes online, I present to you the Carla Valentine Collection in my first official fashion show!"

The crowd cheered, then Carla pulled Josephine off the stage. She pressed a remote and blaring music came out of speakers attached to the walls. She nodded at the models off to the side, then they prepared to strut their stuff.

Sasha smiled and mouthed something that looked like "finally." Swaying her hips, she made her way onto the stage as the first model. She was magnetic as she started her walk, and the crowd watched with huge smiles. Josephine made her way back over to us, watching the show from the crowd.

"What a waste of time," Inspector Esposito said to Josephine. He had to talk loudly over the music.

Josephine sighed. "I'm so sorry, Inspector. When I couldn't find Carla, I just assumed the worst. Better safe than sorry, right?"

"I should charge you for wasting our resources,

Signora," Inspector Esposito replied. "This is not America. The *polizia* do not mess around!"

Josephine continued to apologize, but the inspector was irate. The music drowned out his voice as the show continued. I glanced at Uncle Henry who wasn't even looking at the models. No, his focus was on Carla entirely.

"She looks the same as she did years ago," Uncle Henry murmured. "It's good to see her again, even after all this time."

"What's your history with Carla? Just how close were you two?"

Uncle Henry sighed. "It's a long story, but—"

The crowd gasped and made our heads turn around. When Sasha reached the end of the runway, she slipped. Her right foot—covered in a diamond-encrusted Carla Valentine heel—lifted, then she fell on her back with a loud thud. The crowd gasped as Carla turned off the music and rushed to her side.

"My back!" Sasha cried. "Someone, help!"

"Call an ambulance!" Carla said, scanning the audience. "Quickly!"

As the bodyguard nearby dialed for an ambulance, Inspector Esposito pushed his way through the people to approach the stage. I followed with Ben and Uncle Henry right behind me. When we reached Carla, she ran her finger along the runway before sniffing it.

"*Mio Dio*," Carla swore. "This is cooking oil! This isn't supposed to be here. This is a fashion show, not a kitchen for crying out loud!"

"How did it get there?" I asked.

Carla thought for a moment. "Someone must've put this here on purpose. Coated the runway in oil to make it slippery. It's the only explanation. They wanted my models to fall!"

I looked over at Sasha, who groaned. Her blonde hair sprawled around her, almost like angel wings. With her dress torn and face twisted in pain, tears formed in her eyes. As she looked up at Carla, her tears turned to rage.

"Listen to me carefully, Carla Valentine," she snarled. "If this hurts my modeling career in any way, I'll make you pay for this!"

"Really? Me?" Carla shook her head. "I had no part in this, Sasha! Do you think I'd want my own fashion show to fail?"

Sasha didn't reply, probably because she was in so much pain. The other models looked on in fear but kept their distance. The crowd swarmed the runway, eager to see Sasha's injury.

As everyone turned quiet, I looked a little closer. Someone *had* coated the stage in cooking oil, but only at the very end. The back of Sasha's dress was completely covered in the brown oil.

Someone in the audience tried to help Sasha to her feet, but Carla swatted their hand away. "Don't touch her! If she broke her back, it's too dangerous. Just keep your distance—"

And then the lights went out.

The crowd screamed. Everyone ran toward the exits, people bumping into me and probably everyone else. Uncle Henry reached for me, and I grabbed Ben so no one could separate or trample us. The entire room was pitch black.

"What's going on?" Ben asked to my left.

But the lights came back on a few seconds later. The crowd paused then began to trickle back to their seats.

As I looked up, I noticed the banner hanging on the wall above the runway. Written in red paint, it read: *QUIT FASHION OR ELSE, CARLA. SIGNED, THE CRIMSON CAPER.*

Inspector Esposito gasped and swore in Italian under his breath. The name "Crimson Caper" stuck out to me. Was it related to the person I chased before in the red trench coat and fedora? Or was it just a coincidence?

Josephine rushed over, staring up at the banner with wide eyes. "My God, who would do such a thing?"

"I don't know," Carla said, turning to us. "This is sabotage! Someone's trying to ruin me *and* my fashion show. I just know it! Too many things have happened to be a coincidence."

"What a shame," a male voice said, approaching us. "But it seems like karma, *sì*?"

I turned around to see two men. The one who spoke was young, maybe in his early thirties, with brown hair, hazel eyes, and a reporter badge around his neck. He had a camera in his hands and took several pictures of Sasha, the banner on the wall, and the snarl on Carla's face.

"Stop snapping pictures!" Carla said. "I don't want this in the papers."

"I have every right to photograph this event, *Signora* Valentine," the man said, smirking. "You can't stop me."

Carla huffed in response.

The man next to him looked the same age with black hair, a goatee, and a fancy sequin tux. He stroked his mustache as he smiled at Carla, not saying a word. His face seemed familiar, but I couldn't put a name to it.

"I should've known you two would be here," Carla said, placing her hands on her hips. "Your obsession with me is unhealthy. Maybe you should get a hobby or something."

"Don't flatter yourself," the man with the goatee said. "I'm simply here to keep an eye on the competition."

"Who are these men, Carla?" Uncle Henry asked.

"That's Vincent Rossi, fashion critic and so-called journalist." Carla pointed at the man with the camera around his neck. “He writes bad reviews about me on a daily basis. It’s harassment.”

“What can I say?” Vincent asked, shrugging. “I’m offended by bad fashion, and I feel obligated to tell everyone about it. My mother was a seamstress, and a talented one at that. I learned so much from her. If she was still alive, her work would put yours to shame.”

Carla rolled her eyes and looked at the other man. “And this is—”

“Allow me to introduce myself,” the man replied. “My name’s Enrique Bello. I’m sure you’ve all heard of me by now.”

Ben and Uncle Henry probably hadn’t, considering the confused looks on their faces, but I’d heard his name before. The Bello Brand was a large fashion company in Spain. I had a few hats from his online store. Not that I’d ever tell Carla that.

According to the media, Enrique Bello was a long-time rival of Carla, and the two never got along. It was tough trying to compete in the fashion industry. Designers were always trying to outdo each other. And maybe they’d even sabotage someone to gain an edge.

“Look no further for suspects, Inspector,” Carla said, “because, without a doubt, I’m sure these two men are behind this.”

The ambulance arrived a few minutes later, and I sighed in relief. Sasha hadn’t moved, the expression of pain on her face unchanged. As the paramedics carefully lifted her onto a stretcher, she glared at Carla one last time.

“This isn’t over, Carla,” Sasha muttered. “You’ll be hearing from me—and a lawyer!”

As they carried her away, the inspector pulled out his badge. "You claim *Signore* Bello and *Signore* Rossi are responsible?"

Carla nodded. "I know they are. It's more than obvious. I bet they're working together."

Enrique scoffed. "Preposterous! I barely know *Senor* Rossi."

Carla laughed. "You can't fool me, Enrique. Vincent's always writing great reviews about your designs! There *is* a connection."

"The man has good taste. Never met him before tonight," Enrique replied. "Besides, I wouldn't stoop so low. Your fashion simply isn't worth it, Carla. You haven't even been in the business as long as me. I was holding fashion shows while you were still selling your pitiful clothes online. Why would I be threatened by you?"

"Because I'm better than you, and it scares you," Carla said, her tone taunting. "And we both know it."

Enrique just rolled his eyes but stayed silent. But I wondered if it was true.

"And what do you have to say for yourself, *Signore* Rossi?" the inspector asked.

"I feel the same as Enrique," Vincent replied. "I don't know the man personally. Ask yourself this, Inspector—why would I jeopardize my career over one woman?"

"They're lying. Arrest them!" Carla said, pointing her finger at the men.

"On what charges? We have no proof." Inspector Esposito turned to his officers. "I want this palazzo searched. If there's evidence of tampering, I need to see it."

The officers nodded and rushed off.

Josephine sighed. "What a disaster."

"I don't pay you to criticize me, Josie," Carla snarled. "I pay you to work!"

Josephine took a deep breath. "Then, what would you like me to do, Miss Valentine?"

Carla waved her hand in dismissal. "Oh, just go home, Josie. I don't need you."

Josephine stormed off, tossing her clipboard aside. The audience stood around, waiting for an explanation. Would the show go on?

"I'm terribly sorry, everyone," Carla began as she turned to the audience. "It pains me to do this, but my debut fashion show must be canceled."

The crowd groaned. Some even swore and huffed in anger. After a few minutes, the Fashion Palace started to clear out. Even the models left. What should've been a happy event was now deserted and ruined.

"*Grazie*. Our investigation will run more smoothly without an audience," Inspector Esposito said. "Excuse me, but I must find my officers. *Ciao*."

As the inspector rushed away, Vincent chuckled. "Oh, nothing makes me happier than seeing you crash and burn, Carla."

"Get out," Uncle Henry said, coming face-to-face with Vincent. "And if I hear you make one more snide comment, you'll be doing so with fewer teeth."

I'd never seen Uncle Henry so aggressive before. Carla must've meant more to him than just an acquaintance or old friend.

Vincent smiled at him. "You haven't seen the last of me. The entire world will know what a catastrophe this show was, Carla. I'll make sure of it."

As Vincent left, Enrique nodded. "I must be going, too. But what a tragedy. What's that charming American expression? 'That's show business for you?' Very fitting. *Hasta la vista, Señorita* Valentine."

Uncle Henry glared at Enrique as he followed Vincent

out the front doors. I watched them leave together in the same tinted black European car, looking to be more than chummy. Had they lied to the police before? Were they working together? I scribbled their names in my notepad for later.

Carla sat on the stairs of the runway, sighing. "Josie was right. This fashion show *is* a disaster! Never should've thought I could pull it off. I should've just stuck to what I was good at—online sales and small trade shows—and stayed out of the big leagues."

"Don't say that, Carla," Uncle Henry began, sitting down next to her. "Everything will be—"

Carla rose to her feet, sighing. "Don't try to comfort me, Henry—not now, not when someone's after me. The threat on the banner proves it!"

"But who would go so far to ruin your show?" Uncle Henry asked.

Carla scoffed. "I already told you—it was Vincent and Enrique. They had the perfect opportunity!"

Carla was right about that. They also had a motive. They seemed to despise her for whatever reason. But I had to stay objective about this and consider all the angles, as Julia Joy would.

"And the media will be all over this, thanks to Vincent," Carla muttered. "Just wonderful."

"Let's say for a minute it isn't them," I said. "Just for argument's sake. Anyone else?"

"*Mio Dio*, I don't know. My head hurts too much to think right now," she replied. "Who are you, anyway?"

Uncle Henry stood up. "This is my niece, Jessica. I told you about her years ago."

Carla shook my hand. "*Sì*, I remember—sorry. But I recall her being much younger when you mentioned her."

Uncle Henry laughed. "Yes, she's sixteen now. Kids have a tendency to grow up with time, Carla."

"She's grown into a beautiful young lady. But you're right—time takes everything from us."

I detected a hint of sadness in her voice. Uncle Henry looked down, clearing his throat.

Carla turned to me. "Forgive my rudeness, *per favore*. My emotions are all over the place right now, and I've never been calm under pressure. It's been a long day."

I smiled. "Don't worry. I get it. This is my best friend, Ben Clark."

He waved. "Hello, Miss Valentine. Sorry this happened."

"*Grazie*." She nodded politely at him before turning to Uncle Henry. "I'd like to spend some time with you, Henry—and your niece and her friend. Why don't you stop by my house tomorrow morning for tea? You remember where it is, don't you?"

"Of course, I remember," Uncle Henry said, holding her gaze. "I'd never forget."

They continued to stare at each other wordlessly. I glanced at Ben. He looked as awkward as I felt. Were we intruding on something intimate?

Carla cleared her throat and looked away. "Well, I should get going. *Ciao* everyone, and see you—"

"*Madame* Valentine? May I speak with you, *s'il vous plaît*?"

I turned to find an elderly man in front of us. He had graying hair and a neat beard, and held a bedazzled cane. He wore a top hat with a black suit. I recognized him immediately. He was the biggest fashion designer in the world—and it surprised me that I didn't squeal in excitement. I was wearing his perfume right now.

I couldn't help but wonder why he'd decided to stay

when everyone else had left. Maybe he had hung around to speak with us.

"*Mio Dio,*" Carla swore. "You're Lance LaDoux! Weren't you just in France for a fashion show?"

He nodded, shaking her hand. "*Oui*, but I insisted I'd travel to Milan to see your show, *Mademoiselle* Valentine. You have excellent taste in fashion. I believe you'll go very far in this industry. You've already done so well with your online shop, I've heard."

Carla smiled. "*Grazie, Signore* LaDoux—although, I'm afraid you've caught me at a bad time."

He sighed. "I know—people were gossiping outside and I heard what happened. And I'm terribly sorry. Sabotage is unacceptable, and the culprits must be brought to justice." He smiled. "I know how hard it is to start out as a fashion designer. I pledge to fully reimburse you for your troubles."

"That is very generous of you, *Signore* LaDoux, but you don't have to. You're not responsible—"

"Oh, but I insist. It's the least I can do. I like your work, Carla, and I want to help. If you're interested in holding another show, I'd be delighted to arrange it." He tipped his hat. "*Au revoir.* We'll be in touch, Carla."

As he walked away, Ben leaned in to whisper. "Who was that old guy again?"

"Lance LaDoux. Pretty famous in everything from cosmetics to clothes." I shook my head, chuckling. "You're out of touch with the fashion world, aren't you, Ben?"

He nodded. "Couldn't tell you what was designer around here to save my life."

As Carla collected her purse, Inspector Esposito walked over to us. "Ah, I'm glad I caught you, *Signora*. We found a man lurking in the dressing rooms."

"What? Who is it?" I asked.

"He claims to know *Signora* Valentine very well," Inspector Esposito replied. "I think it's best if you see for yourself."

Four

ALIBIS AND LIES

As we followed the inspector, Carla looked puzzled. "I have no idea who it could be, Inspector. Only those I approve of are allowed backstage. And I don't approve of many. No one I know would lurk around like a criminal."

"This one was. And somehow, this man made it past security," Inspector Esposito replied. "And he refuses to give us answers."

"Man?" A look of recognition spread across Carla's face. "No, it can't be him."

"Who is it, Carla?" Uncle Henry asked. "Who do you think it is?"

Carla remained silent. When the inspector opened the door to the backstage area, a tall man in handcuffs greeted us. He had dark hair that was heavily gelled, green eyes, and a scruffy beard. The officers held him back, making him squirm against his cuffs.

"*Mio Dio*, I told you already," the man began, "I'm innocent! I don't know a thing about the show's sabotage."

Carla sighed. "I should've known you'd come around, Tony. You can't stay away, can you?"

"You do know this man, don't you, *Signora*?" the inspector asked.

Carla nodded. "*Sì*, very well. *Too* well. Antonio Rossi is my ex-husband."

"Ex-husband?" Uncle Henry asked, wide-eyed. "You were married *and* divorced, and you didn't think to tell me? You could've sent me a postcard, at least."

"I haven't seen you in over a decade, Henry," Carla replied. "We don't speak anymore. Why would I tell you anything?"

Henry looked hurt by that. He quieted and took a step back as I spoke up. "His last name is Rossi? Is he related to—"

"Vincent Rossi, the thorn in my side?" Carla asked. "*Sì*. They're brothers—and Vincent blames me for the divorce. He claims I broke Tony's heart."

"You *did* break my heart, Carla," Tony muttered. "I've never been able to get over you, *amore*."

"I didn't mean to hurt you," Carla replied, "but my career must come first if I want to succeed. You knew this when you started dating me, Tony. When I blew off dates to fill orders for my website, you were warned."

Uncle Henry crossed his arms. "I know that better than anyone."

I scribbled down the information about the new suspect. Vincent's dislike of Carla ran deep—and it was personal. It gave him another motive to ruin her debut fashion show. But was Tony responsible in some way, too?

Carla sighed. "Release him, Inspector. He's innocent."

"Wait a second," Ben said. "How can you be so sure?"

Carla laughed. "For starters, my ex-husband isn't smart enough to pull off sabotage. He got himself caught, didn't he?"

"You have a point, *Signora*," Inspector Esposito replied, turning to Antonio. "Why are you here, *Signore* Rossi?"

"I wanted to see the fashion show, but Carla didn't invite me. I was worried she'd see me coming in through the front door. And then she'd kick me out," Antonio replied. "So I snuck in through the back alley."

The back alley? That was where I had chased the Crimson Caper. Was it just a coincidence?

"Where were you during the sabotage, *Signore* Rossi?" the inspector asked. "Do you have an alibi?"

Antonio shook his head. "No alibi, Inspector. I hid in the shadows to watch the show. But listen, I'd never do this. I still care about Carla."

Carla smiled. "You have a good heart, Tony. Let him go, Inspector."

The police officers looked at the inspector for approval, and he nodded. They removed Antonio's handcuffs, and he rubbed his wrists. Out of the corner of my eye, I noticed Uncle Henry shooting glares at him.

"Did you see anything suspicious?" I asked. "Maybe the person who was responsible?"

"No, I didn't see anything like that. Wait." Antonio paused. "I did see someone in a red trench coat before the show started. Couldn't see their face, though."

"And what were they doing, *Signore* Rossi? Could you tell?" the inspector asked.

"They were poking around the stage area. They seemed to know their way around the Palazzo. They could work here, *sì*?"

"I'll speak with all the employees and see if they know anything," Inspector Esposito replied, tucking his notepad in his jacket pocket. He turned to me. "It appears you were right, *Signorina*. I'm sorry I didn't take the glove and scarf seriously before."

"It's all right," I replied. "It did sound pretty far-fetched. I'm just glad someone else saw them."

"Just great," Carla muttered. "Some freak in a red trench coat's trying to ruin me."

"And they're trying to make it known," I said. "By leaving the glove, they wanted to draw attention to themselves—to make a statement for some reason."

"I'll have my officers ask around for someone who matches that description. We'll be in touch, *Signora* Valentine," the inspector said. "I hope we'll find the culprit soon."

The inspector and his officers left, and Carla looked at Antonio. "I know you still care about me, Tony, but it's been a year since we divorced. You need to move on and leave me alone. If you don't, I'll call the inspector and report you for stalking."

Antonio shook his head. "I can't do that, Carla. If you love someone, you never stop protecting them. Ever. We'll meet again, *amore. Ciao.*"

When Antonio was gone, Carla sighed. "I should get going, too. I need a long nap after today. Perhaps a bubble bath, too."

"Wait, Carla," Uncle Henry said. "We need to talk."

"Tomorrow, Henry. We can talk then," she replied softly. "I need to go—I need time to process everything. *Ciao.*"

Before Uncle Henry could stop her, Carla picked up her purse and rushed out the front door. We stood in silence for a few minutes in the empty Palace as Uncle Henry stared at her spot on the floor.

"I think Carla was right. That art critic guy seems guilty to me," Ben said. "What do you think, Jess?"

I shrugged. "I don't know yet, but I plan to find out. Right now, actually."

Ben raised his eyebrows. "What are you talking about?"

"I need to prove my theory right," I replied. "Come with me."

Uncle Henry wasn't in the mood to talk, but he sighed and followed me anyway. I led them outside to the back of the building, near the alleyway and the exit door. It was empty except for the three of us.

I tugged on the door to walk back inside, but it wouldn't open.

"You can't open it from the outside," I murmured. "There's no way anyone—Antonio *or* the Crimson Caper—could've snuck in through this door. It's impossible!"

Uncle Henry's eyes lit up. "Do you think Antonio was lying then?"

"I don't know. Maybe there's a simple explanation," I said. "But right now, I'm putting everyone on my suspect list."

It was sometime in the afternoon when we left the Fashion Palace. The three of us were exhausted from the long flight and the fashion show, so Uncle Henry told Larry to drive us to our hotel. As the limousine pulled up to the luxury hotel, Ben whistled.

"What a beauty," he said. "Better enjoy this while it lasts."

"I think our stay will be a little more extended than planned," Uncle Henry said. "I don't want to go home until this situation with Carla's resolved."

"Then I'd better call my dad," Ben said, glancing at me. "You know the sheriff. He'll get mad if he's not kept in the loop."

His father could be so uptight and demanding. I hoped Ben wouldn't get in trouble for staying with us a little longer than planned. It was bad enough he was already grounded when he got home. What else could the sheriff do—super ground him?

"What about me, sir?" Larry asked. "I can't afford to stay in Milan any longer than a day."

"Don't worry, Mister Kibbler. Your food and lodging will be paid for, and your family will be compensated while you're away," Uncle Henry replied, turning to us. "Come on, kids. It's been a long day. I'm told this hotel has the best buffet. Let's get some grub."

While Larry parked, Ben and I followed Uncle Henry into the lobby. He spoke with the concierge, who gave him four separate keycards. He then gave one to me and one to Ben, and while he didn't give us any instructions, his pointed look spoke volumes.

"We get our own rooms? You're the best, Uncle Henry!"

Ben opened his mouth to speak, but Uncle Henry interrupted him. "Oh, no, you don't, Mister Clark. I won't hear that you can't accept this. Please, take it."

Ben nodded, grinning. "Then, I'll just say thank you instead. You have no idea what this means to me, Mister Prince."

By then, Larry had joined us. He also got a keycard and looked overjoyed to have a room by himself. We headed as a unit to the elevators.

After we separated to find our rooms, I changed out of my fancy pink dress and put on a simple skirt and blouse instead. The room was everything I could've hoped for. It had a small kitchen area, a flat-screen TV and couch, a gleaming bathroom, and delicious-looking mints on the pillows. On the balcony, I spotted a hot-tub and several hors d'oeuvres sitting on a table.

Uncle Henry took the middle room—another unspoken message about us being on our best behavior—but it was also a safety issue. We could both get to Uncle Henry if there was a problem in the night. Ben's key opened the room to the left, leaving me the one on the right.

As I snacked on the hors d'oeuvres, I looked over the balcony's railing and smiled at the beautiful view of Milan. We were staying on the fourth floor, and you could see everything from this height.

If the sabotage wasn't weighing on my mind, I would've enjoyed the view a lot more.

I heard arguing coming from Ben's room even though we were far away from each other. The walls were thin, and it sounded like he was on the phone. A minute later, the door that connected Uncle Henry's room to mine opened. Ben came in wearing blue jeans and a tank top, much different than the nice suit he wore earlier. He sighed and shook his head.

"Well, that went as bad as I thought it would," Ben muttered. "Dad wouldn't stop yelling after I told him I was staying in Milan for a little longer than expected with you. Besides being grounded, I know he'll punish me some other way."

"Sorry, Ben. Do you want me to get Uncle Henry to talk to him? He could convince him it's not your fault."

He scoffed. "Don't bother. Dad hates rich people—especially Henry Prince, as you know. It'll just make things worse."

"Right. Well, speaking of phone calls," I said, pulling out my cell phone, "I should call Tiffany and Madison and let them know where I am. Do you want to say hi?"

He shrugged. "Sure, but I don't think they like me very much."

I scoffed. "Oh, come on. They like you just fine!"

But Ben was right, although I'd never tell him that. Tiffany and Madison thought Ben was a little weird, as most of the people at Blackwood Academy did. It might've bothered Ben, but I didn't care what people had to say. They would gossip no matter what.

I called Madison first, then she picked up after a few rings. It sounded like she was somewhere with a lot of cars and wind in the background. "Hey, Jess. What's up?"

"I could ask you the same thing. Where are you?"

"In Mom's car. We're almost to Louisiana," she replied. "What's up?"

"I'm in Milan. Hang on, let me get Tiffany on the other line," I said, inputting her number for a three-way call.

Tiffany answered quicker than Madison. I could hear silverware clanging and voices in the background. "Oh, I'm glad it's you, Jess. Hanging out with my family is torture! I'd kill for someone else to talk to."

"No killing necessary. By the way, Mads is on the other line. Ben's here, too," I said. "Say hi, girls."

Tiffany didn't say anything, but Madison did. "Wait a second—you're in Milan with that weirdo Ben Clark and not us? I'm hurt, Jess."

"See? They don't like me," Ben whispered, and I made a face at him.

"Hang on. Why are you in Milan?" Tiffany asked before she gasped. "Wait. Did you go to see Carla Valentine's show? I heard about it on TV."

"Oh, that's right. I also heard it was sabotaged. Is that true, or just another stupid rumor?" Madison asked. "Spill it, girl."

I told them everything about the sabotage—the suspects, the Crimson Caper individual, and Carla's weird relationship with Uncle Henry. Ben stayed silent and shook his head as we gossiped. He didn't understand girls at all.

"You love mysteries. This'll be perfect for you," Tiffany

said. "Only wish I could be there instead of at this dumb family reunion."

"Me too. Hey, let's tell Holly where Jessica is right now. We need to *really* rub it in," Madison said.

Tiffany laughed. "Good idea. She'll be so jealous! Can't wait to see the look on her stupid face."

"Same. We're almost in Louisiana so I have to go," Madison said. "But I'll tell you this—thanks to my years of watching *CSI: Las Vegas*, I've learned a few things. The person who committed the crime always seems the least likely to. That's how it works in fiction, anyway."

"I'll keep that in mind. See you later, girls," I said and hung up.

I expected Ben to make a snide comment about Tiffany and Madison. He wasn't too crazy about them, either. But he didn't. The room was quiet. I glanced over at him, and he wore a worried expression.

"Ben, what's wrong?" I asked. "You look deep in thought."

"I, uh, I am. Do you remember on the plane, right before the turbulence?" Ben asked. "How I was trying to tell you something?"

I nodded. "Yeah, of course. Is everything all right?"

"Well, actually—"

Uncle Henry burst through the door. He still hadn't changed out of his suit. Come to think of it, I never saw him wear casual clothes. He probably felt like he had to be CEO-worthy all the time.

"Great news, kids. The buffet's still on downstairs," Uncle Henry said. "They've got everything, too—burritos, pizza, burgers, sushi. It's included with our stay, so don't feel bad about eating too much, Ben."

Sushi was my favorite. I couldn't help but squeal in excitement.

I turned to Ben. "Let's talk later, okay? I'm starving."

Ben nodded, giving me a smile. "Yeah, sounds good. It's not that important, anyway."

"Go ahead downstairs, Ben. Larry should be there already. We'll meet you in a few minutes," Uncle Henry said. "I need to speak with Jessica."

Ben nodded and closed the door as he left. I looked up at Uncle Henry, worried. He rarely used my full name unless I was in trouble—or the situation was serious.

"Everything's fine, Jess. No need for the frown," he said. I relaxed a little. "I know you're curious about Carla and me. I would be too."

"I am, but only if you're comfortable sharing it."

He sighed. "I have no choice. Given my history with Carla, the inspector might consider me a suspect. It *does* look suspicious, considering I arrived right before the sabotage."

I knew Uncle Henry was innocent, but I saw his point. "All right. Go on. I'm listening."

He took a seat on the bed. "Carla and I were once engaged."

My jaw dropped. "What? When? How?"

"Twelve years ago. I was in Milan on business. It was a whirlwind romance. Never expected to fall so hard. We got engaged after a month of dating, but I thought it would last."

"Why don't I remember her?"

"You were just a kid. It was years before your parents' accident."

I swallowed the lump in my throat. I didn't like to talk about Mom and Dad's deaths. "Why didn't you marry her?"

"Our jobs got in the way. Back then, she was just launching her online shop and doing some small trade shows. She wanted to make it in the fashion world, and I'd just inherited Prince Enterprises," Uncle Henry replied. "It wasn't a good time for us. We were too busy, so we broke up. Barely kept in touch. When I learned you were a fan of her, and that she was hosting a fashion show at the Palace...well, maybe the tickets were a gift to you *and* me. A chance for me to see her again and make sure she was okay after all this time apart."

"Oh. Do you still love her?"

Uncle Henry turned silent for a few seconds. "You never stop loving someone, Jess—no matter the time or distance between you. But if we'd gotten married, I think we would've divorced by now, just like her and Antonio. Maybe our break-up was a good thing."

"Maybe. But do you know anyone who'd want to hurt her?"

Uncle Henry shook his head, rising to his feet. "Not at all. Back when I knew her, everyone loved her. Obviously, things have changed. Her personality is completely different now. Like Josephine said, Carla's bossy, demanding, and downright rude at times. Must be the stress from the fashion industry. I know how much the pressure can get to you as a businessman." He walked to the door. "Anyway, come on. We don't want Ben to think we abandoned him, now do we?"

I followed him into the hallway before I paused, checking my pockets. "Oh, shoot. Forgot my phone. Go ahead without me."

Uncle Henry nodded and left. I entered my room, spotting my phone on my bed, right where I'd left it. As I picked it up, I decided to take a picture of Milan before I joined the others. I could send it to Tiffany and Madison, and they'd have proof to show Holly.

As I snapped a photo from the balcony, something on the ground level caught my eye. It was a person in a red trench coat—and they were looking up at me, their face hidden by that large scarf.

Five

TEA AND TERROR

When we made eye contact, the Crimson Caper sprinted into the crowded street. This was my only chance to catch them. Even though I knew Uncle Henry wouldn't approve, I had to do it anyway.

I raced out of my room and down the stairs, bumping into hotel staff and other tourists. I rushed out into the street where the Crimson Caper had stood, looking up at me.

But they were gone. I saw no hint of red in the crowd.

There was only another red glove on the ground, most likely left for me to find. It was almost as if they were taunting me—playing a game of hide and seek. As I stared down at the glove, standing near the doors of the hotel, an employee walking inside saw me.

"Excuse me, *Signorina*? May I help you?" one of the staff members asked.

"Did you see anyone hanging around the hotel? Someone in a red trench coat, maybe? They tend to stick out in a crowd."

"I saw no one. I can ask the other staff if you'd like."

I nodded, and he rushed off inside. I stared out into the

busy streets of Milan, hoping to see the Crimson Caper again, but they were gone. How could they vanish without a trace?

When the staff member returned, he shook his head. "No one knows anything, *Signorina*. I'm sorry."

I sighed but thanked him anyway. The Crimson Caper had a real knack for disappearing—but how much longer would this last?

I caught up with Uncle Henry, Ben, and Larry in the dining room. When I showed them the glove, their faces turned white with fear.

"The Crimson Caper knows who and where we are. They might be after us," I said. "We need to be careful."

No one said a word about it after that. We were too terrified to think we might be in danger. As I scarfed down some pizza *and* sushi, I mulled over my whirring thoughts.

How did the Crimson Caper know where we were staying? And why were they so concerned with us, anyway?

We spent the rest of the day in the hotel. I read more of my mystery books, Uncle Henry caught up on some extra work, and Ben watched TV in Italian. A news reporter sat behind a desk as pictures of Carla Valentine, Sasha's fall, and the inspector flashed across the television screen. People in the audience had taken lots of pictures on their phones.

I didn't know what the reporters were saying, but it couldn't have been anything good.

Some of the images caught my eye. Someone took them backstage, in areas where journalists and regular people couldn't go. It meant one thing.

Someone involved in the show's production took these pictures and sold them to the media. It didn't mean they were behind the sabotage, but it was still suspicious. But who—and more importantly, why?

Ben decided to stay on the pull-out sofa in my room—with Uncle Henry's permission and the adjoining room's door left ajar—and I was glad. I didn't want to be alone with the Crimson Caper on the loose, and despite being several stories up, made sure to lock my balcony door. Even after all that, I didn't sleep very well. And when I did, my dreams consisted of a faceless individual in a red trench coat. The flash of crimson was enough to keep me awake.

The next morning, I put on a lot of concealer to cover the dark bags under my eyes, then met with Uncle Henry and Ben in the hallway. Larry rushed downstairs to collect the limousine for us.

"Should we stay here?" I asked Uncle Henry. "I'd understand if you wanted to see Carla alone. You know, given your history."

Uncle Henry shook his head. "This isn't a date, Jess. We're going over there for one purpose—to find out more about the Crimson Caper. Carla could know something helpful."

"Not to burst anyone's bubble, but is it a good idea?" Ben asked. "I'm not a scaredy-cat or anything, but the Crimson Caper's stalking us. Maybe we should stay out of it and let the inspector do his job."

Uncle Henry scoffed. "The inspector doesn't know Carla like I do. She might not open up to him. If something bad happened to Carla and I wasn't there to help her, I don't think I'd forgive myself."

As we walked downstairs and headed into the lobby, Larry burst through the revolving doors. He hunched over, trying to catch his breath. It looked like he ran over from the parking lot.

"Larry, what are you doing here? Did something go wrong with getting the limo?" Uncle Henry asked.

Larry nodded, taking a deep breath. "The limo's outside, sir, but there's something on it you should see. I wanted to warn you beforehand."

Alarmed, I looked at Ben who had a similar expression. We followed Uncle Henry past the revolving doors where tourists were coming and going. Larry had parked our limousine a few feet away. As we approached, I saw what he was talking about.

In red, someone had written, *STAY AWAY FROM CARLA*.

I ran my finger along the letters and nodded when they smudged. "It's lipstick."

"Then the Crimson Caper has to be a woman," Ben said. "The trench coat, the scarf, the lipstick. Girly stuff."

"Or it could be a man pretending to be a woman to throw us off," I replied. "And guys can like makeup too."

"Hmm. Good point. See, I never would've thought about that."

As they talked about the lipstick, I bent down. When I ran my fingers along the ground, I found something that felt like a plastic tube. Someone threw it underneath the limo.

I pulled it out and discovered it was a tube of red lipstick. But the label was missing as if someone scratched it off on purpose. I doubted there would be any fingerprints on it—especially if the Crimson Caper used gloves. They didn't seem stupid enough to leave such obvious evidence behind. They were no amateur.

Using my sleeve to not get further fingerprints on it, I held the lipstick up for the others. "See? I was right."

"Poor Carla." Uncle Henry ran a hand through his hair. "She deserves better than this."

"Am I still driving you to Miss Valentine's house, sir?" Larry asked.

Uncle Henry nodded. "Yes. I won't let some lunatic threaten me—not when it comes to Carla."

After snapping pictures of the evidence, I used a napkin from my purse to wipe off the lipstick marks. Uncle Henry took a seat in the front with Larry and Ben, and I hopped in the back. As we drove away, I scribbled a few thoughts down in my notepad.

"What are you writing?" Ben asked, leaning over.

"A possible clue. I think I know what brand of lipstick this is."

"But there's no label. How can you tell?"

"For one thing, I take my makeup very seriously. And second, I'm pretty sure I have this shade back home."

"Anyone can buy lipstick, Jess. Why would it matter what brand it is?"

"Because," I began, "this lipstick's manufactured by Lance LaDoux's cosmetic company. See the little LL on the bottom? It could be nothing, but I don't believe in coincidences."

"Which means?"

"A possibility of three things—Lance LaDoux's the Crimson Caper, he's working with the saboteur, *or* someone's trying to frame him by using his particular brand of lipstick."

I didn't know which one was worse.

Carla lived in a beautiful house in Monferrato, a historical region of Piedmont in Northern Italy. The house sat tucked away, hidden in the countryside of endless fields, farmland, and vineyards. It was an important wine district in a territory cut in two by the river Tanaro, about an hour and a half from downtown Milan. The perfect escape after everything that's happened.

Except for the slew of cars and journalists in front of the house. They snapped pictures, shouted questions, and crowded Carla's lawn. Her curtains were closed, trying to hide the inside of the home.

I noticed Vincent Rossi in the front of the crowd. He wore a smirk as if he was enjoying all the pandemonium. He was still a high suspect on my list.

"What the hell's going on?" Uncle Henry asked.

"Media vultures," Larry muttered, slowing the limo. "Just as bad as the reporters back home."

"It was all over the news last night," Ben said. "At least, I think it was. Hard to understand in Italian. And I was too lazy to get up and turn on the subtitles."

Uncle Henry sighed. "We have to get in there, Larry. Do what you must."

Larry nodded. "We'll go around the back, sir. I hope Miss Valentine doesn't mind if I trample her grass and lovely flowers."

We sneaked around the side of Carla's home, Larry maneuvering the limo through the nearby field, banging into flowers and grapes being grown for wine. None of the journalists were back here. They seemed too busy trying to catch a glimpse of Carla near the front. Their mistake.

"I'll text Carla and tell her we're here. With all these journalists outside, she probably won't answer if we knock," Uncle Henry said. "I hope her number's still the same after all these years. That it hasn't changed like her personality."

He sent off a quick text and, a minute later, the backdoor opened with a quiet squeak. Carla poked her head out. She was dressed in a robe and slippers with no makeup on and messy hair.

For a fashion designer, this was rock bottom.

"Henry? Are you there?" she whispered.

Uncle Henry, Ben, and I exited the limousine, shutting our doors quietly. It was a miracle the journalists hadn't heard us yet, but it was impossible to hear anything over their shouting. A lucky break for us.

"I'll wait right here for you, sir," Larry said. "Good luck. I hope you find some useful information."

"Thanks, Larry. Here's hoping."

Carla locked the door behind us once the three of us were inside. Her house was glamorous and expensive, but also messy and disheveled. The yelling quieted in here. Carla flicked on a light while smoothing down her uncombed hair.

"You've caught me at a bad time. I completely forgot about our tea!" Carla said, sighing. "Between the fashion show, the Crimson Caper, and the journalists stalking me, I'm starting to feel like a failure."

Uncle Henry reached for her hands and caressed them. "You're not a failure, Carla. I'll help you. I'm personally going to find the Crimson Caper and teach them a lesson."

"*We*," I corrected. "*We're* going to help you."

When Ben didn't say anything, I elbowed him. "Ow! Yeah, of course, we'll help you, Miss Valentine."

Carla pulled her hands from Uncle Henry's and looked away. "I'm not sure that's such a good idea, Henry. I've been doing a lot of thinking, and maybe we should let it go."

Uncle Henry scoffed. "What are you saying? You're going to let this criminal win?"

Carla shrugged. "If it keeps us safe, why not? What if this person is dangerous? I won't have murders on my conscience."

"We don't know they'll resort to that. I can't believe you'd back down from this. The Carla I knew was strong and determined—not someone who gives up."

"Things have changed," she replied, walking closer. "Don't act like you know me, Henry. It's been years!"

The room turned quiet. Uncle Henry glared at Carla, but then his eyes softened. I looked at Ben awkwardly.

Carla cleared her throat. "Take a seat, *per favore*. I'll be right back with that tea I promised yesterday."

As she scurried into the kitchen, Uncle Henry took a seat on the couch and crossed his arms. "I can't believe her, Jess. If someone was out to ruin my business, you're damn right I'd hunt them down."

Ben shrugged, taking a seat next to him. "I don't know, Mister Prince. I'd be a little scared to go after this person, too. Uh, in a manly way, of course."

I shook my head at Ben trying to sound macho. Beside the kitchen archway sat a little table with an answering machine. A relic from the past I had never seen before. A call was coming through—and I was curious. I walked over as the message played through the room.

A male voice echoed through the machine. "Good morning, Miss Valentine. I'm calling from the *New York Times,* returning your call regarding an interview—"

Carla rushed into the room with tea in her left hand and used her right to stop the message on the answering machine. She looked up at me with an angry scowl. "What do you think you're doing?"

"Oh, sorry," I stammered. "But we couldn't help but overhear the message."

Carla sighed. "No, it's fine. Just don't do it again. I value my privacy, you know."

"I understand," I said. "Josephine said that was why you disabled the security cameras at the fashion palace. But now that I've heard it, I have to ask. What was all that about?"

"More journalists bothering me. I just delete them and move on," she muttered, setting out the tea for everyone. "If they're not breaking down my front door, they're calling my home phone. I've gotten calls from all over the world. I bet that weasel Vincent gave them my number and house address!"

"Maybe he did. Anyway, you have a lovely home, Miss Valentine," I said, trying to butter her up for questions. "What can you tell us about it?"

"*Grazie*. My grandparents bought this house—used to make wine here and ship it to Milan. That earned my family their money. Sadly, I've spent most of it on my fashion career. To start up my online shop and travel to trade shows. I have very little left."

Uncle Henry sat forward. "If you need a loan—"

"No, Henry," Carla said. "While that's nice of you, I need to do this on my own."

He nodded, dropping the subject. I sipped my tea and cleared my throat. "Can I ask you some questions, Carla?"

Carla shrugged. "I guess so. Don't know what more I can tell you, though. I've given all my information to the inspector."

I pulled out my notepad. "Vincent said something at the fashion show. He mentioned karma—like you deserved this."

"It's just as I said before—he blames me for divorcing his brother. It takes two to ruin a marriage, you know," Carla muttered. "I still think Vincent's guilty."

"How did you and Antonio meet?"

Uncle Henry balled his fists. Clearly, he didn't want to hear it.

"Oh, don't remind me...." She trailed off, shaking her head before she continued. "Tony was an obsessed fan. Followed me around, sent me love letters. He bought an order online, saw my picture, and became enamored. After a while, I found it endearing. It was nice to be wanted. But my career became too busy, and I divorced him. Anyway, that was years ago. I've moved on. Sadly, he hasn't."

"Is he an art critic like his brother?"

Carla shook her head. "Tony, an art critic? *Mio Dio*, don't make me laugh. He doesn't know the first thing about fashion. Tony's done some odd jobs—mostly maintenance and construction. Kind of a freeloader, actually."

Uncle Henry made a disgusted face at me, but Carla didn't notice. No doubt she could do better.

"Where's Josephine? Doesn't she live with you?"

"No, she lives in an apartment in the city. I've been paying her rent since she came here to help me with my fashion show. Come to think of it, I don't know where Josie is. I haven't heard from her since the fashion show."

"Isn't that weird?" Ben asked. "I mean, she's your personal assistant, right?"

Carla nodded, pulling out her cell phone. "*Sì*, you have a point. Give me a second."

As she fiddled with her phone, Uncle Henry leaned over. "What are you doing?"

"Tracking Josie. There's an app for that."

"You're tracking your personal assistant? Isn't that, like, illegal?" Ben asked.

Carla scoffed. "Oh, don't be ridiculous! As her employer, I have every right to know where she is. I haven't been paying her rent for nothing, you know."

"You have a smartphone *and* an answering machine?" I asked. "Pick a century."

Carla snorted. "Very funny. I love that answering machine. My grandmother got it for me. I'd never let it go, no matter how old it is. And it still works, so why get rid of it?"

"Ah, I get it," I replied. "Well, where does it say she is right now?"

Carla gasped. "It lists her current location at the airport! Her apartment's nowhere near there. She has no business at the airport that I know of."

Uncle Henry rose to his feet, setting his teacup down. "Only a guilty person would try to flee the country after a crime. We need to follow—"

A loud crash echoed from the kitchen. It sounded like glass breaking and a thud landing on the floor.

Carla put her teacup down and clutched her robe. "*Mio Dio*, I think someone's broken in!"

"Stay here—all of you," Uncle Henry whispered. "If the person's dangerous, I'll yell for you to run outside. The journalists might be annoying, but at least you'll be safe in the crowd."

"You can't go back there!" I said. "What if they have a gun?"

But Uncle Henry wouldn't listen to me, as usual. And he had the nerve to wonder where I got my stubbornness from. Carla, Ben, and I huddled by the front door in case we had to make a break for it. A man yelped in surprise before two sets of footsteps approached us.

Uncle Henry dragged Antonio Rossi around the corner. He released Antonio and tossed him to the floor. Antonio didn't resist or fight back. He looked guilty as sin.

"Tony? What are you doing here?" Carla asked, crossing her arms. "I thought I told you to leave me alone!"

"Seems your ex-husband has a listening problem," Uncle Henry teased. "Or would he prefer to answer to the inspector?"

"No. Please don't call the *polizia*!" he cried. "I don't want to go to jail."

"Then why are you here?" Ben asked.

Antonio looked up at Carla. He hesitated.

She shrugged. "Go on. Tell them the truth."

Antonio sighed. "I'll admit it. I have an obsession with my ex-wife. I guess I was going to steal some of her clothes."

"Why?" I asked. "To sell them?"

"No." Tony looked down. "To... to keep. As a keepsake. Didn't expect anyone to be home with all the journalists outside. But they didn't see me sneak in through the back."

"Oh, Antonio." Carla placed a hand on her forehead. "You're such a fool!"

"*Sì*, possibly. But answer me this—if you loved someone, would you be able to let them go?"

Uncle Henry pulled him to his feet. "No, of course not, but I wouldn't stalk them, either. Seems a little suspicious if you ask me. Especially in light of all this Crimson Caper business."

"He's not the Crimson Caper. He doesn't have the intelligence to pull off something like that," Carla said. "But if he comes around again, and he's caught, I'll have no choice but to call the police. Let him go, Henry."

Uncle Henry shrugged. "If you insist."

He opened the front door and shoved Antonio toward the swarm of reporters. They pounced on him and started shouting questions. On his back, I noticed something peculiar. A piece of red fabric. It could've easily been from a red scarf or a trench coat.

The journalists shouted more questions, nearly trampling Antonio as Uncle Henry slammed the door shut. I looked out the window as Vincent helped his brother to his feet, shielding him from the mob. I'd question Antonio about the red fabric soon, but I had questions for Josephine first. Time was of the essence with her. I didn't want her to leave the country. And I didn't want to risk getting trampled in the crowd to speak to Antonio right now, anyway.

I closed the curtains and turned to Uncle Henry. "Anyway, we'd better find Josephine. If she's responsible, we can't let her get away."

Uncle Henry nodded. "You must've read my mind, Jess. Carla, get dressed, and we'll escape through the back."

Carla nodded and disappeared into her bedroom. When she returned, fully dressed, Uncle Henry opened the back door to find a crowd of journalists waiting for us. I couldn't even see the limousine anymore. I turned around, noticing journalists still on the front lawn. Some of them must've seen us and rushed around the back.

"Oh my gosh," I cried. "We're trapped in here."

FLIGHT RISK

Carla paced, on the verge of tears. "I can't believe this! First, these journalists stalked my house, now they won't let me leave?"

"Everything will work out, Carla," I said. "We'll find a way to—"

Uncle Henry's cell phone rang, then he held it up to his ear. "Hello? Larry? I can barely hear you!" He nodded and put the phone down, turning to us. "The journalists swarmed the limousine. It was too dangerous to stay, so he drove back through the field. He's waiting a few blocks down."

"Great. Now our ride's gone!" Ben said. "Can't you call the police?"

Carla scoffed. "The *polizia*? They don't care! If we're not in danger, they won't lift a finger around here."

"We can't get out the front or the back," I said, "but there must be another way. Do you have any ideas, Carla?"

She stopped pacing and nodded. "*Sì*, my wine cellar has an emergency escape. That's where my family used to store their bottles of wine. I barely use it, but I know it can get us out of here."

"Where does it lead?" Uncle Henry asked.

"To the vineyard. And eventually the street. We'll be far away from everything, including the limo."

Ben shrugged. "We don't have any other choice. Come on. I need to get out of here. I'm feeling a little claustrophobic. In a manly way."

I rolled my eyes. "Ben's right. Show us the way, Carla."

Carla nodded and flicked on the light switch that led into her cellar. It was even messier and darker down here, with old, discarded clothing scattered around. I spotted several bottles of old wine and design supplies. On a dirty workbench in the corner, I noticed something odd.

A red fedora sitting on the table. It looked like it could've belonged to the Crimson Caper.

"Is this your hat, Carla?" I asked.

Carla shook her head. "No. My fashion line doesn't make hats. Not yet, at least. We stick to dresses and lingerie. I don't know how it could've gotten down here."

Antonio could've left this here. He proved he could break into her house. What else is he capable of? And how many times has he sneaked into the house without getting caught?

Uncle Henry opened the door that led to the surface and looked up. The sunlight's warmth poked through, and the journalists' shouts were far away.

"The coast is clear," he said. "Let's be quiet, okay? We don't want to draw their attention."

After we'd walked up the stairs, Carla locked the door, then pulled it closed behind her. "I don't want anyone to sneak in while I'm gone, but locking the cellar means *I* can't get back inside, either. I don't have a key. *Mio Dio*, what a mess."

"Don't worry, Carla. I'll book a room for you at my

hotel. Free of charge for your troubles," Uncle Henry said. "I'll take care of you until the Crimson Caper's found."

Carla shook her head. "That's sweet, but I can't take advantage of you like that, Henry. I'll find another place."

"I want to make sure you're safe, Carla. Do me a favor and stay with us, okay?"

Carla sighed. "You always knew how to drive a hard bargain. All right, Henry. I agree."

I glanced at my surroundings. I saw nothing but vineyards, growing olive trees, distant farmhouses, and the bright sunshine. The only upside was that I didn't see any more journalists. In the distance, I heard farm animals.

But the countryside in Italy was beautiful, and despite our problems, I forced myself to enjoy it.

"Larry said he parked that way," Uncle Henry said, pointing a mile ahead of us. "Don't know where exactly, so we'll have to search for it."

Ben sighed. "This is going to be a long walk, isn't it? Aw, man, I'm already tired."

I scoffed, pointing down at my heels. "You think *you* have it bad? These are brand new shoes!"

After half an hour of walking through the warm, sunny countryside, all four of us sweated and panted. We found the limousine a little while later, and Larry looked at us with concern and pity. We took our seats with sighs of relief, then I leaned my head on Ben's shoulder.

Larry blasted the air conditioning when he saw our skin gleaming with sweat. "Rough day, sir?"

Uncle Henry nodded. "You don't know the half of it, Larry."

"I'm really sorry I abandoned you back there. I swore I had a good reason, sir. You should've seen those journalists. Wide-eyed and shouting, just like wild animals. They were rocking the limo back and forth to try to get to me inside. They thought Miss Valentine might be in there!"

Uncle Henry shook his head. "I'm not angry with you, Larry. You had every right to protect yourself. Can you drive us to the airport and make it quick? We need to stop someone from getting on a plane."

Larry nodded, stepping on the gas. "Right away, Mister Prince. Whoever's trying to escape, do you think they're responsible?"

"I don't know yet," I said, "but I consider Josephine Arias a suspect. She has motive, means, and opportunity. And boarding a plane right after the fashion show was sabotaged looks pretty suspicious."

Carla scoffed. "If my own personal assistant's out to get me, I swear she'll pay for this."

I thought we'd be too late by the time we made it to the airport. Between fighting through the paparazzi, walking on foot for a while, *and* driving through the crowded streets, we'd wasted a lot of time already. But I crossed my fingers anyway and hoped for the best.

As we pushed through the swarm of people, a voice overhead made an announcement in Italian before it translated into English. "Now boarding for flight 212 to New York City."

Carla gasped. "That's probably Josie's flight. Hurry!"

We rushed toward the long line of people at the various desks, searching for flight number 212. The crowd made it difficult to see, and the loud sounds from the planes drowned out our voices. Glancing around, I noticed a familiar woman in the crowd.

Josephine. She dragged her suitcase behind her and had her passport ready in her hands. We called her name, but she couldn't hear us over the noise.

"She's about to pass through security!" Ben said. "If we don't catch her now, she'll be gone forever."

"Not on my watch!" Carla said, pushing her way to the front of the line. Some people cursed at her in Italian. "One ticket, *per favore*. And hurry!"

The woman at the desk handed her a ticket after viewing her passport, then Carla sprinted and dove on top of Josephine. They both landed on the floor with a loud thud, then Josephine's suitcase went flying. It seemed like the entire airport—including the staff—stopped what they were doing to stare at them.

"My God. Carla!" Uncle Henry said. "What are you doing?"

"You sabotaged my show, didn't you?" Carla asked, still on top of Josephine. "Admit it!"

Josephine scoffed. "That's ridiculous. Get off me!"

"Not until you admit it!"

Several security guards sprinted around the corner, tearing Carla off Josephine. Both Carla and the security guards argued in Italian, so I couldn't understand what they were saying. They restrained Carla as Josephine rose to her feet, collecting her suitcase. In the scuffle, the luggage blew wide open.

And a red trench coat—exactly the same kind the Crimson Caper wore—fell out. But it didn't look finished.

"There's the proof we need!" Carla said, noticing the suitcase. "You're the Crimson Caper, aren't you?"

Uncle Henry crossed his arms. "It does look bad. Care to explain yourself, Josephine?"

Josephine sighed. "This is exactly what I was trying to avoid! Ugh."

"What? Going to jail?" Carla asked, fidgeting in the guards' grasp. "You can't cover it up any longer, Josie. We know it's you!"

"Let her go," Josephine said to the guards. "Carla's not a danger to anyone. At the very least, I guess I do owe her an explanation."

Carla nodded, breaking free from the guards. "*Sì*, you do. You can start by explaining why you betrayed me."

Josephine shook her head. "No, you've got it all wrong! I'm not the Crimson Caper. I don't know who it is, either."

"Then why do you have their outfit with you?" I asked.

Josephine sighed. "It was my blueprint—my first copy. A few months ago, I received an anonymous phone call. They used a voice changer, so I don't know who it was. Anyway, they demanded I make them two sets of a red trench coat, fedora, scarf, and gloves. Had to make a rough practice coat to figure out what I was doing."

"You never knew who they were?" Ben asked.

Josephine shook her head. "I asked, but they wouldn't tell me. They told me to leave the clothes on a nearby park bench, and they'd put the money in a tree. I was only allowed to collect it a few hours later."

"And you didn't think that was odd?" Uncle Henry asked.

Josephine shrugged. "Well, yes. But somehow, they knew I wanted to be a fashion designer. They paid me in cash—a lot of it. I couldn't refuse an opportunity like that, whether I knew who they were or not."

"A red trench coat is a weird outfit to request," I said. "Did they say why they wanted it?"

Josephine shook her head. "Not at all, but I didn't ask. When you held up the red glove at the fashion show and told me about the trench coat, it clicked. I realized they hired me for it months in advance."

"And instead of coming to me and explaining yourself, you decided to take off like a coward?" Carla asked, crossing her arms. "Pathetic."

Josephine put her hands on her hips. "Come to you? Why would I do that? The red trench coat wasn't the only reason I wanted to leave for New York."

"Spit it out, Josie. No more secrets and lies," Carla said. "Tell us everything."

Josephine sighed. "Fine. You're a terrible boss, Carla. Controlling, demanding, arrogant. You know how much I want to be a fashion designer—how much I look up to you. But you've done nothing but treat me like a servant! I do a lot for you, and I'm tired of your disrespect. Why shouldn't I leave?"

"That's nothing like the Carla I remember," Uncle Henry said, turning to her. "What happened to you?"

Carla sighed. "I'll admit, I've changed a lot in the last twelve years. I was never perfect, but the fashion world can change you, Henry. And not for the better, either."

"Wow. Who knew clothes could turn someone into a terrible person?" Ben whispered to me.

"Look, you have to stay in Milan, Josephine," I said. "You have to tell the inspector what you know."

"I wanted to, but I was scared he'd think I was guilty. Worst of all, I was scared the Crimson Caper would come after me."

"I have a solution," Uncle Henry said. "I'll book you a room at the hotel we're staying at. Carla's coming too. We'll keep an eye on you. Trust me—the Crimson Caper won't get you there."

I nodded. "If we stick together, we should be safe."

Josephine sighed. "Fine. I *have* grown fond of Milan. It's a beautiful city."

"Has the Crimson Caper ever contacted you again? To place another order or for any other reason?" I asked.

"No, not at all. I thought my job was finished."

"Do you know their number?"

"Sorry, no. It said unknown number."

I thought for a moment. "If they *did* call you again, could you agree to make them new clothes? We could ambush them and find out who they are."

Josephine hesitated. "I'd have to think about it. Sounds dangerous. And I really don't want to be involved any more than I already am."

I nodded. "I know, but it might be our only lead to the Crimson Caper. You can help catch this person. For good."

"I'll decide if they ever call again. Can we get out of here? I'd feel much safer in a hotel right now."

Uncle Henry nodded. Before we were allowed to leave, he smoothed things over with airport security—I was surprised they hadn't already detained us—and they finally let us go. As the five of us walked out of the crowded airport, I felt like someone was watching me. And as soon as we reached the front doors, I realized why. A swarm of journalists huddled near the entrance, blocking us in. It was like Carla's house all over again. She groaned, placing her hands on her hips.

Larry waited for us in the parking lot with the engine running. It was hard to see the vehicle with the flashing lights from the cameras.

"*Mio Dio*, not again!" Carla cried. "They're everywhere! Why can't they just leave me alone?"

"Hate to say it, but sabotage makes a good story," Josephine said. Carla glared at her. "What? It's the truth."

The security guards followed us, helping us push through the mob. I blocked my ears as they shouted intrusive questions. Carla didn't seem to mind the questions. She looked cool, calm, and collected, much different from this morning.

"How are you feeling, Carla?" one journalist asked.

"Your fans want to make sure you're okay!" another said.

"Do you know who sabotaged your show?"

If this was the lifestyle Carla had to put up with, I pitied her. Journalists never even bothered us this much back home with my uncle as the CEO of a famous company.

Carla paused when we neared the limousine. She turned to the reporters, plastering a big smile across her face. They shoved their microphones at her, desperate for anything she had to say.

"*Grazie* for your concern," she said. "This difficult time has taken a lot out of me, but knowing the fans and journalists care makes me smile. I promise once this is over, I'll give proper interviews."

"She knows how to handle the media," Ben whispered. "Guess she's feeling better."

The reporters asked more questions, but Carla hopped into the back of the limo. The four of us followed her, then Uncle Henry tapped the back of Larry's seat.

"Get us out of here, Larry. Before they can follow," he said. "Leave 'em in the dust."

The limo screeched and sped away. Carla glanced back at the journalists. She smiled to herself, leaning her head against the window.

"Who knew the public loved me that much?" she asked. "*Mio Dio*, I never imagined they'd be *this* concerned."

"Why did you talk to them?" Uncle Henry asked, glancing at her in the back seat. "I wouldn't give these journalists the time of day."

"If I don't, they'll continue to hound me. I hope I satisfied them for now," Carla replied. "Maybe they'll leave us alone."

"Well, I didn't sign up for any of this," Josephine muttered. "I wanted to get to New York to avoid the media circus, thanks."

"Fashion designers thrive in the spotlight, Josie," Carla replied. "You should learn that if you want to be in this business. Without fame, we're nothing. And all publicity is good publicity."

"If you say so." Uncle Henry checked his watch. "It's almost dinner at the hotel. Maybe a good meal will take our minds off the situation. Once the Crimson Caper's behind bars, we'll be able to eat out for a change."

"Good idea. I'm starving," Carla replied. "Anyway, I wanted to visit Sasha at the hospital tomorrow. I hope her condition isn't serious. I wanted to give her some time to calm down before I saw her again."

"Sasha doesn't know *how* to calm down," Josephine said. "She's threatening revenge to destroy your reputation."

Carla scoffed. "What an attention-seeker. Models are so dramatic. Anyway," Carla turned to me, "would you like to join me tomorrow?"

I nodded. "I would. Sasha might know something about the Crimson Caper—something we missed."

"We shouldn't bring it up. Sasha's traumatized from the fashion show and mentioning the Crimson Caper could make her angry. She hates me already, so we're treading on thin ice. We need to be careful with her."

Josephine nodded. "Asking questions could get us hurt. What if the Crimson Caper's violent?"

Carla agreed. I said nothing, but I knew I couldn't contain my questions. Carla didn't want us to get involved—

and neither did Josephine, for her own safety—but it was too late. I was already curious.

I wanted to ask Sasha about the mysterious scarf in her dressing room. Either she was guilty or someone was going around planting evidence to throw off the police.

Which made finding the person responsible even harder.

Seven

NO SAFE PLACE

Larry took us back to the hotel and we ate our dinner. Uncle Henry booked two separate rooms for Carla and Josephine, ones that were down the hall from us. The women thanked him and took their key cards, but Josephine looked a little guilty.

"Mister Prince, this is very generous," she began, "but I can't take your money."

Uncle Henry shook his head. "Nonsense, Miss Arias. You and Carla deserve to be safe. No harm will come to you here, not with us staying down the hall."

Considering how I'd seen the Crimson Caper lurking below my room yesterday, I wasn't so sure.

Ben decided to sleep in my room again tonight, so we took turns in the bathroom, changing into our pajamas. Uncle Henry didn't mind as long as we promised no funny business and kept the adjoining door cracked open. I glanced over the balcony, but I saw no Crimson Caper. I breathed a sigh of relief. Would they return? More importantly, would they get violent?

"Another day in Milan comes to an end," Ben said, setting up pillows and blankets on the couch for himself, "and we're not any closer to finding this Crimson Caper, are we?"

I shrugged. "I have some theories, but I can't prove any of them right now. I hate to say it, but this mystery's kind of exciting. Can you believe we're in the middle of one? It's like I'm Julia Joy. I want to write to Emily Pratt and tell her."

Ben shook his head, chuckling. "Only *you* could find sabotage fun, Jess. Hope you find the Crimson Caper for our sakes. Sweet dreams."

I turned off the lamp and lowered my eye mask. "Goodnight, Ben. Sleep tight—and don't let the Crimson Caper bite."

"Thanks, Jess. Now I'm for sure going to have nightmares."

I giggled before I felt my eyes closing. After a few minutes, I was sound asleep, exhausted from the adventures we'd had.

Until a scream down the hall startled me awake.

I sat up in bed and turned on the light as Ben rose to his feet. "Jess? Was that you? Are you okay?"

I shook my head. "I'm fine, Ben. That scream wasn't me."

"Then who was it?"

"It sounded like a woman, and it was really close." I pulled on my pink robe and slippers and grabbed my cell phone. "We better find out. Come on!"

We exited our room, joining other tourists standing in the hallway, dressed in their pajamas. They looked half asleep. The scream must've woken them up too.

I knocked on Uncle Henry's door, then he opened it a second later. "Jess, is everything okay?"

"Someone screamed and woke half the floor. It's why I came to get you, actually."

"I heard it too. I thought it was some kid or something. Who could it have been?"

Carla exited her room a moment later, out of breath. "*Mio Dio*! That sounded like Josie. Oh, I hope she's not in any trouble."

"Are you okay, Miss Valentine?" Ben asked. "You look like you're having trouble breathing."

"Just having a panic attack. Don't worry about me. Let's get to Josie!"

We approached Josephine's room. I twisted the handle on her door and found it locked. I pounded on the door. "Josephine? It's Jessica. Are you okay?"

When I heard nothing, Uncle Henry sighed. "Stand back, kids. I'll handle this."

As Carla, Ben, and I took a step back, Uncle Henry kicked open the door. It took a few tries before it went flying forward with a slam. I was the first to rush inside the hotel room, my curiosity getting the better of me.

The room was a mess. Furniture sat overturned, the curtains were knocked down, and someone left the balcony door wide open. Josephine was huddled on the bed, crying into her hands. A streak of red lipstick was smeared on the wall.

It read, *DON'T MESS WITH ME. SIGNED, THE CRIMSON CAPER.*

Another threatening lipstick message. My mind went to Lance LaDoux and his makeup brand immediately.

I walked over to the balcony door and the breeze hit me. We were staying on the fourth floor, so it would've been possible for someone to enter Josephine's room that way. With the proper climbing equipment, they could have come up from the ground or down from the roof. It wouldn't have been easy, but it was possible. A smudge of lipstick was on the door as if the person had gotten some on it and then fled in a hurry. I closed the door and locked it, just in case they returned.

"Josie, are you all right?" Carla asked.

Josephine eyes were glossed over. The poor woman looked terrified, rocking herself back and forth on the bed. Tears rolled down her cheeks.

"What happened, Josephine? Can you speak?" Uncle Henry asked, bending down next to her.

Josephine shuddered with fear. "The Crimson Caper was here. I forgot to lock the balcony door, and...." She cried into her hands harder.

I walked over and put a hand on her shoulder. "You're safe now, Josephine. Please, tell us what you know. We might be able to help."

She sniffled. "I woke up to someone in a red trench coat standing over me. When I screamed, they began turning over furniture and tossing my drawers around. I screamed again, then they wrote that message and fled."

"That's it? They didn't say anything to you?" I asked.

"No, nothing at all. I couldn't tell who it was, either—not with that hat on their head. I knew I should've taken that flight to New York."

Security entered the room next, and Uncle Henry rose to his feet. "Call Inspector Esposito, please. He needs to know about this."

The security guards reached for their phones while I thought about the Crimson Caper. If they ran when Josephine saw them, then maybe they had no desire to hurt her. Or anyone else.

But what were they planning instead?

———

When Inspector Esposito arrived with his officers, he looked exhausted. I checked the clock on the wall, and it read a little after one a.m. The Crimson Caper obviously planned this attack, hoping everyone would be asleep so they could flee. But the fact that Josephine wasn't harmed proved one thing.

The Crimson Caper wanted to scare us, not hurt us. But why?

Carla helped Josephine onto the bed, then they sat together. It seemed Carla's compassion for Josephine had grown since the Crimson Caper had broken in. Inspector Esposito stood beside them, nodding as he wrote down Josephine's account of the night. A few tears slipped out of her eyes again as she described the Crimson Caper and how scared she felt. I would've been scared too if I saw a stranger in my room, standing over me and wrecking my room.

I sent Ben off to bed—only because it looked like he was going to pass out—while Uncle Henry and I stayed behind. The other tourists returned to their rooms when security told them they were in no danger. I wanted to stay to make sure Josephine was okay, but I also wanted to learn more about the intruder.

"How did the Crimson Caper know you'd be at this hotel? Did you tell the public anything?" the inspector asked.

Josephine shook her head. "No one knew we were staying here. Mister Prince arranged it for us. The Crimson Caper must be following us—and eavesdropping or something."

"Perhaps. I'm disappointed you didn't tell me of your past with the Crimson Caper, *Signora*. When they hired you to make their outfits, it seems clear they planned this for a while."

Josephine sighed, nodding. "I know, I know. It's all my

fault. I should've never agreed to work with them in the first place."

"None of this is your fault, Josephine," I said. "You couldn't have known what the trench coat would be used for. No one could've."

"Ah, *Signorina* Prince," the inspector said, turning to me. "Whenever the Crimson Caper strikes, there you are."

"I hope you're not accusing my niece of anything, Inspector. She isn't capable of something like this," Uncle Henry said, crossing his arms. "My Jess is a good person."

I smiled at that.

"Not accusing, no. But there's a connection here. Don't you think?"

I shrugged. "Yeah, I guess. Maybe I just have bad timing. Or maybe the Crimson Caper's toying with me. Sure, Josephine's room was broken into, but the lipstick message on the limo was meant for me. It was left on my car, after all."

I thought for a moment. *Was* it possible the Crimson Caper was trying to tell me to back off?

"If they wanted to send you a message, why write it on Josephine's wall and not your own?" Inspector Esposito asked. "It's quite the leap, *Signorina*."

"Yeah, it is. But crazier things have happened. Oh, wait. I locked my balcony door. The Crimson Caper couldn't have gotten to me. Maybe they settled for Josephine? She was close to my room. The Crimson Caper could've even been spying on me or something."

"Maybe. But why not Carla?" Uncle Henry asked. "She's the one they're sabotaging, after all. Seems to me they should've broken into her room instead."

"That's the mystery," the inspector replied, putting his notepad away. "Was anything stolen, *Signora* Arias?"

Josephine shook her head. "No, I don't think so. My wallet was untouched."

"Just as I suspected—burglary wasn't the motive. Interesting," the inspector replied, tapping his chin. "Well, I think I have enough evidence and statements for one night. But I wanted you all to know I'll be holding a press conference on television tomorrow afternoon. With two attacks, the Crimson Caper could be a bigger threat than the *polizia* realize. We must address the public and warn them. Perhaps someone out there will know this strange person."

A press conference? I knew we had to go, just in case something happened. It was a good thing I liked spying and eavesdropping.

The inspector collected his things and approached the door. "Anyway, *grazie* for all your help. In the meantime, an officer will guard the hallway. Don't hesitate to contact me if the Crimson Caper returns. *Ciao*."

As he left, Josephine turned to Carla. "Carla, would it be too much to ask if you could sleep in here tonight? I know we're not that close, and I said all those things about you, but I'm scared. I'd just really appreciate some company right now."

Carla looked hesitant, then eventually sighed and nodded. "All right, very well. It's the least I can do since the Crimson Caper is after me. But I'm taking the bed, Josie. You can have the couch."

We were fortunate—nothing else happened that night. After I returned to my room, I had a restless sleep, but there wasn't any more screaming. It was like the Crimson Caper learned their lesson.

Or they'd return later, when we let our guards down again.

When dawn poked through the curtains, I gave up on sleep altogether. I rose to my feet and tossed my clothes over my pajamas. I squinted through the darkness at Ben but couldn't tell if he was sleeping or not.

"Are you awake?" I whispered, turning on the lamp.

Ben nodded, stretching on the couch. "Yeah. Rough night. Did the inspector find out who the Crimson Caper is yet? I'm dying to know. Tired of living in fear like this, wondering when and where they're going to attack next. It sucks."

I shook my head. "Not yet, but maybe we can share theories soon. I'm really eager to talk to him. He must have some tips he can share with me about investigations."

There was a knock on the adjoining door, then Uncle Henry stepped in. "Hello, Jess. Are you ready to go?"

"Oh, right. We're going to see Sasha today," I replied. "Almost forgot. How's Josephine doing this morning?"

Uncle Henry sighed. "Not good. You'd better see for yourself."

Ben and I got ready quickly, then we all headed for the corridor. When we got near Josephine's room, Carla exited. The door slammed shut behind her. I spotted an officer at the end of the hall, keeping an eye on everyone who passed. It made me feel a little safer, but still, a part of me knew—if the Crimson Caper wanted to get us, they could. They already proved that last night.

"Are you sure you don't want to come?" Carla asked, addressing the half-open door.

Josephine kept the door open an inch to chat with her. "No, I'd feel much better if I stayed here. I don't want to go outside. Not right now."

"Well, fine. Be stubborn," Carla muttered, glancing at

us. "She's a little traumatized after last night. Whimpered in her sleep. I guess that's normal, though."

"Poor Josephine," Ben mumbled. "All of us would probably be the same."

"Yeah, true. Come on, everyone," Uncle Henry said. "We'll eat breakfast first and then head to the hospital. Larry's waiting for us in the dining hall."

During the limousine ride to the hospital Sasha was staying at, I looked over the suspects in my notepad. I had to consider every angle, every possibility, which meant Josephine was still a suspect. She could've easily staged a break-in, trashed the window and room, and faked a scream. She knew how to make the red trench coat, after all, and could've been lying about everything.

I sighed. This mystery got harder every day.

As we pulled up to the parking lot of the hospital, I noticed several cop cars outside, including the inspector's. I frowned. What would he be doing here?

"Something must've happened," Ben murmured. "Look at all the cops."

"I hope Sasha's all right," Carla said. "She's the most high-maintenance model I've ever worked with, but she doesn't deserve to get hurt."

We exited the limousine and walked into the large, crowded hospital. Carla went over to the front desk and spoke with the receptionist in Italian. It looked like they were arguing. Carla turned around, sighing.

"She won't let us inside Sasha's room. It's restricted to family members and police only."

But I never took no for an answer so I walked up to the

front desk. "Hello, my name's Jessica Prince. Look, we're really concerned about Sasha—"

The receptionist woman just shrugged. I didn't think she understood English. She pointed at the telephone and mumbled something in Italian.

"She's threatening to call the *polizia* if we don't leave," Carla said, translating for us. "I guess we have no choice but to go—"

"It's all right." The inspector walked around the corner. "I'll let you see *Signora* Simpson. I don't see the harm in it. I'll give your names to the front desk so you can stop by any time you'd like."

We waited as he spoke with the receptionist in Italian. She glared at us but didn't argue, though she muttered something when he turned from her.

The inspector gestured down the hall. "Follow me. Though, you must be warned—*Signora* Simpson's not in the best mood."

"Why not?" I asked as we followed him. "And what are you doing here?"

"Those two questions are intertwined," the inspector replied as we reached Sasha's room. "See for yourself."

As the inspector opened the door and let us inside, a handful of officers greeted us. They stood by the window, staring at the red lipstick mark on the wall that read STOP LOOKING FOR ME OR ELSE.

They didn't sign their name this time, but it was obvious this was the Crimson Caper's handiwork. It matched the handwriting left on Josephine's wall and it was the same shade of lipstick. But did they leave this here before or after Josephine's break-in? And why would they target Sasha?

It seemed like no one and no place was safe.

"Two break-ins in one night," the inspector said. "My job has gotten a lot busier these days."

I walked over to the red lipstick, shaking my head. "How did the Crimson Caper get in? Weren't they caught on the security cameras?"

"I'm afraid not, *Signorina*. This Crimson Caper knew how to avoid being seen," the inspector replied. "Our people are getting worried. We may have a riot on the streets if we can't stop this criminal—which makes my press conference even more necessary."

Sasha lay in the hospital bed across the large room in front of the lipstick-covered wall, several pillows around her propping her up. A police officer stood next to Sasha while asking her questions. She seemed irritated and wouldn't look the officer in the eyes. "I don't know anything. I was asleep when it happened. Aren't you listening?"

"Sasha, are you all right?" Carla asked, stepping forward. "I'm sorry I didn't come sooner, but—"

"You!" Sasha said, pointing her finger at Carla. "I want this woman arrested. Right now."

Eight

THE PRESS CONFERENCE

"Do you know what she's done to me, Inspector?" Sasha continued. "Do you?"

Carla crossed her arms, scoffing. "Oh, what are you talking about, Sasha?"

"You know what you did," Sasha snarled. "You invited me to star in your fashion show. But when I got out here, I found out there were other models lined up."

"Is that true, Carla? Did you tell her that?" Uncle Henry asked.

Carla scoffed, turning to Sasha. "Hardly. I never said you were *the* star of the show. I said you were *one* of the stars. Take it up with your manager if you have an issue."

"Star or not, look at me, Carla!" Sasha said, her eyes filling with tears. "My back's injured. The doctors say it could be serious. What if it never heals? What if I can never model again?"

Carla sighed, her tone softening. "I'm truly sorry, Sasha. I never wanted this to happen to you."

"Well, it did," Sasha replied, drying her eyes. "I knew I shouldn't have come to Milan. It might've cost me everything. Aren't you going to arrest her, Inspector?"

"No, *Signora* Simpson. She hasn't done anything wrong," he replied. "The sabotage was unfortunate, but rest assured, we're doing everything to find this Crimson Caper."

I pulled out my notepad and scribbled into it. Sasha was once a suspect, but could she have been behind this? Would she really go so far as to hurt herself to sabotage Carla?

"Finding the Crimson Caper or whatever they call themselves won't help me now," Sasha said. "If my career's over, yours will be, too, Carla. I'll make sure of it myself."

Carla didn't reply. She stepped forward, then walked over to the door. "I think I need some fresh air. Be right back."

"You can run now, but not for long," Sasha called out. "I'm going to sue those clothes right off your back!"

As Carla left, the inspector cleared his throat. "I'm sorry for your injury, *Signora* Simpson, but I must ask you a few questions. Is that all right?"

Sasha rolled her eyes. "Fine. I don't really have a choice while I'm stuck in this bed, anyway."

The inspector pulled out his notepad. "You didn't see or hear the Crimson Caper last night?"

"Yeah, that's right. Finally, someone around here's listening," Sasha muttered. "I only saw the writing on the wall when I woke up. I yelled for the nurse, then she ran in and called the police. But I wouldn't have heard an explosion outside, Inspector. The doctors have me on some pretty heavy pain meds."

"Why would the Crimson Caper come here, Sasha? Why would they threaten you?" I asked. "Any ideas?"

Sasha scoffed. "How should I know? The police get paid to figure that out, not me. And honestly, if this Crimson Caper *is* real, they have bigger problems than me. Coming here was a big waste of time for them. They're supposed to be after Carla for some reason."

"What about security cameras?" Ben asked. "There have to be cameras in this hospital, right?"

"Correct. I already checked them out," the inspector said. "We saw the Crimson Caper enter the hospital, but we couldn't make out any features. They left the message and then ran outside. They escaped down the back alley and didn't return. And since it was so late, fewer nurses were on duty and didn't see them."

I sighed. So much for finding them today.

"Anyway, let's talk about the fashion show," the inspector continued. "Do you remember anything from that night? Perhaps something you might've forgotten until now?"

Sasha thought for a moment. "Well, come to think of it, I *do* remember Lance LaDoux poking around the Palace. This was way before the show started—before people were allowed inside. Didn't think it was weird until after the sabotage."

"Lance LaDoux?" the inspector asked with a quizzical look.

"A fashion designer and cosmetic maker from France. Biggest, richest one in the world. He flew in to see Carla's show," I replied before I turned to Sasha. "Did he say anything to you?"

Sasha shook her head. "He didn't speak to anyone. He was just looking around the Palace—looking at the stage, too. No one told him to leave. I mean, it was Lance LaDoux, for crying out loud. Would you tell a famous fashion designer and make-up mogul to go away? He goes to these fashion shows all the time."

Ever since I'd connected Lance's lipstick to the writing, I hadn't been able to stop thinking of him and a possible motive. While I didn't have one yet, Sasha's testimony proved he had the opportunity to sabotage the show.

"Sasha, who do you think sabotaged the show?" I asked. "If you had to guess?"

She shrugged. "No clue. All I know is it wasn't me. But if I were you, I'd be looking into Carla's ex-husband. Wasn't he lurking around backstage like a creeper, too?"

I nodded. Where was Antonio? We hadn't seen him since he tried to break into Carla's home. No matter what he did, Carla didn't see him as a threat. What made her so sure he wasn't the Crimson Caper? Was he really as stupid as Carla made him out to be?

"Just one more thing," I said. "I found a red scarf in your makeshift dressing room, much like the one the Crimson Caper wore. Josephine told me the entire room belonged to you. Since you demanded a dressing room. How do you explain it?"

Sasha scoffed. "Hang on. Am I a suspect?"

"Everyone is a suspect, *Signora*," the inspector replied. "Jessica raises a good point. Please answer the question."

"I can't," Sasha replied. "I don't know how the scarf got there. Honestly, it wasn't mine."

If the scarf didn't belong to Sasha as she claimed, then someone planted it there. But who could it be? Who else had access to the backstage area?

The inspector put his notepad away. "I think I'm finished here, *Signora*. A security guard will stand outside your room to make sure the Crimson Caper doesn't return. Feel better."

Sasha shook her head, staring out the window. "I don't know if I *can* feel better. Everything I worked hard for was taken from me, in the blink of an eye. All because of Carla's stupid fashion show."

And then she lowered her head and started crying.

"Man, this is depressing," Ben whispered to me. "I thought the Crimson Caper was just about sabotage, but now they've hurt someone. I wonder if it was on purpose? You know, if I were Carla, I'd feel really guilty."

I nodded, thinking the same. Speaking of Carla, she still hadn't returned. Where had she gone?

"I'm going to find Carla," I said. "I'll be right back."

As I left the room, I walked down the hallway. I glanced over at the front desk and noticed Carla had her cell phone up to her ear. She was speaking in hushed Italian as I approached, but she didn't notice me.

I tapped on her shoulder. "Carla, can I talk to you?"

She jumped and put the phone down, turning to me. "*Mio Dio*, Jessica! You scared me. I guess I've been a little jumpy since the show. What is it?"

"I just wanted to check on you. Sasha's injury can't be easy to hear, considering it happened at your fashion show," I replied. "Plus, you were gone a long time. Who are you talking to? Weren't you going outside for air?"

"I called Josie. I *did* go outside, but then I started to worry about her at the hotel," she replied, bringing the phone up to her mouth. "*Ciao*, Josie. Hang in there, okay?"

"How's she doing?" I asked after she hung up the phone.

Carla shrugged. "How do you think? The Crimson Caper scared the life out of her. I've never seen her so terrified before. Not even when we found a giant spider on the runway."

I snorted. "Ha, really?"

"Oh, yes. I screamed bloody murder." Carla sighed and leaned on the desk. "I miss the days when that was my only problem."

I felt like I should say something encouraging. "It's not your fault, Carla. You didn't mean for any of this to happen."

She nodded, rubbing her temples. "You're right. I didn't —but I *still* feel responsible. If Sasha had died, I don't want to think about it. I made a huge mistake with this fashion show, Jessica. *Grazie* for trying to cheer me up but we both know it's true. I should've just stuck to selling fashion online."

"Don't talk like that. I'm sure everything will work out."

"*Signora* Prince?" the inspector asked, walking over to me. "Ah, there you two are. I was about to return to the police department. The news conference is scheduled in one hour. I'll see you both later."

"Wait, Inspector. Can I come with you to the press conference? I'd love a ride. Never been in a police car before. In America *or* Italy."

The inspector thought about it for a moment. "All right, I suppose. As long as you promise to stay out of the way."

But I couldn't promise that.

"Cool. Just let me ask my uncle for permission so he doesn't worry."

But as I turned to Carla, she was gone. I frowned, looking around for her, but didn't see her anywhere. As the inspector waited for me, Uncle Henry and Ben came around the corner.

Ben smiled, holding up a bag of chips. "They have vending machines in Milan. Can you believe that, Jess? Total score!"

I laughed. "I'm happy for you, Ben. And your snack addiction." I turned to Uncle Henry. "Did Sasha say anything else while I was gone?"

"She was too upset to speak. But she still blames Carla for everything." Uncle Henry shook his head. "If she pursues legal action, I know some great lawyers who could defend Carla. But I hope it doesn't come to that."

"I see. Well, the press conference starts in an hour. I'll be going with the inspector to the police station to watch. If that's okay."

Uncle Henry nodded. "All right—I'll call the inspector and tell him I said yes. As long as you stay close to the inspector and don't cause any trouble."

"I'll try not to. And I'd like you both to be there too," I replied. "With luck, I'll be able to find the real culprit—and Sasha can blame them instead."

As I rode with Inspector Esposito, an awkward silence lingered for the first few minutes. I didn't know much about him or what to say. As I glanced in the rear-view mirror, I noticed Larry, Uncle Henry, and Ben in the limo behind us.

But where was Carla? She disappeared at the front desk, and I was sure I hadn't seen her get into the limo. Maybe she had another vehicle waiting somewhere or something.

"You seem to care a great deal about Carla Valentine," the inspector said as we weaved in and out of the Milan traffic. His vehicle was much smaller than the ones back home, fitting in better on the tight Italian streets. "From my experience, she is a difficult person to get along with. Constantly changing emotions. It makes my head spin."

"Ha, you can say that again." I shrugged. "Well, to tell you the truth, I barely know her. She and Uncle Henry were engaged years ago. I'm mostly helping because of him."

"Oh? And why did they end their relationship?"

"They were both workaholics. I know Uncle Henry. When he gets an idea, you can't talk to him," I replied. "It was probably for the best, but I think they still care about each other."

"A scorned ex-lover. Hmm. That would be the perfect motive for sabotage," the inspector said, glancing at me for a moment. "Don't you think so?"

"I guess. Wait a second. You think my Uncle Henry could be guilty?"

The inspector shrugged. "And why not? I must consider all the possibilities, *Signorina* Prince."

"Yeah, I know. I am, too," I replied, "but I know Uncle Henry. He wouldn't do this. He couldn't. It's just not his thing."

"Then who else could it be?"

I pulled out my notepad. "Well, I have some theories. Let's start with Sasha. She had access to the show, plus I found a red scarf in her dressing room. Means and opportunity right there."

"And her motive?"

"She was angry Carla didn't make the show all about her. I heard she has a reputation for being a drama queen. Maybe the shock of not being center stage forced her to do something about it?"

"But she was injured, *Signorina*. If she put the oil on the stage, wouldn't she be careful to avoid it?"

I shrugged. "Maybe she planned it, to throw investigators off? Or maybe to gain sympathy? Maybe she didn't plan to fall? There're a bunch of reasons."

The inspector nodded. "An interesting theory. Do you have another suspect?"

"Antonio Rossi, Carla's ex-husband. We found him hanging around backstage, and he broke into Carla's home," I replied. "Carla thinks he's innocent—and too stupid to be a saboteur—but he clearly has means and opportunity. His motive is anger over his divorce. He's still in love with Carla, but she wants nothing to do with him."

"Ah, another scorned ex-lover," the inspector said. "Next, *Signorina*?"

"Vincent Rossi, the journalist, and Enrique Bello, the rival fashion designer. I saw them at the show, taunting

Carla, so they have means and opportunity. They left in the same car so they could be working together to ruin her career or something. It'd make the fashion world easier for Enrique. And Vincent hates Carla for divorcing his brother. Two good motives."

"Hmm," the inspector replied. "Well, it's possible. Anyone else?"

"Josephine Arias, Carla's assistant. She says she's been mistreated by Carla, and she wants to be a fashion designer herself. There's her motive. She had designs for the red trench coat in her suitcase, plus she said she spoke with the Crimson Caper. She also has means and opportunity."

"But her room was attacked, and I saw *Signora* Arias. She looked traumatized," the inspector said, glancing at me. "Certainly, she's a victim, no?"

"Maybe, maybe not. It *could* be an act, just like Sasha's injury. While I thought the Crimson Caper *was* Josephine for a while, another suspect jumped up on my list. They're sitting at the top now."

"And who would that be?"

"Lance LaDoux, the famous fashion designer from France. He was at the show and Sasha said she saw him poking around," I replied. "The Crimson Caper wrote a threatening message on my limo. I found red lipstick near it, the brand LaDoux makes. It can't be a coincidence. There's only one thing bothering me about him, though."

"Do tell, *Signorina*."

"Well, Lance promised to reimburse Carla for her troubles. He seemed sad her show was sabotaged," I replied. "It could mean two things. One, he *did* sabotage the show and feels guilty. Or two, he *didn't* sabotage the show and truly wants to help."

The inspector smiled. "Ah, very good. You've clearly given this a lot of thought."

I smiled. "I have. And thank you, Inspector. Maybe I'll even follow in your footsteps and become a detective one day. For now, though, I'll settle for being an amateur sleuth. Who do *you* think's guilty, Inspector?"

"I can't afford to make assumptions, *Signorina*. Detectives must stay impartial," he said. "I'll let the evidence speak for itself. Until then, I'll remain suspicious of everyone."

"Even Uncle Henry?"

The inspector glanced in the rear-view mirror, nodding. "Even him."

A crowd of people gathered outside the police department, shouting things in Italian. I couldn't understand many of the words, but two stood out the most. Crimson Caper. The public looked angry and frustrated with the situation. If I lived here, I would've been afraid, too.

The inspector helped me push through the chanting people as we entered the station. The police department in Milan was busy with police officers and detectives hard at work. I followed Inspector Esposito to his cozy office where an officer sat with a sketchbook and a pile of pencils.

"This officer is a sketch artist, *Signora*," the inspector explained. "I'd like you to describe the culprit so he can draw a composite sketch. If it's all right with you and your uncle, of course. I thought we could kill two birds with one stone while we're here. As that charming English saying goes."

I nodded. "Let me call my uncle and find out. Just one moment, Inspector."

I pulled out my smartphone, calling Uncle Henry. He spoke with the inspector personally and gave him permission. He even promised not to sue the department if any harm came to me during all this—and I hoped it wouldn't.

"Ah, good. That's settled." Inspector Esposito handed me back the phone. "Once the portrait is finished, I'll show it to the public during the press conference. Try to remember what you can about the Crimson Caper. Even small details could help."

I took a seat beside the officer. As I gave the best description of the Crimson Caper that I could, Uncle Henry and Ben entered the office. The inspector nodded politely at Uncle Henry, his eyes lingering on him. I wondered if my uncle knew he was a suspect.

"There you are." I frowned when I didn't see Carla with them. "Hey, where's Carla?"

Uncle Henry furrowed his eyebrows. "We thought she rode with you? We just assumed she was in the back seat or something."

I shook my head. "No, I haven't seen her since the hospital. When I turned around, she was gone."

"Well, that can't be good," Ben said. "Where could she have gone?"

We hushed when the inspector's phone rang. He picked it up and nodded before he turned to us. "The journalists have arrived. The news conference will begin in a few minutes. You all may watch if you'd like."

"Of course, Inspector. In the meantime, I'll try calling Carla on her cell phone. Maybe she had something to do," Uncle Henry said. "Good luck out there, Inspector."

Inspector Esposito thanked him and headed outside. As Uncle Henry tried to call Carla on his smartphone, we followed the inspector and stood in the crowd. A larger crowd formed this time, except with more journalists—including Vincent Rossi who smirked from the front row.

The inspector walked up to the podium as we watched from a distance. All the journalists lifted their cameras to video him, eager for the press conference to start.

"Greetings, everyone," the inspector said in English, then repeated everything in Italian. "I'm here to debrief you on the Crimson Caper, take questions, and give tips on how the public can stay safe during our investigation. Especially during such a high-profile case."

As the inspector rambled on, I took the opportunity to scan the crowd. Nothing looked out of the ordinary except for one person. I'd recognize their red clothes anywhere. The Crimson Caper was here, hidden within the crowd.

And they were staring at me.

Nine

THE ARSONIST

I tried to chase after the Crimson Caper, but Uncle Henry grabbed my hand. "Where do you think you're going?" he whispered.

Naturally, I resisted. "I just saw the Crimson Caper. I have to stop them."

But when I looked back, the Crimson Caper was already gone. Uncle Henry glanced around. "Really? I didn't see anyone."

"Oh, they were here. But they got away." I huffed. "Again."

The inspector finished his debriefing, then glanced around at the journalists. "I can take questions now if anyone has any. But remember, this is an ongoing investigation. Much of the details remain confidential—"

Vincent Rossi pushed through the people, not giving the inspector a chance to finish. "How will Carla Valentine answer for this? Will you be charging her with negligence?"

The inspector wrinkled his eyebrows. "Pardon me, *Signore* Rossi?"

"If it weren't for Carla's fashion show, the Crimson Caper wouldn't have attacked," Vincent replied. "Surely, she bears some of the responsibility, don't you think? She's brought a criminal to our streets."

I rolled my eyes. Of course, Vincent would try to accuse Carla of something criminal right now. I pulled out my notepad and scribbled his name down at the top of my list. His readiness to divert the blame to Carla was suspicious—like something a guilty man would do.

As the crowd loudly agreed, the inspector shook his head. "Nonsense. *Signora* Valentine is a victim, not a criminal. May we have another question, *per favore*?"

"How will you keep the people of Milan safe, Inspector?" another journalist asked. "What if this Crimson Caper escalates?"

"We're doing everything in our power to protect Milan," the inspector replied. "We've already taken numerous measures. Increased security, further resources to investigate, and—"

A nearby police officer walked over, stopping the inspector. He leaned in to whisper in the inspector's ear. Inspector Esposito nodded and turned to the podium.

"*Mi scusi*," the inspector said, "but I have an urgent police matter to attend to. Rest assured, the public will be informed of the situation as it unfolds—"

A small, expensive sports car pulled up to the street corner, then Enrique Bello opened the driver's door and exited. He pushed through the crowd, rushing toward the podium. He was out of breath by the time he'd made it over to the inspector.

"There's been a fire at the Fashion Palace, Inspector," he said, and the journalists turned around to look at him. "You should see the flames."

The inspector sighed. "I know, I was just informed by my officer. Stay away from the Palazzo, everyone. Allow the *polizia* to conduct their investigation—"

But it was too late. The journalists abandoned the press conference, hopping in their tiny European cars to drive to the crime scene. After a few minutes, not a single soul remained in front of us. Inspector Esposito sighed and mumbled something that sounded like an Italian curse word.

"No one ever listens," he muttered. "I must head to the Fashion Palace now. I'll see you all later."

Before I could ask any questions, the inspector rushed away with his officers behind him. Uncle Henry and Ben shook their heads.

"Gosh, now the fashion building is on fire?" Ben asked. "Sounds pretty serious."

"I guess so. But it's a little strange how Enrique knew about it, right? Even before the other journalists did?"

Uncle Henry nodded. "You must've read my mind, Jess. Anyway, let's head back to the hotel. The police can handle this."

"We should go too, Uncle Henry. To see what's going on." When Uncle Henry looked skeptical, I knew I had to do something to convince him. "What if Carla's there? What if she's hurt?"

Uncle Henry sighed. "All right, good point. She didn't answer any of my calls."

"Maybe she's in danger," I said. "I told you I saw the Crimson Caper in the crowd during the press conference. It could all be connected somehow."

Uncle Henry balled his fists. "I swear, if they did something to Carla—"

A taxi pulled up to the building, then came to a stop with a loud screech. Carla got out of the vehicle a second later and scanned the police courtyard for us. When she noticed us, she rushed over.

"Oh, there you are! Glad I caught you," Carla said, bending over to catch her breath.

"Where did you go?" I asked. "We couldn't find you for a while."

"Back to the hotel. Even though Josie and I spoke on the phone, I was still paranoid. I had to make sure she was okay," Carla replied. "She's doing fine. A little frazzled, but what else can you expect?"

Uncle Henry stepped forward, crossing his arms. "You can't run off like that, Carla—especially not with the Crimson Caper on the loose. We were worried. I was about to report you as missing, you know. You wouldn't answer my calls."

Carla scoffed. "Don't be ridiculous, Henry. I'm fine. I was just busy with Josie. Anyway, I went for a walk to clear my head and saw that the Fashion Palace was on fire. And so soon after the Crimson Caper sabotage. Can you believe that?"

I shook my head. "I really can't. Why would someone set it on fire? And why now?"

Carla sighed. "Your guess is as good as mine. They've already ruined me, so what's the point of destroying an old piece of Italy's history?"

I spotted Larry down the road, waiting with the limousine running. "Come on. Maybe we'll find some answers at the Palace."

The Fashion Palace was a disaster when we arrived. From police officers to journalists and curious passersby, I could barely see the building. But I noticed right away the thick, grey smoke in the air, the burning flames, and the stench of fire.

The police officers put up police tape to hold the screaming journalists and frantic citizens back. Behind them, firefighters were hard at work, using their hoses to put out the blaze.

Carla gasped and fell to her knees. "*Mio Dio*, not the Fashion Palace! It looks even worse in person. How could they do this? Not just to me, but to our beautiful city?"

I pulled out my notepad and scribbled my thoughts down. I'd just seen the Crimson Caper in the crowd, but was it before or after the fire started? And were they responsible for this?

Uncle Henry helped Carla to her feet. "I know this is traumatic, but you must stay strong. The Crimson Caper wants to break you, Carla. Don't let them win."

Carla nodded, wiping away her tears. "You're right, Henry. I can't give them the satisfaction."

"Do you think the Crimson Caper's here?" Ben whispered to me.

I did a quick scan of the crowd. I didn't see anyone in a red trench coat, so I shrugged. "I don't know—but with the Crimson Caper, you can never be sure."

I did see two familiar faces in the crowd, though—Vincent Rossi and Enrique Bello. Vincent shouted questions at the officers as he always did but Enrique seemed distracted. He glanced down the street in the direction of the back alley. When I looked, I realized what he was staring at.

Lance LaDoux. He walked around the side of the building with his cane, shaking his head as he made his way over to us. "How awful, *Mademoiselle* Valentine. This building is a prominent fixture in Milan, *oui*?"

She nodded. "It's over a century old. Countless famous fashion designers have shown their work here. And now it's just gone. What a tragedy."

"What are you doing here, Mister LaDoux?" I asked.

"I came to see the damage, of course," he replied. "When I heard the sirens, I was curious."

"The Crimson Caper's been leaving threatening messages around town—all in red lipstick," I began. "Did you know they're using your lipstick brand, Mister LaDoux? It had your logo on the bottom of the tube. Care to explain that?"

Carla gasped. "You aren't suggesting he's had anything to do with this, are you?"

I shrugged. "A good detective looks at all the possibilities. I learned that from Inspector Esposito."

Lance smiled at me, but it was disingenuous. "*Oui*, I think I'll let that accusation slide, *mademoiselle*. Teenagers say such silly things, don't they?"

"Don't talk down to my niece," Uncle Henry said. "She may be a teenager, but she's not a fool."

"And you never answered her question," Ben said, crossing his arms.

Lance shrugged. "How should I answer it, *Monsieur*? My lipstick's very famous. Anyone could've gotten their hands on it, *oui*? Many pharmacies sell it across the world. It doesn't prove anything."

"Well, yeah," I began, "but you *do* have a connection to this case. Isn't that a strange coincidence?"

Lance ignored me, turning to Carla. "*Mademoiselle* Valentine, I promised I'd help you—and I *always* keep my promises. Join me at my mansion tomorrow evening for dinner. I'll present my check to you then."

"That's very kind of you," Carla began, "but I can't accept your money."

"*Au contraire*," he replied. "I'd hate to see an up-and-coming fashion designer's career come to an end. Consider it a favor. You can pay me back by putting on a show in my honor—when this Crimson Caper's apprehended and it's safe, of course."

Carla sighed. "Very well, *Signore* LaDoux. And *grazie* for all your help."

He bowed. "It's my pleasure. You may even bring your friends—if they don't accuse me of something so criminal again."

Carla replied before I could say anything. "They won't."

I couldn't make the same promise.

Lance waved before he walked past the building toward a dark limo that waited for him. If the limo was over there, why had he come from the back alley? As he drove off, I wondered about it.

Carla turned to me. "You'd better be on your best behavior tomorrow, Jessica. You could ruin his generosity before he has a chance to use it."

I crossed my arms. "But you said you didn't want his money."

She sighed. "What other choice do I have? As I told you before, I spent most of my family's fortune on my fashion career. And it took a lot of Euros to get the fashion ready."

"Right. Well, if you're so worried I'll mess it up, why even invite us?"

"I'm doing it as a favor to you. Your uncle told me how much you love fashion, and I want you to see everything you can. And I'd like for Henry to be there. As added protection these days." Carla's pleading eyes fell on me. "Just...be careful with what you say."

"All right. Anyway, I'm going to find the inspector. Come on, Ben."

Ben nodded and followed me. The inspector stood behind the police tape, talking with several firefighters. As I approached the crime scene tape, an officer blocked my path. He started to mumble in Italian.

"What? Sorry, I don't speak Italian," I replied.

"No entry," he said in rough English. "Turn back."

I sighed, stepping back. It was clear I was going to have to get creative.

Ben turned to me. "Well, this blows. Now what?"

I gestured at the back alley. "Follow me. We're getting into that building one way or another."

Ben hesitated, then followed me anyway. I managed to slip through a window that had been opened by the police. Fortunately, the fire had been put out in that area, making it safe for us. Ashes sat along the windowsill from the fire. When Ben paused, I gestured at him.

"Come on," I whispered. "Before someone catches us."

"The things I do for you," Ben muttered, then slipped through the window.

Once we were inside, we watched the Palace burn closer as firefighters frantically rushed back and forth with their hoses. The inspector looked up and noticed us when he heard footsteps before walking over.

"Jessica Prince?" he asked. "What are you doing here? How did you get inside?"

"I came to check on you, Inspector. Make sure you were okay."

"That's kind of you. Truth be told, I'm devastated. Italy's lost a monumental building, *Signorina*. What a tragedy."

"I'm sorry. This is really awful. Do you know how the fire started?"

The inspector shook his head. "Not yet. Until the fire's extinguished, it isn't safe to enter and investigate. I don't like to get ahead of the evidence, but...."

"But what?" Ben asked.

"I believe this was arson. All I need is the evidence to prove it."

A firefighter walked around the side of the building,

holding a piece of paper in his hands. He gave it to the inspector who glanced down at it. As they spoke in Italian, I waited impatiently to hear what was going on.

The inspector turned to me, showing me the note. "The firefighter found this in the back alley. Someone left it near the dumpster."

On the note, in red lipstick read I WARNED YOU. The paper looked singed with black soot, burned slightly to a golden-brown color. It was a miracle the fire hadn't burned it up completely.

Was it a coincidence Lance had come from the back alley? And if the Crimson Caper *had* started the fire, where were they now?

"Well, there's your evidence," Ben said. "Definitely arson."

The inspector nodded. "It's a good start. And when I'm allowed inside by the firefighters, I hope to find more evidence that can prove—"

An officer ran over to us, out of breath. He spoke quickly to the inspector, whose eyes widened. When they finished speaking, the inspector turned toward the front doors almost as if he were waiting for something.

"What's going on?" I asked.

"My officer claims a person was found inside the building," the inspector replied. "The firefighters are bringing him out now."

A second later, the front doors to the Palace burst open. A group of firefighters carried a burly man, unconscious and full of black soot. He had light burn marks on his arms, but it didn't seem fatal. I gasped when he came closer and I recognized him.

"That's Antonio Rossi," I said. "Carla's ex-husband. Back again."

"Indeed," the inspector replied. "How peculiar."

The firefighters handed Antonio to a group of paramedics nearby. They placed him on a stretcher and put him in the back of the ambulance. As the paramedics got in the driver's seat, Vincent went chasing after them.

"Wait, *per favore*. That's my brother!" he cried and then mumbled something in Italian.

The paramedics let Vincent enter the ambulance, then it drove away with its sirens on. I checked to make sure no one else was coming out of the building, but it seemed like Antonio was the only one.

What would he be doing at the Fashion Palace? And unconscious inside, of all things?

"Carla needs to know about her ex-husband," Ben said. "We'd better go tell her."

The inspector nodded. "Meet me at the hospital, *Signorina*. When he wakes, I'll arrest him for arson, trespassing, and sabotage."

"Shouldn't you wait until you can question him? It doesn't prove he started the fire."

"He had no business being inside the Fashion Palace. That's suspicious enough," the inspector replied. "We need something to do in the meantime while the fire's put out. Perhaps there'll be evidence inside that can link Antonio to the crime. *Ciao*."

As the inspector hopped into his car, Ben and I walked over to Carla and Uncle Henry. They both had the same confused and worried look on their faces.

"What happened?" Uncle Henry asked. "Who was that man they pulled out of the building? We couldn't see his face."

I sighed, looking at Carla. "You aren't going to like this, but it was Antonio."

Carla gasped. "Tony? Why was he here in the first place?"

"That's what I want to know," I replied. "Come on. The inspector said to meet him at the hospital. He's going to arrest Antonio there."

Carla shook her head. "They can't. Tony's innocent. You must believe me, Jessica."

"I'm not the one you need to convince," I replied. "The inspector thinks this was arson, and they found a threatening note in the back alley. Tony being here makes him look pretty guilty."

"You're wrong. Dead wrong," Carla cried, rushing over to our limo. "Hurry, everyone. We can't let the inspector do this."

As Uncle Henry and Ben followed her to our limo, I sighed and pulled out my notepad. Carla swore Antonio wasn't behind this, but I wasn't so sure. And besides Lance, Antonio was the highest suspect on my list. As the days went by, his name only seemed to climb. Did he know how guilty he acted?

I glanced back at the building, watching it burn. If the Crimson Caper could resort to arson, what else were they capable of?

I had a bad feeling in the pit of my stomach when I thought of the possibilities.

Ten

ACCUSATIONS AND SUSPICIONS

The reporters beat us to the hospital, following the sirens of the ambulance. Security guards held them back and forbid the press from entering. After some cajoling —and swearing up and down that I knew the inspector— they let us pass.

As we pushed through the crowd of people and walked inside the hospital, I noticed Inspector Esposito speaking with the nurse at the front desk. Several of his officers surrounded him with their handcuffs out. When they saw me, they tapped him on the shoulder, then he turned around with a polite smile.

"Ah, *Signorina* Prince," the inspector said. "Good to see you again. I suppose you've come to see me arrest *Signore* Rossi?"

"Yeah, I have," I began, "but I'm not sure Antonio's guilty. There are a lot of suspects, Inspector."

"See, Inspector? Tony's innocent," Carla said, pushing past me. "Listen to Jessica if you don't believe me."

The inspector shrugged. "I suppose we'll see, *Signora* Valentine. Your ex-husband has a lot to explain first."

"I want to see him. Where is he?" Carla asked, crossing her arms.

"Down the hall to the right. I was just on my way to see him," the inspector replied. "But this is a sensitive police matter. I'd rather not have a civilian inside the room just yet—"

Carla rushed down the hallway before he could finish, disobeying a police order, and then disappeared inside the room. Inspector Esposito didn't look too happy with her before he started walking after her. As Uncle Henry, Ben, and I followed the inspector, shouting came from Antonio's hospital room. It sounded like Carla's voice, but I couldn't make out the other one.

When we entered, Carla and Vincent Rossi were arguing. Antonio laid on the bed, still unconscious. Nurses checked his vital signs but rushed out of the room when the arguing became louder.

"This is your fault, Carla," Vincent sneered. "Now the Crimson Caper's targeting my brother, too."

She scoffed. "I had no part in this. Do you think I wanted him to get hurt?"

"Perhaps I do," Vincent replied. "You broke his heart when you filed for divorce. You took everything from him. Why not take his life now, too?"

Carla took a step closer. "I'll make you pay for saying that, you little—"

"Pardon me," the inspector said, stepping between them. "Let's not fight. We have enough issues already, don't you think?"

"The only issue is this, Inspector," Vincent began. "Carla's a threat to our city—and now my brother. The Crimson Caper's bound to hurt more people because of her. Just give it time."

"And that's why I'm here," the inspector replied, "to find

this Crimson Caper and bring them to justice. I know what's at stake, *Signore.*"

"Speaking of which, how's Antonio doing?" I asked.

Vincent sighed. "The doctors are confident he'll survive. He was treated for smoke inhalation and minor burns, but nothing too serious. A miracle."

Carla reached for Antonio's hand, caressing it. "*Mio Dio*, Tony. Why were you even there? You could've gotten killed."

Antonio was still motionless and unresponsive. Vincent rolled his eyes but didn't start another argument. It was clear Carla still cared about her ex-husband, and I knew he still cared about her.

I saw the look on Uncle Henry's face. He seemed sad—but I couldn't tell if it was pity for Carla or because he wished he were the one who married her. I wondered if he felt a pang of jealousy every time they shared an intimate moment.

The inspector pulled out his notepad. "My officers locked down the Fashion Palace after the sabotage. Do any of you know why *Signore* Rossi was there?"

Carla shook her head. "Not at all, Inspector. He had no reason to be."

"Me, either," Vincent replied. "The last I heard from him, he was at his apartment downtown. Shouldn't have been anywhere near the Fashion Palace, unless...."

"Unless what?" I asked.

"Well, I know about his unhealthy obsession with Carla," Vincent muttered, looking up at her. "He'll do anything to get her attention—and her pity."

Carla scoffed. "What are you suggesting? That he saw the building burning and ran inside so I'd come see him?"

Vincent shrugged. "Hey, it's possible. His love for you blinds him—makes him stupid. He'd do anything for you."

His eyes hardened when he looked at Carla. "I wouldn't be surprised if this was a trap to lure you here. I bet you delight in his foolish, love-sick ways, Carla. It gives you a thrill, doesn't it? To have a man obey your every command?"

Carla shook her head. "You have it all wrong, Vincent. I don't want to see Tony hurt. If anything, I want him to move on with his life. Find happiness elsewhere."

Vincent scoffed at that, clearly not believing her. But he didn't start another argument in front of Inspector Esposito. I was glad too—I was sick of all the fighting. It wasn't getting us any closer to the Crimson Caper.

The inspector sighed. "We'll only have the answers when he awakes. I'll ask the doctor when that will be."

As the inspector left, an uncomfortable silence spread across the room. Ben shifted awkwardly, Uncle Henry's face still twisted with sadness as he stared at Carla, and Vincent and Carla glared at each other.

For once, I wished it was me who was unconscious right now.

A minute later, footsteps approached the room. As I turned, expecting it to be the inspector, it was Enrique Bello instead. He had several drinks and snacks from the vending machine in his hands.

"I'm back, Vinny. Brought some food, too," he said before he looked up at us and gulped. "Oh, everyone's here."

"Enrique Bello? What the hell are you doing here?" Carla asked, crossing her arms.

He paused, at a loss for words. "Well, I was... you see, Carla... why shouldn't I be here? I have every right to visit the hospital."

"As if I believe you. You're the Crimson Caper, aren't you?" Carla asked, getting in his face. "You probably set the fire and put Tony inside to frame him. Wait until Inspector Esposito gets back. You'll be in jail by the end of the—"

"Enough!" Vincent sighed. "You can tell her the truth, Enrique. It's fine."

He lowered his voice. "But Vinny, it could ruin us. Think of the consequences—"

Vincent turned to Carla. "Enrique and I... are partners."

"Partners in what? Business?" Carla asked.

Enrique shook his head. "No, Carla. *Romantic* partners. We've been dating for five years."

The room went quiet.

"Then you lied about knowing each other," I said. "I saw you two get in the same car when you left the fashion show."

Vincent nodded. "We had to keep it a secret—not to deceive you, but for our own protection."

Carla scoffed. "But why? Same-sex relationships are legal in Italy. We even have a gay pride parade held every June in Milan. I've been before—The Milano Pride is beautiful."

"Legal perhaps, but not widely accepted," Vincent replied. "You know how the Catholic Church feels about the topic. Many share their opinion. Some people can be violent in their protests. We were afraid."

"And it's not just that," Enrique added. "I work with fashion brands around the world. Some countries are extremely homophobic. If the news spread about me, I could lose it all."

"*Mio Dio,*" Carla muttered, looking down. "I see."

"And now you have leverage," Enrique said, crossing his arms. "You can destroy our careers by using this against us. Your competition in the fashion world would be gone with a few words."

"Use it against you? Why would I do that? I'm not cruel —and it's none of my business who you date," Carla replied. "But I'm still convinced either one of you is the Crimson

Caper. Now that I know how close you two are, it seems obvious you're working together to sabotage me."

"As I've said before, neither of us is the Crimson Caper," Vincent replied. "When you accuse us, the *real* culprit gets away—and my brother's hurt in the process. As always when it comes to you."

When I thought another argument would break out, the inspector returned. He carried his notepad, glancing down at it. "Both the doctor and his medical records confirm *Signore* Rossi will live. The doctor believes he'll wake any moment now."

Everyone looked at Antonio. His eyes were still shut.

"Well, what are we supposed to do in the meantime?" Ben asked. "Just hang around and wait for Sleeping Beauty here to wake up?"

The inspector nodded. "Indeed—it appears we have no choice. *Signore* Rossi has information for us. And it could help to bring the Crimson Caper to justice. But until then...." The inspector leaned forward, placing handcuffs around Antonio that tied him to the bed. "He's under arrest."

"You can't do this," Carla huffed. "For one, you have barely little evidence. And I know in my heart he's innocent."

"For once, I agree with her," Vincent muttered. "My brother's not capable of anything criminal, inspector."

"That's not exactly true. He broke into Carla's house," I said. "And he was sneaking around backstage after the sabotage. He's not entirely innocent, you know."

Vincent and Carla glared at me.

The inspector nodded. "*Signorina* Prince is right. If anything, his presence at the Fashion Palace proves his guilt —as both the arsonist *and* the show's saboteur. I'm eager to hear his explanation, but my stance is clear. Antonio Rossi is the Crimson Caper."

Uncle Henry, Ben, Vincent, and Enrique sat in the waiting room while we killed time. Only an hour had passed and I was already bored. Carla excused herself to go to the bathroom as I flipped through an Italian magazine, looking at the beautiful fashion inside.

I felt bad Carla might never get to make fashion again. Or, at least, get another chance at a high-profile fashion show.

The inspector paced the floor, looking over his notepad. A second later, his cell phone rang. He excused himself and left the room to answer it. I tip-toed after him, listening around the corner. Fortunately, he was speaking in English.

"Matches? They burnt down the Palace?" the Inspector said into his phone. "Awful. *Si*, the signed matches inside would prove it. And the Crimson Caper signed the matchbox near the back door in red lipstick? How strange..."

The red lipstick made me think of Lance again. And since he was there at the Fashion Palace, it made him look pretty suspicious.

"Yes, I agree," he continued, not noticing me. "I'll wait until *Signore* Rossi wakes and ask him questions, then you can bring him to the station. I'll investigate the Palace again shortly after. Just in case we missed something. *Ciao*."

I needed to keep an eye out for someone with matches. And get away before the inspector noticed me.

He lingered behind to grab a cup of coffee, giving me enough time to make it back. He joined us a minute later. I took my seat again as the inspector sat across from me, but I couldn't read magazines anymore. My mind had filled with the Crimson Caper and what they'd do next.

Carla sighed and rose to her feet. "I need some fresh air. My anxiety's bothering me again. Be right back."

"Don't go too far," the inspector replied. "Stay close in case the Crimson Caper returns."

As Carla nodded and left the hospital, I decided to wander the halls until I found my way to Sasha's room. And possibly overhear more gossip. Had Carla bothered to check on her again? Or was she left here alone to suffer?

As I knocked on her door, someone opened it on the other side. It was Sasha but she was up on her feet now with the help of crutches. Fully dressed and with make-up on, she looked much better than the last time I'd seen her. She noticed me immediately. My high heels had a habit of giving me away, especially on marble floors.

"Jessica...Prince, right?" she asked. "What are you doing here?"

"That's me. I wanted to check on you."

She scoffed. "Yeah, right. You're only here because of Carla's ex-husband. I heard the Fashion Palace burned down. The nurses were gossiping about Antonio. You know, I feel sorry for him—but a part of me thinks he's guilty. I mean, he has the perfect motive or whatever, right?"

She was right, he did. But a part of me felt like I didn't know the whole story—as if some pieces of the puzzle were missing. I looked down at her hospital bed. She was packing her clothes and personal items into a suitcase.

"Are you going home?" I asked.

She nodded. "Well, sort of. I'm going back to the hotel. I hope to return to New York in a few days."

"Maybe you shouldn't. What if the inspector needs your help on the case? The investigation is still ongoing."

She snorted. "Do you think I care? I've put up with

enough. Besides, I have nothing to tell him. Seems Antonio what's-his-name is the main suspect, anyway."

"But what about the doctors? Did they say you're okay to leave?"

She sighed. "The doctors think I should stay a few more days, but I can't. I'm going crazy staring at these white walls. I'm home-sick—and I want to get away from the Crimson Caper as soon as possible."

"All right, I get it. I'd probably feel the same way. How are you feeling?"

"Sore," she replied, touching her back, "but I'll live. Still haven't forgotten my promise to sue the pants off Carla. Just gotta find a good lawyer."

As she continued to pack, something small inside the suitcase caught my eye. It was a single box of matches—and several of them were missing.

"Are those your matches?" I asked. "Where did you get them?"

She slammed the suitcase closed. "Brought a few boxes with me from New York. You never know when you might need one, right? It's not illegal, Jessica."

"Yeah, I know," I replied, "but the police found evidence that matches were—"

Footsteps approaching caught my attention. As I turned around, the inspector stood in front of me, holding up his cell phone.

"*Signorina* Prince, may I speak with you a moment?" the inspector asked.

I nodded. "Of course. Bye, Sasha—and feel better."

"Thanks, Jessica. Here's hoping."

"How are you feeling, *Signora* Simpson?" the inspector asked, glancing at Sasha.

"Angry, Inspector. Can't believe someone would do this to me," she replied. "When you find them, make them pay."

"I'll certainly do my best. *Ciao* for now."

As the inspector and I left the room, Sasha closed her door. I couldn't stop thinking about her matches. What would she need them for? And was it a coincidence similar ones burned down the Fashion Palace? Since she said she brought a few matchboxes with her, why was there only one box left?

Sasha looked injured, but it would've still been possible for her to set the fire. *Anything* is possible if you're angry and vengeful enough.

I was about to tell the inspector what I'd learned but he spoke first. "*Signorina* Prince, there you are. Where is your uncle?"

"Still out in the waiting room, Inspector. What's going on?"

"As I was going to tell him, I'd like you and your friends to return to your hotel. For safety reasons, mostly. Please pass the message along that there's been an incident."

"What kind of incident?"

He shook his head. "I can't say—it's a police matter. But it would be best if you stayed out of the way."

I was just about to argue when an officer approached Inspector Esposito, then they walked away to whisper. Some of it was in English while other words were in Italian. It was enough for me to figure it out. Especially with an Italian dictionary on my smartphone.

"It came from a blocked number," the Inspector was whispering. "The phone call I just received. When I answered it, the person was using a voice changer."

"A blocked number and a voice changer," the cop murmured, making me think back to Josephine. "It was the Crimson Caper, right?"

"Very good. They called to taunt me—to tell me I'll

never find them. After a few seconds, they hung up. I doubt my officers can trace the call."

"Then it couldn't have been Antonio. He's still unconscious."

"Indeed. *Signore* Rossi must be innocent. In light of this confession, I have no choice but to drop the Crimson Caper charges against him. But he still must explain why he was at the Fashion Palace."

As I took in all the information from my eavesdropping, Carla approached from around the corner. She was so quiet, almost like a prowling cat. "Sorry—couldn't help but overhear. Did you say you're not going to arrest Tony anymore?"

He turned around, sighing. The officer he was speaking to walked away. "Indeed, *Signora* Valentine. He has an alibi for the Crimson Caper crimes. I was so certain he was guilty. I thought I had a breakthrough in the case."

She scoffed. "You've wanted to pin this on him from the beginning, Inspector. How does it feel knowing you almost put an innocent man in jail?"

"I'm terribly sorry for any pain I might have caused. But I was only doing my job—"

Vincent and Enrique rushed past us, heading straight for Antonio's room. As I wondered what was going on, Uncle Henry came running up to us, out of breath. "There you are. The doctor said Antonio's awake now. Figured you and the inspector would want to know."

The inspector nodded. "Good—then we'll have all the details soon enough. If *Signore* Rossi *isn't* the Crimson Caper, I hope he'll have some theories on who is."

Eleven

WHAT LITTLE REMAINS

Carla ran down the corridor as soon as she heard Antonio was awake. Uncle Henry, the inspector, and I followed her, entering the room. A moment later, Ben, Vincent, and Enrique joined us.

Antonio looked exhausted and groggy, but he seemed to be okay. Carla threw herself on him and Vincent rolled his eyes. As she hugged him tight, he furrowed his eyebrows and sat up.

"Where am I? What happened?" He glanced around, noticing us. "Why are you all here?"

"You're at the hospital in Milan. Someone started a fire at the Fashion Palace, and you were found unconscious inside," I replied. "We came to check on you. Do you remember?"

He shrugged. "Bits and pieces. *Mio Dio*, my head hurts."

"Tony, I'm so glad you're alive!" Carla said, pulling away from him to give him a glare. "But what were you doing there in the first place?"

"That's a question I'd also like to know," the inspector said, pulling out his notepad. "Do tell."

"I was out for a walk. I do that sometimes to clear my head," he muttered. "When I saw the fire, I ran inside."

"You did?" the inspector asked. "And what was the reason for that?"

"It might sound silly, but I wanted to save some of Carla's designs," he replied. "The *polizia* closed off the Palace and she wasn't able to get back inside. I had to try to save *some* of her clothes."

Carla turned to glare at the inspector. "That's true. Your officers refused to let me grab my things, citing safety concerns. Do you know how hard I worked on those clothes?"

"The lockdown was for safety reasons, *Signora*. We can't be too careful with the Crimson Caper still on the loose. If you'd been there, perhaps your fate would be similar to your ex-husband's—or worse," the inspector replied. "Did you happen to save any article of clothing, *Signore* Rossi?"

Antonio shook his head. "I almost did, but then I fell unconscious. Must've inhaled too much smoke. The last thing I remember was darkness."

"The clothes are important, Tony, but they're not worth your life," Carla said. "Remember that."

"Tony, you could've been killed," Vincent said. "You did all this for her? A woman who broke your heart?"

He nodded. "I did. But can you blame me, Vinny? Wouldn't you do the same for someone you love?"

"Only if they loved me back," Vincent muttered, glaring at Carla, "and only if they were worth running into a fire for."

Carla stepped forward, gritting her teeth. "I've had enough of your remarks, Vincent—"

"We're getting off-topic here. The arguing can wait," I interrupted. "Antonio, do you know who started the fire at the Palace?"

He shook his head. "No, sorry. But now that I think about it, no, it sounds crazy."

"Tell us, *per favore*," the inspector replied. "Every bit of information helps."

"Well, I thought I saw someone in a red trench coat fleeing the area," he replied, "but I can't be sure. The smoke was too thick and I was distracted trying to get to the clothes."

The inspector nodded. "That makes sense. I believe the Crimson Caper's responsible for this. The note in the alley proves it."

"Probably." Antonio tugged at the handcuffs, noticing them. "What are these for, Inspector?"

"Allow me to remove them," the inspector replied, stepping forward and releasing him. "You were my primary suspect."

"*Were*? So now you're letting me go?" Antonio asked, perking up.

The inspector nodded. "For now."

Antonio looked up at Carla. "For the record, Inspector, I wouldn't ruin my ex-wife's career. I'd never want to do anything to hurt her. I'd follow her to the ends of the Earth."

Carla sighed. "It was a risky thing you did, Tony—running into a burning building. Although I appreciate what you tried to do, don't do it again."

He didn't say anything. He just slumped farther in the bed, almost like a child getting scolded.

"How long do you have to stay at the hospital?" Vincent asked.

"Twenty-four hours. The doctors want to keep me here for observation," Antonio replied. "Then I'll be allowed to go home."

"You'll stay with me at my apartment, Tony," Vincent

said. "I don't think it's safe for you to be alone right now. Just in case this individual comes back."

"That's good to know," the inspector said, writing it down in his notepad. "Do you own matches, *Signore* Rossi? Either on you or at home?"

Antonio frowned. "Uh, no. I don't smoke or light candles so I don't need them. Why would you ask me that?"

The inspector put his notepad in his pocket. "Curiosity. I believe my questions have been answered. Now I must take my leave. My officers are waiting on me to investigate the Palace once the fire is safely out."

"I want to come, too," Carla said. "As painful as it'll be, I need to see how damaged the Palace is."

"And we'll go with Carla. For moral support." Really, I just wanted an excuse to get inside that place again and investigate. I glanced at Uncle Henry. "Right?"

"Yes, of course." Uncle Henry turned to Carla. "If she'll have us there."

"It couldn't hurt. *Grazie*, everyone."

We glanced at the inspector for permission. "I'll allow it again as long as you don't tamper with evidence. And remain on your best behavior."

"Cross my heart and hope to die," I said.

"While you're all gone, I'll stay with Tony," Vincent replied, glaring at Carla. "Someone should."

"Me too," Enrique said, "in case the Crimson Caper returns."

Carla crossed her arms. "I still think the Crimson Caper's in this room. Wouldn't put it past you, Vincent."

Vincent barked out a laugh. "Do you honestly believe I'd commit arson? And then get my brother hurt in the process? *Mio Dio*, you're a real piece of work, Carla. I'm glad you divorced my brother. I only wish he'd learn his lesson and move on. Before it kills him."

"Vinny, that's enough." Antonio glared at him. "Don't speak to her like that. For me."

Vincent glared at Carla but didn't say another word. It was clear he loved and respected his brother, but I still wasn't convinced he couldn't do something like this—or his lover, Enrique.

The inspector sighed. "Petty accusations will get us nowhere—only evidence will. And I hope the Fashion Palace will give us something to work with."

"Same. Enrique, I never had the chance to ask you this before," I began, "but how did you know the Palace was on fire? You even knew about it before the journalists."

He looked down before he met my gaze. "Are you kidding? You'd have to be blind not to notice the smoke. I was out for a drive and saw it myself."

His story seemed plausible, but why did I have trouble believing him? And was it a coincidence both Lance and Enrique happened to be in the area while the building burned?

As the five of us left the hospital room and walked outside, I noticed Sasha standing near the side of the road with her suitcase. It looked like she was trying to hail a cab. She had something in her mouth, but I couldn't make out what it was from far away. She tried to cover it by keeping her hand over her lips.

"Jess, are you coming?" Uncle Henry asked as he walked toward the limo.

"In a minute," I replied, my eyes still glued to Sasha. "Wait for me. I just need to do something first."

As Uncle Henry, Ben, Carla, and the inspector got into their vehicles, I walked over to Sasha. As I tapped her on the shoulder, she turned around, startled. And I noticed a fat cigarette in her mouth.

"Sasha, are you smoking?" I asked.

"Shh!" she whispered. "Don't say it so loud!"

"Why not?"

She sighed, blowing smoke from her mouth. "Because my modeling agency doesn't allow smokers. They say it ruins your body or whatever. To them, image is everything."

"But you do it anyway. Why?"

"It's my stress reliever. I know it's not healthy, so spare me the lecture," she said, stomping her cigarette on the ground. "Did you come over here to tell me it's bad for me?"

"I mean, it is. Smoking is terrible. But no, I came to get answers—and I think I just did. How do you light your cigarettes?"

"With matches. How else?"

"Not a lighter?"

She shook her head. "I prefer matches. They remind me of my late grandpa who smoked too. In a way...I guess it makes me feel closer to him. I guess we both had the same bad habit."

"Oh. Well, I'm sorry for your loss then. But how often do you smoke? Enough to go through several matchboxes?"

She nodded, hanging her head in shame. "Yeah, way more than I should. You won't tell anyone, will you? If my agency finds out I'm smoking, it'll be a breach of contract. They could fine me. Maybe even fire me. And I've been through enough these past few days!"

I shook my head. "Don't worry—your secret's safe with me. It's none of my business, anyway. Thank you, Sasha. You've been very helpful."

"Helpful?" she asked as I walked away. "How? What are you talking about, Jessica?"

I only smiled.

When we arrived at the Fashion Palace, the building was still standing. The fire was serious but not big enough to completely destroy it. I wondered if that was done on purpose by the Crimson Caper. To scare us off but not kill anyone or completely destroy anything—just like before. The smell of smoke still lingered in the air and several police officers guarded the singed doors.

The inspector spoke with a nearby firefighter before he turned to me. "They said it's safe to go inside. Follow me, everyone."

As Uncle Henry, Carla, and Ben followed us, the inside was a sad scene. With the runway crumbled, the walls stained black, and soot on the floor, nothing looked salvageable. The racks of clothing left behind were completely burned. Not one single article of clothing survived. I had a feeling the culprit wanted it that way.

"*Mio Dio*," Carla cried, looking around in horror. "My fashion's ruined. Some pieces I worked on for years."

"I'm sorry, *Signora* Valentine. I'm sure the firefighters did all they could," the inspector said, "but it wasn't possible to save them."

Carla rolled her eyes. "It might've been if only you would've let me in before. If you ask me, you should be partly responsible for this, Inspector. I'll find a lawyer and sue you for the destruction of my clothes. And that damned Crimson Caper. Just wait and see."

Carla rushed to the backstage area as Uncle Henry shook his head. "Sorry about that, Inspector. She's probably just blowing off steam and didn't mean that. This can't be easy for her. Her show's sabotaged, now she loses the majority of her clothes in a fire?"

"I'll go find her," I said. "And I think I should go alone. Maybe some girl talk will cheer her up."

Uncle Henry sighed. "All right but be careful. Let me know if you need me."

I promised I would. As I followed Carla, heading down the hallway, I heard crying coming from one of the dressing rooms. When I entered the room, I saw Carla sitting on a burned piece of furniture, crying into her hands. There were piles of clothes around her, ruined by the flames.

"Carla, are you all right?" I asked, walking over to her.

She shook her head, wiping her tears away. "No, I'm not all right, Jessica. Some madman sabotaged my show. And now they've burned the city's greatest fashion building to the ground. I just... I'm at a loss as to what to do."

I frowned. "I know. I'm so sorry, Carla."

She sniffled. "*Grazie*, Jessica. I apologize if I've been rude to you and your uncle before. It's just been a stressful time for me."

"Don't worry—I understand. But I do have some questions if that's okay?"

"Sure, I guess it couldn't hurt. What do you want to know?"

"Are you sure it wasn't your ex-husband? He's broken into your house before. Vincent said it himself—Antonio would do anything to get your attention. Maybe even sabotage."

She looked up at me with her bloodshot eyes. "No... no, there's no way. He's completely innocent."

Before I could respond, the inspector knocked on the door and then entered the room. "Sorry to interrupt but I found something suspicious. It's over where *Signore* Rossi was found unconscious."

I turned to Carla. "You were saying?"

She shrugged. "I don't know what the inspector's talking about. Tony couldn't have done something like this."

"You might change your mind when you see this, *Signora* Valentine," the inspector said. "Follow me."

Carla trailed behind as I walked with the inspector. I found Uncle Henry, Ben, and a handful of officers standing near the exit door.

"It was here the firefighters claimed they found *Signore* Rossi," the inspector said. "And a few steps away, we found this."

The inspector handed an article of clothing to Carla to observe. It looked heavy and was badly scorched in her hands, almost unrecognizable. But there was no mistake about it.

She was holding a red trench coat—the same one the Crimson Caper wore. Yet another one.

"How weird is it that this was found near Antonio's body?" Ben asked. "That just screams guilty to me."

"It's not weird—it's ridiculous," Carla said. "So what if it was found near his body? It still doesn't mean he's the culprit. Maybe it was a set-up?"

The inspector nodded. "That theory's very possible. And I'll tell you why. I received a phone call while *Signore* Rossi was unconscious in the hospital from a person claiming to be the Crimson Caper."

Uncle Henry sighed. "Then I guess the culprit isn't Antonio. Too bad. It would've been easy to pin this on him. He certainly hasn't made himself look innocent."

The inspector nodded. "Indeed. In the meantime, I won't arrest him—not with conflicting evidence. But I still consider him a suspect."

"Was there any other evidence?" I asked.

"None, *Signorina*—which I believe the Crimson Caper was counting on," the inspector replied. "However, the matchbox with the red lipstick still remains. I've ordered my officers to dust it for prints. It might be too badly burned but we could get a partial."

"Oh, take this too." I reached into my purse and pulled out the lipstick that was still wrapped in a tissue to prevent DNA from getting on it. "I found this under my limo. Right after someone wrote on my limo door with it. It's Lance LaDoux's brand. Could have DNA on it, maybe."

The inspector carefully took it, then passed it along to a nearby officer. "Will do. *Grazie.*"

"What now? When will you find my saboteur, Inspector?" Carla asked, placing her hands on her hips. "I'm getting impatient."

"With luck, *Signora*, soon," he said. "Let's hope the Crimson Caper makes a mistake. If not, we have no other evidence."

"I'll keep my fingers and toes crossed." Uncle Henry checked his watch. "It's nearly dinnertime, and I'm starving. Let's head back to the hotel and grab a bite to eat."

The Inspector nodded. "Good idea. My wife's likely preparing dinner as we speak. I'll be in touch, everyone. Take care in the meantime."

As he left, I grinned. "I hope the lipstick I found will help. Or some of my suggestions. I really hope the inspector appreciates me."

Carla shook her head. "An investigation is no place for a child, Jessica. If you don't mind your own business, the Crimson Caper might come after you. And I have enough on my conscience."

As she stormed off outside, we followed Carla, making our way toward the limo as Larry waited for us. As I opened the door to get in, I saw someone walking around the side of the Palace. When I looked closer, I realized it was Sasha, crutches and all. She went from a possibly broken back to crutches pretty fast. She had a camera in her hands and was snapping pictures of the building. Why would she want to document this? And why was she even here at all?

As I stared at her, Ben noticed. "Hey, Jess? Are you getting in or not? The breeze is cold, you know."

"Sorry," I muttered, shutting the door. "I'll be right back."

Ben rolled down the window. "Wait! Jess, where are you going?"

As I walked toward Sasha, Ben's voice must've alerted her. When she turned around and noticed me, she froze, her eyes wide in fear.

"Sasha! What are you doing here?" I asked. "What are you taking pictures of?"

A second later, she grabbed her crutches and ran away from me. I didn't bother to chase her—my high heels were too tight and expensive to break. But as she sprinted off, I noticed something odd.

Something had fallen out of her pocket. And she was in much better shape than I realized, well enough to run. Did she even need the crutches? Or was she faking her injury this whole time?

When she reached the end of the street, a taxi waited for her. She hopped in the back seat and sped off into the distance. I sighed, not even knowing where Sasha was staying to contact her.

As I looked down, I noticed something sitting on the ground. It was a small card that had fallen out of Sasha's pocket as she took off. I thought it was a tissue or something at first. When I bent down to pick it up, I realized it was a business card with Vincent Rossi's name, email, and phone number. It said to call if someone was a witness to breaking news or wanted to leak a story.

But why would Sasha have this? What was she planning to do with it, and did it relate to the photographs she took? I wasn't even aware Vincent Rossi and Sasha knew each other.

As I pulled out my notepad and scribbled in my findings, I realized one thing—this case was getting stranger. But was it possible Sasha was the real Crimson Caper?

Twelve

A MATTER OF FINGERPRINTS

When we returned to the hotel, everyone made their way toward the dining hall. We didn't speak much, still shocked someone would set the Fashion Palace on fire. It took someone really spiteful and angry to do that. As we chowed down on some amazing Italian pasta, my cell phone rang. I excused myself to answer it.

"Hello?"

"*Signorina* Prince," the inspector said. "How are you doing?"

"I'm fine, Inspector. No sign of the Crimson Caper yet. Did you get the fingerprints off the matchbox?"

"We did—and it isn't good. All we could manage was a partial print, as I suspected. Not enough to run it through our database. The lipstick tube you provided was clean. I thought I'd call and check on you. Make sure the Crimson Caper hadn't returned. And to let you know the results since you provided evidence for us. *Grazie* again."

"Of course, Inspector. Anytime." I sighed. "So, where do we go from here?"

"I'd like to enlist your help. I know this is unorthodox, but you know the suspects and they may let their guard down around a civilian. And a teenager at that. If you found a fingerprint for me, I could do a comparison from there," he replied. "I think you know the list of six suspects. Since I don't have cause to issue warrants for their fingerprints, they must voluntarily give them to me."

"I'll do my best to convince them, Inspector. Or maybe I'll happen across something left out in the open, like a cup or something. I'll let you know. And thanks for including me."

After I hung up, Ben gave me a funny look. He knew I was up to something.

"Who was that?" he asked.

"Oh, just the inspector," I replied. "There wasn't enough fingerprint evidence to find a match, but he could run a comparison if someone volunteered. Or if I found a fingerprint somewhere. Uncle Henry, will you give your fingerprints?"

He nodded. "Yes, of course. I have nothing to hide."

"I'll do it, too," Larry said. "Only to clear my name. My wife would kill me if I went to jail in Milan."

"Great, thanks. Ben?"

Ben shrugged. "Sure, why not? Anything for you, Jess."

Everyone looked at Carla but she wasn't saying anything. I sighed, realizing I'd have to come right out and ask. "Carla, will you volunteer your fingerprints?"

She took a sip from her wine glass and shook her head. "No, I'm sorry. I'm the victim here. Do you think I want to be treated like a common criminal?"

"It's not like that," I replied. "This could help the inspector's investigation."

"Will *you* have your fingerprints taken, Jessica?"

"Yeah, of course. I want to help the inspector in any way I can."

Carla stood up, throwing her napkin on the table. "I

respect that. And I hope you can respect my decision too, for obvious reasons. I need to go relax now. *Ciao*."

As she walked away, Uncle Henry shook his head. "Why can't we have one nice, normal dinner?"

After we finished eating, I brought a plate up to Josephine's room. As I knocked on the door, I heard footsteps approach and the chain rattle. I could hear her heavy breathing on the other end.

"Who's there?" she asked. "You can't get in. I have a chain lock!"

"It's me—Jessica. Look through your peep-hole if you don't believe me."

She must've realized it was me because the door opened a second later. She left only enough space for me to enter, then shut the door behind us. I handed her a plate of food, and she took it with a sad smile.

"Thanks, Jess. Sorry I haven't been around much lately," she said, taking a seat on the bed. "I've just been too scared to go downstairs."

I nodded. "Don't worry about it. I understand."

As I walked into the room, I noticed the television was on. Josephine was watching some Italian soap opera with the English subtitles on. I glanced outside her balcony window, but I didn't see the Crimson Caper.

Would they return without their red trench coat? Or did they have an extra set of clothes somewhere?

"So," Josephine began, shoveling spaghetti into her mouth, "anything exciting going on?"

I thought about the Palace fire, Sasha's strange behavior, and Lance's lingering. "Well, where do I start?"

"I know the Palace burned down. Saw it on the news," she replied. "I don't speak a word of Italian, but the pictures were hard to misinterpret."

"It was pretty bad. But one more thing," I said. "This is a

little uncomfortable to ask, but would you consider giving the inspector your fingerprints?"

She froze. "Me? Why? Am I considered a suspect?"

"Well, everyone's *technically* a suspect. But that's not important. What's important is helping the inspector get what he needs."

"I *do* think it's important. Giving away your fingerprints is a big deal! What if it's used against me?"

"It won't be. Trust me—this could help narrow the list to find the culprit."

She sighed. "I can't do it, Jess. I know I'm not the Crimson Caper. You'll just have to believe me."

I nodded, rising to my feet. "I see. Well, enjoy your dinner, Josephine. I'm glad the Crimson Caper hasn't stolen your appetite, at least."

She thanked me as I reached the door. When I turned the handle, she called out to me. "Hey, Jess?"

I turned around. "What's up?"

"If the Crimson Caper could burn down an old building, do you think they'll resort to murder?"

I paused to think. "I hope not, but anything's possible. The culprit hates Carla, but do they hate her enough to kill? And who would it be? I'm still not sure."

"Do you have leads? You know, who you think it might be?"

I smiled. "Oh, a few. I'm still investigating—and you've been a great help."

"I have? How? And are you sure you should be investigating this?"

Before she could ask any more questions, I left the room and closed the door. Whether she knew it or not, Josephine had just given me a big piece of the puzzle.

A very important piece.

As I walked to my room, I heard footsteps behind me. I

spun around, startled before I noticed it was Carla. It looked like she'd been on the phone.

"Sorry. Didn't mean to scare you," she said. "I just wanted to remind you about the dinner tomorrow night with Lance. He called to make sure I remembered."

"Right, *that* dinner. I'll be there. But why is Lance acting so shady? First, his lipstick brand left threatening messages, then I saw him poking around before the fire. Not to mention he was there when your fashion show was sabotaged. What gives?"

"Look, Jessica, LaDoux has no reason to sabotage me. If anything, he's been the most helpful and supportive. So drop it. Please."

As she turned to walk away, I followed. "My friend, Madison, told me the culprit's always the person you least suspect."

"Maybe that's true. But I'm sure it's not him. Now, I'd like to get back to my room and relax like I said."

"Wait—just one more thing. It's not about Lance, I swear."

She sighed, turning to face me. "What now, Jessica?"

"Sasha checked out of the hospital today. Do you know where she's staying in Milan?"

Carla shook her head. "No, I'm afraid not. While I booked the other models at a hotel a few miles from here, Sasha insisted on a fancier one, much like how she insisted on a dressing room. We had to get her a makeshift one since the Palazzo doesn't have dressing rooms. Anyway, she never told me which hotel she chose, just demanded a stipend for it. Can you believe that? *Mio Dio*, what a spoiled little princess."

"That's too bad. Speaking of the other models, have you heard from them? Or the stage crew?"

"No, of course not. They'll probably never speak to me

again. The Crimson Caper knew how to scare them off. But Inspector Esposito told me he spoke with the stage crew and other models and didn't see anyone suspicious. They all had alibis."

"Hmm, that's good to know. Isn't there any way we can get in contact with Sasha?"

Carla raised an eyebrow. "I have no idea. Why is it so important, anyway?"

"I've seen her do some questionable things. I wanted to ask her about them."

Carla thought for a moment. "While I don't appreciate your theories on LaDoux or my ex-husband, you could be right about Sasha. Wouldn't put anything past that little attention-seeker—even sabotage. I hope you find her."

"Me too," I replied. "Look, about the fingerprints. If you gave them to the inspector, it could really—"

"Jessica, I've already given you my answer." Her tone was much harsher now. "Leave it alone."

Carla rushed inside her room and closed the door in my face. I sighed.

"Really help," I mumbled, finishing my sentence.

I walked over and entered my room, feeling exhausted after today. I flicked on the light switch and collapsed onto my bed that the hotel staff had made. A minute later, there was a knock on the door. I opened it slowly in case it was the one person I didn't want to see. The crimson kind.

"Hey," Ben said, carrying a blanket and pillows with him. "Mind if I bunk with you again? I already asked your uncle, and he said it was cool. Gave me the 'no funny business' speech again though."

I smiled, opening the door wider. "Ha, that sounds like Uncle Henry. And of course. After the fire, I don't think anyone wants to be alone. Why didn't you come through the adjoining room?"

"Your uncle was on the phone. A work call. I didn't want to disturb him, so I walked through the main hall. And as for being alone? Yeah, you got that right. At least about me. Can't believe I thought Milan would be relaxing." He set up his blankets on the couch. "So, how goes the search for fingerprints?"

I sighed. "No one's cooperating, not even Josephine. You'd think they'd want to. Fingerprints on the matchbox could find the Crimson Caper. That means the sabotage and threats would finally end."

"Well, I believe you'll find them, Jess," Ben said, yawning as he laid down. "You're smart enough to figure it out."

"Thanks, Ben. And you know what? I think I know where to look next."

At breakfast the next morning, Carla and Josephine didn't show up. I could understand Josephine's reluctance, but Carla's seemed mean-spirited—and I'd need her for the next stage of my questioning.

"Do you think Antonio checked out of the hospital yet?" I asked the breakfast table.

Uncle Henry checked his watch. "Most likely. It's almost been twenty-four hours. Why do you want to know?"

"I wanted to ask him some questions. I know he's staying with Vincent, so I wanted to drop by. If that's okay."

"You couldn't have done that at the hospital? We were just there with the inspector. I thought you asked all your questions then."

I shook my head. "No. And anyway, this *has* to be at Vincent's place."

Ben gave me a sideways glance. "You have that look in your eyes again, Jess. What are you planning?"

I grinned. "Nothing. Nothing at all."

"Uh-huh. As if I believe that," Ben said.

"Fine. We can go, but we'll need Carla. She knows where Vincent lives," Uncle Henry said. "I'll bring Josephine some food since you did it yesterday. Ask Carla to join us at the limo."

We nodded and went our separate ways. As Uncle Henry filled a plate for Josephine, I took the elevator and knocked on Carla's door. When she opened it, she looked less than thrilled to see me.

"*Mio Dio*, it's you again," she muttered, crossing her arms. "I hope you haven't returned to pester me about giving my fingerprints."

"No, I haven't. Antonio's out of the hospital today, and he's staying with Vincent. Don't you want to check on him?"

She sighed. "I do. But it's complicated."

"How?"

"Seeing him brings back old memories," she replied, sitting on her bed. "I'm mostly angry at him for running into the Palace while it was on fire. What kind of an idiot does that? Ugh, he never listens to me."

"Do you still love him?"

"Love? Oh, I don't know. It's such a strong word, especially when fashion takes up a large chunk of my heart. But I know he loves me. And it doesn't hurt to have a man at your beck and call. I try to spare his feelings, at least."

"And what about my Uncle Henry? Do you love him, too?"

Carla sighed. "Henry's a very special man, as I'm sure you know. Kind, intelligent, thoughtful. I'm glad to know him."

"Yeah, but you didn't answer my question."

"Henry will always be a part of me, but our lives are too

hectic for love. It's why it didn't work with Tony," she replied. "Besides, you wouldn't want me as your step-aunt, Jessica. I can be very difficult to live with."

That's what everyone tells me, I wanted to say.

I cleared my throat, changing the subject. "So, will you come with us to see Antonio?"

She nodded, rising to her feet. "All right, I will. I think I still remember where Vincent's apartment is—not that Tony wouldn't tell me if I called and asked. But why do you want to come?"

"Well—"

"If you intend to interrogate him, I won't take you," Carla interrupted. "He's been under enough stress. And I've told you before that he's innocent."

"Then I won't. I do have questions," I said, "but for Vincent. Do you remember when I asked you what hotel Sasha was staying at?"

She nodded.

"I don't know where she is, and I have no way to track her down. But it doesn't matter—not when I know where Vincent is."

Carla frowned. "I'm confused. How does Sasha relate to my ex-brother-in-law?"

I smiled, making sure the business card was still in my pocket. "Oh, you'll see."

Half an hour later, we pulled into a swanky neighborhood. A tall apartment building sat in the distance, sparkling in the sunlight. It looked very expensive, but Vincent and Enrique had good jobs to pay for it.

"It's that one," Carla said. "Vincent threw us an engagement party here once—in happier times, of course."

"Well, it's nice to know everyone got an invite but me," Uncle Henry muttered from the front seat.

After Larry parked the limo, Carla sweet-talked the guard into letting us enter the secure building. We took the diamond elevator to the top floor, right up to the penthouse apartment.

Ben whistled as he looked around. "Nice digs."

Carla nodded. "Vincent's quite rich. He's one of the most popular art critics around—much to my dismay."

As the elevator dinged, Carla got off first. She knocked on the door to Vincent's apartment. "Vincent, it's me. Let me in."

The door opened a second later, but only a crack. Vincent's face poked out and frowned once he saw Carla. "*Mio Dio*, it's you again. What do you want, Carla?"

"To see Tony. He's here, isn't he?"

"He is. We just got back from the hospital. He's resting right now."

"Good. Now move out of the way."

Vincent shook his head. "No, I don't think I'll be doing that. You know I don't approve of your... fraternization. I don't understand why you care so much, either. Your marriage is over, Carla. Stop stringing him along."

Carla balled her fists, cursing in Italian. "If you don't let me in, I swear I'll—"

"Vinny? Who is it?" a voice asked, one that was very familiar.

Vincent sighed, turning over his shoulder. "It's no one, Tony. Just those door-to-door salesmen. I'll get rid of—"

As Vincent looked away, Carla slipped under his arm and made her way into the apartment. When he looked back and noticed, he scoffed.

"Hey! You can't burst in here!" he said, following her. "Breaking and entering is illegal the last time I checked."

I motioned for Uncle Henry and Ben to follow me inside as we pushed past Vincent. He sighed, closing the door. That was when I noticed Antonio lying on the couch, watching an old movie on a big-screen television.

Carla bent down and hugged him. "Tony, how are you feeling? Any better?"

He nodded. "A little, but my brother has me on bedrest. You know how he gets."

Enrique walked out of the kitchen with an apron on. "Breakfast is served, so come and get it whenever—" He paused when he saw us. "Oh, we have guests. Again."

"They were just leaving. Carla shouldn't be here, brother," Vincent said, looking down at Antonio. "She does nothing but cause you heartbreak. And now real, physical pain. Don't you realize you need to move on?"

"Actually, Carla wasn't the one who wanted to come here," I said. "I convinced her."

Vincent frowned. "You? You're Jessica Prince, aren't you? That American billionaire's niece?"

I nodded. "Yeah, and I'm looking into the Crimson Caper. Much to my uncle's disappointment. But I think you already know all about me, Vincent. Someone's been feeding you information, haven't they?"

When Vincent didn't say anything, Carla stood up with a scowl. "What the hell's going on here?"

"A good question," Enrique said, untying his apron. "I'd also like to know, Vinny."

There was a knock on the door, but Vincent didn't move. I smiled. "Don't worry—I'll get it. I think I know who it is, anyway."

And lo and behold, when I opened the door, I saw exactly who I imagined.

"Sasha? What are you doing here?" Carla asked, crossing her arms.

When Sasha saw us, her face turned white and she zipped around. But I was quicker this time, expecting her reaction. I grabbed her arm, preventing her from running.

"Let go of me, Jessica," she cried. "My back still hurts from that nasty fall. You'll end up making it worse!"

I shook my head, throwing her crutches away. "Oh, I don't think your back's as bad as you told us. Come inside, Sasha. You can explain to everyone how well you know Vincent."

Thirteen

AN UNCOMFORTABLE DINNER PARTY

Sasha glanced at Vincent, a look of terror spreading across her face. The room turned silent. That was when I looked down and realized Sasha was standing by herself—without the use of crutches.

I was right. Sasha had faked her back injury—and I had a few theories on why.

When Sasha wouldn't say anything, Vincent scoffed. "I don't know what you're talking about. I've never met this woman before."

"Yes, he's right. I don't know Vincent at all," Sasha stuttered. "I was lost, and somehow, I ended up here."

"I don't think anyone in this room believes that, Sasha. Right?" I looked around. "Pretty awful excuse, too."

Everyone except Vincent nodded, then I looked back at Sasha. "Whether you admit it or not, I can prove you know him."

Sasha crossed her arms. "How?"

"Let's back up for a second. I need to explain something first. We all saw that you don't need your crutches." I gestured at them in my hands. "You don't look like someone who has a back injury. Or any injury at all."

She froze for a second. "Well, I must be healing faster than I thought. Even the hospital thought I should stay a bit. In case it got worse. But it still hurts sometimes, I swear."

"Maybe it does." I nodded down at Sasha's purse. "And I bet if I went through that bag, I'd find those pictures you took earlier. You know, the ones of the Fashion Palace? Right before you ran from me?"

Sasha scoffed. "I don't know what you mean."

"Oh, I think you do." I circled her. "And I think I know why."

"Then what foolish conclusion have you come to?" Vincent asked.

"You're working together to get back at Carla. Sasha's been threatening to do it all this time," I replied. "Here's what I think happened. Sasha agreed to fake her back pain and get pictures of the Palace. She already sold pictures to the media before—pictures that ended up on the news—but she wanted revenge. Taking the pictures would've looked suspicious if you did it, Vincent—given your history of hating Carla—but not Sasha. You're trying to ruin Carla, aren't you?"

When Vincent didn't reply, Sasha moved closer to him. "What's the point in lying, Vincent. They already know. And something tells me this girl will harass us if we don't admit it."

"So it's true?" Carla asked, crossing her arms.

"How could you keep this from me?" Enrique asked Vincent.

"And me, too," Antonio added angrily.

Vincent sighed. "I was compiling an exposé to use against Carla—to show the public that Carla's dangerous. It would finally prove my point that she's a horrible woman. I had to keep it from you two. You never would've supported it—especially you, Tony. I had to do something to get back at her for the way she treated you."

"And the fake back injury?" I asked Sasha.

"It was Vincent's idea. We met at the fashion show after it was sabotaged. That was when we planned it," she replied. "I suggested suing Carla, but Vincent wanted something more personal. I was taking pictures of the Palace for the exposé, but you caught me. And with my testimony that Carla was rude and self-centered, it would've ruined her reputation for good."

"Part of this was for my brother—to watch his ex-wife go down in flames with the ruined fashion show and the story," Vincent said, "but also for you, Enrique."

"For me?" Enrique asked. "How?"

"With this story published, Carla's career would be destroyed. You wouldn't have competition anymore. You'd be the biggest fashion designer around."

"I don't need your help, Vinny—and I don't need someone keeping things from me, either," Enrique snarled. "Yes, Carla's my competitor. But I'm above sabotage and secrets. You should be, too. I'll stay at my own apartment tonight. I need some time to think about all this."

"And if I wasn't still feeling off, I'd leave, too," Antonio said. "I can't believe you'd go to this much effort to make my ex-wife look like a villain. *Mio Dio*, her show was sabotaged. She's been through enough."

Vincent shook his head and lowered his eyes.

"Are you the Crimson Caper?" Uncle Henry glanced around the room. "Any of you?"

"No, absolutely not. I wanted to cash in on the story, sure, but I don't do sabotage," Sasha replied. "No way."

"Me either," Vincent said. "This partnership was simple research for a story, and that's all. When the Fashion Palace burned down, I saw it as an opportunity to make Carla the bad guy. I had nothing to do with the arson or the sabotage."

"And I'm not guilty," Enrique said. "I didn't even know what these two were doing."

Antonio nodded. "My answer's the same. I'm not the Crimson Caper either."

"I'm sorry, Vincent," Sasha muttered. "I know you said I wasn't allowed to see you in person, but I had to give you these photographs. I was tired of waiting around. I wanted the exposé on Carla now."

"Why not just email them?" I asked.

"I wanted to see Vincent in person, maybe get a cash bonus or something. Figured he couldn't turn me down if I showed up and refused to leave."

"If you print anything about me, I'll sue you for libel," Carla said. "And I have witnesses to this, too. It's harassment."

Vincent sighed, nodding. "There's no point in the story now. You can stop pretending you're injured, Sasha."

"So, *that* was the reason you wanted to come here?" Ben asked me. "How did you know Sasha would show up?"

I shrugged. "I didn't. I only knew she had photographs, and my best guess was that she planned to sell them to someone—maybe a journalist. When Sasha ran from me, she dropped Vincent's business card. It started to make sense after that."

Vincent opened the door. "Are you happy now? You've ruined my story and exposed my only witness. Now get out."

"One more thing," I said. "Matches were used to burn down the Palace. A matchbox was left inside. The inspector found a partial fingerprint on it, but he needs something to compare it to. Will you give your fingerprints?"

Vincent scoffed. "Nice try, but I'll have to decline. Too

much of an invasion of privacy. Unless I'm being charged with something, the answer's no."

"Antonio?"

He shook his head. "My name's already been cleared. The inspector said so. And I'm too comfortable on this couch to move, so...."

I looked at Enrique, but he also shook his head. "Sorry, Miss Prince. What if Carla were to use it against me? Can't risk my reputation. Besides, I'm not the Crimson Caper."

"Before you ask, I'm saying no," Sasha said. "I've seen how those fingerprints are taken on CSI. Don't they use gross black stuff?"

"I'm not sure—"

"Nope! Not going to happen. Do you know how much I paid for these nice nails?" she asked, showing us her pink bedazzled nail polish. "I'm not risking messing them up. No freaking way."

I sighed. "Fine, I guess we'll have to find the Crimson Caper the hard way. Before I go, does anyone have any matches?"

Sasha glared at me. She'd never admit her smoking habit out loud.

"Only Vinny does. In the kitchen," Antonio said. "Mostly for birthdays."

Vincent nodded. "I do. Do you need one?"

"Interesting. I don't need one, but thanks." I turned to Uncle Henry and Ben. "Come on. Let's get to the police station so we can give our fingerprints."

"I'll be watching you, Vincent," Carla said as she made her way to the door. "I won't hesitate to call the *polizia* if you try anything else."

"*Mio Dio*, relax. You're so dramatic." Vincent rolled his eyes. "I'm not the Crimson Caper. And the last time I checked, writing an exposé on someone wasn't illegal."

As much as I wanted to believe him, he had made himself look pretty guilty. But if he was innocent, then who could it be?

When we arrived at the police station, it was just as crowded and hectic as before. Several journalists swarmed the building, shouting dozens of questions, but the officers held them back. I felt bad for the inspector. His job wasn't easy.

Larry parked the limousine around the back and came in with us. One of the officers guarding the front door recognized me and let us pass. Carla wasn't too thrilled about coming along, but she had no choice. We were her only ride back to the hotel.

The secretary at the front desk pointed toward the inspector's office, then we walked over and knocked on his door. A second later, the inspector emerged with a smile on his face.

"Ah, *Signorina* Prince," the inspector said. "You brought the whole gang. Here to have your fingerprints taken?"

I nodded. "Yep. We're ready."

"We'll need to be quick," Carla said. "Remember, LaDoux's dinner party is tonight. We can't be late."

"We'll have plenty of time. It's almost noon," Uncle Henry said. "Why do you like Mister LaDoux so much anyway?"

"Because he can help me, Henry. He has money and influence."

"So do I," Uncle Henry replied. "I'd be more than willing to—"

Carla shook her head. "I won't take anything from you, Henry. You know that."

The inspector cleared his throat. "Sorry to interrupt, but will you also give your fingerprints, *Signora* Valentine?"

She shook her head. "I've been over this with Jessica, Inspector. My answer is the same. Absolutely not."

"But surely you want to assist in my investigation. The process of elimination is important."

She laughed. "Assist? Of course. Have my rights violated? No. You might not understand it, but it's a matter of principle, Inspector."

I sighed. "Carla, come on—"

"You know what? I'll wait in the limo. I don't need this right now."

As she walked outside, the inspector sighed and turned to me. "What about the other suspects, *Signorina*? Did they agree?"

I shook my head. "Sorry, but no. They all pretty much had the same excuse. And I didn't see an opportunity to take something they put their DNA on. Not yet, at least."

"Interesting," the inspector muttered, scribbling in his notepad, "and very suspicious."

"But I agreed to cooperate," Uncle Henry said. "My niece told me you consider me a suspect, Inspector. If I can help clear my name, I'll do anything."

The inspector smiled. "If only the others were as helpful as you, *Signore* Prince. Follow me, *per favore*."

The inspector led us into an enclosed laboratory where fancy science equipment was set up. He walked over to a small desk, then I noticed the ink pad, gloves, and a piece of paper waiting for us.

"Police mostly use digital readers now to take fingerprints," he explained, "but I like to do things the old-fashioned way. My father was an inspector too, you see, and he solved many difficult cases. If it was good enough for him, it's good enough for me."

As the inspector pulled on his gloves, I stepped forward. "Interesting. I'll go first, Inspector."

The inspector nodded and began. The ink felt cold, the pad a bit sticky. Both Ben and Larry had their fingerprints taken without issue, even though Ben looked a little nervous. When it was Uncle Henry's turn, he took a deep breath and stepped forward, jutting out his hands.

"Here's to being innocent," he said.

When we finished, the inspector removed his gloves and smiled. "*Grazie*, everyone. You've been a big help. My team will treat this as a high priority. These will be analyzed within twelve hours. We have a special lab that can rush it."

"And whoever's fingerprints match is the Crimson Caper?" Ben asked.

The inspector nodded. "Quite possibly, *Signore*. I'll contact you when I receive the results. *Ciao* for now."

As we left the building, Ben's face turned completely white. "Look, I know I'm not the Crimson Caper, but what if the lab techs get it wrong? What if I end up in jail?"

I shook my head, laughing. Ben was always a big worrier. "No one here's going to jail. You know why? None of us is the Crimson Caper, and I know that for sure. You don't have to be scared, Ben."

"Hey, I'm not scared," Ben said, forcing himself to look tough. He even puffed out his chest. "I'm just... concerned. Yeah, that's it."

As he panicked, I noticed Carla near the limousine. She spoke on the phone again in the same hushed Italian as before. As we walked toward her, my heels clicking on the pavement, she noticed us and tucked away the cell phone.

"Was that Josephine again?" I asked.

"What? Oh, yes, it was," she replied. "I don't like leaving her alone. We may not always get along but the Crimson Caper's dangerous."

I nodded, hopping in the back seat. "Good point. Take us to the hotel, Larry. We have to get ready for our dinner tonight."

A few hours later, I applied the finishing touches to my hair and make-up. I chose the nicest dress I owned—pink, of course—as Ben put on his tux. I had to help him with the tie. Just as we were about to leave, Carla banged on our door.

"Come on," she said. "We can't afford to be late."

I rolled my eyes, grabbed my purse, then opened the door. "We're ready, Carla. Lead the way."

She had dressed in tight clothes, her cleavage leaking out of her top. She had overdone it with make-up and hairspray. It seemed like it was all an act for Lance, just a game to her to win his money and support.

"Never seen her so desperate before," Ben whispered. "This Lance guy already promised her money. Why drag us to a long dinner party? Just hand over the check, old man."

I shrugged. "I don't know, but it's a good thing we're going to his house. I can't help but find him suspicious."

Ben gave me a funny look. "Please tell me you're not going to snoop."

I kept my mouth shut and avoided his eyes.

Ben groaned. "Jess! What if you get caught?"

"I won't, Ben. Pinky swear."

"What if Lance takes his check away and Carla freaks out on you?"

"I promise I'll be careful," I muttered. "Look, Ben, I have to do this—"

Uncle Henry left his room in his nicest suit and sighed. "I already asked Josephine if she wanted to tag along. Unfortunately, she's still not in the right frame of mind to go anywhere right now."

"Man, the Crimson Caper hit her hard," Ben said. "I feel bad for her."

"I do too. It seems the Crimson Caper is out to traumatize us all." Carla shook her head. "Are we ready to leave now?"

Uncle Henry nodded and took us to our limousine. As Larry drove us closer to Lance's mansion—one of the most expensive houses in Milan, Carla told us—my heart raced.

What if Lance was the Crimson Caper? Was it a smart idea to spend time alone with him?

Larry pulled up to the sidewalk of the luxurious mansion and my jaw dropped. It was several floors high with sports cars and motorcycles sitting near the garage. Carla walked up to the front gate and spoke into the small intercom.

"We're here to see Lance," she said, fixing her top. "He's expecting us for dinner."

When the gate opened, we walked to the front door. We found it unlocked so we opened it and entered. As we followed Carla into the foyer, I noticed how dark, quiet, and empty the house was. It didn't look like anyone lived here. But as I looked around a little closer, I noticed things that seemed strange to me.

The foundation had cracks, the furniture looked old and falling apart, and the red wallpaper was torn at the edges. Even the chandelier above us looked a little worse for wear.

How could this be the house of one of the most successful fashion designers and cosmetic moguls in the world? The same one worth millions of dollars?

"Where is he?" Ben asked. "Not a very good host."

"My apologies, *monsieur*," Lance said, walking around

the corner with a champagne glass in his hands. "I had other business first. Follow me to the dining area, *s'il vous plaît.*"

As we walked into the dining room, I noticed a long glass table. Exactly five chairs waited for us, then Lance took his seat at the head of the table. Several glasses of champagne sat on the table for Uncle Henry and Carla.

"My butler, Manuel, will be here in a moment," Lance said, taking a sip of his champagne. "Make yourselves comfortable in the meantime."

"Hi, Mister LaDoux. How often do you stay in Milan?" I asked. "Is it a regular thing?"

"I stay a few times a year, but I can't stand hotels so I purchased this house. I spend all my time in Paris," he replied, glancing at Carla, "but some things are worth sticking around for, don't you think?"

Carla grinned. So far, everything was going according to her plan.

"May I use the bathroom, Mister LaDoux?" I asked.

Lance nodded. "*Oui*. It's down the hall to your left. Be quick, though. Dinner will be served shortly."

Ben gave me another one of his looks like the be-careful-and-don't-get-caught kind. I winked and fled the room as the others took their seats. But I didn't have to go to the bathroom. It was time for snooping Jessica Prince to come out for a visit.

As I wandered the mansion, looking for clues, the property damage worsened. Why didn't Lance take better care of his house? Did he just not care? If so, why not hire people for that?

Down the hall, I noticed a private room, maybe an office. The door looked open a crack, almost as if Lance forgot to lock it. I gasped after I pushed it open and entered the room.

A picture of Enrique and Lance, shaking hands and grinning, hung on the wall.

Fourteen

THE MAN WITH THE SCAR

Lance and Enrique knew each other after all—and they were much closer than I thought. The picture looked taken at Lance's house, right in his office. It seemed recent, judging by the wrinkles on Lance's face. But why hadn't Lance or Enrique mentioned their connection?

The office itself was very plain, cluttered with drawings for new fashion designs and cosmetics. It seemed to serve as a back-up office in case something happened to his Paris workspace. Countless medals and trophies in Lance's name decorated the room. Pictures of Lance and famous celebrities he'd met and worked with sat on the walls.

The neat desk caught my eye. With several folders on future fashion projects, there wasn't anything special about it—except a lipstick sat on top of it, the same brand and color as the ones the Crimson Caper used. It looked identical to the one I found near our limousine.

I picked it up using a napkin from my purse, careful not to get any fingerprints on this one. As I removed the cap, I noticed someone used it recently. The stick was much shorter than the new one I purchased at home.

I slipped it in my purse and opened the drawer to the

desk. The left drawer had a piece of paper with a list of names. It also had dates and price tags, ranging from two hundred dollars to a thousand. I couldn't understand any of it. I skimmed the list, trying to recognize the names, but they didn't look familiar.

When I opened the right drawer, I gasped. There was a briefcase inside, filled with what looked to be tens of thousands of dollars. I knew Lance was a millionaire—a super successful fashion designer and make-up mogul. But would he really leave this much money here? And in a briefcase instead of a safe? I had learned from Uncle Henry's business talks that probably wasn't a good idea.

As I shut the drawer, someone cleared their throat. "May I help you, *mademoiselle*?"

I spun around, startled to see a dark-haired man in a butler uniform. He stared at me with one eyebrow raised, then glanced down to realize I'd just snooped through the desk. There was no doubt about it—he'd caught me.

Better talk fast. Or else.

"I got lost," I sputtered. "I was just trying to find the bathroom, but then I wandered in here. Sorry about that."

"It's down the hall to the left," he replied, coldly.

I nodded and approached the door. "Thanks. With a house this big, the rooms can get confusing. My mistake."

As I walked by, he grabbed my arm. He said nothing for a few seconds, and I looked up at him in fear.

"Dinner is served," he finally said.

He released me and I quickened my pace down the hallway, not wanting to be alone with that man anymore. When I reached the dining hall, I sighed in relief to see Uncle Henry, Ben, Carla, and Lance waiting for me. There was always safety in numbers.

The butler wasn't lying. Platefuls of steak, lobster thermidor, rice, rich cheesecake, and a dozen other snacks crowded the table. My stomach growled at the sight of it all.

"Jess, are you okay?" Ben asked. "You were gone for a while."

I faked a smile and took my seat, draping the napkin across my lap. "I'm fine. Just got a little lost."

Lance chuckled. "*Oui*, I can relate. When I first moved in, I got lost more times than I'd care to admit."

Carla laughed a little louder than usual. I rolled my eyes at her. She wanted Lance's money, but did she have to be so obvious about it?

The butler entered the dining room and Lance nodded. "This is Manuel, the butler I mentioned. We have him to thank for this wonderful meal."

The butler didn't say anything. His eyes glanced at the living room and Lance seemed to understand the secret message. He rose to his feet and placed his napkin on the table.

"Excuse me for a moment," Lance said. "In the meantime, *bon appétit*!"

As Lance and the butler disappeared, Carla, Ben, and Uncle Henry dug in. Despite how hungry I was before, it seemed I'd lost my appetite. Because in the pit of my stomach, I knew one thing—the butler was telling Lance he'd seen me snooping in his office.

Lance returned a moment later, but the butler was gone. I lowered my eyes and reached for some of the rice, filling up my plate. I could feel Lance's eyes on me as he took his seat, but he didn't say anything. Not yet, anyway.

"We really appreciate you asking us over for dinner, *Signore* LaDoux," Carla said, breaking the silence. "You've been so wonderful to me since the show was sabotaged. If it weren't for you and my friends, I would've gone insane by now. I know I've been a bit difficult, but everyone at this table truly has my gratitude."

Lance smiled. "It's no trouble at all, Carla. I promised I'd help you, *oui*? We must look out for each other in the fashion world. And as we agreed, by the end of the night, you'll have your check. I'll see to it myself."

Carla nodded and looked less tense. She had gotten what she'd come for. We only needed to make it through dinner.

Lance turned his attention to me. "So, *mademoiselle*. You're Jessica Prince, *oui*?"

I nodded, nervously swallowing my food. "That's me, yeah."

"I've heard your uncle is a famous businessman in America," he replied. "We're a lot alike in many aspects."

Uncle Henry took a sip of champagne and chuckled. "I see my reputation precedes me. Yes, I've been a businessman for fifteen years. Prince Enterprises has an office in Venice, actually."

"I see. And you, *mademoiselle* Prince? What do you do?"

"Me? Oh, I'm just a high school student," I replied. "Nothing special."

Lance scoffed. "Oh, I don't believe that, *mademoiselle*. I've seen you with the inspector. You're helping him with the Crimson Caper case, *oui*?"

Uncle Henry looked at Lance in confusion. He had to know there was something fishy about his line of questioning. Where was Lance going with this?

"Well, not in any official capacity or anything like that. I'm no cop. But I've tried to give him tips, sure. I was the first one to see the Crimson Caper after all."

"Well, *mademoiselle*, if you two are so close," Lance said, cutting into his steak, "perhaps you can tell him I had nothing to do with this sabotage business. And if he were to, say, come to my house and search my office, perhaps it would not end well for him."

I swallowed again. There was no doubt he knew what I did—and that sounded like a threat. When I didn't speak, Lance looked up at me.

"Will you tell him that, *mademoiselle*?" he asked.

I nodded. "I can tell him that, yeah."

Lance smiled, but it looked forced. Carla didn't seem to catch on but it looked like Uncle Henry and Ben had. Their eyes flitted between me and Lance. They couldn't have known I'd gone to Lance's office, but they knew something wasn't right.

I couldn't bring myself to look away from Lance. His eyes were so piercing, so cold. While I still wasn't sure if he was the Crimson Caper or not, I knew he was up to something.

"Uh, can someone pass the salt?" Ben asked, breaking the silence.

We ate the rest of our meal in uncomfortable silence. Lance didn't bring up the inspector again, nor did I ask to go to the bathroom. Manuel returned a few minutes later to collect our plates and bring them to the kitchen.

"What a delicious meal, *Signore* LaDoux," Carla said, patting her stomach. "You must thank Manuel for us."

"I will," Lance replied. "And please, call me Lance. We're friends now, *oui*?"

Carla smiled. "*Grazie*, Lance. I mean that."

He rose to his feet nodded. "No, it's *moi* who should thank you all for a delightful evening. Carla, would you accompany me to my office? It's where I keep my checkbook."

As Carla stood up, tires screeched in the distance. Bright headlights shone through the dining room window, nearly blinding us. When they faded, I looked outside, noticing who it was.

A tall, dark-haired man in an expensive suit exited a black-tinted vehicle. Several other cars pulled up with more men in fancy suits. They wore sunglasses—which I found odd at night—and white headsets in their ears. It was almost as if they were bodyguards or something.

As the first man fixed his suit, I noticed the gleam of a pistol on his belt. My eyes widened. I reached for my cell phone, ready to dial the inspector's number if necessary.

Who were these men? If not police officers, why did they have guns?

"Who's that?" Carla asked, turning to Lance. "Another guest for dinner? He's a bit late. We're finished now."

"Stay here, everyone," Lance said, glancing out the window. "I won't be long."

Lance left and closed the dining room door behind him. But before he walked away, I saw the look in his eyes.

It was pure fear—and it was unmistakable.

The men pounded on the front door. I watched from the window as the group of men waited impatiently, checking their watches and tapping their feet. Lance opened the door a moment later but I couldn't hear what they were saying. They spoke in low, hushed tones.

"They have guns," I whispered to the table. "I saw one for sure, but I bet they all have them."

"Guns? *Mio Dio*, that's insane," Carla whispered. "It's dark outside. You're probably seeing things, Jessica."

"I know what I saw, Carla."

She still looked skeptical.

Ben nodded. "I believe Jess. What if these guys are dangerous?"

"Stand behind me, all of you," Uncle Henry said, shielding us with his body. "Just in case."

"This is absurd," Carla whispered. "These men are probably friends of Lance or something."

"I don't have any friends with guns," Ben muttered.

Footsteps echoed in the foyer, then the front door slammed shut. I heard yelling and it was coming from a voice I didn't recognize. Was it from the first man I had seen?

The door to the kitchen opened behind us and I jumped. Manuel stood there with the same dull expression on his face. "It's time to leave. Come with me to the back exit, everyone. Mister LaDoux was prepared for a situation like this."

"Prepared for what situation, exactly?" I asked. "Did he know that guy outside would show up?"

Manuel glared at me. "There's no time to explain, but you're in danger. Follow me or—"

The door to the dining room swung open. A second later, the group of men entered. The first man who looked to be their leader smirked at us. I saw him better in the light this time. He had black hair, brown eyes, and a knife scar across his left cheek.

"Well, well, well. Seems like there's a nice dinner party going on," he said, turning to Lance. He spoke perfect English and had a thick Italian accent. "Why wasn't I invited?"

Lance was quiet for a moment. "Pardon me, *monsieur*, but I assumed you were too busy to—"

"Oh, you're probably right. I have better things to do than go to parties," he muttered, looking at us. "Everyone looks like they're leaving. We haven't missed anything, have we?"

"Just dinner," I replied. "Who are you?"

The man glanced at me, his stare colder than Lance's. "Isn't it past your bedtime, kid?"

"It's past *all* our bedtimes," Lance said. "Let my guests go home, *monsieur*. We can discuss our business in private."

"And there's a lot to discuss. I'm not too happy with you, Lancey-boy," the man muttered, turning to me. "You're free to go. Get out of here."

Uncle Henry grabbed my arm and led me past the scary man. The man smirked at Carla, giving her a wink once he saw her.

"We'll be in touch, Carla," the strange man said. "I look forward to seeing you again."

She furrowed her brows. "I don't even know who you are."

He smiled. "You will soon. Don't worry."

"I don't think so," Uncle Henry said. "I don't know who you are, but I won't let you harass her."

"Hey, nobody's harassing anybody," the man replied, reaching for his belt, "but I don't like someone up in my face."

I grabbed Uncle Henry's arm as panic spread through me. "Come on, Uncle Henry. We need to leave."

"Smart kid," the man replied. "Listen to her, *Uncle Henry*."

Uncle Henry glared at the man and pulled us out of there. But as we left, I knew the man was watching us. Larry pulled up in the nick of time. As I entered the limo, I glanced through the window and saw Lance's face.

His arrogant, threatening demeanor faded. Now, he looked terrified and lost like a little child. As Larry drove away from Lance's house, I saw the man with the scar close the curtains.

Carla was livid as Larry stepped on the gas, taking us as far away as possible from Lance's house. When I glanced over at her, she crossed her arms and her face turned bright red.

"Why did you force us to leave?" she asked, directing her anger toward Uncle Henry. "He hadn't given me the check yet."

"Are you kidding?" Ben asked. "I'm pretty sure someone was about to get killed. That scary dude had a gun! Did you seriously want to stick around?"

"Not exactly," Carla grumbled, slinking down, "but I wanted Lance's money."

"Isn't anyone wondering why Lance wanted us to have dinner with him? Or why he wanted to give Carla the money alone, in his office?" I asked. "It's just weird."

Carla shrugged. "*Signore* LaDoux's a private man. He's also a legend in the fashion world, so I'd appreciate it if you didn't accuse him of anything."

"When I was gone, I snuck into his office. He had a picture of him with Enrique, for starters," I began. "But I also found red lipstick, a briefcase filled with cash, and a weird list of names."

Carla scoffed. "I'm sure he's met Enrique before. He's in the fashion world, after all. The lipstick's from his cosmetic company and the money was there because he's a millionaire. Simple explanations."

"And the list?"

Carla shrugged. "It could be anything. You're overreacting, Jessica. I think everything's fine."

I shook my head. "No, some things don't add up. Larry, please take us to the police station."

"Don't, please," Carla said. "It could jeopardize my friendship with Lance. And his money."

"I'd hate to agree with Carla," Ben began, "but you

heard what Lance said at dinner. If you meddle in his business, you'll pay for it, Jess."

"No. Jessica's right," Uncle Henry said. "Your suspicions aside, Lance could be in danger. What if that man kills him? Could we live with that on our conscience?"

No one said anything. Uncle Henry was right—we couldn't. We needed to do something.

When we arrived at the police station, it was well past eight in the evening. As we made our way inside the building, I walked toward the inspector's office and hoped he was still here. I only trusted him with this.

The door opened, then I breathed a sigh of relief when it was Inspector Esposito. He looked down at me, curiously. "*Signorina* Prince. I was just about to head home for the evening. My wife called and said she made some delicious lasagna. What are you doing here?"

"Lance LaDoux's in trouble. We had dinner at his house tonight and some guy came to visit him. It looked aggressive," I said. "He had dark hair, a business suit, and a nasty scar on his face."

The inspector paused for a moment. "A scar? Are you certain, *Signora*? Did this man travel with several bodyguards?"

"Well, yeah. Why?" Ben asked. "Is he some kinda celebrity?"

The inspector looked over our shoulders and opened the door a little wider. "Step inside my office, *per favore.* We have something very important to discuss."

Once the four of us were in the small room, the inspector shut and locked the door behind us. We waited in silence for him to speak, but he didn't. Instead, he walked over to his desk, opened the bottom drawer, and pulled out a grainy photograph.

He held up the picture. "Is this the man you saw tonight? The one who came to visit *Signore* LaDoux?"

I gasped, nodding. The picture looked like someone took it from far away, hidden behind a pile of bushes. The man in the photograph spoke to someone in a business suit near a warehouse and it looked very suspicious.

"Yes, that's him," Uncle Henry said. "Do you know him, Inspector?"

"Know him? I've been trying to arrest him for years, *Signore*," the inspector replied. "His name is Bruno Salvatore —and he's known for his mob connections and drug operations."

Fifteen

SHADY BUSINESS DEALS

Carla gasped. "That's impossible! Lance wouldn't hang around someone like that."

"I'm surprised to hear they're friends," the inspector said. "I had no idea *Signore* LaDoux was involved."

I took a seat. As I thought in silence, I remembered something and gasped. "That explains the sheet of paper I found. It had names, addresses, and money amounts. It must've been a list of drug orders. In hindsight, it makes sense now."

The inspector nodded. "Really? Good. That means there's proof. Quite foolish of them to write it all down, but this works in the *polizia's* favor. I bet they never thought they'd get caught. Foolish, foolish men."

"And I found a picture of LaDoux and Enrique Bello shaking hands. Could he be involved, too?"

The inspector shrugged. "It's possible. Seems a lot of fashion designers have ties to Salvatore, for whatever reason. Perhaps he has a personal stake in it."

"And the briefcase of money...." I trailed off. "It was probably from a drug deal or something."

"Very possible. Did you rummage through LaDoux's entire house, *Signorina*?"

The others looked at me. They knew I was guilty.

My face reddened and I looked down. "That's... that's not important, Inspector. If you know Bruno's a mobster, why have you never been able to arrest him?"

"He's very good at covering his tracks," the inspector said, sighing. "We've tried going undercover, planting bugs, spying with surveillance. But he's very clever. Eluded us for years. I've been waiting for the right piece of evidence to get him, but I've never found it."

"Maybe with LaDoux's help, you can finally put him in prison—where he belongs," Uncle Henry said. "God, I can't believe I threatened a mobster."

"It was pretty badass, actually," Ben said, making me nod in agreement.

"You're very lucky to have escaped, *Signore* Prince. The Salvatore family has generations of shady business deals and drug operations. I've been working on this case for a long, long time."

"Hold on a second," Ben said. "Why would the greatest fashion designer in the world—Jessica's words, not mine—have ties to a mobster? What could Lance want from him?"

"Unfortunately, crime *does* pay," Uncle Henry said. "He's most likely making a substantial amount of money for working with this Salvatore thug."

Ben shrugged. "Maybe, but it seems like LaDoux has everything he needs already. Isn't he an ultra-millionaire or whatever?"

I had a hunch—but I didn't want to say it out loud in case it was wrong. I needed more information first.

"All the little details remain uncertain. Perhaps LaDoux will give us the answers we seek," the inspector replied. "And you mentioned he was in danger?"

I nodded. "Yeah, this Bruno Salvatore guy's at his house right now. When we left, he closed the curtains. I've got a bad feeling about it."

The inspector grabbed his car keys and jacket off the wall. "Then we'd better hurry, *Signorina*. With a man like Bruno Salvatore, things often end in tragedy. Trust me."

"I still believe Lance's innocent," Carla said as we rushed out of the station. "There's no way he'd get caught up in something criminal. He's way too smart for that."

"If there's one thing I've learned about mysteries," I said, "is that people will surprise you." As I watched the inspector get into his car, I frowned. "Aren't you bringing back-up, Inspector?"

He shook his head. "No, *Signorina*. A slew of cop cars could make Salvatore run. Please, return to your hotel where it's safe and let me handle this. I've come too far to let him slip through my fingers again. *Ciao*—and take care."

As the inspector rushed out of the station, Carla turned to Uncle Henry. "Lance could be in danger. I need to find out for sure. We should go after the inspector, Henry."

Uncle Henry glanced at me and Ben. "And if there's a massive shootout? What about Jess and Ben?"

"We'll stay far behind the inspector and be discreet. I promise—we'll be fine."

"No. I'll come with you, but my niece and her friend will stay out of it." Uncle Henry turned to me. "And you will stay out of it, yes?"

"Of course," I lied.

Carla nodded. "Fine. Now, come on, Henry."

When Carla took off to our limo, Uncle Henry sighed and followed. For Carla, it seemed like Uncle Henry would do anything. As I watched them leave, Ben turned to me.

"You're going to follow anyway, aren't you?" he asked. "And I'll be tagging along?"

I smiled. "If you'd like."

"Oh, I'm coming. Just to make sure you don't get into trouble. Besides, where Jessica Prince goes, Ben Clark goes too."

"Just as it should be. Now, come on—they're getting away."

Ben and I grabbed a taxi, following Larry's limo with Uncle Henry and Carla inside. They were following the inspector's car and didn't notice a taxi trailing them. As we pulled into Lance's laneway behind them all, we heard silence. Had Salvatore killed him already?

The inspector had already made it to the front door when we arrived. I rolled down my window to listen in. As he banged on the door, it opened a second later. Lance stood there with a pipe in his mouth and a robe around his body. He looked relaxed and ready for bed.

Not a single hair on his head looked harmed.

"Inspector... Esposito, *oui*?" Lance asked. "I remember seeing you at the fashion show. A tragedy what happened. But to what do I owe the pleasure?"

"What are you talking about, Mister LaDoux?" I asked, running up behind the inspector. "A man was just at your house threatening you. We were there! I asked the inspector to make sure you were okay."

Inspector Esposito eyed me. "I thought I told you to head back to your hotel, *Signorina*?"

"And I thought I told you to stay out of it this?" Uncle Henry asked. "For your own safety?"

"No time for that." I waved them both off. "Well, Mister LaDoux?"

Lance shrugged. "I have no idea what you mean, *made-*

moiselle. There was no man here."

"Will you at least admit we had dinner tonight?"

Lance nodded. "*Oui*, of course. The five of us had a lovely dinner, served by my wonderful butler, Manuel. Once the evening was finished, they left and I retired to bed."

Once the others caught up, Ben's eyes widened. "He's alive! Man, I thought he was done for."

Uncle Henry crossed his arms. "What's going on here?"

"Besides you not listening to my orders?" Inspector Esposito demanded, exasperated.

"Forgive us, but we had to make sure Lance was okay," Carla said. "He's my friend, Inspector. Surely you can understand that."

Inspector Esposito nodded, backing down. It was a good thing we had such a kind, understanding inspector. But there was still the issue of Lance.

"He's lying," I said. "He told the inspector there was no man. You guys remember, right?"

Uncle Henry nodded. "Yes, I clearly remember a man threatening me. You don't forget that sort of thing."

"Carla?"

She shrugged. "I don't know. I *did* have a lot of champagne."

"Oh, please. You're only saying that to get Lance's money," I replied, and her face burned. I turned to the inspector. "You have to believe us. Why would we make this up?"

The inspector turned to Lance. "Good point. And there are at least three witnesses to this altercation. What do you have to say to that?"

"It's all hearsay, Inspector," Lance replied. "You can't prove it one way or another, *oui*? And since no crime was committed, I don't see what the problem is."

The inspector thought for a moment. "May we come in, *Signore*?"

Lance opened the door a little wider. "*Oui,* Inspector. Be my guest."

As I followed the inspector inside the home, no one was inside. Manuel poked his head around the corner, watching us with curiosity, but he was the only one here. Bruno Salvatore and his thugs were gone.

"Do you mind if I look around, *Signore*?" Inspector Esposito asked.

Lance shrugged. "Why not? I have nothing to hide."

As the inspector checked the foyer and dining room, searching for clues, Uncle Henry, Ben, and Carla entered the home after us. Carla sighed and reached for Lance's hands.

"I'm so sorry for everything, Lance," she said. "I told them not to come here. I didn't want them to treat you like a criminal."

He smiled, placing a hand on her shoulder. "*Oui*, I know, Carla. None of this is your fault."

His eyes slid to me and held my gaze. He knew more than he let on—I was sure of it.

As the inspector snooped, I couldn't stop myself. I entered the kitchen, almost bumping into Manuel. He didn't say anything when he looked down at me, but his gaze was hard.

"Hello, Manuel. You agree there was a man here, right? He had a scar?" I asked. "Big, scary guy?"

Manuel shrugged. "I'm not at liberty to say, *mademoiselle.*"

"Even if Lance's life is in danger? Don't you care about him, your boss?"

He pushed past me, walking toward the door. "*Monsieur* LaDoux was clear at dinnertime. Investigating where you're not supposed to can and will get you in trouble."

And then he vanished into the hallway. I sighed. There was no doubt they were acting suspicious, but how could I prove any of it?

Something in the distance caught my eye. There was a brown smear of mud on the tile near the backdoor. As I bent down, I realized it was fresh. Several footprints left through the back, almost in a hurry.

But it wasn't a smoking gun. If I said it might belong to Bruno Salvatore, Lance could've easily taken the blame himself.

I walked down the corridor, approaching Lance's office. Someone had left the door open so I entered and looked around. All the evidence I'd seen before was gone—the picture, the briefcase, and the list of names. I still had the lipstick I'd stolen, but it wasn't exactly implicative.

Again, it left me without proof. So frustrating.

I returned to the foyer and found the inspector, Uncle Henry, Ben, Carla, and Lance waiting for me. The inspector looked at me with hopeful eyes, praying I'd have something for him.

"Did you find anything, *mademoiselle*?" Lance asked.

I shook my head. "No. There's nothing here."

"I found nothing as well." The inspector turned to Lance. "I'm terribly sorry to have bothered you, *Signore*."

Lance smiled. "It's no bother at all, Inspector. I appreciate you checking on me. You were only doing your job, *oui*?"

The inspector nodded. "I was. But may I tell you something before I go?"

"Why, of course."

"If we were to say, hypothetically, a man was here," the inspector began, "I assure you, it's not a man you'd wish to get involved with. Certain business deals—no matter how attractive—can end poorly. Do you understand?"

Lance forced a smile and gestured to his door. "Have a good night, Inspector. You too, *Mademoiselle* Prince."

As we left Lance's house, the door slammed behind us. I sighed and turned toward the inspector. "Sorry, Inspector. I really thought Bruno would still be here."

He shook his head. "Don't apologize, *Signorina* Prince. You did the right thing by asking me to come here."

"And what about Enrique? It's a long shot connecting him to this based on one picture, but maybe he knows something?"

The inspector checked his watch. "Possibly. And it's nearly nine. Not too late to make one last pit stop and see what he says."

"Great. Enrique's staying with his boyfriend, Vincent Rossi. Our driver, Larry, knows the address. Follow us and we'll take you there."

As we got into our limo and the inspector waited to follow us in his vehicle, Carla sighed. "I suppose any hope of a check is long gone by now."

Uncle Henry turned from the front seat to look at us. "I promised you before, Carla. I'd be willing to help you financially—"

"And I told *you* I won't accept your help," she said. "I truly am grateful, but the savior routine is getting old, Henry."

As Uncle Henry sighed, I glanced at Carla. "Maybe you don't need Lance's money. Maybe you could find another way to finance your next fashion show. In a world of social media, anything's possible."

She raised an eyebrow. "What are you talking about, Jessica?"

"Well, instead of renting a big venue," I began, "think smaller. Hold it at your house. Or maybe your workshop?"

"My house is too risky. I don't need the Crimson Caper knowing my address. But the workshop's a good idea," she replied. "I'd have to think about it. I'm not even sure I want another fashion show. With the number of threats I've received, maybe I should quit before someone gets hurt. Permanently. No more online fashion, no more small trade shows. Nothing at all."

"Come on, Carla. You can't let the Crimson Caper stop you from living your dream!" Ben said. "That just sucks."

Uncle Henry nodded. "Ben's right, Carla. The old you wouldn't admit defeat—and she wouldn't let anyone stand in her way."

Carla sighed. "Maybe you're right. I'll need a day to sort out some things, but, yes, I think I'm ready to move forward with my life. The Crimson Caper can't stop Carla Valentine —not like this."

When we arrived at Vincent and Enrique's apartment, it was pitch black outside. We led the inspector into the building—he got past the doorman with his police badge—and went to the top floor.

I knocked on the door, then Vincent answered it a second later. He sighed when he saw me again. "Oh, it's you. Why are you back again? To bother me?"

The inspector pushed in front of me, holding up his badge. "I'm Inspector Esposito, *Signore* Rossi. May we come in?"

Vincent gulped, opening the door a little wider. "Of course, Inspector. Can I ask what this is about?"

As we entered the large apartment, the inspector closed the door. I noticed Antonio was still lying on the couch, watching television. He glanced up and saw Carla and grinned.

"Back so soon, *amore*? Did you miss me that much?" he asked. "I'm flattered."

Carla shook her head. "No. We're here on police business, Tony. It's important."

"I must speak to Enrique. Jessica told me he lives here," the inspector said. "He could be involved in something dangerous."

Vincent frowned. "Enrique? Are you sure? I can't believe he'd do anything—"

Enrique exited the bathroom a second later in his pajamas. He removed the toothbrush from his mouth when he noticed the inspector, glancing around at the rest of us.

"You're Inspector Esposito from the fashion show, right? What are you doing here?" he asked.

"I told the inspector to come. I found a picture inside Lance LaDoux's home office. It was of the two of you, shaking hands," I said. "Pretty weird."

Enrique shrugged. "And? Is that a crime?"

"No, *Signore* Bello—but being involved with the mafia is." The inspector turned to Vincent. "Are you aware someone in your household might be involved in drug deals?"

"What's he talking about, Enrique?" Vincent demanded, crossing his arms.

"I have no idea. You're all *loco*. Totally *loco*."

"Enrique's right. He wouldn't do something like this." Vincent turned back to us. "Do you have any proof? Other than a simple photo?"

I shrugged. "Well, not exactly."

"Is it possible you were wrong, Jess? That the picture of

them really *was* innocent?" Uncle Henry asked. "They do run in similar circles."

As I racked my brain for an answer, thinking of all the information I had, an old memory flashed across my mind.

"Wait a sec. When the Fashion Palace burned down, you were the one to tell the journalists," I replied. "When we were there, I saw Lance LaDoux coming out of the back alley. But the weird part? You were watching him—almost nervously like you knew why he was there. Like you were afraid to get caught."

Enrique paused. "I don't understand."

"Me, either," Ben muttered.

"This might be a crazy theory, Inspector, but it's all I have. Please hear me out," I said. "Lance LaDoux was selling drugs in the back alley during the fire. I don't know how Enrique fits in, but he definitely knows about it."

"Enrique?" Vincent turned to him.

But Enrique didn't say anything. He stared down at the floor, wordlessly.

"*Signore* Bello?" the inspector asked. "Is she correct?"

Enrique sighed, taking a seat in the nearby chair. "Yes, she is."

Vincent's eyes widened. "What? Enrique, how could you?"

"I'm not involved in the drug business. I swear," Enrique replied. "A few months ago, while I was visiting Vincent here in Milan, I was approached by Bruno Salvatore. I didn't know who he was."

"Approached? Why?" I asked.

"Well, he said he knew how financially hard the life of a fashion designer could be. It's very unstable, as I'm sure Carla knows," he continued. "He offered to make me lots of money if I helped him with his... business ventures."

"How does *Signore* LaDoux fit into this?" the inspector asked.

"I'm getting to that. Salvatore set up a meeting between the two of us at Lance's house. I thought Salvatore was an investor or something, so I went," Enrique replied. "That night, I learned he was a mobster. He asked for my help in selling narcotics, his preferred method of moneymaking, but I refused."

"And then what happened?" I asked.

"What do you think, *chica*? I was followed and harassed every day. I didn't tell Vincent because I wanted to keep him safe," Enrique replied. "Salvatore told me if I went to the police, he'd take everything from me—even my life. And I believed him."

"Why hasn't he done anything to retaliate if you refused?"

"We came to an agreement of sorts. I wouldn't help him sell drugs," Enrique said, "but I had to be their look-out. You know, the guy who makes sure these back-alley deals are successful? That's why I was watching the alley during the fire. I knew a deal was going down between Lance and some drug addict."

I glanced at Carla, getting an idea. "That's probably why Lance wanted to speak with you in private. He knew you were struggling financially and wanted you involved. Could've been Salvatore's idea."

Carla scoffed. "Then he can keep his blood money. I don't want any ties to the mob *or* drug trade."

The inspector's cell phone rang, then he reached for it in his pocket. "Excuse me, everyone."

As he left the room, an uncomfortable silence spread over us. No one knew what to say. Enrique looked ashamed, Vincent looked disappointed, Carla looked angry, and Antonio just looked confused.

"This is crazy," Ben whispered in my ear. "But does any of it have to do with the Crimson Caper?"

I shrugged. "It could. What if Bruno Salvatore's the one who sabotaged her show? He *does* have a motive. Leaving Carla penniless and ruined *could* inspire her to join the drug-selling business for some quick cash. Really makes you wonder."

When the inspector returned, he looked at me and sighed. "We matched the fingerprints, *Signorina*. We know who touched the matchbox at the Palazzo."

"That's great. Who is it?"

He approached Uncle Henry, placing handcuffs around his wrists. "Henry Alexander Prince, you have the right to remain silent."

Sixteen

THE FALSE ARREST

Uncle Henry struggled against the handcuffs, squirming in the inspector's arms. "This is absurd, Inspector. I'm innocent."

I gasped, tears filling my eyes. "No, you can't arrest him. He didn't do it, Inspector. He couldn't have."

"Listen to Jessica, Inspector," Carla said. "I don't believe for a second Henry did this to me. You shouldn't, either. I demand you let him go, right now."

"The evidence doesn't lie, *Signora* Valentine," the inspector replied. "And there's no logical reason for his fingerprints to be on the matchbox that started the blaze in the Palazzo. It looks incredibly suspicious."

Antonio sat up, shaking his head. "I had a feeling it was him, Inspector. He was at the fashion show, right? The perfect opportunity."

Carla glared at him. I did, too.

"*You* were at the fashion show, too," I said, crossing my arms.

Antonio shrugged. "True—but my fingerprints weren't found, now, were they?"

"That's because you didn't give elimination fingerprints."

He shrugged. "My point still stands."

I scoffed, making Antonio grin.

"He'll be taken to the police station for an interrogation," the inspector said. "Do not interfere, *per favore*."

As the inspector dragged Uncle Henry away, I followed like a lost puppy. "Uncle Henry, what do I do?"

"Everything will be fine, Jess," he replied. "Don't worry, sweetheart."

And then he disappeared, and there I was, crying in a stranger's apartment. Ben, with his mouth wide open in shock, pulled me into a hug as Vincent, Enrique, Antonio, and Carla watched us.

"Your Uncle Henry's right, Jess. Everything will be okay," Ben whispered, patting my hair. "I believe that."

I wiped away my tears. "I hope so. Anyway, there's no time to cry. I have to meet Uncle Henry at the police station, even if the inspector told us not to interfere. Maybe I'll be able to help him somehow."

"I'll come with you," Carla said, grabbing her purse. "I won't let Henry go down for this, Jessica. I know he's innocent. You have my word that I'll prove it."

"If he's *so* innocent, then why were his fingerprints on the matchbox that started the fire?" Antonio asked. "Innocent or not, it looks bad, *amore*. Don't you think?"

Carla glared at him again. "I don't know for sure yet—but I intend to find out, just so you know." She turned to me, softening her gaze. "Come on, Jessica."

As the three of us rushed out of the apartment, Vincent reached for his cell phone.

———

When we told Larry about Uncle Henry's arrest, his eyes widened in shock. No one believed he could do something like this. It just wasn't in his nature.

And he certainly wouldn't risk leaving me on my own. Uncle Henry was all I had—my sole caretaker since my parents died. He loved me too much to put me *or* our family name in jeopardy.

When we arrived at the police station, endless journalists and TV reporters mobbed us. Vincent must've called them and told them all about Uncle Henry's arrest. I'd seen him reach for the phone just before we left. Uncle Henry and the inspector were gone inside so they hounded us instead.

"Jessica Prince, right?" a nearby journalist asked. "How does it feel to see your uncle arrested?"

"Did he do it because of jealousy, *Signorina*? Envy?" another shouted.

"You're billionaires, aren't you? Do you intend to post bail? How will this affect Prince Enterprises?"

And they didn't stop there. Others shouted in Italian at us as Ben, Carla, and I tried to make our way through the swarm. The police officer at the front door let us in and I breathed a sigh of relief.

Quiet. I could finally hear myself think again—and my mind filled with worry for my uncle.

"Man, what a disaster," Ben muttered. "But the journalist back there was right. Won't your company take a hit? Suffer losses or lose partnerships, or whatever?"

I nodded. "Probably. It's even more reason to prove Uncle Henry's innocence. Now all I have to do is get to him somehow. Never thought I'd be visiting him behind bars—"

"*Signorina* Prince? I thought I recognized you. I was with Inspector Esposito when the Crimson Caper first struck," an officer said, walking up to us. "Look, I've got a niece I'm raising by myself. I know she'd be upset if anything happened to me. So I'll tell you this—Henry Prince was just brought in. He's waiting in Interrogation Room B down at the end of the hall. If the inspector allows it, maybe you can watch from the window or something."

I nodded and rushed down the corridor, taking Ben and Carla with me. As we reached the door, I looked through the small, glass window. I saw Uncle Henry sitting behind an interrogation desk across from the inspector. The handcuffs were still around his wrists, chaining him to the table. He looked defeated and somber.

When I saw the inspector's face inside, I filled with rage. How could he do this to my Uncle Henry? Especially after all the time we'd spent together, investigating this case? I forced my anger down inside and convinced myself to keep a clear head. If I wanted to help Uncle Henry, I couldn't let my emotions take control.

"This can't be easy," Ben whispered. "I'm so sorry, Jess."

"Thanks. And right now, Uncle Henry needs me. I'm going in—approval or not."

I stormed inside the interrogation room, then the inspector looked back at me. Carla and Ben followed. "*Signorina* Prince. What are you doing in here?"

"Coming to see my uncle. Look, I'm worried about him, Inspector. He's the only family I have left after my parents died. Can you please let me stay in the room with him? I promise I'll be on my best behavior. If he's going to jail, this might be the only time I have left with him."

The inspector sighed. "I'm not without a heart, *Signorina*. Fine—you may stay but be quiet. I was just about to begin the interrogation. Your friends may watch from behind the glass if they also agree to remain silent."

Carla and Ben walked around the side of the room, watching from the one-way mirror. I took a deep breath and closed the door behind me. Uncle Henry perked up as soon as he saw me, giving me a small smile. He was always trying to cheer me up.

"Thank you for letting her stay, Inspector," he said. "But a part of me doesn't want her to see me like this."

The inspector pulled up a chair for me, then I took a seat in front of Uncle Henry. I reached for his hand and squeezed it tight. "Don't be ashamed, Uncle Henry. I know you didn't do this."

"Thanks, kiddo." He smiled. "If I go to jail for this, I've left all our money to you, Jess. You don't have to worry about your future."

I shook my head. "Of course I do. I'd give up all the money in the world if it means you're free. It's all worthless without you, anyway."

The inspector cleared his throat. "To be clear, the official charges are arson and sabotage. The judge has been notified and the bail is being determined."

"Sabotage? So that means you think he's the Crimson Caper, too?" I asked.

The inspector nodded. "That's right, *Signorina*. The note we found in the back alley during the fire was written in red lipstick, the same kind the Crimson Caper uses. While we can't officially link the arson and the sabotage, it does seem there's a connection, doesn't it?"

"Sounds like a lot of theory to me. And by the way," I said, reaching into my pocket, "I have lipstick from Lance LaDoux. It's been recently used and it was left in his office."

"Did you steal it, *Signorina*? If so, it can be deemed inadmissible in court."

"I was a guest in Mister LaDoux's house, and that's how I found it. I'm not accusing LaDoux of anything—I just want to know if the lipstick's a match."

The inspector nodded and rose to his feet, taking the

lipstick from me. "All right. Further testing can't hurt. I'll pass it along to my lab technician. Be right back."

As the inspector left, Uncle Henry took a deep breath. "I can't believe they'd arrest me for this, Jess. I swear on my brother's life—I didn't do anything. I'd never hurt Carla."

"Should I call our lawyer?" I asked. "Bruce... Greenberg, right?"

He nodded. "It'd probably be a good idea to get in touch with him, yeah. Can you call him for me while I'm stuck in here? I don't care what the bail amount is, either—we need to pay it. You have the number for my accountant, right? If you call him and explain everything, he'll know what to do."

Uncle Henry hushed when the inspector returned and took his seat. "*Signore* Prince, you claim you're innocent. How do you explain your fingerprints on the matchbox, then?"

Uncle Henry shrugged. "I don't know, Inspector. I don't even own matches. I've never touched one a day in my life. And if I did all this, I'd like to think I wouldn't be dumb enough to leave such an obvious clue behind."

"Is it possible the fingerprints were planted?" I asked. "In the last Julia Joy novel I read, the culprit used tape to plant someone else's fingerprints on the murder weapon. It *can* be done, Inspector."

"True, that's always a possibility. How could they get his fingerprints?"

I shrugged. "Uncle Henry's been to a lot of places—the fashion show, the hotel. Maybe he left a coffee cup or something with his fingerprints on it behind. It could've happened anywhere. But I guess that means someone's out to get him—and they've been watching for the right moment."

"And that raises one question. Why would anyone want to frame Henry Prince? Do you have any enemies, *Signore*?"

Uncle Henry shook his head. "None that I can think of."

"I can," I replied. "Bruno Salvatore. You *did* just threaten him at Lance's house."

Uncle Henry put his head in his hands. "You're right—that was just a few hours ago. That's what I get for playing the hero."

"And who knows—he could've been planning this for a while. Tampering with evidence or something. Maybe he saw you with Carla and decided to frame you."

"I'll have my officers look into Salvatore's whereabouts for the show's sabotage and arson," the inspector replied. "However, Salvatore's very good at covering his tracks. Until then, you're our only suspect, *Signore* Prince. Fingerprints on the matchbox could be enough to convince a jury of arson."

"You're forgetting something, Inspector. Uncle Henry's been with me the whole time in Milan, during the arson *and* the sabotage. I think I would've noticed if he did something criminal."

The inspector nodded. "I'm aware of how close you two are. But surely you don't spend every waking minute together. Do you share a hotel room?"

I sighed. "The suite has adjoining rooms."

"With private spaces for each of you?"

"Well, yeah."

"And as *Signore* Rossi pointed out, Henry was at the fashion show before the sabotage, right?"

"Yes, but—"

"Then it would've been possible for him to sneak away at any moment, either at night or for a bathroom break," the inspector said. "Or he has an accomplice—someone to do the work for him."

Uncle Henry scoffed. "That's ridiculous, Inspector—

both theories. I'm not the Crimson Caper *or* the arsonist. And I don't know who is."

An accomplice? I'd never thought of that before. I assumed the Crimson Caper was only one person, but what if it were two? They'd be able to alternate, making each other look innocent.

And it would explain why Josephine made *two* sets of apparel for the Crimson Caper. I figured they wanted a back-up.

"As we speak, my officers are raiding your hotel room, *Signore* Prince," the inspector said. "The judge granted me a search warrant. And fast, considering the high-profile case. We're looking for any evidence pertaining to the arson or the sabotage."

"With all due respect, Inspector, all you have is *one* piece of evidence," I said, "and it's flimsy. Uncle Henry could've come into contact with that matchbox without realizing it, or someone could've put his fingerprints there on purpose."

"Indeed, *Signora*. However—"

"No. Listen to me, Inspector," I demanded. "You have nothing else—no red trench coat, no red lipstick, and no oil that could've made Sasha slip on the runway. The Crimson Caper would have all that."

He nodded. "That is true."

"And if he *were* the Crimson Caper, Uncle Henry isn't an idiot. He has an IQ of one fifty! Why would he cover his tracks up until this point? And the Crimson Caper wears gloves, in case you forgot!"

The inspector nodded, scribbling into his notepad. "You do have a point."

"I won't let you pin this on Uncle Henry with only one piece of evidence. I'll fight you, Inspector—I'll get a lawyer and take you to court if I have to. But I won't stand by and let you insult my uncle like this."

The inspector sighed. "I hear you, *Signorina*. I'm not trying to be unreasonable or cruel. This isn't easy for me to do, but I must follow the evidence. And so far, Henry Prince is the only one with something against him."

Uncle Henry shook his head. "What a nightmare. I never should've come to Milan."

The inspector rose to his feet. "This interrogation's over. I may bring him back if I gather more evidence. In the meantime, Henry will be placed in the holding cells for now. In the morning, you'll be able to collect him and post bail after he briefly appears in court."

"What about the lipstick analysis? Or what the police officers found in his hotel room?"

"You may stick around to hear the results if you'd like. A team of officers are working on this case, so it shouldn't take long, *Signorina*."

"Thank you, Inspector. I hope you find evidence that exonerates him."

"For his sake—and his freedom—I hope so, too."

As the inspector left, I gave Uncle Henry a big hug across the table. "Stay strong, okay? I'll find a way to get you out of this."

He smiled. "Jess, as long as you're on my side, I have nothing to worry about."

Ben and Carla heard everything from behind the glass, and I was grateful I didn't have to explain what happened in the interrogation room. It made me upset just thinking about it. Ben held my hand tight as we watched Uncle Henry get dragged away by the officers, pulled to the holding cells like a common criminal. He gave a nod to reassure me, but it didn't make me feel any better.

Nothing could—except finding the real Crimson Caper.

Carla and Ben took a seat in the waiting room. Carla bit her fingernails in anticipation, Ben's knee shook, and I paced the floor. Waiting to hear about the evidence was nerve-wracking and it was already past midnight.

When the inspector returned, I rushed over to him with Ben and Carla. "Well, Inspector? What are the results?"

"Let's begin with the hotel room search," he said. "We searched his entire room, suitcases, and limousine, which *Signore* Kibbler allowed us access to. There was no evidence of a trench coat or anything relating to the Crimson Caper or the arson."

I smiled. That was good news, but I did have some questions. Did whoever set Uncle Henry up plan to do it, or was it a last-minute idea? The fact that they only had one piece of evidence against him suggested the latter.

"And the lipstick analysis is complete," he continued. "You were right with your suspicions, *Signorina*. The lipstick you found in LaDoux's home matches the shade used by the Crimson Caper. However, there's no way to prove it was this particular lipstick that wrote the threatening messages. Lipsticks are extremely common. My wife's large make-up collection proves that."

"LaDoux? Are you serious?" Carla asked before she shook her head. "I suppose after his involvement with Salvatore, he's capable of anything."

"Speaking of *Signore* Salvatore, my officers can't get in touch with him. He certainly knows how to hide," the inspector said. "His company, Salvatore Industrial, has a building downtown. Perhaps I should visit and see if I can speak to him."

"He won't talk to a cop, Inspector," I said. "But maybe I could ask him a few questions. He might let something slip around me."

"Jess, come on. He's a mobster," Ben said. "Even *I* know that's a bad idea."

The inspector nodded. "Your friend's right, *Signorina.* It's far too dangerous. I forbid you from speaking to him. In the meantime, I'll ask my officers to search common spots in Milan for him. He's bound to show up sometime."

I said nothing. If Salvatore had information, I was going to get it one way or another.

"After a brief arraignment in front of a judge, the bail will be determined," the inspector continued. "My officers will call you once that's happened and let you know the amount."

I nodded. "Thanks. Then I'll get Uncle Henry's accountant to send the money as soon as possible."

"As I said before, once bail has been approved, he'll be free to leave until his court date," the inspector replied. "But as of right now, *Signorina*, his fate doesn't look good. I suggest you spend as much time with him as you can before it's too late."

As the inspector walked away, Carla balled her fists. "Can you believe that idiot inspector? Who cares about fingerprints? They don't prove he started the fire. Or that he's the Crimson Caper."

I sighed. "Yeah, I know. But if we don't find something to help him, it'll put him in jail. Maybe for good."

"I'll do everything in my power to save your uncle," Carla replied. "I won't let him go to prison, Jessica. Not like this."

I checked the time on my phone, nodding. "Thanks. Well, we'd better get back to the hotel. It's late and I'm tired. Uncle Henry will be safe here, but we should watch our backs. The Crimson Caper's still out there—and we could be their next target."

Seventeen

THE MARKET ATTACK

Sleep didn't come easy for me that night.

An officer from the station called and told me that bail had been set at two-hundred-thousand Euros. After hours of tossing and turning, I decided to get out of bed. I spent the rest of the early hours of the morning on my cell phone, calling the accountant, lawyer, and a few family friends back in Willowbrook. Given the time difference, no one was happy to hear from me. But the accountant and lawyer jumped into action, and Madison and Tiffany grew more and more sympathetic as we spoke. They couldn't believe anyone could frame someone as kind as Uncle Henry and I didn't, either.

Uncle Henry was probably the ideal scapegoat. The Crimson Caper couldn't have planned on him being in Milan but, once the opportunity presented itself, it was too good to pass up. But why would they choose Uncle Henry rather than someone who was supposed to be here? It seemed like there should have been a plan in place before the Princes showed up, and deviating from a plan always posed risks. Was it his money? Fame? Or something else?

I took a peek in Uncle Henry's suite from my adjoining

room. The police had turned it upside down in their search for evidence, tossing over furniture, emptying his suitcases, and messing up the bed. But the fact that nothing came up gave me hope.

That maybe they couldn't pin the crimes on Uncle Henry after all.

As I stepped outside the room to take a deep breath, I heard footsteps. They came from Carla's room. It sounded like she was pacing, and I sighed. This had to be rough on her, too—considering Uncle Henry was going to jail for her show's sabotage and arson.

And then I heard whispering, but it sounded angry. Was she talking to someone?

I pressed my ear against her door but didn't hear another voice. She must've been on the phone. But who would she be talking to? And at this late hour? It couldn't have been Josephine this time.

When I entered my room again, Ben was still asleep on the couch. He hadn't slept once in his room this week, and I couldn't blame him. If the Crimson Caper would go to the trouble of framing Uncle Henry, were we in danger, too?

When dawn colored the sky, Ben woke up and rubbed his eyes. "Jess? What are you doing up?"

"Couldn't sleep," I muttered, grabbing a bottle of water out of the room's small fridge. "Too much on my mind."

"Yeah, I get that. I had more nightmares," he whispered, and looked down in shame. "The Crimson Caper took you away. I couldn't save you in time. Man, it felt so real."

I sat on the couch beside him, giving him a smile. "I'm fine, Ben. We all are. When we find evidence that gets Uncle Henry out of jail, the Crimson Caper will pay."

"Good. With all those mystery books you read, I know you'll catch them," Ben said, pulling his sweater on. "I heard you on the phone last night. Did you find people that could help?"

I nodded. "Our accountant's getting the money together right now. Should be sent in a few hours. In the meantime, our lawyer, Bruce, is taking a private jet to Milan. I hope he'll be here later today. I could really use his advice."

"So, what? We just let Mister Prince rot in a cell until then? That's not right."

I shrugged. "What other choice do we have? It's a waiting game now, Ben."

Ben looked out the window, scanning below. I'd already looked for the Crimson Caper earlier and hadn't seen anyone outside. "Well, I can't stay in this hotel room all day and wait, Jess. I'm already going insane."

"We could go shopping to kill the time," I suggested. "Shopping helps me think, you know. And I saw a market a few blocks from here."

"Shopping? Yeah, sure," he said, turning around with a shrug. "It's just...never mind. Let's go."

I narrowed my eyes at him, but he looked away. Ben had been acting strangely lately—as if he were hiding something from me. And he should know by now that I *always* found out the truth.

I slipped on my heels then grabbed my phone as we locked our door. "Let's ask Josephine and Carla if they want to come. We're safer in numbers."

I knocked on Josephine's door first. She opened it a second later, nervously. "Jessica? I looked through the peep-hole to make sure it was you. Still paranoid. And I heard what happened to Henry. It's all over the news. For the record, I don't believe he'd do such a thing. And I'm sorry you're going through this."

I nodded. "Thanks—and you're right. He's being set up

by the Crimson Caper. Sorry I didn't tell you last night. It was really late when we got back from the police station."

"Don't worry about it. I feel awful he's going down for this. Is there anything I can do to help?"

I shook my head. "Not really. Do you want to come with us to the Markets? It's not far from here. Maybe it'll distract us. We haven't been able to do much sightseeing with everything going on."

"No, I don't think that's a good idea, Jess," she whispered. "What if the Crimson Caper comes back? They framed Henry for sabotage, but what if they have something more fatal in mind for us?"

I shrugged. "They could. But I won't live my life in fear, Josephine. You shouldn't, either. We should be safe in a big crowd. But I want to catch the Crimson Caper. A part of me hopes they follow us."

She shook her head, shutting the door. Her voice was muffled from within. "Sorry, Jessica. I just can't. But stay safe, okay? I'm crossing my fingers Henry's off the hook soon."

When she was gone, I sighed and turned to Ben. "Come on. Maybe Carla will want to come."

"She has a point," Ben said. "This *does* sound dangerous, Jess. Maybe we should just stay at the hotel after all. I'm sure your uncle would agree."

"Everything's dangerous, Ben. But if the Crimson Caper *does* show up, I owe it to Uncle Henry to try and stop them. If not, he could go to jail for years. And I'm too stubborn to let that happen. I'm also not ready to take over the family company just yet."

It took Carla a few seconds to answer the door after I knocked. She looked exhausted as if she'd been up all night. "Oh, hello, Jessica. Hello, Ben. Any news on Henry? Is he still the prime suspect?"

I sighed. "As far as I know, yeah. The police haven't found anyone else."

"I can't believe this. *Mio Dio*, this was all a mistake," she cried, placing her head in her hands.

"What was a mistake?"

She rubbed her temples and looked up at me. "The fashion show. None of it should've happened. It's my fault. If it wouldn't have happened—if I'd stopped it, somehow—Henry wouldn't be in jail because of me."

"Look, you can't blame yourself," Ben said. "You didn't want Mister Prince to go to jail, did you?"

Carla dried her tears. "No. Not at all."

"Then Ben's right—you're not at fault. Uncle Henry doesn't blame you, either. The only one to blame is the Crimson Caper."

Carla balled her fists, her anger scaring me sometimes. "You're right, Jess—and they need to pay."

"I'm onboard with that. Anyway, we have a few hours to kill before the bail money arrives. Do you want to come shopping with us?"

Carla shook her head, glancing back at the phone. "No. I have a few calls to make—people to get in touch with. Mostly old friends concerned with what's going on. They've been calling nonstop to say how sorry they are for this whole fiasco. I never knew so many people cared—it's almost flattering. I've been trying to tell them Henry's innocent, but the news reports are convincing."

"Well, if you change your mind, we'll be at the Markets," I replied. "It's a few blocks from here. You can't miss it."

She nodded, shutting the door halfway. "The Markets? I'll think about it. *Ciao*, Jessica."

As Ben and I walked down the hallway, my cell phone rang. I dug it out of my purse and held it up to my ear when I realized it was Alan Hampton, Tiffany's father. He was the temporary CEO whenever Uncle Henry was out of town. If he had to call me, something wasn't right.

"Jessica? Glad I've gotten in touch with you. We've heard about Henry's arrest," he said. "It's all over the news, in case you weren't aware."

I sighed. "Yeah, I know. How's Prince Enterprises doing?"

"Not good, Jessica. Our stocks have gone down. Prominent business partners—billionaire investors—are threatening to leave us," he replied. "I'm really worried."

"Is there any way you can stall the investors? To make sure we don't lose any more money?"

"We're trying. We keep telling them Henry's innocent. That's why I called," he replied. "The team wants him to know we're on his side. None of his employees thinks he's guilty. We're here for you, Jess—no matter what. Prove he's innocent over there and I'll handle things from here. See you soon."

As I hung up, I turned to Ben, sighing. "You were right before—our company's losing business. If we can't prove Uncle Henry's innocent, Prince Enterprises will go under."

We stood there in silence for a few seconds, thinking about the magnitude of what was at stake. It made me wonder—had the Crimson Caper chosen to frame Uncle Henry, hoping his business would tank in the process? It seemed a little too coincidental.

Ben shook his head. "I don't know what to say, Jess. Man, this whole vacation's been a disaster. I wish I could make it all better for you."

"You can," I replied, linking his arm with mine. "Let's go buy a lot of clothes. Sometimes, retail therapy is just what you need."

When I found Larry at the breakfast buffet and told him about our plans, he protested. After I convinced him it could help—and pinky swore to watch out for anyone in red—he relented and drove us to the Markets. As he parked on the side of the road, he turned to give us both a worried look.

"Please be careful, Miss Prince. And you too, Mister Clark," he said. "Your uncle would never forgive me if I let something happen to either of you. Or that ornery Sheriff Clark."

"Everything will be fine. Stay close," I replied, hopping out of the limo with Ben by my side. "We won't be long. See you soon!"

The Markets were exactly as advertised—dozens of stalls in a block-wide space, all selling different products. I marveled at the jewelry, clothes, and trinkets, but Ben didn't seem to care. He wasn't a shopper like me and the girls.

Some of the vendors and people passing by seemed to recognize us from the news. Some snapped pictures of us, probably to sell or post online. Ben looked uncomfortable, trailing behind me with his head down.

"Wow. News travels fast," Ben muttered. "Feels like everyone's staring at us."

"Just ignore them. I've had some practice with paparazzi back home," I replied, admiring some handmade bracelets. "Hey, you know what we should do? Let's get matching friendship bracelets. It'll be fun!"

Ben laughed. "Come on, Jess. Isn't that a little girly?"

I placed the bracelet on his arm, smiling. "Nah. It looks nice. What do you say?"

Ben's eyes widened when he glanced at the price tag. He removed the bracelet, putting it back. "For that much? Pass. Not that you can put a price on our friendship, of course."

"Nice save," I said, smiling up at him, "but I insist. I'll buy it for you. A token of our adventures together."

He ripped his arm away, shoving it in his pocket. "No, Jess. You've done enough. Don't waste your money on me."

And then he had that look in his eyes again—the same look he had on the plane. Something was troubling him. And because of that, it was troubling *me*.

I pulled him away from the vendor, sighing. "First of all, you're not a waste. I like buying things for you. Secondly, you've been acting weird lately. Spill it."

"I...can't," he said, looking everywhere but my eyes. "You have enough on your mind. I don't want to burden you some more."

I sighed, taking a seat on the ground. "Fine. If you won't tell me, I'll just sit right here until you do."

People passed, giving us strange looks. I probably looked weird sitting on the street, but I didn't care.

"Jess, don't be crazy," he muttered, trying to pull me up. I resisted, keeping my butt firmly planted on the ground. "Come on—people are looking!"

"So? They were looking before. Tell me what's on your mind. You know how persistent I am, Ben."

He sighed. "You really won't get up until I do, huh?"

I crossed my arms to prove I was serious.

"Fine. Have it your way," he mumbled, playing with a nearby necklace. "I'm sure you know I'm different from the other kids at Blackwood Academy. Have you ever wondered how I got accepted into some snazzy private school?"

I rose to my feet, wiping the dirt off my pink dress. "Yeah, of course. I mean, I was curious, but I didn't want to ask if you weren't ready to tell me."

He smiled. "And that's why we're friends, Jess. No one respects me like you do." He looked down, his smile fading. "But I'm poor. Like, really poor. My dad and I have almost been homeless for not being able to pay our mortgage. But when Mom died, Dad used her life insurance money to get me into private school. He said it's what she would've wanted for me—a good education."

I frowned, placing a hand on his shoulder. "Oh, Ben. I'm so sorry."

He nodded, sadly. "Yeah. And when I hang out with you it's just a reminder that I'm only here, bumping shoulders with the rich because Mom's gone. If she was still alive, we probably wouldn't have met, Jess."

I didn't know what to say. Ben and I were really close—we shared secrets all the time—but he never told me anything like this before. He barely mentioned his mother or the cancer that claimed her life years ago.

"Don't get me wrong—I like hanging out with you. You're the best friend I've ever had," he said, grinning. Then his smile faded again. "But I'm not like you, with private jets and fashion shows and purchases at an over-priced Market. Sometimes...sometimes, it hurts when you drag me to all these fancy places."

"I'm sorry. You're so right. I've been a jerk, and the worst part was that I didn't even realize it," I replied. "We don't need an expensive friendship bracelet, anyway. We have each other's company, and that's enough."

Ben smiled from ear to ear. "Jess, you have no idea how much that means—"

The screech of tires startled me. A black European car with tinted windows spun around the corner, blowing up smoke and dust as they sped toward the Markets. The crowd stared at the car, murmuring.

My heart pounded. "Ben, I have a really bad feeling right now."

The driver's side window rolled down, then I caught a hint of red inside. When their gloved hand reached out the window, clutching something small and shiny, my adrenaline kicked in.

"Ben, run!" I cried, reaching for him.

"Jess, what's going on?" he asked, his face white with fear.

"No time for questions. Follow me!"

And then the Market exploded with cracking and popping sounds. I pulled Ben down behind a nearby Market stall while the vendors inside fled. Children cried, people screamed, and loud pops exploded around us.

When the popping sounds slowed and came to a stop, I figured it was safe. I poked my head around the corner of the stall, looking for any sign of the mysterious black car. Most of the people were gone—escaping into the frantic streets. I heard police sirens wailing in the distance and breathed a sigh of relief.

Someone had called them. Maybe we'd be okay after all.

"Are you all right?" I asked Ben.

"Yeah, I think so," he replied, taking a deep breath. "Are you okay? And who was that?"

I nodded. "I'm fine—and I think the Crimson Caper decided to pay us a visit."

"But why? And how would they know we were here?"

As Ben trembled behind me, my eyes roamed down the street and finally noticed the car. When I heard the engine revving and the tires turning, I realized something.

The driver was coming right at us.

Eighteen

UNCLE HENRY'S FREEDOM

Ben and I dove out of the way as the black car plowed through the Market stalls, leaving destruction everywhere I looked. The stalls toppled over, jewelry went flying, and the hanging clothes ripped into shreds.

It was a good thing the majority of the Markets cleared out, or the car would've killed a bunch of people—including Ben and me.

The two of us hid behind the remnants of a Market stall of fresh produce. I listened in silence, too terrified to look around the stall. I heard something that sounded like paper hit the ground before tires screeched and the car took off.

And then everything went quiet.

I poked my head around the stall, but it was too late to see the car's license plate. The car was long gone by now. I walked around the stall, looking for clues on the ground. I found several firecrackers, used and discarded, still sizzling with smoke.

As I looked to the left, I noticed what fell out of the driver's window—a piece of paper. And in red lipstick—the Crimson Caper's trademark—read YOU'LL NEVER CATCH ME.

As I held it in my hands, I started to giggle. Ben got up slowly, walking over to me with a concerned look on his face. His clothes looked scuffed and dirty from the pavement, but he seemed to be fine otherwise.

"Uh, Jess?" he asked. "Why are you laughing?"

I held up the piece of paper. "Because, Ben—this is proof Uncle Henry's innocent. He can't be the Crimson Caper, not after all that."

Ben rubbed his neck and shoulders, nodding. "Good. Wish we could've found another way to prove his innocence without almost dying, though."

A moment later, a black, tinted limousine pulled up to the Market stalls, driving over the curb. Ben grabbed me and jumped for cover, but I pushed him off when I realized who it was.

"Larry! Are you okay?" I asked, running over.

He got out of the driver's seat, nodding. "I could ask you the same question, Miss Prince. I heard screams and a car taking off. What happened?"

"A car drove through the markets, tossing fireworks at us. The good news is everyone lived—no serious injuries. The even better news is now we have proof Uncle Henry isn't the Crimson Caper," I said, showing him the piece of paper. "But the bad news is... well, the Markets are destroyed. I hope we won't get blamed for it."

Several police cars with their sirens blaring pulled up to the Markets a second later. Police officers got out of their vehicles with their guns raised, pointing them at us. We held up our hands as they shouted in Italian.

"Wait, we're innocent," I cried. "Please, don't shoot. Let us explain everything."

Inspector Esposito pulled up in his car and got out of the driver's seat. He rushed in front of us, forming a shield. As he yelled at the officers in Italian, they lowered their guns and put them away. Citizens on the street watched and murmured. Even I was in a state of disbelief.

The inspector turned to face me, pulling out his notepad. "*Signorina* Prince, are you all right? We know it was the Crimson Caper who attacked the Markets. A witness saw their red trench coat behind the wheel but couldn't see the license plate."

I nodded. "Yeah, everyone's fine. I don't think the Crimson Caper wanted to hurt us. They could've easily killed us all, but they decided to trash the Markets instead. It was like they were making a statement."

"A fine point. Did anything stand out, *Signorina*? Either the vehicle or the person driving it?"

I shook my head. "No, I didn't see it very well. All I know is that it was a black European car with tinted windows. I saw someone in red behind the wheel. They set off some firecrackers before ramming into the Markets. And they left this note too."

The inspector took the note from me. "Hmm, just like all the other threats. I doubt there will be any evidence on this. We have so little on the Crimson Caper. But in the meantime, the city will be alerted of the vehicle, and we'll ask the public to keep their eyes open. As for the firecrackers, how could the Crimson Caper have gotten their hands on them?"

I shrugged. "A vendor, maybe? How many places sell firecrackers in Milan?"

The inspector thought for a moment. "Not many, *Signorina*. I'll get my officers to track them down. I want every vendor in this city questioned."

"Good idea. You know, you got here pretty fast," I said. "It only happened a few minutes ago."

"Indeed, but not fast enough," he replied, sighing. "Ten minutes ago, the station got a call from an unknown number. It was the Crimson Caper, and they told us they planned to attack the Markets. We mobilized as fast as possible. It was just like the call I received at the hospital."

"Were you able to trace the number this time?"

"No, *Signorina* Prince. They hung up too fast again. I hate to say it, but we weren't prepared for a case like this."

"Despite that, this is good news. It proves Uncle Henry isn't the Crimson Caper. He couldn't have been in two places at once."

"Unless there are two Crimson Capers."

I hadn't thought of that before, so I nodded, pointing at the note. "Maybe, but we don't know that for sure. At the very least, the note casts doubt on his guilt. So, will you let Uncle Henry go now?"

"It isn't that simple, *Signorina*. We'll discuss this at the station," he replied. "My officers will close off the scene and take statements from the civilians. In the meantime, I want to speak with *Signore* Prince himself."

Larry drove me and Ben back to the police station as the inspector followed us in his car. I felt safer knowing he was right behind us. As I glanced out the window, I noticed the morale in the city changed. Word spread fast about the Market attack, leaving Milan paranoid and afraid. The streets were nearly deserted.

"Man, this Crimson Caper's insane," Ben muttered. "And they just keep escalating. Sure, no one died in the fire or the Market attack, but they could've. What's next?"

"I agree with Mister Clark," Larry said from the driver's seat. "We might not be able to help Mister Prince. It'd be much safer if we returned to Willowbrook."

"We can't leave," I said. "If we do, Uncle Henry could go

to prison forever. No, I have to stay and figure this out. A good sleuth wouldn't run when things get hard. Julia Joy wouldn't, that's for sure."

Ben scoffed. "But he was behind bars when the lunatic drove at us, and we have the note. That screams innocent to me. Why can't the inspector just let him out?"

I shook my head. "The inspector thinks we have two Crimson Capers. No proof of it yet, but if a lawyer can convince a jury that—plus the matchbox evidence—it doesn't look good for Uncle Henry. At best, they could still convict him as an accomplice with knowledge of the crimes."

Ben sighed. "Then what can we do in the meantime? I'm getting tired of walking around in fear, Jess."

"Me too, but it's working. We got the Crimson Caper to come out of hiding. Speaking of that, I don't think the Market attack was random," I replied. "The Crimson Caper's targeting us—me. They left the note in red lipstick, knowing I'd find it and understand. Just like the kind on our limo."

"But why? What's so special about you?"

I shrugged. "That's another mystery to solve. And there's another thing bothering me."

"What is it?"

"Well, it seemed like the Crimson Caper went to all this trouble to frame Uncle Henry. That was clear when they planted the fingerprints," I said. "If they wanted to pin this on him and get away with it, why attack the Markets while he's in custody? If anything, that would help his case. It doesn't make sense. They've changed up their M.O. so fast. It's really weird."

Ben and Larry didn't say anything. This case just continued to become more confusing as the days passed.

When we arrived at the police station, there were no reporters waiting for us this time. If I knew journalists, they were most likely at the Markets, trying to get all the information they could. Forget field day—the Crimson Caper had made it a field *week* for them with the sabotage, arson, and Market attack.

Larry let us out near the front doors, then we met up with the inspector. He nodded and gestured for us to follow him into the busy police station where all the available officers were working on the Crimson Caper case. You could tell by their frantic voices it had shaken them, too. I bet they'd never seen a case like this before.

The inspector walked into his office and grabbed a set of keys from his desk. "It's time to see what *Signore* Prince has to say about this. Perhaps he'll have some information for us."

He led us to the row of cells where a slew of criminals looked up at us. When they saw the inspector carrying keys, they seemed hopeful but lowered their heads when the inspector approached Uncle Henry's cell. It hurt to see my uncle treated like a common criminal, especially when I knew in my heart he was innocent. He rose to his feet and smiled at me.

When the cell unlocked, I flung myself into his arms. "Uncle Henry! How are you?"

"Well, I don't like the fact that I have to do my business in public now," he said, pointing at the toilet in the corner of his cell, "but I'm okay. What's going on? The officers were running around earlier. They looked terrified."

"It's why we've come to speak with you, *Signore*," the inspector said. "The Markets were attacked by the Crimson Caper. They damaged several stalls and almost ran over dozens of citizens. Did you know about any of this?"

Uncle Henry shook his head. "No, of course not. I've been locked in this cell since last night, Inspector. It wasn't me."

"Indeed, but perhaps you have someone on the outside," the inspector replied. "This could be a ploy to make you appear innocent."

"I thought that too, Inspector," I said, "but it isn't Uncle Henry's fault. The Crimson Caper—for whatever reason right now—wants to prove Uncle Henry's innocent. I don't know why they've changed their minds after going to the trouble of putting his fingerprints on the matchbox."

"Look, Inspector, as I explained when you first dragged me in here," Uncle Henry said, "I'm not responsible for any of this."

"We'll see about that, *Signore*," the inspector replied, turning to me with his notepad open. "What were you doing at the Markets in the first place, *Signorina* Prince?"

I cleared my throat. "Well, we went shopping for new clothes."

"Wait a second. You two went shopping even though there's a Crimson Caper out there?" Uncle Henry asked. "Are you two insane?"

"Hey—it was Jessica's idea, not mine," Ben muttered. "I don't even like shopping."

"Thanks for that, Ben. For the record, we were just killing time. The bail money and our lawyer are both on their way, and we didn't want to sit around the hotel," I said. "And I was also testing out a theory. The Crimson Caper knew where we were, so it proves they're following us. Following *me*, like I told Ben earlier."

"Hmm. Who knew you were going to the Markets?" the inspector asked.

"Well, Larry Kibbler—our chauffeur. He took us to the Markets. And don't be angry with him, Uncle Henry. I had to beg him to drive us," I said, noticing Uncle Henry's look of disapproval. "I told Carla to come, but she didn't think it was a good idea. And of course, I asked Josephine to tag along, but she was too traumatized. But personally, I think the Crimson Caper's watching us—maybe our hotel or limo. I've caught them watching my room before."

"Would you like me to assign an officer to follow you around, *Signorina*? It may be safer for you."

I shook my head. "No thanks, Inspector. If anything, I want them to do something again. We need more evidence—and the Crimson Caper's getting reckless."

"There you have it. Witnesses saw this car drive into the Markets, right?" Uncle Henry asked. "The Crimson Caper's identity is a mystery, but there's one thing I know for sure—it's not me. Let me out, Inspector."

The inspector sighed. "I'd like to let you go, *Signore*. I really would. However, the evidence says—"

"Your evidence is weak and won't hold up in court," I heard a familiar voice say behind us. "Any jury knows that."

I turned my neck to see a balding man with thick glasses and an expensive suit standing behind us. Bruce Greenberg—Uncle Henry's lawyer. He represented him for years, ever since I was a little girl. He could come across as condescending and abrasive, but I guess that came with being a top lawyer.

"Thank goodness you're here, Bruce," Uncle Henry said. "Wait, how did you get here so fast?"

"I was already in Europe for another client."

"Well, I'm grateful. More than you know. You need to get me out of this place. I didn't do anything."

"I know, Henry—and I will." Bruce handed the inspector a piece of paper with a bunch of numbers on it. "I spoke with Henry's accountant. The bail money was received twenty-two minutes ago. Why has my client not been released yet?"

The inspector scoffed. "We simply hadn't gotten around to it, *Signore*. With the Market attack—"

"Which wasn't Henry's fault, clearly," Bruce interrupted. "Unless you'd like me to complain to your superior, I suggest you allow my client to return to his hotel."

The inspector nodded, stepping aside. "Very well. *Signore* Prince, you're free to leave. However, the charges still stand. You must not leave Milan while our investigation's ongoing."

"Go back to the hotel and rest, Henry. You'll have some dignity back for now, at least," Bruce said, looking at the toilet with disgust. "And Inspector, I'd like to go over a few things with you."

Inspector Esposito shook his head. "I'm far too busy for that, *Signore*—"

"Oh, no, I insist," Bruce said, leading him to his office. "Let's begin with this matchbox. I have a few theories on how someone could plant fingerprints."

As they walked away, Uncle Henry laughed. "Good old Bruce. I know he'll get me out of this mess. Where's Carla? Is she all right?"

I nodded. "She's fine. She's been at the hotel all day, worried about you."

"I'm glad she's safe—as I am with you two. But don't think I haven't forgotten you snuck away to the Markets."

I rolled my eyes. "Oh, please. If we hadn't gone, the Crimson Caper wouldn't have attacked us. You'd still be in jail, you know."

Uncle Henry sighed, relenting. "I suppose you're right. Come on, kids—let's get back to the hotel. I'm craving some real food instead of the slop they've been feeding us here."

Larry looked relieved to see Uncle Henry out of jail, and I was too—but he wasn't in the clear yet. There was still the matter of the fingerprints, something he couldn't explain. Market attack or not, that could land him in prison.

When we got back to our suites, Uncle Henry suggested we order room service. While Larry, Ben, and I ordered small, modest meals, my uncle nearly ordered the entire menu. Everything from pizza to steak to pork chops sat in front of him, and he dug in like it was his last meal.

After a few minutes, I couldn't stomach watching him eat all of that. I was pretty sure I'd vomit. Instead, I decided to visit Carla and Josephine and tell them the good news of Uncle Henry's freedom. I knocked on Carla's door first and she answered it quickly.

"Jessica, hello. I thought I heard your voice in the hallway," she said. "What happened? Has the situation with Henry changed?"

I nodded, smiling. "Uncle Henry's been set free—for now. The inspector's suggesting Henry has an accomplice, though. He refuses to let the fingerprints slide."

Carla shook her head. "*Mio Dio*, I hate that Inspector. Why does he ignore what's obvious? Henry's innocent."

"Yeah, I know. But I guess he's just doing his job. Anyway, did you hear about the Market attack? Some lunatic drove right at us. Ben and I hid until it was over."

"I did—it's been all over the television. It's very fortunate for Henry, but I'm glad you and your friend are okay," she said, opening the door a little wider. "Why don't you come in? I'm making tea. I had room service bring up a kettle and a few bags since I'm too scared to go home."

I entered and shut the door behind me, taking a seat on the nearby couch. Carla walked over to the small pantry and grabbed two cups of steaming hot tea. As she handed one to me, I noticed a red burn mark on her hand.

"Ouch. That looks painful," I said, gesturing at the burn. "You okay?"

She nodded, wincing. "I'm fine, *grazie*. I burned myself on some hot tea before you knocked. It was my fault. I've been distracted by Henry's arrest and wasn't watching what I was doing—"

I almost dropped my cup as a bloodcurdling scream ripped through the hotel. As I placed it down on the coffee table, Carla glanced at me with fear in her eyes.

"What was that?" she asked, rising to her feet.

"I think it was Josephine. Sounded like her, anyway. Come on—we need to make sure she's okay!"

Nineteen

THE BLACK CAR

Carla and I joined the slew of other concerned guests outside Josephine's door. Everyone knew it was her—we'd gone through this before. Was it the Crimson Caper again? Had they returned for another attack?

Uncle Henry, wiping his mouth on the bib around his neck, rushed over with Ben and Larry behind him. I pushed through the people, making my way toward him.

"Did you hear that scream?" I asked.

"Hard not to. I'm sure it was Josephine," Uncle Henry replied. "Get us in there, Jess. Time to find out what's going on."

I knocked on the door. "Josephine? It's us. Is everything all right?"

Silence. I sighed, turning to Uncle Henry for help.

"I could run downstairs and ask the concierge for a key," Larry said.

"Josephine could be in danger. We don't have time," Uncle Henry replied. "Everyone, take a step back. We're coming in, Josephine."

With one swift kick—his second of this trip—the door flew open. I rushed inside, but nothing in the room seemed out of the ordinary. The curtains sat closed, the balcony door looked locked, and it was neat and tidy around the suite.

But the phone was dangling off the coffee table. In the corner, Josephine rocked herself back and forth. I rushed over, kneeling beside her.

"Josephine, what happened? Are you all right?"

She shook her head and pointed at the phone, half-hanging off the table. I glanced over at it, the entire room silent until I heard heavy breathing on the other end of the line.

Someone had called Josephine. And if I had to guess, I knew who it was.

Uncle Henry, Ben, and the others looked at me in confusion. Carla entered the room, bending down beside Josephine to comfort her. I picked up the phone and pressed it against my ear.

"Hello?" I whispered.

"As I was saying to Josephine, before she rudely screamed in my ear," the deep voice on the other end began, "midnight tomorrow night. She knows what I need from her."

The voice sounded altered in some way. I couldn't tell if it was a woman or a man, but I knew one thing for sure.

"You're the Crimson Caper," I muttered. "It's you, isn't it?"

"*Molto bene*. Very perceptive, Jessica. It's true what they say about you—you *are* a good detective... for a teenager."

"What do you want? Why are you trying to ruin Carla? Why did you almost kill us in the Markets?" I asked, my voice growing louder and angrier. I had a million questions.

"Midnight tomorrow, Parco di Trenno. Bring two sets of new clothes," the Crimson Caper replied. "Come alone. I want you to deliver everything by yourself, Jessica. And no cops, either—or people get hurt."

"Why not Josephine like last time?"

The Crimson Caper snorted. "You've been so eager to be involved in this case. I'm giving you an opportunity to see it up close. Josephine will make the clothes and you'll deliver them."

"How generous. What are you planning?"

And then the phone went dead. As I put it down, Josephine wailed. I turned around, looking at her with a mix of pity and sadness. She'd been through so much. Carla wasn't the only one tormented by this Crimson Caper.

"Who was that, Jess?" Uncle Henry asked.

"The Crimson Caper," I replied, turning to Josephine. "They want more clothing, right?"

Josephine nodded, her voice a whisper. "My phone rang. I picked it up, and I heard their familiar voice, and I freaked! They wanted me to make more clothes, and they wanted you to deliver them."

"More outfits? Why?" Ben asked. "Josephine made them once already. Don't they have enough?"

"Well, with all the clues they've left behind, I'm not so sure. Think about all the clothes we've found so far. They have to be in need of new stuff by now," I replied. "And I can't help but think the timing of this phone call is suspicious."

"What do you mean?" Uncle Henry asked.

"This is the second time the Crimson Caper's made their presence known. I still think it's a ploy to make you look innocent, Uncle Henry. Right after you were released from jail."

"Why would they frame me just to make me look innocent?"

"That's a good question," I said. "No idea yet."

"You could be right about the Crimson Caper's motives." Carla rose. "Perhaps this person doesn't want Henry taking credit for their work? Or maybe they don't want their plans to include him?"

"Anything's possible—but why they want him to look innocent's still bothering me," I muttered. "And another thing. The Crimson Caper called me out by name on the phone. They know who I am for sure—and they want me to deliver the new clothes at midnight tomorrow. Somewhere in a place called Parco di Trenno—wherever that is."

"That's an American graveyard park," Carla replied. "Lots of American soldiers are buried there. How sadistic they'd want to meet there of all places."

"And more proof you can't go, Jess," Ben said. "Seems like an obvious trap to me. What if they try to kill you?"

"And I'm not making clothes for them ever again," Josephine snarled. "Not when I know what they plan to use them for. I want to be left out of this mess for good."

I sighed. "First things first. How are you feeling, Josephine?"

Josephine shook her head. "Still shaken up. There's nothing this Crimson Caper won't do. I regret ever making clothes for them. Why can't they just leave me alone?"

"A good question," Ben replied. "Why does the Crimson Caper still harass us when Carla's fashion show was sabotaged, and Henry's charged for their crime? Seems like they got away with it to me. Anything else would be overkill. And a waste of time."

"There's still a lot we don't understand. But for now, we need to get to the police station. It's not too late, so Inspector Esposito might still be there," I replied. "I want to see him in person and see the look on his face. Come on. He needs to know about this."

"Do I have to go?" Josephine asked. "It's not safe leaving the hotel. The Market attack I saw on TV proved it."

I nodded. "You have to go, Josephine. You might have information that could help the inspector."

She glanced out the window at the night sky, shaking her head. "I don't know. The Crimson Caper could be lurking —waiting for me."

I placed my hand on her shoulder. "I know this is hard, Josephine. But if the Crimson Caper gets away with this, it'll never end. Do you want to live your whole life in fear?"

She turned to me, sighing. "I don't. I might regret this, but... let's go, Jessica. I'm ready to speak with the inspector."

"Great, thanks. Maybe we'll get lucky and they'll show themselves again. That's why it's good to go in person. And if they do appear, get ready, everyone. We need to catch them."

Ben patted his biceps, or lack thereof. "Bring it on."

Josephine looked nervous and paranoid the entire ride to the police station, but we made it there in one piece. Uncle Henry told Bruce what we were doing, and he agreed to come with us. He really hated we were talking to the cops—especially with Uncle Henry already looking guilty—but this was necessary.

As we entered the station, we caught the inspector just as he was about to leave. I almost felt bad he'd miss another family dinner, but our information could help his case. He didn't seem to mind either.

Once I told him about the phone call, he escorted us into the interrogation room. Bruce set his briefcase down on the table and cleared his throat.

"Despite my objections, Henry decided we should be

here," he muttered, glancing in Josephine's direction. "And he asked me to represent you as well, Miss Arias."

Josephine shook her head. "Thank you, but I can't accept. I don't have the money to pay him back for your services."

"Don't worry. I'll pay for it," Uncle Henry said. "Doesn't hurt to have a lawyer around. And before you say no, it's already a done deal."

Josephine smiled. "Thank you, Mister Prince. Someone as kind as you could never be the Crimson Caper."

If only a courtroom would believe that, then Uncle Henry would be off the hook.

The inspector pulled out his notepad. "This is the second time the Crimson Caper's called you, right, *Signora* Arias?"

She nodded. "Yes. I haven't heard from them in a while —not since the night I gave them their clothes."

"Did the Crimson Caper mention why they needed more clothing? Or what they planned to do with it now?"

"No, not at all. They've never told me their plans," Josephine said, gesturing toward me. "Jessica spoke with them more than I did this time. I dropped the phone and screamed when I realized who it was."

"Ah, *Signorina* Prince. It all comes back to you," the inspector said. "Isn't it a little odd how often the Crimson Caper includes you?"

"Miss Prince is my client, too. Watch how you speak to her, Inspector," Bruce said. "I don't appreciate you framing your questions in an accusatory manner."

"It wasn't accusatory, *Signore* Greenberg," the inspector replied, "but a mere observation. Every step of the investigation, *Signorina* Prince has been involved in some capacity. She was the one who saw the Crimson Caper fleeing the fashion show, right before the sabotage occurred."

"Well, I hope everyone in this room knows I'm not the Crimson Caper," I said. "But you're right, Inspector. With the attack on the Markets, I think the Crimson Caper's obsessed with me. A few days ago, I saw them looking up at my hotel from the street."

"It's irrelevant. I haven't been informed of any charges pending against Miss Prince, so let's drop the questions," Bruce said, leaning forward. "We came here to report the phone call. Address your questions to my other client, Inspector."

The inspector nodded, sighing. "The Crimson Caper requested a clothing transfer in Parco di Trenno tomorrow at midnight, right?"

Josephine narrowed her eyes. "Yes, Inspector. Why?"

"It seems obvious what you must do, *Signora* Arias. This is our best lead—our only opportunity to catch the Crimson Caper," Inspector Esposito replied. "You must prepare the clothes. Then I'll deliver them myself."

I shook my head. "That's no good, Inspector. The Crimson Caper requested me. If you deliver the clothes, you could scare them off. I have to do this."

"Wait a minute," Uncle Henry said. "Jessica, can't you see the risks? This is your life we're talking about here."

"Yeah, *my* life. And I'm choosing to do this." I glanced around the room. "Either give me permission or I'll sneak out and do it. At least this way, I'm letting you all come too. To watch from a distance."

Bruce sighed. "Jessica...please, rethink this."

"No. I want to do this. I want to meet the Crimson Caper."

Ben scoffed. "The Crimson Caper wants to meet you in a graveyard, Jess. All the better to kill you in. Can't you see that?"

"Excuse me?" Josephine asked, rising to her feet. "Don't I get a say in this? I'm the one who has to make the clothes."

"But you won't be the one who delivers them. You'll be safe, Josephine," I replied. "It's me risking my life."

"I don't think anyone's safe, Jessica," Josephine began, "but you don't understand. I don't want a role in any of this. What if the Crimson Caper uses more of my clothes to kill someone? I'll feel like an accomplice. I'd probably never sleep again. Not like I'm sleeping much these days, anyway."

"No one will blame you if that occurs, *Signora*," the inspector said. "But that's all the more reason to do it. This could be our only chance to lure the culprit out. It's unorthodox and I don't like involving a teenager in a police investigation, but we have an opportunity. As much as it pains me to admit...Jessica must deliver the clothes. While we watch from a distance like she said."

"And if Jess dies?" Ben asked. "No. We can't ask her to do this."

"I agree with Henry and Ben. It *is* risky," Carla said, "but think about what Jessica told us. The Crimson Caper knows where we're staying. If they really wanted to hurt Jessica, wouldn't they have done it already?"

I nodded. "She's right. I'm in."

But Josephine shook her head. "I can't do it. I can't make the clothes knowing the Crimson Caper could use it for violence."

"Then we'll be throwing away our only hope of catching them," I replied. "You made the clothes in the first place for them. You got us into this mess. At the very least, don't you want to try to make things right?"

I knew it was harsh blaming her, but I had to sound convincing. If she wouldn't make the clothes, we wouldn't be able to meet the Crimson Caper.

Josephine sighed, stomping her feet. "Fine! I'll make two more trench coats if it gets you all to shut up. I'll order some supplies sent to my hotel room and get started right away."

"Good. Now, what about the measurements, Josephine? What specifications did they ask for? We can use that to narrow down the suspect list if we know their size."

"They asked for extra-large clothes. The bigger, the better."

"Hmm. Maybe they're trying to hide their shape. That could be anyone," I said, thinking of the suspects. "Hardly narrows it down. Hopefully, I'll be able to find out more in person."

Uncle Henry gave me another one of his famous I-don't-approve looks. "Jess...."

"Don't worry, Uncle Henry. I know what I'm doing," I replied. "I got you out of jail, didn't I?"

He couldn't argue with that. "All right. I might regret this, but you can go. But Inspector, watch out for my girl."

"I will." The inspector rose to his feet. "*Grazie.* Tomorrow night, I'll arrive early to hide in the park. When you make the exchange, I'll attempt to capture the Crimson Caper."

I nodded. "Sounds like a plan, Inspector. I just hope this works. If not, we may never catch them."

We returned to the hotel, exhausted and in need of a long sleep. As I crawled into bed, saying goodnight to Ben on the sofa, I could hear Josephine down the hall. Her sewing machine was on full blast, working on the trench coat she didn't want to make. I could hear her cursing under her breath as she worked.

When early morning came, I sneaked out of bed and dressed. I looked back at Ben who seemed so peaceful sleeping. I felt bad not telling him where I was going, but I had to do this—alone. Larry would never drive me, and the others would never approve, but I needed to follow a hunch on something I couldn't stop thinking about.

The black car. The inspector hadn't mentioned if he found the car's owner yet, but I had a few ideas of my own. Sadly, the police couldn't check it out. It had to be me. But I wasn't complaining.

I caught a taxi at the front of the hotel and gave the driver my destination. When we arrived, I paid him with the allowance in my purse and looked up at the big letters on the building.

Salvatore Industries. Just the place I needed to be.

As I approached the front doors, I glanced at the parking lot. Sure enough, dozens of black European cars sat out front, just like the night Bruno Salvatore arrived at Lance's home and intimidated us. I shuddered thinking about it.

He had more than enough black cars at his disposal. Sure, those cars were common, but did it mean he was the Crimson Caper? Or was he just connected to them? I didn't know, but I *did* know he had motive, means, and opportunity.

Motive? Leaving Carla broke and desperate, looking to turn to drugs to fund her career. Means? Of course—he's a gangster. He could easily get a black car and whatever else he needed to pull off a crime. And opportunity? He had all the opportunity in the world. He was becoming a high suspect on my list—and his past in the mob didn't help his case.

As I entered the building, I glanced around. Men and women in black suits and dresses typed on their computers, looking up at me as I passed. In truth, I didn't know what

Salvatore's company did. Was it a computer company like Uncle Henry's? Or was it just a front for drug operations?

I'd bet all my fortune on the latter.

I approached the front desk then placed my pink purse on top of it. "Hello, I'd like to see Bruno Salvatore."

The secretary barely looked up from her computer. "He doesn't accept visitors. He's a very busy man, in case you don't know," she spat, avoiding my gaze. "And we don't appreciate random people walking in from off the street."

"Oh, but I'm not someone random. My name's Jessica Prince, niece of billionaire Henry Prince," I said. "And my uncle's very interested in your... business."

It was a lie, but I needed to say something to get me a meeting with the man himself. It made the secretary look up, intrigued. She nodded toward a row of chairs. "Wait over there."

I drifted away from her desk but didn't sit. She kept me in her sights while placing a phone call. Despite my attempts at eavesdropping, she spoke too softly and kept her mouth covered. After hanging up, she said, "Elevator around the corner. Fifth floor."

"I thought he didn't accept visitors?"

Judging by the glare on her face, it was clear she didn't appreciate my snarky comment.

"Thanks." I hurried away before anyone changed their minds.

The elevator ride was smooth and fast. I stepped out into a large waiting space furnished with a reception desk and another row of chairs.

The assistant seemed every bit as surly as the one downstairs. She glared at me and said, "Mister Salvatore is in a meeting right now. I'll let you know when he's ready."

"I'll just sit right here." I took a seat against the wall.

But the waiting didn't take very long. A few moments later, the door to what I presumed was his office opened. And lo and behold, Bruno Salvatore and Lance LaDoux walked out. But they weren't the only ones.

Sasha—without her crutches—stood by their side.

Twenty

ALL THE WRONG PLACES

It was clear Bruno, Lance, and Sasha hadn't seen me because they continued to talk as if I wasn't there. I grabbed a magazine to hold over my face while slinking down in my seat, wanting to overhear their conversation without being seen.

"I'm telling you, *Monsieur* Salvatore," Lance began, "Carla can't be persuaded. She'll never join our alliance."

"Yeah, Lance is right," Sasha said. "Carla's capable of a lot, but not this. She has limits, I think."

He turned, giving them a smirk. "I'm not a man who takes no for an answer—and the two of you should know that. Carla *will* join us, given her current monetary situation. It's inevitable."

Given that revelation, I decided it might work to my advantage if they knew I'd overheard them. I stood and cleared my throat. "Excuse me, Mister Salvatore? I'm pressed for time. Can I have a word with you now?"

The three of them turned, looking at me. Lance gulped and Sasha's eyes widened so big, I thought they were going to pop out of her head. She immediately opened her bag and pretended to root through it, letting her hair fall to curtain her features. But it was too late for either of them to hide from me. While she and Lance looked terrified, Bruno seemed amused. As always.

"Henry Prince's niece, yes?" Bruno asked, lighting his cigarette. "I remember you from the dinner party. When my secretary phoned ahead, I knew I had to let you in to see what you wanted."

"That's me. I thought Lance might be with you, but I never thought I'd find Sasha here." I stared right at her.

She pulled her hand from her bag and clutched the strap tight in her balled fist. As she met my gaze, her complexion paled.

"We're having a simple conversation. That isn't against the law, is it?" Bruno asked.

It is when you're talking about selling drugs, I wanted to say, but it was probably best I kept my mouth shut instead.

"Uh, I should get going," Sasha muttered, slipping past me. "I have a lot of stuff to do."

"Don't go too far, Sasha," Bruno said. "I might need you in the future for an important project."

As she nodded and walked by, she placed something in the palm of my hand. It felt like paper. If Bruno noticed, he didn't say anything. I discreetly stuffed it in the pocket of my dress, saving it for later.

"What can I help you with today, *Signorina*?" Bruno asked, puffing his cigarette. "And if it's so important, why isn't Henry Prince himself here to talk about it?"

"Well, I don't know if you've heard, but he was arrested for arson and sabotage. The inspector thinks he's the Crimson Caper," I replied. "He was released on bail but isn't allowed to leave the hotel."

"How sad," Bruno muttered, puffing his cigarette again. "Step inside my office, *Signorina*. We can talk in private."

"I should be leaving, too, *monsieur*," Lance said. "I have many business matters to attend to. Au revoir."

"So soon? Come on, Lance—stay a little longer," Bruno urged. "As my business partner, I think you should be present for this meeting. Don't you agree?"

Lance sighed but before he could protest, Bruno draped an arm around the old man's neck and led him into the office. I followed, taking a seat in one of the plush chairs. Bruno locked the door before sitting in front of me.

In hindsight, it was probably a bad idea getting locked in a room with a gangster, but I had questions. Questions he'd never answer truthfully to the police.

"If you're seeking to join our organization, you must know the full extent of what we do," Bruno said, leaning back in his chair. "I can't admit it out loud for legal reasons, *Signorina* Prince—so I trust you know I can't confirm or deny anything."

"Then I'll say it. I know you're selling drugs," I replied, "and I know Lance is helping you. Seems obvious to me."

"It is? How so?" Bruno asked, amused. "Do tell."

"Well, if I had to guess, there are a lot of business possibilities in the fashion industry. Models want drugs for a little edge, and fashion designers need the sales to pay the bills," I said before I turned to Lance. "And you, Mister LaDoux—you need this partnership. How long have you been broke?"

Lance scoffed. "Broke? *Moi*? That's preposterous, *mademoiselle*!"

I shook my head. "No, I don't think it is. I've seen how much your house is falling apart. You don't have the money to put it back together, do you?"

"I don't know what to say," Lance muttered.

"And I bet the money you promised Carla was just a ploy. It was never yours in the first place, was it? It was Mister Salvatore's. Probably from a drug deal," I continued.

"You wanted to give Carla the money, but it comes with a catch—she has to join your organization to keep getting payments. Isn't that right?"

Lance gaped at me like a fish out of water. Bruno smirked and seemed impressed.

"But Bruno arrived, and you couldn't say anything in front of us," I said. "He came to see if Carla agreed to join, but he didn't expect to see us there. He couldn't admit the truth, either—and he couldn't stop Carla from leaving."

Bruno chuckled, stubbing out his cigarette. "You're observant, *Signorina* Prince. I'll give you that."

"*Very* observant," I replied. "It's why I'm really here, Mister Salvatore—and it isn't to talk business. A black car attacked me and my friend at the Markets yesterday. The driver left a threatening note behind, the same kind the Crimson Caper uses."

"I heard about that," Bruno said. "It's a miracle you survived. I would hate to see your pretty little blonde head splattered all over the pavement."

I cleared my throat, feeling like that was a threat. "I'm glad it didn't come to that. But I can't help but think about your cars, Mister Salvatore. When you arrived at Lance's house the other night, you had a dozen black European cars. There are more in your parking lot."

His smirk faded. "What are you getting at, *Signorina*?"

"Nothing. Just pointing out a coincidence," I replied. "The Crimson Caper's someone ruthless who wants Carla ruined—for her to be poor and desperate. I wonder why that is?"

Bruno rose to his feet. "If you're not here to talk business, then we have nothing to discuss. You should know I don't like wasting time. You're smart enough to find your way out, I'm sure."

I refused to move. "Was it your black car, Mister Salvatore? Did you attack the Markets?"

He unlocked the door and opened it. "*Ciao, Signorina* Prince. Perhaps one day, we *will* be business partners. Wouldn't that be exciting?"

Don't count on it, I thought. But I saw the gleam of the gun on his hip and decided not to argue.

I looked over at Lance who stared at me. His eyes seemed to say *get out while you can*. But whether he partnered with Bruno on his own or got coerced into it was still a mystery.

I nodded, rose, then walked to the door.

Bruno grabbed my arm. "Also, I don't care for accusations, *Signorina*. And in this city, you must be careful with whom you choose to go snooping around. You may just make a powerful enemy. *Ciao.*" He shoved me into the hallway then locked the door behind me.

I rushed through the building, rattled by the attention I drew from everyone I passed. Once I'd made it outside, I took a deep breath, grateful to still be alive.

Stupid, I thought to myself. This was pointless and risky. If Bruno was the Crimson Caper, there's no way he'd admit it. Or his drug operations.

As I dug through my pocket to find the local taxi number, my hand touched whatever Sasha gave to me. When I pulled it out, it was an address and room number with three words on it. It read COME SEE ME.

As the taxi I called pulled up to the curb, I handed him the address Sasha gave me. "Do you know where this is?"

"I do, *Signorina*," the taxi man said. "A hotel. Only a few blocks from here."

A hotel—so that's where Sasha had been staying. Whatever she wanted to tell me was obviously important if she was willing to give me her address. But was it more than a coincidence her hotel was close to Bruno's office?

When the taxi arrived, I paid the man and followed the information on the card—fourth floor, room 213. I knocked on it once before the door flung open, then Sasha's head poked out into the hallway.

"Were you followed?" she asked.

"Um, I don't think so," I replied. "No one knows I'm here, either."

"Good. We have to talk fast," she said, opening the door. "Come in. Hurry."

When I was inside, she locked the door behind us. She had about four extra locks to keep the place secure. Was she expecting trouble?

"What's this all about?" I asked. "Why did you want to meet me?"

"It's about Bruno Salvatore. I figured you'd want to know why I'm working with him," she said, taking a seat on the sofa. "And I should explain myself."

I sat down beside her. "I'm listening."

"First, I'm sure you know what he's up to—illegal drug operations. He's hoping the fashion industry will make him richer. You'd be surprised how many people are junkies in this line of work." She shook her head in disapproval. "Secondly, I'm not working with him. Never in a million years."

"No? Then why were you there today?"

"I'm working undercover," she replied, "for Interpol."

"The world's largest international police organization? Why are they involved?"

"Bruno Salvatore has a long list of criminal activity. It doesn't stop at drugs, and it won't end there, either," she said. "He wants to control the entire fashion industry—in every country. He's like a disease, and it's spreading. Fast."

"Does Inspector Esposito know about this?"

"Yeah, but he knows not to say anything. Me being undercover could be our only chance to catch Bruno," she said. "Look, I *am* a model. I didn't want to get into this undercover fiasco."

"So why did you end up doing it?"

"Because I had no choice. Right after my fall, I wanted to get home to New York, but Bruno contacted me. He wanted me to join his drug operation—and threatened my life if I didn't. He set me up in this hotel and tried to bribe me. And as you heard him say, he doesn't take no for an answer."

"Then how did you get involved with Interpol?"

"I went to the inspector as a last resort, and he got me in contact with an Interpol agent. He told me all about the case. It doesn't pay well, but at least they'll protect me as long as I gather evidence against Bruno."

"What about that exposé you were doing on Carla? Is that related?"

"No, not at all. That story was for my own benefit—for money and publicity. It's why I faked my injury. Stupid, I know, but not illegal. Vincent and Antonio aren't involved in the drug trade because they're not important in the fashion world," she said. "But Enrique got caught up in it. When Bruno asks you to join, well, you have no choice. He's approaching a lot of high-profile people in the fashion industry. Apparently, he has a niece who's really into fashion. He got the idea from there."

"And Lance? Why do I get the feeling he has no choice, too?"

She nodded. "You're right. He was in a sticky situation —losing money, declaring bankruptcy. He felt like he had to join. Bruno has a sixth sense for this sort of thing—like who's poor and desperate. Lance isn't working undercover and I don't think he knows I am, either. Believe me, I wasn't thrilled to hear my fashion and make-up hero was working with a mobster."

"And how does Carla fit into all this? I heard Bruno talking about her while I was in the waiting room."

"Then it should be obvious. Bruno has his sights set on Carla next," she replied. "Interpol hasn't contacted her in case she agrees to work with Bruno. They don't want to give our operation away, but they can't intervene, either. Too risky."

"Is she in danger?"

She shook her head. "No, but Bruno desperately wants her help in the drug trade. He's confident she'll say yes because she needs the money—after the Crimson Caper sabotage and stuff. And how she wasted her family's fortune trying to make her fashion dreams come true. Everyone knows that."

"Tell me honestly," I said, leaning forward, "do you think Bruno's the Crimson Caper? He has a good motive for wanting to work with Carla."

Sasha shrugged. "I don't know, Jessica. If he is, Interpol won't care about that. It's small compared to his drug affiliations. They have me concentrating on catching him for that, not arson and threatening notes."

I sighed, rising to my feet. "Well, thanks for telling me. You know, for a while I thought *you* were the Crimson Caper."

"I'm not, but I hope you find the culprit."

"I'll try my best. For now, I should get going," I said, approaching the door. "I hope you can put Bruno Salvatore away for a long time."

"Me too. One more thing, Jessica," Sasha said, following me. "I invited you over to warn you, but truthfully, we're risking both our lives here. Bruno Salvatore's a dangerous man. Visiting him today was brave—but now he knows who you are. I'd be careful if I were you."

"I won't let anyone intimidate me, Sasha—not even a mobster," I said, unlocking the door. "You focus on him and I'll catch the Crimson Caper. Hopefully, after this, Milan will be safe again. For the most part."

I quickly hailed a taxi outside the hotel where Sasha was staying. When it pulled up to my hotel, I glanced down at my watch. It was almost noon and I knew it was too late to sneak back inside. Everyone must've realized I was missing by now.

As I unlocked the door to my room, the couch was empty. Ben was nowhere in sight and I started to panic.

"Where were you?"

I gasped and turned around, seeing Ben hiding behind the door. He had his arms crossed and looked furious.

"Ben! You scared me," I muttered, placing a hand over my heart.

"Yeah? Good because you scared me this morning," he replied. "When I didn't see you here, I thought the worst! Where did you go?"

"Sorry, but I had to do something important," I replied. "Does Uncle Henry know? Is he mad at me?"

Ben shook his head. "I lied to him when he asked where you were. I told Mister Prince you were sick. You know, with girly problems. He took the hint and backed off."

"You're a life-saver," I said, putting my purse down. I glanced up, noticing Ben was still standing there, staring at me. "What?"

"Well? Aren't you going to tell me where you went?"

I sighed. "You won't like it."

"What else is new, Jess? Just tell me."

"I was at Bruno Salvatore's office—the mobster."

Ben's mouth widened. "What? Jess! You can't. That's crazy!"

"I know, I know!" I replied, taking a seat. "It was dangerous, but I had questions. The black car at the Markets *could* belong to him. I saw him driving one when he pulled up to Lance's house."

"Well, what did he say? Did he admit he's the Crimson Caper?"

"He wouldn't say yes or no. But don't worry," I replied. "Sasha's working undercover for Interpol. They're going to bust him with drugs sooner or later. I'll be fine, Ben."

He sighed. "You'd better, Jess. If something happens to you...."

A knock on the door startled us both.

"Who is it?" I asked, hesitant to open it. I feared it was Bruno Salvatore.

"It's Inspector Esposito, *Signorina*. I wanted to speak with you in person."

I rushed over and opened the door, relieved to see it was him. He bowed and took a step inside the suite. I closed the door behind us. "I hope I'm not disturbing you."

I shook my head. "Not at all, Inspector. What's going on?"

"I found out how the Crimson Caper acquired the firecrackers. When the news of the Markets attack spread, we received a phone call," he said. "A vendor sold firecrackers to a sketchy-looking man right before the attack. He paid in cash and wanted the firecrackers quickly."

"Who was the man?"

"We found him. He isn't the Crimson Caper, *Signorina*," he replied. "Turns out, someone paid him to buy the firecrackers for them. When I asked for a description of the person, take a guess at what the man said."

"That it was a mysterious figure in red garments? Impossible to tell if it was a man or a woman?"

"Indeed. Unfortunately, the lead ends there. The man had no further contact with the Crimson Caper since then and couldn't tell us anything more."

I sighed. "Then we're back to square one. You could've told me that on the phone, Inspector. Why do I get the feeling you came all this way for something more important?"

"You're right, *Signorina*. I finally found out who the black car belongs to and wanted to tell you in person."

Twenty-One

THE MYSTERIOUS CAR OWNER

"Then I want to go with you to meet the owner, Inspector."

He shook his head. "I don't think that's a good idea—"

"Then I'll follow behind in my limo," I replied. "Look, this Crimson Caper framed my uncle and nearly killed me and my friend. I want to see who they are. And you might need me as a witness to confirm it's really the car from the markets."

The inspector sighed. "You're a stubborn girl. Fine—you may come. But I'll take the lead. Don't do anything dangerous and listen to me."

I promised I would, then Ben agreed too. Was the black car really the key to finding the Crimson Caper? Or was it just another dead-end, like the firecrackers?

As the three of us left the suite and I locked the door behind us, Josephine's door opened. She poked her head out a second later, her eyes darting down the hallway.

"Jessica? Is that you?" she whispered.

I nodded, walking over. "It's me, Josephine. You don't have to be scared. The inspector's here with me."

She took a deep breath and opened the door a little

wider. "Good. I finished the clothes. It's all here, in double—the red trench coats, the hats, the gloves, and new scarves. All oversized like they wanted."

I looked over her shoulder, noticing the red clothing lying on the bed. Her hands looked red and raw as if she had overworked them. I felt bad for Josephine and everything she went through, but she was still a suspect on my list.

And as I learned, you couldn't trust anyone.

The inspector nodded. "Very good, *Signora* Arias. *Grazie* for all your help."

"I didn't mention it before, but I've been thinking," Josephine said, crossing her arms, "is it a good idea to give the Crimson Caper new clothes? It isn't an invitation to do more bad things?"

"You misunderstand, *Signora* Arias. It was never my intention to give the Crimson Caper more apparel," the inspector replied. "When *Signorina* Prince gives the Crimson Caper the briefcase, I intend to attack. The only way the Crimson Caper will leave the park is in handcuffs."

"Then I didn't need to do this at all! You could have had Jess carry an empty garment bag. Do you know how this has tortured me? Not to mention how much work this was... and on such short notice!"

"Please, calm down. Yes, this is all an act. Everyone must play their parts, as you did. In case the Crimson Caper gets suspicious and checks the bag before we move in, it's important to have what they expect. We can't let them know about our deception before we're ready to move."

Josephine sighed. "I hope that works, Inspector. If I know one thing about the Crimson Caper, it's that they're very good at getting their way—*and* putting on a show while doing it."

We found Uncle Henry, Larry, Bruce, and Carla downstairs, shoveling breakfast into their mouths. When Uncle Henry saw me and the inspector, he rose.

"Jess, there you are! Are you feeling okay?" he asked. "You're not one to miss breakfast."

Ben nudged me, and I remembered. "Oh, right. Yeah, I'm feeling better. Nothing to worry about. Well, that's not true. The inspector has something important to say."

Carla rose to her feet. "Oh? What's going on?"

"We've located the black car—the one used to attack the Markets, *Signora* Valentine," the inspector said. "I was on my way to meet with them. *Signorina* Prince managed to convince me to come along."

"Of course she did," Uncle Henry grumbled. "Sounds like my niece. Well, if she's going, I am too."

The inspector nodded. "Very well. But as I said, let me take the lead."

"I'm coming too, whether you like it or not," Carla said, picking up her purse. "I want to meet the Crimson Caper face to face. I want them to know how much pain they've caused me."

As Larry followed the inspector's car, my stomach twisted into knots. Was this it? Were we on our way to meet the culprit, the same one who sabotaged a fashion show, set fire to the Palace, framed Uncle Henry, and stalked Josephine?

They had a very long rap sheet.

The inspector put his signal on and turned right, pulling into the parking lot of Vincent's apartment complex. When he turned his engine off, Larry pulled up beside him and did the same.

"Why are we at Vincent's apartment?" Carla asked.

"Just following the inspector's car, ma'am," Larry replied.

Carla huffed. "If that foolish Inspector accuses Tony again, I think I'll scream. Tony's innocent."

When I saw the inspector get out of his car, I followed him. "Inspector! What's going on?"

The others got out of the limo and slammed their doors shut. The inspector nodded at me. "Vincent Rossi claimed he went to his car shortly before the Markets attack only to find it stolen. Can you guess what car he owns?"

"A black car?" I asked. "Oh, that's right—I forgot. At the fashion show, he left in one with Enrique."

"Indeed, *Signorina*. A black car. He reported it missing, but right after the attack, the car returned—badly damaged. He didn't witness who left it here. When he heard about the Markets attack, he realized what happened."

I'd been wrong—the black car didn't belong to Bruno Salvatore. Was it nothing more than a coincidence?

"I told you, Inspector. I knew Vincent was behind this," Carla muttered. "Where is he now? I want to see what he has to say for himself."

"He's bringing the vehicle to us as we speak," the inspector replied. "In addition to this parking lot, there's also an underground facility. *Signore* Rossi keeps his car underground for safety reasons."

"Well, if his car was stolen, it doesn't seem too safe to me," Ben muttered.

A few moments later, the underground parking garage opened to reveal a black car. It was the same one I'd seen in the Markets. And judging by the extensive damage to the paint, front bumper, and windows, it wouldn't be hard to prove.

"That's it. That's the car that rammed into the Markets," Ben said as I nodded beside him. "I'd never forget it. Man, that thing still haunts my dreams. Like the car Christine from that Stephen King novel. Oh, what was the name of it?"

"*Christine*?" I asked.

"That's it!"

Vincent parked his car next to us and got out of the driver's seat. "Glad you're here, Inspector. I'm also a victim of a crime."

"Victim? Don't make me laugh," Carla spat. "You're the Crimson Caper, aren't you? You had us going for a while but it's time to admit it. To end this little charade."

Vincent shook his head. "As much as you'd love to see me hauled off to jail, I'm not the Crimson Caper. You're not worth sabotaging. You're not even worth a second thought. You believe me, Inspector, right?"

"I'm considering all the possibilities, *Signore*," the inspector replied, pulling out his notepad. "If you weren't the driver, why would someone steal your vehicle?"

"To frame me, I guess," Vincent replied. "Someone wants me to look like the Crimson Caper—someone like Carla."

Carla shook her head. "More lies, Inspector. What else can you expect from a man like Vincent?"

Vincent balled his fists. "I won't stand here and be treated like a criminal, Inspector. This comes as a surprise to me, too. I assumed the underground garage was safe. Seems I was wrong."

"Explain what happened again, *Signore*."

"I took a week off work to look after my brother," he replied. "I came out to use my car to buy groceries, but it was gone. I called the police, but the car returned—and in this condition. Couldn't believe it at first."

"If you're innocent, who else had access to your vehicle?" I asked.

He sighed. "Anyone in the building. You can access the parking garage through the basement level. But if someone was determined, they'd find a way."

As he glared at Carla, I looked down at the car. "Was it hot-wired, or did someone steal it using a key?"

"I think someone used a key. Didn't look hot-wired to me."

"Hmm. Then perhaps someone broke into your apartment to steal the keys," the inspector said. "Any guesses?"

Vincent shook his head. "None. Because it isn't possible, Inspector. When Enrique and I went out, Antonio was still there. He would've noticed if someone broke into our apartment."

"Where do you keep your keys, *Signore*?"

He sighed, rubbing the back of his neck. "In hindsight, it seems foolish to leave them out in the open, but... in the kitchen, near the telephone. But as I said, it isn't possible someone broke in and stole them."

"May I have a look inside the vehicle, *Signore*?"

He nodded, stepping back. "Of course, Inspector. I have nothing to hide."

The inspector opened the back door first, revealing a stack of firecrackers lying on the seats and the floor. The upholstery, stained black and scorched, looked damaged from the firecrackers.

Vincent sighed. "*Mio Dio*, look at the damage. It'll cost me thousands of Euros to repair all this."

"You aren't the only one victimized, Vincent," Carla muttered. "At least this is fixable. How can I possibly repair the Fashion Palace?"

Uncle Henry placed a hand on her shoulder. "Don't worry, Carla. You'll find a way."

She sighed and looked down. "I really hope so."

The inspector opened the driver's door and pulled out a

magnifying glass. As he ran it over the driver's seat, I saw several red fibers sitting there. It looked like it could match the red trench coat or scarf the Crimson Caper wore.

"I'll have my officers collect this as evidence. They can compare it to the gloves *Signorina* Prince found," he said, rummaging through the rest of the vehicle. "But in my mind, the Crimson Caper was definitely here, *Signore*."

Vincent groaned. "And they had to use my vehicle to do it? I feel so lucky."

As the inspector looked under the seats, he noticed something near the pedals. When he pulled it out, I realized it was a tube of red lipstick. It was probably the same one used to write the threatening note.

But I had Lance's red lipstick in my purse and the one taken from the hotel parking lot. He either had more, or he wasn't the Crimson Caper.

"More evidence. The science lab will analyze it for fingerprints," the inspector said. "Where are *Signore* Bello and your brother? I'd like to ask them questions."

Vincent nodded. "Wait here, I'll get them."

As he rushed off, Carla turned to the inspector. "What more do you need? That's two pieces of evidence you found, plus the damaged car. You have to admit it looks suspicious, Inspector. Vincent Rossi's the Crimson Caper."

"It's a possibility," the inspector replied, bagging the red lipstick, "but I must hear all sides of the story, *Signora*. As a detective, I can't afford to be biased."

"But if he's the Crimson Caper, why would he use his own vehicle?" I asked. "And then, most of all, why would he report it to the inspector? It'd make more sense to get rid of it—you know, demolish the car and hide the evidence?"

"You're smarter than that, Jessica. It's to cover his crimes," Carla cried. "If he makes it look like the car was stolen, he won't be a suspect. He's lying to you all. I just know he is."

As Carla tried to convince us of his guilt, Vincent returned. He had Enrique and Antonio by his side. Antonio looked much better and I wondered how much longer he'd stay with his brother. At least Enrique and Vincent seemed like they made up.

"Ah, there you two are," the inspector said, pulling out his notepad again. "Were you aware *Signore* Rossi's car was stolen?"

"Not at all, Inspector," Enrique replied. "Just found out. Vincent rushed inside to tell me before he called you to report it."

Antonio nodded. "And that was when I heard about it too. I was shocked. This is a safe building—we don't get much crime here."

"Have you heard or seen anything suspicious in the past few days? Perhaps in your apartment building or the underground facility?"

Vincent, Antonio, and Enrique shook their heads.

I sighed. They couldn't tell us anything, but I knew one thing for sure—this was the Crimson Caper's car, the one they stole to use. And I didn't think they chose Vincent's car at random. They must've had a reason—and a plan.

"No, Inspector. We've never had a burglary before," Vincent replied. "We don't have any other information for you."

"*Grazie* for your time," the inspector replied, slipping his notepad into his pocket. "I'll call a tow truck to collect your car. I'll wait for them to show up and see if off myself. You don't mind, do you?"

"Not at all. Do what you must, Inspector—as long as it proves my innocence."

Carla scoffed. "You're just going to leave, Inspector? Why aren't you arresting him?"

"My brother's innocent, Carla," Antonio spat. "I'd appreciate it if you didn't accuse him anymore."

As she glared at him, I realized he'd be dead if looks could kill. But this was the first time Antonio had snapped at Carla. He usually seemed desperate for her approval so he must've really believed his brother was innocent. Was his love for his brother stronger than his love for Carla?

She continued to glare but didn't argue. She turned around and hopped into the limo, slamming the door behind her. Antonio shook his head.

"We'll be in touch, *Signore*," the inspector said. "And try not to worry. I'll assign an officer to watch your building."

As the three men nodded and walked away, I turned to the inspector. "Isn't it weird how the Crimson Caper returned the car? I mean, why wouldn't they just dump it in a lake or something? Why risk bringing it back here and possibly getting caught?"

The inspector nodded. "I thought that as well. I'm starting to believe your Uncle Henry is being framed. And he isn't the only one. Something very strange is going on here."

Carla said nothing the entire way home. Uncle Henry stole glances at her, but she was staring out the window into a world of her own. I couldn't imagine how frustrating this whole process must've been for her. I would've been angry, too.

When we returned to the hotel, she sprinted to her suite and slammed the door. Uncle Henry went to chase after her, but I stopped him.

"Don't. She's upset, and nothing you say will make her feel better," I said. "She just needs time."

He nodded. "I see your point, Jess. Ready for your meeting with the Crimson Caper tonight? You don't have to do it, you know. We can find another way. And I won't have to spend all night worrying."

"The black car was a dead-end. Meeting the Crimson Caper in person could be our only chance. I have to do this, Uncle Henry."

He wasn't completely onboard, but he respected that. We gathered for dinner that night, but Carla still wouldn't come out of her room. As I passed by her door, I heard pacing. Something was clearly bothering her.

But I had bigger things to worry about. Uncle Henry, Larry, Bruce, and Ben decided to wait in my room with me. Bruce protested again, but I told him I had to do this.

When eleven p.m. rolled around, I received a call from Inspector Esposito on my cell phone. "*Signorina* Prince? There were no fingerprints on the lipstick found in the car. And those red fibers matched the Crimson Caper's apparel. However, there was no DNA evidence found. I had every technician at the lab working hard and fast to get it all processed."

I sighed. "So we don't have much to go on. Great."

"True, but don't worry. I've arrived at the Parco di Trenno. I'm not certain where the Crimson Caper intends to meet you, but I'm sitting at a park bench in disguise. I have the perfect view of everything from here."

"That's great, Inspector. But what if the Crimson Caper tries to hurt me?"

"My gun's attached to my hip, *Signorina*. I won't let any harm come to you. Italian police don't always carry guns, but this was a special occasion," he replied. "You should get here soon. Perhaps the Crimson Caper will arrive early, and we can ambush them first. *Ciao.*"

I hung up the phone and took a deep breath, turning to Uncle Henry and Ben. "Well, this is it. I'm ready to head to the park, Larry."

"I'll be close by if you need me," Uncle Henry said. "I'll stay with Larry and keep out of the way."

Ben pulled me into a hug. "Be careful, Jess. I know you can't leave a mystery unsolved, but it isn't worth dying over."

"Trust me—I have no intention of that."

"Are you ready, Miss Prince?" Larry asked.

I nodded, taking a deep breath. "I'm ready. Let's go meet this Crimson Caper."

As Larry, Uncle Henry, and I left my suite, Josephine opened her door. "Tonight's the night, isn't it? The meeting?"

I nodded. "It is. Thanks for all your help, Josephine."

She handed me a thick garment bag of clothes, sighing. "Don't thank me. It was the right thing to do. But Jessica? Catch this Crimson Caper. I want this to end for good."

As she shut the door, I walked over to Carla's room and knocked twice. "Carla? It's almost midnight. Wish me luck?"

No response. Considering it was so late, she was probably in bed by now. I shrugged and followed Larry out of the hotel, carrying the duffel bag with me.

And as Larry, Uncle Henry, and I pulled away from the hotel, I had a horrible feeling in the pit of my stomach.

Twenty-Two

CRIMSON CONFRONTATION

The park was pitch black when we arrived. I stared out the window but didn't see a single living soul. Where was the inspector? Was he still here?

As Larry pulled up behind a tree, hiding the limousine, my heart raced. I couldn't believe I was about to meet the Crimson Caper in person. I hadn't seen the culprit since the marketplace. And even then, it hadn't been up close, not since the fashion show when I chased them on foot.

"Are you sure you still want to do this, Miss Prince?" Larry asked, turning around to glance at me. "It isn't too late to tell the inspector you've changed your mind."

Uncle Henry nodded. "Larry has a good point, you know."

I shook my head, glancing at the duffel bag in my hand. "No, I have to do this, guys. I've come too far to quit now. Besides, I can't pass up a chance to find out who the Crimson Caper is."

Larry sighed, nodding. "All right, Miss Prince—but please be careful. I'll wait for you here. And if anything goes wrong, I'll be driving through the park to get you."

"Right beside me," Uncle Henry added.

I smiled. "Thanks, you two—but I think I'll be fine."

"How can you be so sure?" Larry asked, concerned.

"Well, I guess the Crimson Caper *could* kill me," I replied, "but then they'd have a whole other crime on their hands. And something tells me they're not the killing type."

"I hope your theory is right," Uncle Henry said. "Good luck, kiddo."

I opened my door, clutching the garment bag in my hand so hard my knuckles turned white. I tightened my pink sweater around my waist, shivering from the cold night. Several street lamps illuminated the way and allowed me to see in front of me.

Parco di Trenno was beautiful with miles of green grass sprawled out in front of me. Owls cooed in the trees as I rushed down the trail, noticing the row of graveyards in the distance. I read online that the park had a war cemetery with many American soldiers buried here from World War II.

It was almost as if the Crimson Caper chose this location as a warning—that if I made one wrong move, I'd join these graves.

As I glanced to the right, I noticed the inspector sitting at a park bench. He dressed in all black and I almost missed him. He had a magazine covering his face, but he lowered it when he saw me and gave me a nod.

It didn't do anything to calm my nerves.

I wasn't sure where the Crimson Caper wanted to meet, so I wandered near the trees. "Crimson Caper? I'm here. Where are you?"

Silence. I sighed, sitting down near the tree. *I could be here a long time.*

"You're early," a voice behind me said.

I jerked, jumped up, then whirled around. The street-lamp helped to illuminate their face, covered by a red scarf and sunglasses. But since I had their accessories and trench coats, it forced them to wear a black jacket instead. They had put on a spare set of black gloves to hide their hands.

"Crimson Caper," I muttered. "It's been a while since I saw you."

They nodded, their voice disguised by a voice changer. "Did you bring the clothes? The ones Josie made for me?"

"Everything's here," I said, keeping my distance, "but I want to ask you a few questions first."

"That wasn't the deal," they replied, creeping closer to me.

Out of the corner of my eye, I saw the inspector rise from the bench. He tip-toed toward the trees, watching the two of us. He was waiting for the right moment to attack.

"Well, since I'm the one who has your stuff, I think you're at my mercy," I said. "Why are you trying to sabotage Carla Valentine's career?"

"Why do you care so much about her?"

"For starters, she means a lot to my Uncle Henry," I replied. "And I don't like seeing people hurt."

"My reasons are irrelevant," they replied. "Give me the clothes."

"Why did you frame my uncle?" I asked. "He's a good person. He doesn't deserve to go to jail for your crimes."

"It was a mistake," the Crimson Caper replied. "That much I can admit."

"A mistake? So what, you just accidentally framed him? You stole his fingerprints, for crying out loud. Seems pretty deliberate to me."

They sighed. "You'll never understand, Jessica—and I don't have time to explain it. Give me the clothes or else."

"If I give them to you, what will you do with them?"

"What's necessary. Everything I've done has a reason behind it. I don't expect someone like you to get it, Jessica. You're just a teenager."

"It's not a good idea to underestimate me," I replied. "Why do you wear red when you sabotage Carla? Why do you only wear what Josephine makes for you?"

"To make a statement. Again, it's too complex for a kid like you," they replied. "And I wouldn't be so sure Josie's innocent."

I sighed. It was clear the Crimson Caper wouldn't answer my questions, and I was getting tired of talking in circles.

"Do you want the clothes?" I asked.

The Crimson Caper nodded.

"Fine," I replied, shrugging. "Then go get them."

I threw the garment bag toward the trees where the inspector hid. The Crimson Caper huffed before walking over. They bent down and were inches away from grabbing the bag when they paused and cocked their head.

I held my breath.

The inspector sprang to his feet, but the Crimson Caper was faster. They grabbed the bag, slung it over their arm and took a step back while stuffing their hands in their pockets. "Nice try, Inspector—but I knew you were there the whole time."

But how was that possible? The park was as black as night. If I could barely see in front of me, then the Crimson Caper couldn't, either—and not with sunglasses on.

Unless the Crimson Caper knew of our plans tonight. Someone could've warned them.

"You won't get away with this, Crimson Caper." The inspector drew his gun. "You've done enough harm, don't you think? Now, put your hands up, *per favore*. Nice and slow."

They withdrew their hands from their pockets but didn't raise them. "Not this time, Inspector. You can't stop me—not now."

Before Inspector Esposito could react, the Crimson Caper lit a firecracker then threw it at the inspector's feet. It sparked and smoked. The ground around us lit up, and fog billowed, hiding the Crimson Caper.

"Inspector!" I cried. "Watch out!"

But as I stepped forward, the Crimson Caper threw a few more firecrackers. As the rank cloud grew, the Crimson Caper's foot emerged from the thick of it to land a kick on the inspector's shins.

He dropped to his knees, but I continued forward. It was like a minefield trying to wade through the explosions. The park burst with colors, making everything smoky and bright.

The inspector lay on the ground, shielding his face from the blasts. I tried to reach him, but another firecracker exploded right in front of me. I dove for cover. As I looked up, I could just make out the Crimson Caper running into the distance.

They were getting away—and with the new clothes.

"Inspector, quick," I said. "We have to stop them."

The inspector mumbled something, but I couldn't hear it over the firecrackers popping. As I covered my face and coughed, the roar of an engine overpowered the explosions. Bright headlights barreled toward me from behind.

Please don't let it be the Crimson Caper coming back. This night could only get worse if someone ran us over.

Thank goodness. It was Larry's limousine. He pulled beside me, carefully avoiding the firecrackers on the ground, and rolled down his window. He and Uncle Henry peered out at me, concern etched on their faces.

"Get inside, Jessica," Larry said. "It isn't safe."

"Hang on," I yelled. "I have to get the inspector first."

Coughing and wheezing, with my eyes stinging and tears streaming down my face, I tried waving aside the smoke while searching for Inspector Esposito. When I found him beside the path, I pulled him to his feet. He was also struggling to breathe through the smoke, and he placed his arm around my shoulders for support. His body felt limp, and I worried he was seriously hurt.

"*Signorina* Prince? Is that you?" He squinted through the darkness. His voice sounded deep and groggy with pain.

"It's me, Inspector. Keep your head down," I said, dragging him with me. "My limo's right over here."

I opened the back doors and flung the inspector inside before I jumped in and took my seat. "Go, Larry. Get us out of here!"

Larry stepped on the gas, barreling through the park. Uncle Henry was looking back at us and making sure I was okay. As I glanced out the window, I watched the firecrackers burst and taper off. I prayed it wouldn't start a forest fire.

When I looked back at the inspector, his eyes fluttered open and closed. His arm looked bloody and bruised, and the skin hung on by a thread. It looked painful.

"Inspector, what happened?" I asked, placing a napkin from my purse over the wound. "Why are you bleeding?"

"The firecracker, *Signorina*," he murmured. "It struck my arm. Gah, the pain's unbearable."

When he started to mumble incoherently—words in English and some in Italian—I turned to the driver's seat. "Larry, we need to take the inspector to the hospital. He was hit by a firecracker the Crimson Caper threw at us."

"I saw the Crimson Caper go this way, Jessica," he said. "We could catch them if we follow their trail."

"It's tempting—I won't lie. I want nothing more than to catch the Crimson Caper. But we both know the inspector's health is more important," I said, placing the seatbelt around Inspector Esposito's waist. "We should get him to the hospital."

"I understand. I'll drive us to the closest hospital—"

A second later, Larry slammed on the brakes. I skidded off the seat, smacking my head on the floor. Uncle Henry reached back and helped me up. As I groaned, I looked back to make sure the inspector was all right.

He was fine but still bleeding pretty badly. It was a good thing I'd put his seatbelt on first or we could've added a concussion to his list of injuries.

"Jess, you all right?" Uncle Henry asked.

I nodded. "Yeah, yeah. I'm fine. Just wasn't expecting that."

"Oh, my goodness, I'm so sorry," Larry said, staring back at me with wide eyes. "Miss Prince, are you sure you're okay?"

I clutched my throbbing head. "I think so. What happened, Larry?"

"A man jumped in front of the limo," he replied. "I had to slam on the brakes or I would've hit him."

"Man? What man?"

I heard a tapping on my window and looked up. Lance LaDoux stood outside, knocking on the door. "*Mademoiselle* Prince, is that you?"

I groaned and opened the door, looking up at him in confusion. "Mister LaDoux? What are you doing here? It's past midnight, you know."

"You see, *mademoiselle*—" He stopped mid-sentence when he glanced inside and saw the inspector. "*Mon Dieu*! What happened to Inspector Esposito?"

"The Crimson Caper threw firecrackers at us," I replied. "We're taking him to the hospital."

Lance shook his head. "A senseless tragedy. You must stop this Crimson Caper, *Mademoiselle* Prince."

"I'm trying. Do you need a ride home, Mister LaDoux?"

"*Oui, mademoiselle*. But I'll accompany you to the

hospital first, seeing as it's urgent," he replied, slipping in the back seat. "Is he awake?"

I snapped my fingers in front of the inspector's face, but he didn't respond. "No, I think he's unconscious from the pain. That isn't good. Step on it, Larry."

As Larry pressed his foot on the gas again, and we took off with a screech, I looked out the window for any sign of the Crimson Caper. I sighed.

They were long gone.

Uncle Henry shook his head. "I knew this was a bad idea."

"Perhaps it's a good thing I ran into you, *Mademoiselle Prince*," Lance said, interrupting Uncle Henry's frustration. "With the inspector unconscious, we can speak freely."

"About what?" I asked, rubbing my temples.

"What you said before, in Salvatore's office, it was all true."

I stared at him. "So, you're in the drug—"

"No need to say it out loud, *mademoiselle*," Lance muttered, glancing at Uncle Henry and Larry in the front seat, "but *oui*, it's true. You must think I'm some kind of evil person, don't you?"

I nodded.

"Then you don't know the full story. Much like *Mademoiselle* Simpson, I'm working with Salvatore against my will," he replied, sighing. "But due to my financial difficulties, I had no choice. And now it's too late to back out. My life would be in danger if I refused."

"But you're one of the most successful fashion designers and make-up moguls in the world. I've got tons of your products back home, and they sell really well. How could you have financial difficulties, as you put it?"

"I've taken many risks in my career, *mademoiselle*—risks I wouldn't do again if I had the chance," he replied. "I was irresponsible with my money, and now I pay the price. So to speak. I would've left Milan a long time ago for France, but Salvatore kept me here, making money for him."

"Why were you in the park tonight, Mister LaDoux? And at midnight? That seems a little too convenient. And suspicious."

"For a deal. I received a phone call from a potential buyer asking to meet in the park tonight. These exchanges are usually done in remote areas, so it didn't alarm me."

I sat up straighter. "A buyer, meeting in this park? Suspicious, like I said. What did they sound like? Were they male or female?"

He shrugged. "I can't say, *mademoiselle*. It seemed as if their voice was disguised somehow. They didn't tell me their name, either. But they neglected to show. I assumed they changed their mind, so I decided to leave. That was when your driver almost ran into me."

"Sorry about that," Larry said, speeding through the streets. The limo was back on the roads again and I sighed in relief that we were out of the park.

"The Crimson Caper," I muttered. "They wanted you to be here. I bet they were the one who called you. They're trying to set you up."

"Perhaps. Look, I know there's no reason for you to believe me, after everything I've done," he began, "but I'm not the Crimson Caper, *mademoiselle*. I wouldn't do that to Carla Valentine, whom I admire a great deal."

"But what about that lipstick I found in your office? It's the same one the Crimson Caper uses to write their messages. Was it yours?"

He nodded. "*Oui*, it's mine. From time to time, I try on the lipsticks my company makes to evaluate them. It's not an unusual practice, even for men. If you would've asked, I would've gladly told you the truth. As I mentioned before, anyone in Europe could easily get their hands on my lipsticks. They're everywhere."

Was Lance right? Was the lipstick nothing more than a coincidence and he had no role in the sabotage or arson? Being here tonight looked suspicious, but his explanation seemed more than reasonable—considering what I knew about him and Bruno.

"Speaking of deals, do you know if Bruno wants Carla to work for him? Maybe for that check you promised her?"

"*Oui, mademoiselle*. He asked me to offer her the money. He's waiting for the right opportunity to get her alone. He wanted to do it the night of my dinner party," he replied. "But I invited you instead. I knew if others were present, Salvatore couldn't proposition her."

"So you invited us to save Carla?"

He nodded. "As much as I could. I try to look out for her, *mademoiselle*. I only wish I could save her from this monstrous Crimson Caper."

When we arrived at the hospital, the inspector began to wake up. He looked up at me, clutching his bleeding arm. "Where am I, *Signorina* Prince?"

"The hospital, Inspector. You need to see a doctor."

"No, that isn't necessary," he replied, shaking his head. "I feel fine. I must find the Crimson Caper. Did we apprehend them?"

"Sorry, Inspector, but no. They got away. With the clothes Josephine made too."

He cursed in Italian before he looked up and noticed Lance. "*Signore* LaDoux? What are you doing here?"

Lance stuttered, so I stepped in. "He was out for a late-night stroll, Inspector. Everything's fine. Do I have to drag you inside the hospital, or will you come willingly?"

The inspector sighed and stepped out of the vehicle. "Very well. But don't tell my wife about this, *per favore*. She worries about me enough."

I totally understood that. Uncle Henry was already staring at me in concern.

I promised I wouldn't as Lance, Larry, and I helped the inspector inside who stumbled a bit when we reached the front desk. As I explained what happened, a nurse nodded and took the inspector to a private room where he saw the doctor on call.

I followed, watching as they placed the inspector on a white hospital bed. He argued the entire time, swearing he was all right, but the doctor wouldn't listen. They cleaned and bandaged his wound as he rambled on.

"He'll be fine," the doctor said in a really thick Italian accent. "We've patched him up and given him painkillers."

I sighed in relief. We got lucky tonight that those firecrackers hadn't caused too much damage.

The doctor turned to me. "*Signorina*? That bruise on your forehead must be looked at."

I didn't even realize I had a bruise, though my head was pounding. The fall I took in the limo almost knocked me out, but I didn't want an examination. Inspector Esposito was more important.

"Really, Doctor, I'm okay. It's just a simple—"

"Do it, Jess," Uncle Henry urged. "For me."

I sighed and submitted to an exam and a series of questions. When the doctor shone a light in my eyes, I winced.

"You've suffered a minor concussion. You must get plenty of rest and fluids, *Signorina*."

"But I can't rest, Doctor. I'm trying to find the Crimson

Caper. You've seen them on the news, right? They need to be stopped."

He shook his head. "Doctor's orders. If you don't return home and rest, I'll have no choice but to admit you."

"And I'll let them," Uncle Henry added.

I sighed, nodding. "Fine, I'll go home and rest. But can I speak to the inspector first? Alone, please?"

The doctor nodded, then he left the room. I looked back at Larry and Lance who both took the hint and left. Uncle Henry kissed my bruised forehead before walking out of the room. When he had closed the door, I walked over to the inspector's bedside.

"Inspector, can you hear me?"

"I can, *Signorina*. My burn's starting to feel better. *Grazie* for bringing me here," he replied. "If it weren't for you, I would still be passed out in that park. And at the Crimson Caper's mercy. Who knows what they would've done to me." He shook his head. "Anyway, what's on your mind?"

"We have a problem, Inspector. The Crimson Caper knew you were coming tonight. They were prepared for your ambush. They had firecrackers with them and wanted Lance nearby, looking guilty."

His eyes widened. "Which means one thing...."

I nodded. We had both come to the same conclusion. "We have a mole."

Twenty-Three

THE LAST WARNING

After a lot of convincing from the doctor, the inspector agreed to stay overnight at the hospital for observation while he called his wife. They treated him better than an average patient since he was such a beloved inspector. As I left, he told me he was starting to feel better, and I breathed a sigh of relief.

I couldn't let the Crimson Caper kill someone—either on purpose or because of their recklessness. They'd put us through enough already.

Larry, Uncle Henry, and I drove Mr. LaDoux back home to his mansion. He said nothing the entire way. When we pulled into his driveway, he looked back at me.

"When the inspector's feeling better, I intend to tell him about Salvatore's drug operation," Lance said. "I want to help the police gather evidence against him. I've had enough of his manipulation."

"Are you sure?" I asked. "Seems risky."

Lance nodded. "*Oui*, but it's all thanks to you, *mademoiselle*. You've made me realize I don't want my legacy to be linked to a man like Salvatore."

"I'm glad. The inspector will be too. But be careful,

Mister LaDoux," I said. "Salvatore has eyes everywhere. If he finds out you're planning to double-cross him...."

Lance nodded. "I will, *Mademoiselle* Prince. And I must give you the same warning with the Crimson Caper. I don't know if they and Salvatore are one and the same, but I do know they're equally dangerous. *Bonne nuit.*"

I waited until I saw Lance get into his house before we drove off. He was putting himself in danger by working with the police against Salvatore, but I couldn't help but feel proud of him. It was the right thing to do.

When Larry, Uncle Henry, and I returned to our hotel, Ben and our lawyer, Bruce, were still waiting up for me. Their faces were hopeful as we walked into the room and removed our jackets. I almost didn't want to tell them the truth.

"So? Is that awful Crimson Caper in jail now?" Ben asked. "Has your uncle been cleared of all charges?"

"Not exactly," I replied, sighing. "The Crimson Caper got away with the garment bag of clothes—but not before throwing firecrackers at us. We had to take Inspector Esposito to the hospital. He had a bad burn on his arm."

Ben gasped. "Firecrackers? Sheesh, not again. Are you okay, Jess?"

I nodded. "Yeah, I'm fine. And the burns were only minor on the inspector, so he'll live."

"That's it, Miss Prince. You can't work with the police any longer," Bruce said. "I should charge them for recklessly endangering my client."

"You can't charge them, Bruce. I volunteered to go," I replied. "And besides, the inspector needs me. We're close to finding out who the Crimson Caper is—I just know it."

Uncle Henry shook his head. "I agree with Bruce, Jess. Every time you work with the inspector, someone gets hurt.

Including you. The doctor said you have a concussion. You need to rest."

"No, I can't. I need to keep going. Besides, I feel fine. My head is stronger than it looks." I turned to Ben. "You're on my side, right? I need your support, Ben."

He shrugged. "I don't know, Jess. Look, I know you've got a knack for solving things, but it's too dangerous. And you've got a concussion. Sorry, but I think you need to just lay low for now and take it easy."

"Larry?"

He sighed. "I'm afraid I agree with them, Miss Prince. Your health is our number one priority."

I took a seat on my bed, huffing. How could they do this to me? Didn't they know Inspector Esposito needed my help?

I sat up when I remembered something. "I can't quit, guys. Want to know what I found out tonight?"

Uncle Henry sighed. "Jess, please—"

"No, hear me out. Both me and the inspector think we have a mole," I replied. "The Crimson Caper knew the inspector was there. They had to have been warned."

Uncle Henry crossed his arms, thinking. "But who could tell them?"

"Someone who knew about tonight," I replied, "and someone who's only pretending to be on our side."

"I might regret asking you this, but who do you think it is?" Ben asked.

"Well, all of us in this room knew about the meeting. Don't worry—I don't think it's any of you," I replied. "But Josephine knew, obviously. She made the clothes. And then there's Carla and Lance. And if Lance knew, there's a chance Salvatore did, too—even if Lance didn't know he did."

"Hold up. What do you mean, Lance knew?" Ben asked.

"Well, he was there in the park. Another drug deal," I

replied. "Someone with a disguised voice called him to meet in the park. When no one arrived, he started to leave. Larry almost ran him over. I figured he was being set up. The Crimson Caper wanted him there tonight."

"Or Lance *is* the Crimson Caper," Uncle Henry said, "and wanted you to believe someone else lured him there."

I shrugged, rising to my feet. "It's possible. But do you see why I can't walk away? There's too much at stake—for everyone involved. What if the police never solve the case, Uncle Henry? What if Carla's stalked by the Crimson Caper forever? If there's a small chance I could help, I have to take it."

"You have a point, Jess," he said, nodding. "I might regret this, but you can keep assisting the inspector. But be careful, all right? Stop rushing into danger. It really scares me when you do that."

Ben scoffed. "Mister Prince, I really don't think this is a good—"

"I'll be fine," I interrupted. "And the Crimson Caper told me framing Uncle Henry was a mistake. It seemed like they regretted it. Weird, right?"

Uncle Henry furrowed his eyebrows. "Yes, that makes no sense. If it were a mistake, why did they frame me in the first place?"

"Great time for the Crimson Caper to get a conscience," Ben muttered.

I shrugged, yawning. "For now, I'm exhausted. I probably should get some rest. See you in the morning?"

Once everyone nodded and cleared out—except for Ben, of course—I shut and locked the door. After the night I'd had, I needed some good shut-eye. And to give my concussion a break.

While Ben fixed the blankets on the couch to his liking, he shook his head. "I know it's not possible to change your mind, but I'm worried, Jess. The Crimson Caper knows who you are—and they don't like it when people get in their way."

I smiled. "It's sweet you're concerned, but I know what I'm doing. Trust me. But speaking of trust, we can't trust anyone else. And we'll have to be careful with how much information we give to other people. For all we know, the Crimson Caper could be closer than we think."

Early the next morning, I knocked on Carla's door. She opened it a few moments later, rubbing her tired eyes. Judging by the bags under her eyes, she hadn't gotten much sleep, either.

"Oh, Jess—it's you," she said, yawning. "What happened last night? Did you catch the Crimson Caper?"

I shook my head. "No, sorry. They escaped."

The door to Josephine's room opened, then she poked her head out. She looked as exhausted as everyone else. She glanced at the two of us, her face white with fear.

"Did I hear that right? The Crimson Caper escaped?" she asked. "After all that hard work I put into making more clothes? And after the inspector promised he'd catch them?"

I nodded. "It's true. The inspector's beating himself up over it, but it wasn't our fault."

"And I've given them more ammunition to sabotage Carla. Just great." Josephine closed her door, but her voice carried from inside. "Don't ever ask for my help again. I told you this would happen!"

I hadn't forgotten what the Crimson Caper said about Josephine—that she wasn't as innocent as we believed. But was it true, or just another ploy to throw us off track?

When she was gone, I sighed and turned to Carla. "Sorry

about that. Josephine's just upset, but I'm not going to give up. I *will* find this Crimson Caper for you, Carla."

Carla shook her head. "I hope so—because I can't keep living like this, Jess. I'm tired of looking over my shoulder, wondering when the Crimson Caper will attack me or my friends next."

"I know. It's why I came over this morning," I replied. "I have a new plan, and I need your help."

She raised an eyebrow. "What kind of plan? The last one didn't go over so well. And I'm not eager to put myself in danger like you, Jessica."

"The Crimson Caper's getting reckless, Carla. Pretty soon, they'll do something stupid and we'll catch them. Which is why I need you to put on another fashion show. And soon."

"No. Absolutely not," she muttered. "Not after what happened last time. If I plan another show, it'll be a magnet for the Crimson Caper. I'm almost certain they'll attack again."

"Which is why you need to do it. Aren't you tired of waiting around for the Crimson Caper to show up? Why not make them come to us?"

"*Mio Dio*, I don't know," she mumbled, staring at the ground. "I wouldn't feel right putting on another show after Henry's arrest. It was my first fashion show that got him into this mess."

"Jess is right, Carla," Uncle Henry said, leaving his hotel room. "Forget about me for a moment. Fashion's your dream, isn't it? Besides using it as bait for the Crimson Caper, you need to do this show. You can't give up on your career because of some thug in a red trench coat."

"But there's so much to be done," she said, leaning against the archway of her door. "Clothing alterations, finding models, choosing a location."

"And we'll help with it all," I replied. "What do you say?"

She took a moment to think before she nodded. "All right, you've convinced me. After breakfast, we'll head to my workshop to get started. I've got some spare outfits there that didn't make my recent collection. We'll use those and make alterations since there's no time to sew an entire new fashion line. Ugh, I forgot how crazy preparation for a show could get."

As we nodded and turned to walk toward the dining hall, I realized Carla wasn't following. "Aren't you coming with us to eat breakfast?"

"In a moment, Jessica. I need to make a few phone calls first. I hope some of my old models will consider doing another show," she replied. "If not, we'll have to find another solution. The show must go on, as they say."

As Carla shut the door, I nodded. The show must go on because we have a Crimson Caper to catch.

After we ate breakfast, Larry drove us to Carla's workshop. It sat right next to the canal, beautifully overlooking the water, docking boats, and promenade full of tourists and natives. At least we didn't see any journalists waiting to harass us. I could only imagine the pandemonium when they found out about Carla's next show.

As we pulled into the small parking lot behind the building, Carla yelled into her phone. She'd been talking on it for ten minutes and had been annoying me for the last nine and a half.

"Don't be ridiculous, Josie," she cried. "Haven't you been a hermit long enough?"

It was so quiet in the limo that I could hear Josephine's

retort. "I'm not risking my life again—not like this. Sasha got hurt last time. What if it's me next?"

Carla scoffed. "This time, the *polizia* will be involved. I'll request security for the show. I promise it's safe."

I was counting on my hunch that it wouldn't be. I needed to see the Crimson Caper again. I needed to find out what their next step was. And if I knew them as well as I thought I did, this next fashion show wouldn't be safe at all.

But nothing Carla said convinced Josephine. "I can't do it, Carla. You'd understand if you were in my place. If you want to put on another show, that's your right—but leave me out of it. Good luck finding another assistant."

And then the line went dead. Carla grumbled, slamming the cell phone into her purse. Everyone in the limo stared at her, wondering what to say next.

"Didn't sound like a good conversation," Ben muttered.

"It really wasn't. As I told you before, no one in their right mind would agree to be a part of my next show. The last one was a total disaster. I called all my former models at the hotel—including Sasha—and they refused for safety reasons. How can I operate without models and staff?"

"Well, we could be your models," I said.

Carla laughed so hard, it rumbled the limousine.

"Jeez, no need to be so rude about it," Ben grumbled.

"I apologize," Carla said, wiping away tears of laughter, "but none of you know anything about fashion, do you? Or how to strut down a runway?"

I shook my head. "Well, not exactly. But if you want this show to happen, what other choice do you have?"

She sighed. "I suppose you're right. Come along, then. We have much to do—including tailoring my clothes to your measurements."

"Uh, do I have to do this?" Larry asked. "I'm not much of a model."

"It would be helpful. If not, I'll be ruined! Is that what you want? Is it?"

Larry sighed, turning off the ignition. "No, Miss Valentine. I'll help you. Wait until my wife back home hears about this."

"Consider me out, Miss Valentine," Bruce said. "I'll handle the legalities of your show, however."

Carla nodded. "Okay, that's fine. When this Crimson Caper's found, I want them sued for emotional distress."

As we exited the limo, the inspector pulled up in his car. He was looking much better and well-rested except for the bandage around his arm. I knew that burn would take a long time to heal.

"What's he doing here?" Carla asked, placing her hands on her hips. "I can't work if the police interfere. They can join us after everything has been set up."

"I called him after breakfast and asked him to tag along," I said. "He won't interfere. He's going to protect us, Carla."

"Can he really? He couldn't protect us last night. He let the Crimson Caper escape," Carla said. "What good can he do now, Jessica? Maybe we should get another inspector."

I shook my head, defending the inspector. "You weren't there. You didn't see what happened. The inspector tried to stop them, but—"

"No, *Signorina* Prince. She's right," the inspector said, walking over. "I failed to catch the Crimson Caper. Any action from them will be my sole responsibility."

"Just like I told you," Carla said to me. "I'll meet you inside. There's a lot of work to do so hurry, *per favore*."

As she rushed off, I shook my head. "Don't listen to her, Inspector. She's just angry. I know you wanted to catch the Crimson Caper, and we both tried really hard."

The inspector smiled, sadly. "You're too kind, *Signorina*.

Grazie. But in my career, it's too dangerous to make mistakes. When I do, people get hurt—"

And then we heard a piercing scream inside the workshop. I knew right away it was Carla's voice.

"Carla?" Uncle Henry asked, rushing toward the front door. "We're coming!"

As we followed Uncle Henry inside the workshop, I noticed how disheveled it was. Someone knocked racks of clothing over, broke several sewing machines, left a mess of old supplies on the floor, and tossed red paint everywhere.

A banner sat on the wall with red lipstick scrawled on it.

THIS IS YOUR LAST WARNING. DO ANOTHER SHOW AND PEOPLE WILL GET HURT.

Carla put her hand to her mouth, shaking her head in disbelief. "*Mio Dio*, it never ends. How did the Crimson Caper even know I was planning to do another show so soon?"

"That's part of the mystery," I replied. "But yeah, I'd like to know too."

"Well, whatever the reason, I can't do the show. I simply can't!"

Uncle Henry placed his hands on her shoulders. "Listen to me, Carla. The Crimson Caper wants you to be afraid. Don't let them get to you!"

She pulled away from him. "Don't let them get to me? How can I do that, Henry? Nowhere is safe anymore. If I go through with this, someone could get killed!"

"But if you stop, the Crimson Caper will never be caught," I replied. "Then they'd be free to harass you forever. Is that what you want?"

Carla rubbed her temples. "Stop with the questions, *per favore*. Ugh, I have a headache. This all feels like a bad dream."

The inspector pulled out his notepad. "Who had access to the workshop, *Signora* Valentine?"

"Well, me, Josephine, my models... and Lance. I gave him a key in case he wanted to visit," she replied. "And I believe Tony has a key, too. I gave him one when we got engaged. Never got it back in the divorce settlement."

The inspector nodded. "Then the usual suspects. I'll give them a call and see if they have any information—"

Outside, tires screeched in the parking lot.

Twenty-Four

THE SHOW MUST GO ON

We ran out into the parking lot, eager to see who would show up here. As we got closer to the vehicle, I noticed what type it was. A black car. *The* black car that crashed into the Markets, nearly killing Ben and I.

"Get down!" I cried, lunging behind the building. "The black car's back!"

"Calm down, Jessica," Carla huffed. "It's not the Crimson Caper. Look!"

The vehicle came to a halt in front of us, then Vincent Rossi stepped out of the driver's seat. Enrique and Antonio emerged from the other doors, looking relieved they'd found Carla. The car was mostly patched up after its journey through the markets.

"I see you fixed your car, *Signore* Rossi," the inspector said. "It's looking much better than before."

Vincent nodded. "I did—and it cost me a pretty penny. Especially as I insisted on a rush job. I should have Carla reimburse me for it."

Carla scoffed. "Why? I had nothing to do with it. When will you get that through your thick head? If we find the Crimson Caper, you can sue them instead of me."

"What are you guys doing here?" I asked.

Vincent pulled out his camera and journalist badge. "News spread around town about your meeting with the Crimson Caper. Rumor has it they got away again. Is that right?"

"How do you know about that, *Signore*?" the inspector asked. "I told my officers not to speak to the press, and no one was in the park last night. I wanted to keep the Crimson Caper's triumph a secret."

"Anonymous tip. My boss got a call in the middle of the night from an unknown number. They told him about your meeting in Parco di Trenno," Vincent replied. "They also said Jessica Prince gave them new clothes before the Crimson Caper escaped."

"Let me guess," I began. "Was the voice on the phone disguised?"

Vincent nodded. "That's what my boss told me. He wanted me to track Carla down so I'd be the first one to break the story. Everyone in Milan's obsessed with this case —including the journalists. We've never seen anything like this before."

"I'm not telling you a thing, Vincent. Write that in your story," Carla replied, crossing her arms. "How did you even find me here?"

He shrugged. "Process of elimination. We stopped by your house, the hotel, and the local restaurants before we checked out your workshop. *Mio Dio*, I'm nearly exhausted."

"Sorry for making you work so hard," Carla mumbled sarcastically, glancing at Antonio and Enrique. "Why are you two here?"

"I wanted to check on you, *amore*," Antonio replied, placing a hand on her shoulder. "I was worried."

"Well, I'm fine," Carla replied, pushing him away. "And you, Enrique?"

"I wanted to stay updated on the Crimson Caper case. They're a threat to the entire fashion industry, even if they've only sabotaged your show," Enrique replied. "What if it's me next? I must be careful."

"Wise advice for everyone," the inspector said. "I'm afraid you'll have to leave, however. There's been another crime."

"Another crime? What's he talking about, *amore*?" Antonio asked, glancing at Carla.

Vincent already climbed the steps to the front door and entered the workshop. The inspector turned around, chasing after him. "Stop, *Signore*! You can't go in there."

When everyone else rushed into the workshop, I decided to go, too. As I stepped inside, Antonio, Enrique, and Vincent looked around in shock.

"What a mess," Vincent muttered, snapping pictures.

The inspector grabbed the camera from Vincent's hands. "No photographs, *per favore*. I'm confiscating your camera."

"You can't do this, Inspector. I know my rights," Vincent replied, crossing his arms. "Freedom of the press and all that."

The inspector shook his head. "This is a closed area now, *Signore*. You're lucky I didn't arrest you for trespassing through a crime scene."

Vincent said nothing, but Carla looked angry. The inspector tucked the camera in his back pocket as Carla approached him.

"A closed crime scene? Come on, Inspector," she cried. "You can't shut my workshop down. How will I put on my next show without it?"

"I'm sorry, *Signora* Valentine, but the Crimson Caper

may return. It simply isn't safe," the inspector replied. "Besides, there could be evidence here—"

"Hang on, Inspector. Carla has a point," I said. "We asked her to put on another show to try and lure the Crimson Caper. If you shut down her workshop, we could lose our chance to catch them."

The inspector thought for a moment, rubbing his chin. "Interesting."

"Please, Inspector—let Carla do another show," Uncle Henry said. "When it's over, you can shut down the workshop and conduct a proper search. Luring the Crimson Caper here would be valuable to your investigation, correct?"

Ben nodded. "Yeah, and we'll be here the whole time with Carla. If the Crimson Caper shows up, they won't get away again."

The inspector nodded. "I see your point, everyone. Very well, Carla—you may proceed with your second fashion show."

She grinned. "*Grazie,* Inspector. You have no idea how much this means to me."

"But on one condition," he continued. "I want several of my officers undercover in the crowd. I'd recommend doing it sooner than later. I've lost the Crimson Caper once already —and I want to catch them this time, as soon as possible."

"That's fine, Inspector. I was about to suggest the same thing," she replied. "All I need to do is figure out a location for the runway."

I glanced out the window, watching the gondolas in the canal. "What about out there, by the canal? We can model by the pier and set up chairs for the guests. Could be pretty."

"That's a good idea, Jess. I can see it in my head," Uncle Henry said, turning to Carla. "I'll call the property owner to get or pay for his permission. Inspector Esposito can call the city to get a permit rushed. What do you think, Carla?"

Carla sighed, nodding. "What other choice do I have? While it's not the Fashion Palace, I suppose it'll suffice. I still can't believe the Crimson Caper set it on fire."

Antonio linked his hand with hers. "I'm sorry, *amore*. I wish I could do something to make you feel better."

She shrugged him off, pointing at the door. "You can—by leaving. That includes you too, Inspector. We have a lot of preparation to do. And Vincent, I hate to ask, but could you spread the word I'm having another fashion show tonight? I'll use the clothes I didn't take to the Palace. Whatever the Crimson Caper didn't destroy, anyway. Hopefully a few things are salvageable."

"Tonight? Are you sure?" Ben asked. "Isn't that too soon?"

Carla shook her head. "If we get started now, it won't be. Vincent, will you tell everyone?"

"Fine, Carla. But what's in it for me?"

Carla huffed. "You'll be my exclusive photographer, Vincent. No other photography will be allowed. I'll grant you the rights to print them in your magazine. People will pay big money for pictures of my work, especially after the Crimson Caper attack."

He smiled. "Then you have a deal. I'm sure everyone'll be thrilled to hear about your next show. Despite our bad blood, I hope you succeed."

"Me too," Enrique replied. "We may be competitors, but what the Crimson Caper's done to you isn't right. You deserve better."

"I'm still not convinced either of you is innocent," Carla said, narrowing her eyes at them, "but *grazie*. That means a lot. With luck, the Crimson Caper will make an appearance later and we'll stop them."

"A few questions before I leave, *Signora* Valentine," the inspector said. "How long has it been since you visited your workshop?"

She sighed, thinking. "Hmm, probably a week. Not since the night before my fashion show at the Palace. I took most of my clothes with me for the show, leaving my least favorite designs behind. I'll have to pretty them up to use in tonight's show."

"And everything was normal when you left the workshop?"

"It was, Inspector. Do you think I would've left it like this without calling the *polizia*?"

"Right. So the Crimson Caper could've returned any time during the week to leave this message. Perhaps even a few days ago," the inspector muttered. "Did you lock the doors when you left, *Signora*?"

"Yes, Inspector. I always do, and I told you who had keys," she replied. "Are you finished with the interrogation? In case you've forgotten, my show's tonight. If you want the Crimson Caper to make an appearance, I need to get everything in order."

The inspector nodded, putting his notepad away. "Of course. *Grazie* for your time, *Signora* Valentine—and be careful. My officers and I will return a little before the show to blend in with the crowd. By tonight, I pray the Crimson Caper will be in custody."

As Antonio left with Vincent, Enrique, and the inspector, he gave Carla one last glance. She was too busy picking up fallen items to notice.

A few hours later, I stood on a small platform in the workshop. Carla bent down beside me, putting the finishing touches on my dress. She'd managed to scrounge a few materials together from a pile of clothes that hadn't made it, hastily adjusting them for us. I glanced in the large mirror and smiled at my reflection.

The dress I wore was beautiful. It was a deep red which flowed to the floor, trailing behind me as I walked. It fell off the shoulder, showing my collarbone, and I arranged my hair into a pretty bun. It wasn't my usual shade of pink, but I liked it. I did my own make-up, using dark eyeshadow to match the dress. My heels sparkled silver in the light and were three inches high. Ben complained I was taller than him now.

"Ow!" I cried as I felt Carla's needle pierce my ankle. "Be careful."

"Sorry. This isn't easy to do," Carla mumbled, looking up at me, "especially when my model keeps moving."

"Sorry," I mumbled, standing still.

"I brought some pizza. The man who worked there gave me a discount when he heard I was going to be in Carla's fashion show." Uncle Henry set down several boxes. "I got some salad and fries, too."

"Pizza? Models don't eat pizza—especially not before my show," Carla replied. "Everyone needs to watch their figures. I can't have you gaining weight after the alterations."

As Ben picked up a slice, Carla glared at him. He sighed and put it back down. "Fine, whatever. I'll eat some salad. Can't say I'm jealous of the model life."

"This is exciting," Larry said, glancing at his tux in the mirror. "I've never been in a fashion show before. I called my wife, Betty, and told her the good news. She can't wait to see photos."

"Well, it wasn't a simple task fitting all my clothes on you," Carla began, "but I managed to make it work. Jessica's dress is the last item."

"So, we're ready to go tonight?" I asked.

She nodded, checking her watch. "Indeed—and we have an hour to spare. We'd better finish setting up near the canal. Henry, did you get the owner's permission and the city permit?"

He nodded. "I did. The owner was easily... persuaded, and when Inspector Esposito had some trouble, I promised a country-wide discount on Prince Enterprises products if they rushed it. Everything is in order for tonight."

"Wonderful, *grazie*. I need to make a few phone calls to old friends and make sure they're on their way."

"Don't worry, Carla. We'll get everything done," I said, grabbing some of the spare chairs we'd found in the basement. "You can count on us."

"Put that down," she barked. "No one is doing any work in my fashion line."

"Sorry," I said.

We all hastily changed behind sheets Ben had draped over clothing racks at the beginning of the day.

Carla nodded then walked to the back of the workshop to make a few calls. Once we were in our own clothes, Uncle Henry, Ben, Larry, Bruce, and I grabbed the decorations. As we dragged everything out to the pier, I glanced at our surroundings.

"Any sign of any the Crimson Caper?" Ben asked.

I shook my head. "Not yet. Let's hope they show. I'd hate for them to be warned like last time."

As we lined the chairs up, leaving enough space for us to use the pier as a makeshift runway, Carla dragged out several racks of clothing. She placed them behind a large black tarp that served two purposes—a clean backdrop for our "runway" and privacy for us to change during the show. It was like our own private dressing room.

"We only have four models, so there might be some gaps

in the timing," she said. "After you finish your walk and turn, come back here and change into your next outfit. But walk slowly. And change fast."

Ben blushed. "Do we have to change together? I mean, I don't want Jess to feel uncomfortable."

I shrugged. "I'm fine with it. We have no real choice, right?"

"Yeah, it's just...." He rubbed the back of his neck, looking awkward. "I don't want you to see my underwear. They're... Spiderman."

I laughed. Now I understood him hanging the sheets inside earlier. "Ben, I won't look. Does that make you feel better?"

"I'd also appreciate it if you didn't look at Jess either, Ben," Uncle Henry said, crossing his arms. "I trust you'll be a perfect gentleman?"

Ben nodded, clearing his throat. "Of course, Henry. Sir. Uh, Mister Prince. I won't look at Jessica while we change."

As they talked about the show behind me, I glanced down the road. Something bright caught my eye—and it looked like the Crimson Caper. There they stood, dressed in their familiar red trench coat, hat, gloves, sunglasses, and red pants. When they realized I noticed them, they took off running.

"Hey, wait!" I cried, turning to others. "I saw the Crimson Caper. Come on!"

Ben frowned. "The Crimson Caper? Here, right now? Are you sure—"

"Hurry, before they get away!" I replied, already rushing after the saboteur.

"But the show is about to begin," Carla protested. "Wait!"

But I didn't stop. I couldn't—not when we were so close to catching the culprit. The others followed me, sprinting down the long pier, but Carla lagged a bit behind. She was still grumbling angrily that I had run off on her. We pushed through the tourists, searching for anyone red in the distance. As I stopped to catch my breath, I realized it was hopeless.

The Crimson Caper had disappeared.

"Not again," I muttered. "I can't believe they escaped."

"It's not your fault, Jess," Ben said, taking deep breaths. "We tried."

Carla nodded, panting. "We did. And were nearly late for my fashion show. Let's get back to the canal, everyone. We can't let this stop us. Where's that inspector, anyway?"

As we returned to the spot of the canal where the show would take place, we noticed the black tarp knocked over. Carla gasped, bending down to pick up the fallen tarp. Her eyes filled with tears.

"*Mio Dio*, they're gone!" she said.

"What's gone?" Uncle Henry asked.

"My clothes! I left the rack of clothes you were supposed to change into behind the tarp," Carla replied, pointing down, "but now it's not here!"

"The Crimson Caper probably wanted to distract us," Ben said. "While we chased after them, they had plenty of time to steal the clothes."

"But how? I saw the Crimson Caper run off in the complete opposite direction," I replied. "Something doesn't add up. How can they be in two places at once?"

Several cars pulled into the parking lot of the workshop, then the inspector exited the first vehicle. He dressed in plain clothes as did the plethora of officers with him. I rushed over to him, out of breath. He spun around but looked relieved when he realized it was only me.

"*Signorina* Prince? Why are you—"

"I saw the Crimson Caper," I interrupted. "We chased

after them, but they got away—and stole Carla's clothes in the process."

The inspector pulled out his gun. "Which way did they go?"

I pointed north. "That way—but they're long gone, Inspector. Trust me, we already looked."

The inspector turned to his officers, mumbling in Italian. A second later, they spread out in different directions, their guns held high. As they vanished down the block, I turned to the inspector in confusion.

"I've asked them to check our surroundings. If the Crimson Caper's hiding somewhere, we *will* find them," Inspector Esposito said. "Where's *Signora* Valentine? Is she okay?"

I nodded. "She's fine, just shaken up. I'll take you to her."

As we walked over to Carla, she was sitting on the edge of the pier. While she stared out at the boats at dusk, she wiped tears from her eyes. "How can I do the show now? I need to cancel."

"Don't say that, Carla," Uncle Henry said. "We still have the clothes we changed out of to set up. All of us left those outfits inside. Isn't that good enough?"

She scoffed. "Not really. You can't put on a show with only a handful of items."

Dozens of cars started to pull into the workshop parking lot. Citizens who had dressed in formal attire exited their vehicles and made their way over to the pier. Vincent did a good job—it seemed everyone in Milan knew about the fashion show tonight. Speaking of Vincent, shouldn't he have shown up by now? And where were Enrique and Antonio?

Carla rose to her feet, sighing. "The guests are already here. What am I going to do?"

The group of officers returned to the inspector and spoke to him in Italian. He nodded and turned to me. "We found no evidence the Crimson Caper was here, *Signorina* Prince. If they were, they're gone now."

As his words ended, I felt a presence behind me. Clenching my fists, I spun around.

Twenty-Five

THE RED PAINT INCIDENT

Josephine stood behind me, nervously twirling her thumbs as she glanced around the canal. She was looking for the same person I was—the Crimson Caper. When she realized I was staring at her, she forced a smile.

"Hi, Jessica. Hope I'm not too late," she said. "Did the show start yet?"

"It may never start," Carla muttered. "Everything's ruined—again. I told you this was a bad idea."

Josephine frowned. "What's she talking about?"

"The Crimson Caper was here. They made off with Carla's clothes," I replied. "All she has left are the ones she altered right before setting up."

Josephine gasped. "I can't believe it. How does the Crimson Caper keep getting away with this?"

Carla sighed, looking at the group of people near the canal. "I'll have to tell them the show's canceled. And I'm not looking forward to their reactions."

"Hold on, Carla," I said. "It isn't fair you have to cancel the show. We all worked hard to make it happen."

Carla scoffed. "Then what would you have me do? It's

too late to make anything else. I can't pull new clothes out of thin air. It was lucky I had enough leftover in the first place."

"I have an idea," I replied. "We could model what we have on in segments. I can model my dress first, and then the shoes, and the earrings after."

Carla sighed. "Oh, I don't know, Jessica."

"What other choice do we have? Dragging it out seems like the best idea."

Uncle Henry nodded. "Jess is right. We can break down four complete outfits into smaller ones. It'll make the crowd think we have more items than we really do—and make the show longer."

"I guess that's fine. Since I see no other choice," Carla said, pointing at the black tarp. "You can take off some of the things you're wearing back there. We'll show them off one at a time and I'll keep an eye on them. I hope this works."

"As do I, *Signora* Valentine," the inspector said. "In the meantime, my officers and I will spread out and guard the perimeter. If the Crimson Caper returns, we *will* catch them. *Ciao*."

Carla nodded, walking away to greet our visitors as the inspector and his officers blended in with the crowd. Josephine sighed while keeping an eye on the crowd of eager people. The rest of us hurried inside to change.

We finished in record time then met behind the tarp.

Josephine sighed. "I remember when I used to be obsessed with fashion shows. I never would've missed one like this—especially not Carla's. I was a huge fan of her online shop. I guess times have changed."

"They have. All thanks to the Crimson Caper. Anyway, did you come here to help us?" I asked. "Carla could use an assistant right now—someone to cheer her up. And an extra hand would be nice."

Josephine shook her head. "No, I don't think I'm ready

for that yet. I'm surprised I came down here, to tell you the truth. I keep looking over my shoulder, thinking the Crimson Caper's right behind me."

"We all do," I replied. "And I hope they show up—for the inspector's sake."

"Just keep them away from me if they do. Thank goodness the cops are already here. Anyway, I'd better take my seat," Josephine said. "Good luck with the show. Even though I'm not involved, I hope it goes well."

As Josephine grabbed a seat in the audience, I pulled over a chair to set our accessories on. Larry, Uncle Henry, and Ben looked at me for advice as Bruce took his seat.

"We'll model our dresses and tuxes first," I said, "and then we'll come back for the shoes and accessories."

"Good thinking, Jess," Ben said. "Might be the slowest fashion show, but at least we're making it work. You know, Carla always wants to quit. Isn't this supposed to be her dream?"

"I'm sure she's just exhausted, Ben," Uncle Henry said, removing his custom watch. "Carla's been through a traumatic week. I can't blame her for wanting to give up."

I felt so bare without my high heels and jewelry on, but I reminded myself I was doing this for the good of Carla's show. I poked my head around the tarp, watching Carla speak with Antonio. It looked like an intense argument, but I couldn't hear what they were saying over the noise of the crowd. They were likely speaking in Italian, anyway.

Antonio must've just arrived as I noticed Enrique and Vincent a little farther in the crowd. Vincent snapped pictures of the pier and guests as Enrique stood next to him, sipping a glass of champagne Uncle Henry picked up at the store for tonight.

"I remember when that model life used to be mine," a

familiar voice said behind me. "Now I'm busy with other work."

I turned around and noticed Sasha standing behind me, looking down at our clothes. "Sasha? What are you doing here?"

"Just because I'm not in the show doesn't mean I don't want to see it," she replied. "Carla called earlier and asked me to join but I refused. I've got enough on my plate."

"Will you consider modeling again for Carla?"

"Tonight? No way. It's risky enough coming here when I know the Crimson Caper's still on the loose," she replied. "But in the future? Maybe when my other job's finished."

"Speaking of that, how's it going?"

She pulled me away from the others, lowering her voice. "It's the other reason I'm here, Jessica. I have a feeling Lance and Salvatore are going to show up. Salvatore really wants Carla working for him. He told me that himself."

"Why? What's so special about her?"

"Well, for starters, Carla's desperate just like Lance. I figured out he's going broke. Interpol told me he declared bankruptcy," Sasha replied. "But Carla's an up-and-coming fashion designer. He hopes to get her working for him now before she's too big to approach."

When the crowd became quieter and Carla stepped in front of the people, I nodded. "I have to go, Sasha. I think the show's about to start. Catch you later, okay?"

"Of course. You have your job and I have mine. Good luck, Jessica."

As she took a seat near the front, I noticed a familiar black car pull up. Bruno Salvatore stepped out with several security guards by his side. Lance was also there, trailing behind him with his head down. He carried a duffel bag, which I found odd at a fashion show. They took their seats near the back and didn't talk to anyone.

"It's almost time," Uncle Henry whispered as I joined him, Ben, and Larry again. We glanced at the crowd from behind the tarp. "I think Carla's about to give a speech."

Carla grabbed a nearby megaphone and held it up to her mouth. "*Grazie*, everyone, for joining us here tonight. I know the last time we gathered was eventful, but I'm hoping for a smoother show tonight."

As Carla repeated everything in Italian, I scanned my eyes across the crowd, watching everyone. I didn't see any sign of the Crimson Caper, but Bruno Salvatore had a grin on his face. What was he planning?

I didn't see Josephine, Enrique, or Antonio in the crowd anymore. Sasha, Lance, Salvatore, and Vincent were still there, but where had the other three gone?

I found the inspector standing across the way near a little strip of shops. I wondered if he noticed the missing people, too. His officers blended in with the crowd nicely, looking like regular citizens. If I didn't know they were undercover, I wouldn't have guessed.

"Before we begin, I'd like to say *grazie* to my friends—Henry and Jessica Prince, Ben Clark, and Larry Kibbler," Carla said, looking our way. "Without them, this show wouldn't be possible. *Grazie* for being there for me during this time. I'm truly, truly grateful."

Uncle Henry grinned, mouthing "always" to Carla. He still loved her. That much I could tell. And because he loved her, he was willing to do whatever it took to please her.

Just like Antonio. But where was he now? Why would he miss his love's fashion show?

"Without further ado, let's give everyone what they've been waiting for," Carla said, pressing the button on the nearby stereo. It was the same one she had brought from her workshop. "Let the fashion show begin."

Carla stepped off to the side, giving us space to model

near the canal. As the disco music blared, Uncle Henry, Larry, and Ben lined up behind me. I took a deep breath, realizing I was up first.

There's nothing to be nervous about, Jessica, I told myself. *Just do it like you practiced and everything will be fine.*

I focused on not tripping as I strutted out from behind the tarp, following the small path we'd outlined along the canal. Everyone watched with smiles, fawning over my gorgeous gown. I felt so exposed—so uncomfortable—but I forced myself to enjoy the attention.

"The beautiful Jessica Prince models my favorite dress in the collection—an off-the-shoulder chiffon gown," Carla said as I spun for the audience. "It comes in shades of blue, purple, and green, though red's my favorite color."

I smiled at the audience as Vincent snapped my picture. My heart pounded in my chest in front of all these people. I couldn't believe it—I was modeling in my first fashion show. And I was doing fabulously.

As I returned behind the tarp, Uncle Henry strutted out next. Ben grinned as he looked at me, taking my hand in his.

"You look beautiful, Jess," he whispered. "Easily the best-looking model in the whole show."

As I laughed, Larry scoffed. "I'm offended by that, Mister Clark."

I smiled. "Thanks, Ben. It's a little intimidating out there. I'm surprised I didn't trip."

As Uncle Henry did a twirl for the crowd—he was a natural, much to my shock—I looked out again. Josephine, Enrique, and Antonio still hadn't returned to their seats. But now the inspector was missing along with several officers. I wasn't able to see if they were out there as I strutted down. The lights were too bright in my eyes and the adrenaline coursing through my system made it hard to concentrate.

When Uncle Henry returned, Ben took a deep breath. "Guess I'm up next."

"Good luck," I whispered, giving him a kiss on the cheek. "You'll do great."

He blushed and cleared his throat before walking out. He was a little stiff, but I chalked it up to nerves. I smiled as Ben did a little curtsy to the crowd, giving me a wink over his shoulder. The audience clearly loved him, judging by the smiles and cheers.

As Ben posed for Vincent's camera, the music stopped. Carla bent down, pressing a bunch of buttons on the stereo, but nothing happened. The audience began to murmur, wondering what was going on.

Carla laughed, nervously. "We appear to be having some technical difficulties. Let's continue the show anyway."

Ben looked stunned so I waved my arms to catch his attention. I gestured for him to keep going, then he nodded and strutted back to us.

"How did I do? Was I okay?" Ben asked, his hands shaking. "When the music cut out, I thought it was my fault."

I smiled and placed a hand on his shoulder. "You were great, Ben. Don't worry about the music. I don't think it had anything to do with you."

"I suppose I'm next," Larry said, taking a deep breath. "My wife's going to be so proud of me. I can't wait until she sees—"

A booming voice echoed from the stereo. It was the same disguised voice the Crimson Caper used. "Quit the fashion industry or else, Carla. You've been warned. Now you'll pay."

Carla slammed her heel into the stereo, smashing it into pieces. She didn't want the audience to hear the Crimson Caper's voice, but it was too late. The entire pier went silent, frozen in fear.

"Okay, what's going on?" Ben whispered. "How's that even possible?"

As the audience murmured, Carla looked frazzled. She rubbed her temples as I rushed over to her. Everyone on the entire pier stared at us.

"What happened? How did the Crimson Caper get their voice on your CD?" I asked.

She shrugged. "I don't know, Jessica. I told you this was a bad idea!"

"The CD you're using...gosh, that's so ancient."

Carla nodded. "I'm old-fashioned. What can I say?"

"Well, where did it come from? Has anyone else had the chance to use it?"

"It's been in my workshop for ages, along with a few others. I chose it at random for tonight," she replied. "I suppose the Crimson Caper could've tampered with it while they destroyed my workshop. But how would they know which one I'd play?"

"I don't know, Carla. Maybe they recorded their voice over all your CDs? We can keep going without music—"

A piercing scream echoed down the pier. The guests rose to their feet, looking in every direction. A moment later, we noticed someone approaching from the distance, covered in red.

"Is it them?" Ben whispered.

"No," I said, pushing through the crowd. "That's not the Crimson Caper. That's Josephine?"

As she ran closer and hunched over to catch her breath, I realized I was right. It was Josephine—covered head to toe in red paint.

The same red paint the Crimson Caper smeared all over Carla's workshop.

"Josephine, what happened?" I asked.

"The Crimson Caper," she mumbled. "I had to leave the

show, Jessica. I couldn't do it anymore. Too much anxiety, too many thoughts swirling in my head. Maybe running off alone was silly but I just felt trapped and needed to escape—"

"It's okay, Josephine. You don't have to explain yourself. Anxiety sucks and makes us do all sorts of things, and they aren't always logical. Take a deep breath," I replied, as the crowd gathered behind us. "When you left, where did you go?"

"Well, I got halfway down the street when I heard someone calling my name," she replied. "When I turned around, it was the Crimson Caper. They were wearing their red trench coat and hat so I couldn't see what they looked like."

"And then?"

"I looked down and realized what they were carrying," she said. "A can of red paint. They dunked some of it on me and took off. I ran into the inspector and explained what happened, then he told me to come back here for safety."

"I can't believe this," Carla muttered, walking over. She pulled out a napkin from her purse. "I know this isn't much, but you can use it to wipe off the paint. I'm so sorry, Josie."

Inspector Esposito rushed over to us, out of breath. "*Signorina* Prince, there you are. Have you seen any sign of the Crimson Caper?"

I shook my head. "No, not at all. Where did you go?"

"My officers and I decided to walk around and investigate. We didn't see the Crimson Caper during the show, so we thought it was safe to leave the pier," he replied. "We found *Signora* Arias crying and covered in red paint. I have my officers searching the area."

"Did you find the Crimson Caper yet?" Josephine asked.

"Afraid not, *Signora* Arias. It's as if the Crimson Caper vanished."

"The Crimson Caper went that way. I saw them," Antonio cried, rushing up behind us. "Someone in a red trench bumped into me before running off."

"And you didn't try to stop them?" Uncle Henry asked.

Antonio scoffed. "I'm not risking my life. The Crimson Caper's crazy."

The inspector nodded, reaching for his walkie-talkie and speaking Italian into it. It sounded like he was giving orders to his officers. When he finished, he walked past us, staring into the distance.

"Where were you during the show?" I asked Antonio, crossing my arms. "I didn't see you in the crowd."

"I had to go to the bathroom. I used the one in the workshop. Still have my old key," he replied. "That's not a crime, is it?"

I sighed. "Well, not exactly, but—"

Enrique walked over next, clutching his head. He looked around in confusion when he saw Josephine. "*Dios Mio.* What happened here?"

"The Crimson Caper threw paint on Josephine," I replied. "But I could ask you the same question as Antonio. Where did you go?"

"The music gave me a headache. Took a walk to clear my head," he replied. "Why are you looking at me like that? I'm not the Crimson Caper."

I turned to Inspector Esposito. "Isn't it suspicious how Antonio and Enrique disappeared before the paint attack, Inspector?"

He nodded, glancing at the two of them. "Indeed, but *Signora* Arias was missing, too."

Josephine gasped. "You're not saying I had anything to do with this, are you? Look at me, Inspector. I'm covered in paint. I couldn't have done this to myself."

"When I met the Crimson Caper in the park the other

night, they told me you weren't as innocent as I thought, Josephine," I replied. "Do you know what they meant?"

Her face dropped. "No...no, I have no idea what they're talking about. You have to believe me, Jessica. They're lying to you."

As the crowd watched Josephine with murmurs and gasps, the inspector stepped away for a moment. When he returned, he held up his walkie-talkie.

"I've heard from one of my officers," he said. "We found the discarded red paint can."

Twenty-Six

THE HAIR STRAND

We followed the inspector down the street where he turned right. Nestled between a few old buildings sat a bush and several police officers hunched over it. They had set up yellow police tape and snapped photographs, closing off the scene.

"My officers told me they found the red paint can in this bush," the inspector said. "The Crimson Caper must've discarded it here."

The nearby officer pulled back the leaves, allowing us to see the paint can. Someone threw it here, causing it to crack in the process. Most of the red paint was gone, covering Josephine instead. It smeared down the side of the can.

"We believe the Crimson Caper threw the evidence in this bush and ran off," the inspector continued. "We plan to dust it for fingerprints and other evidence."

"What's that, on the side of the paint can?" I asked, pointing at the dark sliver I saw mixed with the leftover red paint. It looked like fur at first.

The inspector put on some gloves a nearby officer handed to him and lifted the paint can. "It appears to be a dark strand of hair. Human, I'd say. Nice work, *Signorina*. My officers will collect it and analyze the strand at our lab."

As the officer collected the strand of hair using tweezers and a plastic bag, I turned to the inspector. "But is the hair from the Crimson Caper or Josephine? She has dark hair, too. Her hair could've accidentally gotten on the paint can when the Crimson Caper threw it on her. How close were they standing to you, Josephine?"

"Very close," she replied. "Less than an arm's length away."

The inspector nodded. "A good question, *Signorina* Prince. Transfer would be possible. Would you be willing to give a sample of your hair, *Signora* Arias? We'd need it to run a comparison."

Josephine hesitated. "Am I being charged with a crime, Inspector?"

"No, of course not. This would be volunteered. I have no intention of getting a warrant as there's no evidence against you."

"Oh, I don't know...." she trailed off, sighing. "You know I hate giving DNA. What if someone uses it against me?"

"I know you're scared, but it'll help the investigation," I said. "And besides, don't you want to prove you're innocent?"

Josephine nodded. "All right, I'll do it. Take what you need, Inspector."

As the inspector readied his tweezers, I thought about everyone who had dark hair—Josephine, Antonio, Enrique, Vincent, and Bruno Salvatore. And, of course, Carla and Ben. There wasn't a shortage of it around. But the evidence, if left by the Crimson Caper, would exonerate Sasha and Lance. And Uncle Henry's golden locks.

"If it doesn't match *Signora* Arias, then we'll know it

was left by the Crimson Caper—an accident while discarding the evidence," the inspector said. "If it does match, then perhaps it was transferred as they emptied the contents onto *Signora* Arias. Just as you suggested, *Signorina* Prince."

The inspector tugged on a strand of hair at the top of Josephine's head. "Ouch!" she cried. "Could've been a little gentler, Inspector."

"My apologies." When he had the hair with a follicle, he placed it in a small evidence bag. Then he handed the evidence to a nearby officer. "*Grazie* for all you've done. You as well, *Signorina* Prince."

"No problem, Inspector. But since the hair is dark, does that mean my Uncle Henry's off the hook? His hair's naturally blond, as you can see. And he was with the rest of us models during the show."

The inspector glanced at Uncle Henry and then back at me. "We can't completely rule him out. He could still have an accomplice or more. Also, this hair could be from a wig, *Signorina*. Forensics can tell if the hair is synthetic or real. I'll know soon."

And somehow, I needed to find out too.

"Can you believe that? The Crimson Caper made a mistake for once," Ben said, grinning. "Maybe we'll finally catch them now."

"But another show has been ruined," Carla muttered, looking toward the canal. "I think the Crimson Caper's right. For whatever reason, they want my career to end. For the sake of everyone's safety, maybe it'd be best if I listened."

"Don't say that again, Carla," Uncle Henry said, reaching for her hands. "We'll help you figure this out. You deserve to do what you love without someone ruining it for you."

"Inspector Esposito?" an officer asked, walking over to

him. He mumbled something in Italian, but I noticed what he was carrying.

A red trench coat, with matching gloves, a hat, a scarf, and sunglasses. It was another set of clothes the Crimson Caper had which I'd handed over after Josephine made them. They only had one set left. Did that mean their reign of terror was coming to an end? Or did they have another plan to get more clothes?

The inspector took the clothes, nodding. "Then it's as we assumed, *Signorina* Prince. The Crimson Caper hid the evidence here to blend in with the crowd."

"Which means the Crimson Caper could still be here," I said, looking around. "And we'd never guess."

As I looked toward the pier, most of the people had left. Antonio, Enrique, and Vincent got into the same car, but not before Vincent snapped more pictures of the disastrous fashion show. I bet he'd make a lot of money selling those photographs. Antonio watched us from his window as they sped away.

"Be right back," I said. "I just want to check out the pier now that everyone's gone. Maybe I'll find something we missed. Come on, Inspector."

As we walked over to the pier, we started to look between the seats, behind the tarp, and through all the decorations. I put on my heels and grabbed our jewelry, which the Crimson Caper hadn't stolen.

Which meant their motive wasn't robbery. They just wanted to stop Carla—for whatever reason.

"My officers will search the area again later, *Signorina*," the inspector said, "but it doesn't hurt to have a fresh set of eyes. What are you looking for?"

I shrugged. "I don't know. Anything that links the Crimson Caper, really."

We continued to look for anything out of the ordinary

for a few minutes. The inspector came up empty, but I saw something gleam on the pier under the moonlight.

And it looked like a spattering of red blood.

I walked over then bent to study it. Interesting. I ran my finger through the red liquid and brought it up to my nose. It wasn't blood at all.

"Did you find something?" the inspector asked, hovering behind me.

I nodded, wiping the red liquid away. "I did. This is red paint, Inspector—the same kind used on Josephine and Carla's workshop."

The inspector glanced at our surroundings. "We're standing where the crowd was seated, *Signorina*. Are you suggesting the Crimson Caper was one of the guests?"

"Yeah, the Crimson Caper was here—probably right in front of us. You were right before," I replied. "After removing their outfit and ditching it, they must've gotten some red paint on them and it dripped down. But do you see how it ends here, in a few small drops?"

The inspector nodded. "I do, *Signorina*. What are you suggesting?"

"The Crimson Caper must've realized they were dripping and wiped it off," I replied, "but it was too dark to see the small mess they left behind already. It ends here, so we can't follow it and find out which way they went. And Vincent only took pictures of the stage, not the crowd, so we don't know who was sitting here."

The inspector swore in Italian. "And most of the people have left. We'll never track them all down."

I nodded, rising to my feet. "You're right, Inspector—but we might not need to. The hair strand could tell us more than the paint trail can."

"True. I hope that evidence alone will help find the

Crimson Caper soon," the inspector said. "*Ciao, Signorina* Prince. And *grazie* for your help. We'll be in touch."

After the inspector left, Lance and Bruno Salvatore headed our way with big smiles on their faces. But Lance's didn't look as genuine. Sasha stayed behind, watching them from the sidewalk.

"Get ready, Carla," I mumbled. "Here comes trouble."

"Carla Valentine. Nice to see you again." Bruno grabbed her hand then kissed her knuckles. "I'd hate to bring up such an unpleasant thought, but what will you do now? Two of your fashion shows were sabotaged, *Signora*. Will you put on a third?"

She shrugged, recoiling as she removed her hand. "I haven't thought about it yet. Seems unlikely, *Signore*. Too dangerous for us all."

"Then your luck's changing, *Signora* Valentine. I enjoy helping fashion designers during difficult times. It's my favorite hobby. My niece is a big fan of fashion so part of me does it for her," he replied, smirking. I was sure the blood money was the other reason he did it. "If you'd like to put on another show, I could help you, *Signora*. I have everything you need—and my bodyguards could stop the Crimson Caper. With lethal force."

"But it comes with a price, doesn't it?" Carla asked, shaking her head. "I don't want your help, *Signore* Salvatore. If I decide to put on another show, I can do it on my own."

The smirk on his face faded. "Can you? The Crimson Caper doesn't seem to think so. But no matter. We *will* work together, Carla—whether you like it or not."

"The lady said no," Uncle Henry said, stepping forward. "Now back off."

Bruno glared at him. "Be careful, *Signore* Prince. Threats have consequences—and I wouldn't want the people around you to get hurt."

When Bruno glanced at me, Uncle Henry balled his fists. I thought he was going to punch him so I stepped between the two men. "We have to leave now, Mister Salvatore. It's late. You should do the same."

Bruno adjusted his suit and tie and nodded. "You're right, *Signorina* Prince—but you haven't seen the last of me. Come along, *Signore* LaDoux."

"Actually, I think I'll stay. I have some business to attend to, *Monsieur* Salvatore. It doesn't concern you," Lance replied. "*Au revoir.*"

Bruno nodded, giving Uncle Henry one last glare before he returned to his car. His security guards hopped in the front seat and drove away. Carla shook her head, scoffing as the black car faded from view.

"How could you partner with a man like that, Lance? A mobster?" Carla asked. "He's evil."

"You wouldn't understand, Carla. It wasn't by choice," he replied, sighing. "I need to leave now. Something requires my attention. Take care of yourself, *s'il vous plaît.*"

"Mister LaDoux, wait," I said. "I wanted to talk to you about—"

He pulled me away from the crowd, lowering his voice. "Fear not, *Mademoiselle* Prince. I plan to speak to the inspector soon. I have some audio tapes on Salvatore that I recorded. He speaks about the drug trade in several of them. A good thing, *oui*?"

"That is. When will you give them to the inspector? What's taking so long, Mister LaDoux?"

He smiled. "All in good time, *Mademoiselle* Prince. I have something to take care of first."

As Lance left, hailing a cab at the end of the street, I noticed what he was carrying. A duffel bag, similar to the one we gave the Crimson Caper. It was the same one Lance arrived with and held onto during the show. None of it made any sense. Lance couldn't have been the Crimson Caper, could he? And where was he rushing off to all of a sudden with something like that?

"Larry, take everyone back to the hotel," I said. "I have something I need to do."

"Such as?" Uncle Henry asked. "The Crimson Caper could be hanging around, Jess. It isn't safe to be on your own right now."

I glanced down the street, watching as Lance's taxi pulled away farther, then I broke into a sprint. I called over my shoulder, "I'll explain later. Just trust me!"

"Jess, stop!"

As I rushed down the street while ignoring Uncle Henry, searching for a taxi, one pulled up beside me. I was just about to ask if I could get a ride before the back seat window rolled down, then Sasha's face poked out.

"Jessica? Did you see him, too?" she asked. "Where's Lance going—and with that big duffel bag, of all things?"

I shrugged. "No idea. Maybe another drug deal?"

"Yeah, maybe. Get in," she said, opening her door. "We need to find out for ourselves."

"Okay. Let me just tell my uncle where I'm going." I sent the text message, got permission, and then hopped in. "Let's go."

As our taxi followed Lance's through the busy streets, I couldn't figure out where he was going. I only knew it wasn't to his house or Salvatore's business headquarters as they were on the opposite end of town. And it certainly wasn't the way to the police station, either.

"How's your investigation going?" I asked, breaking the silence.

Sasha shrugged. "Could be better. Salvatore's been more careful with me lately—making sure he doesn't tell me too much. I can tell he has trouble trusting me. How about your investigation of the Crimson Caper?"

"Same as yours—it could be better," I muttered. "Did you know Lance told me he plans to go to Inspector Esposito? He wants to put Salvatore behind bars."

Sasha shook her head. "No, I had no idea. His testimony could make a big difference. He's been working with Salvatore much longer than I have. You know, I had a feeling he was a victim like me—forced to work for Salvatore. I hope we both break free."

Lance's taxi took a right at the intersection then pulled up to a set of buildings. They looked like offices. To the left, I noticed a sign that read EUROPEAN CENTRAL BANK.

"Pull in here," Sasha said to the taxi driver. "Make sure we aren't seen."

"Why would Lance be at a bank?" I asked.

"I dunno. Depositing drug money for Salvatore?"

"Then why wouldn't Salvatore come with him? Lance said it didn't concern him, remember? It can't be related to their operation if that's true."

Sasha nodded. "Yeah, you could have a point. Something's wrong here."

We saw Lance get out and pay the taxi driver. Given the way the rear lights flashed, it looked like he put the cab in park and planned on waiting. Meanwhile, Lance grabbed the duffel bag then disappeared into the bank. We lost sight of him behind the darkened windows.

"Ugh," Sasha muttered. "We'll never know what he's doing now. You need to get in there, Jessica."

"What? Why me?"

"Because you have a reason to be at the bank. Your uncle's a billionaire, right?"

"Well, yeah, but—"

"And if he tells Salvatore I followed him here, I'll be busted," she replied. "It makes more sense if it's you. I'll wait here for you and keep the taxi ready."

I sighed, opening the door. "Fine. I'll let you know what I overhear."

I tip-toed into the bank after Lance, pulling up my purse to cover my face. He stood near the front desk, speaking with the teller. The duffel bag laid open on the desk, and I saw what was in it. It wasn't the Crimson Caper's outfit as I assumed.

Instead, hundreds of thousands of Euros sat inside—maybe even millions. It was more money than Lance told me he had. How did he get that money? And what was it for?

"Do you understand, *mademoiselle*? Do you speak *Anglais*?" Lance asked the bank teller, groaning. "I want this money to be transferred to my private account. It's in the Cayman Islands."

The teller seemed to finally understand because she nodded and pressed a bunch of buttons on her computer. Then, she took his duffel bag and disappeared into the back area of the bank for a moment.

Lance looked around, nervous. He tapped his finger on the desk and whistled nonchalantly. I turned around, hiding my face behind a stack of envelopes. It didn't seem like he noticed me.

When the teller returned, she mumbled something in a thick Italian accent that sounded like, "Transfer's on the way."

Lance smiled. "*Merci beaucoup, mademoiselle.* You've been a big help."

He turned around, heading for the door. I waited a few moments before I left the bank, watching his cab speed off into the distance. As I walked over to Sasha's taxi, I thought about the situation.

Transferring lots of money into a private account in the Cayman Islands without Salvatore's knowledge and right before speaking with the inspector.

"So? What happened?" Sasha asked as I hopped into the taxi.

"To me, it looks like Lance is sending some money into an offshore bank account," I replied, "and a lot of it, too."

"But why?" Sasha asked. "And how does Salvatore fit into all this?"

"That's what I want to know, too," I replied, "but better yet, how the Crimson Caper fits into it."

"You think the two are related?"

I nodded, staring out the window as we drove down the street. "I don't think anything going on around here is a coincidence, Sasha. The only hard part is proving it."

Twenty-Seven

GIVING IN

It was getting late so Sasha had the taxi take me back to the hotel. After I waved goodbye, I walked up to my room. It was a long night, and I felt exhausted.

The concerned—and angry—faces of Uncle Henry, Ben, Larry, and Bruce greeted me as soon as I entered my suite. They swarmed me as I stifled a yawn.

"There you are!" Ben said, pulling me into a hug. "We were worried. Where did you go?"

"Followed a hunch," I replied, setting down my purse and kicking off my shoes. "It was about Lance LaDoux."

"We'll talk about that in a second," Uncle Henry said sternly. "We really need to discuss the fact that you keep running off when I tell you not to. Are you trying to drive me insane with worry?"

"I'm really not. It was just easier to do this alone. I'm sorry, Uncle Henry. I didn't mean to upset you. I really am just looking out for Carla."

Uncle Henry sighed. "All right. But *I* am concerned about *your* safety. Now, why Lance LaDoux? Is he the Crimson Caper?"

"I'm not sure yet, but he *is* involved with Bruno Salvatore."

"So? We already knew that," Ben replied. "That's not news."

"Yeah, but there's something else—something Lance isn't telling us. I think he's keeping more secrets than we thought."

"Be careful, Miss Prince," Bruce said. "I've heard a little about Bruno Salvatore. He's got a long list of arrests, though no lawyer has ever earned a conviction against him. He's never been charged with murder, but he's capable of evil things. And he might not like a teenager meddling in his business."

"Well, maybe Lance can help put him behind bars," I said, yawning. "He told me he had evidence for the inspector."

Uncle Henry sighed. "That's good. With Salvatore in jail, it'll keep him off Carla's back. I only wish we could find the Crimson Caper."

"Speaking of Carla, where is she now?" I asked.

"In her suite. Didn't want to see anyone," Uncle Henry replied. "I've never seen her so distraught. I think this could be the end of her career, Jess. She was torn for a while but now? I think she's much done with it all."

Poor Carla. This had to be so frustrating for her.

"Well, I'm sorry we haven't caught the culprit yet. But it's getting late. We'd better get to bed," Larry said, approaching the door with Bruce by his side. "Glad to see you in one piece, Miss Prince. Despite everything, at least we're all safe."

"Yeah, true. That's a blessing." Ben sighed, glancing out my window at the darkness. "Can you believe March Break's almost over? Feels like we've done nothing but talk about the Crimson Caper all week."

"It's been one of the most challenging weeks of my life. Can't say I've ever been framed before," Uncle Henry muttered, shaking his head. "See you kids in the morning."

As I locked the door behind him, I turned to Ben. "March Break isn't over yet, Ben. I intend to keep hunting for the Crimson Caper right until the last second. Besides, I don't think Uncle Henry will be allowed to leave the country while he's a suspect, so I'll be staying until this is over."

"I can't! My dad's already furious."

"We'll get you home soon, Ben. And hopefully the case will be solved soon, and Uncle Henry and I will be travelling with you."

"But what if you never find the Crimson Caper, Jess?" He set some blankets out on the pull-out couch.

I sighed. "Then Carla's life *and* career will be ruined—and I can't leave Milan accepting that."

When light filtered in through the curtains, a knock sounded on the door. I sprang up in bed, removing my eye mask to answer it. Uncle Henry stood there.

"Hey, Jess," he began. "Went downstairs to get a drink and heard shouting coming from the lobby. Just wanted to check on you."

Ben woke up on the couch, rubbing his eyes. "Shouting in the lobby? Weird. Is it the Crimson Caper?"

"No idea. But we should check it out." I headed for my clothes.

"You're not going anywhere, Jess." Uncle Henry blocked my door.

"We're safe in a crowded hotel. This could be the break we've been waiting for."

"How?"

"I won't know until I see what's going on."

Uncle Henry sighed. "Fine. But I'm coming with you."

I grabbed a summer dress then tugged it on over my pajamas. "Get dressed, Ben. Let's find out what's going on."

Uncle Henry waited in the hallway. After Ben and I joined him, we hurried toward the elevator, knocking on a bunch of doors to wake Larry, Josephine, and Bruce. They all looked half-asleep.

"Something's going on in the lobby. Uncle Henry said there's shouting," I explained. "We're all going to investigate. Come on."

"Let me check on Carla." Uncle Henry knocked on Carla's door but she didn't answer. He shrugged, turning to us. "Maybe she's still sleeping."

"Lucky her," Ben mumbled. "Wish I was still asleep."

"Follow me," Uncle Henry said, pointing down the hallway. "We'll get some answers."

As we took the elevator down to the lobby, we saw dozens of protestors. They carried signs in Italian I couldn't understand and shouted foreign words at the top of their lungs. Tourists staying at our hotel crowded around them, eager to see what was going on.

"My Italian's a little rusty," Uncle Henry began, squinting at the signs, "but I think it says something about Carla. Maybe...give up?"

I walked up to a nearby protestor and tapped on the woman's shoulder. "Excuse me. What's going on?"

"Protest," she replied in a thick Italian accent. "Carla Valentine is dangerous. The Crimson Caper could attack us—all because of her!"

When the yelling increased, security guards in the building exited the elevator. They walked toward the protestors, yelling something in Italian. Then they began to escort them out of the hotel.

We watched as they chanted in Italian, worried about the Crimson Caper. It seemed everyone thought that Carla was a danger to the city as well. The security guards had a hard time getting them out of the hotel. But where was Carla?

"Man, they sound just like the Crimson Caper," Ben muttered. "But I see their point. The Crimson Caper's scared everyone. Maybe that was their goal all along?"

"You can't blame it on Carla," Uncle Henry said. "She's the one they're targeting. She should have our sympathy, not our anger. The Crimson Caper's responsible for their actions, not her."

"Wait!" a familiar voice cried, walking up behind us. "I have something to say."

I turned around to see Carla, fully dressed and with make-up on. She looked ready for a fancy party. The protestors quieted for a moment, ready to listen.

Carla sighed, looking down. "I hate to admit this, but, after much thought, I'm quitting fashion. Doing shows, releasing clothes online, traveling to festivals. All of it. I'll release an official interview later. *Grazie* for listening."

The protestors stopped shouting, satisfied with her reaction. They'd gotten what they wanted. As the guards continued escorting them out, Uncle Henry turned to Carla.

"You can't be serious, Carla," he said. "Jessica's been fighting hard to find this Crimson Caper. You can't give up now. I'm sure they'll be caught soon. Besides, this is your dream, isn't it?"

"It is. But I'm tired, Henry. So very tired of dealing with this. The Crimson Caper's escaped us twice, and it's obvious we'll never find them. Why shouldn't I give up? At least for now? It's not safe. Not for me or any of these people protesting in the lobby. People are scared, Henry. And I am too."

"Quitting isn't like you. And it's not the right thing to do. The Crimson Caper is a coward—trying to destroy your career from the shadows," Uncle Henry replied. "Please, don't quit. Do it for me, Carla."

"Don't say that! You have no right to tell me what to do, Henry." Carla sneered. "I can make up my own mind. In the meantime, you should start packing your bags for Willowbrook. Once the police have cleared you, then you can leave."

Uncle Henry stepped forward. "Wait a second, Carla. Just listen to me. I'm trying to help!"

"*Ciao*, Henry," Carla replied, stepping back into the elevator. "Have a safe flight home—and do me a favor. Never talk to me about the Crimson Caper again. I'm done with all this drama."

As the elevator closed, Uncle Henry ran his fingers through his hair. "A stubborn woman. If that were me, I'd hunt down the Crimson Caper even if it killed me."

"Well, Carla's *not* you," Josephine said. "If she thinks this is best, then I agree with her. You didn't have the Crimson Caper break into your room. I know how crazy they are! Maybe giving them what they want isn't such a bad idea."

As the lobby turned quiet again, Inspector Esposito pushed through the front doors. He looked over his shoulder and glanced at the mob outside. "What a crowd. Did I miss something, *Signorina* Prince?"

"Just protestors," I replied. "They're afraid of the Crimson Caper. Speaking of them, did you find more evidence?"

"I did. The hair follicle was analyzed."

"Who did it match? Don't leave me guessing, Inspector."

"It isn't a match to *Signora* Arias. It also didn't match any of the hair samples in our database. It's a real hair, however, which excludes the wig theory. We would've been able to learn more—like the gender and hair color of the culprit—but the sample was a bit eroded. Must've happened at the lab."

"That sucks. But it must belong to the Crimson Caper," I muttered, tapping my finger against my chin. "Then our first thought was right—the Crimson Caper accidentally left it behind. A stupid, reckless thing to do."

"Where's *Signora* Valentine? I'd like to collect some hair samples—with permission," he said. "Would she be willing to talk about the case?"

Uncle Henry shook his head. "I'm afraid not, Inspector. Carla's quitting fashion. She asked us to never mention the Crimson Caper again."

He sighed. "That's what I was afraid of. In light of this new evidence, *Signore* Prince, I'm pleased to say all charges against you were dropped. No jury would convict you after this."

As everyone cheered, I gave Uncle Henry a hug. "I'm so glad. I was worried I'd lose you forever."

"That isn't possible, Jess," he replied, squeezing my shoulder. "Thank you, Inspector. With March Break ending and Carla quitting, we'll be leaving shortly. It's a shame we couldn't help further."

The inspector shook his head. "Nonsense, *Signore*. Your niece has been a big help, despite not finding the Crimson Caper. And even if we both tried to keep her out of the investigation."

"That's Jess for you," Ben said. "Always eager to help. Especially if there's a mystery."

I nodded. "Guilty as charged. But what will you do now, Inspector?"

"Speak to our suspects, *Signorina*. If they won't offer a hair sample, I suppose we're back to square one. Despite the Crimson Caper cold case, we've received a lead on something else, actually."

"Oh? What is it?"

"It concerns *Signore* LaDoux," he replied. "He's come into my office with some startling evidence on Salvatore. I almost couldn't believe it. And with *Signora* Simpson's undercover testimony, we have a lot of evidence to convict Salvatore with."

"Will you be able to put him away for good?"

Inspector Esposito smiled. "I hope so—it's certainly the plan. I instructed Lance to lure Salvatore to the police station this afternoon. Would you like to be there to see him apprehended? I know he gave you a lot of trouble. It'll be safe with so many of my *polizia* around."

I nodded. "I'll be there, Inspector. If it's okay with Uncle Henry."

"Yes, it's fine. What's safer than a police station?" Uncle Henry said. "I'll come too."

"Great, thanks. Salvatore threatened my uncle. You bet I want to see him put in jail. Most of all, I want fashion designers to be safe in this city."

"Good. See you then, *Signorina*. At least one case will have a happy ending."

As he left, Vincent Rossi walked through the front doors. The inspector stopped him. "Ah, *Signore* Rossi. Would you care to offer a sample of your hair for my case? We found evidence from the paint can last night and you were at the fashion show. I still consider you a suspect."

Vincent sighed. "Haven't we been over this, Inspector? I

didn't agree to the fingerprints. Why would I agree to something as invasive as a hair sample?"

"I see. A disappointment, but understandable. *Ciao.*"

The inspector glanced back at me, rolling his eyes. I felt his frustration too. After he walked out the door, Vincent rushed over to us. "Is Carla ready?"

"Ready for what?" Uncle Henry asked.

"Our interview," he replied. "I hope she hasn't forgotten. It would be so typical of that woman."

"Hold on a second," I said. "What interview?"

"An interview to tell everyone she's leaving the fashion world. We'll broadcast it live on television. I reserved channel ten. It wasn't cheap, but she insisted she has a few things to say to the public before she quits," he replied. "She called me earlier and practically begged for me to come over. I cleared my schedule for this, so I hope she's grateful. Is she in her room?"

Uncle Henry nodded, sighing. "Yes, I'll show you the way. Look, you can't think her quitting is a good idea."

Vincent shrugged. "Actually, *Signore*, I do. The Crimson Caper's dangerous, as I mentioned after the first sabotage. Carla's the only one with the power to stop them. No more fashion shows means no more opportunity for sabotage. *And* it would erase Enrique's competition."

Uncle Henry glared at him.

"Hey, don't give me that look. I'm not the Crimson Caper," he replied. "Merely pointing out the obvious, *Signore* Prince."

As they entered the elevator, arguing back and forth, Ben shook his head. "Man, I still can't believe Carla's just throwing in the towel. *And* she's doing it on national television. You'd think she'd hate the public attention by now, huh?"

"But she doesn't," I replied. "I think deep down, Carla loves the attention."

"Maybe. She's something else, all right." Ben sighed. "Come on—we can watch the live interview in our room."

———

When we returned upstairs, we found Uncle Henry standing outside Carla's door. He pounded on it, but she wouldn't let him in. As he ran his fingers through his hair again, I approached him.

"Uncle Henry? What's wrong?"

"Carla's mad at me, Jess. I tried to talk her out of quitting again, but she won't listen," he replied, sighing. "She and Vincent won't even let me sit in for the interview. Can you believe her attitude? I'm floored. I thought fashion was her dream, so it's hard to believe she'd throw in the towel so easily."

"Maybe she thinks she's doing the right thing," I said softly. "I'm sorry, Uncle Henry."

"I am too. And we're watching the interview in Jessica's suite, Mister Prince. You can join us," Ben said. "Plenty of room."

"All right. I want to see what she's going to say." Uncle Henry followed us to my suite. "I remember the days when Carla and I used to be inseparable. We told each other everything. I know time has passed, but I realize I don't know her anymore. Or maybe I never knew her at all."

As I locked the door behind us, not knowing what to say, Uncle Henry, Ben, Larry, and Bruce grabbed a seat around the television. Ben turned it on using the remote and pressed a button. "I found a way to turn on the English subtitles. No more trying to figure out what the Italians are saying based on hand gestures and facial expressions."

"Subtitles," I repeated. "I almost forgot...."

"Forgot what? What are you talking about?" Ben asked, raising his eyebrows.

"Nothing," I mumbled. "Let's just watch Carla's interview."

We found the channel the live broadcast took place on and we were just in time, too. We watched as Vincent turned on the camera, then Carla adjusted her hair and make-up. She made sure she was in perfect view at all times. Vincent handed her a microphone and kept his cell phone below him with questions on it.

They spoke in Italian for a few minutes. In the subtitles, it mostly translated to "thanks for doing this interview" and recapping the situation. When that was over, Carla sighed and sat up straighter in her chair.

"I'm sorry to say it but the Crimson Caper's won the battle," she said with the subtitles. "They've put the entire city in danger, and I can't let it continue. If it means giving up the career of my dreams for the safety of Milan, then so be it. Even if I left, the Crimson Caper would probably follow me and cause more mayhem. I'm done dealing with them. I want out now."

"This is very brave of you, *Signora* Valentine," Vincent's subtitles said. "Milan thanks you for ending this nightmare."

"And I want to thank my ex-husband, Tony, for all his support," she said. "Without him, I wouldn't be where I am today."

"Indeed. Have the police found the Crimson Caper yet?"

Carla shook her head. "Unfortunately, no. But I want to make this clear—the investigation needs to stop. It's too risky to keep searching for them. It isn't right what they've done to me, but we have to accept it."

Vincent's cell phone rang. He looked down in embarrassment before confusion spread across his face. "Sorry about that. There, I'll just silence my phone."

"No, go ahead," Carla said. "Take it. I don't mind."

"No, that would be unprofessional. Now—" The buzz of a silenced phone grabbed his attention. "Same number. I apologize." He declined the call. "I was about to ask—"

The phone rang again.

"I suspect this will keep happening. Just answer it so we can move on."

He sighed. "Uh, all right. It's a private number. Hmm."

Vincent answered his phone. A few seconds later, his face dropped. He held his cell phone up to the microphone immediately, then a familiar voice echoed through the television.

"A wise decision to quit fashion, Carla," the Crimson Caper said in their disguised voice. "Glad to see you've finally listened to my warnings."

And then the line went dead. Vincent shook his head. "Sorry you had to hear that, *Signora* Valentine."

"It's fine," Carla said, adjusting her skirt. "I hope that's the last we hear of them."

"What will you do now, without fashion in your life?"

She smiled. "I'll find my way. Maybe I'll go on vacation. You know, I haven't had time off in years. I hear the Cayman Islands are a lovely place to visit."

Her eyes widened, and her face paled. A nervous chuckle burst from her, then she talked over Vincent's next question, her words rushed, her continued laughter forced. "And once I return, who knows."

"I can't watch this anymore," Uncle Henry said, rising to his feet. "It makes me sick she'd give up like this."

As he stormed off, returning to his room, the interview came to an end. After Carla and Vincent said their goodbyes,

Ben turned off the television. We all sat in silence for a few minutes.

I don't know what the others were doing, but my brain raced, making connections with all the evidence.

"Poor Miss Valentine," Larry muttered. "To be forced into a situation like this, it's just awful."

"But at least Carla's a natural on TV," Ben said. "She looked super calm. I would've been a nervous wreck. But in a—"

"In a manly way, right. Whatever you say, Ben," I muttered, checking my watch and remembering the inspector's words. "Larry, can you drive me down to the police station, please? It's almost time for Lance to bust Salvatore. I really don't want to miss it."

"Certainly, Miss Prince," Larry said. "It'll be nice to see him brought to justice."

"I agree," I replied, slipping my purse on my shoulder, "but it's not the only reason I want to go."

"Just what are you planning, Jess?" Ben asked. "You have that look on your face again. The one where you're up to no good."

I grinned. "You're right, Ben. You're absolutely right."

Twenty-Eight

CONNECTING THE CRIMSON DOTS

As Ben, Larry, Bruce, and I left the hotel room, we ran into Vincent out in the hallway. He was leaving Carla's suite, taking his camera and microphone with him. He passed us wordlessly while nodding politely.

"We should see how Miss Valentine's doing," Larry said. "This must be such a difficult process for her—grieving her career."

"Good idea. I need to talk to her," I replied, approaching her door. "Carla, are you in there? It's Jessica."

"You aren't going to try to talk me out of quitting, are you?" she asked from the inside. "I'm tired of explaining myself. The interview was supposed to be the end of it. What's done is done, so leave it alone, *per favore*."

"I just have some questions for you. That's all."

She opened the door a sliver, poking her head out. "Questions? You aren't still searching for the Crimson Caper, are you?"

I nodded. "You know I can't let it go, Carla. I promised I'd help find them for you, didn't I?"

She sighed. "Jessica, I really wish you'd stop. Don't do

me any favors. You're going to get hurt. Even worse than before."

"But aren't you bothered they'll get away? They ruined your life, Carla."

She nodded. "Of course, I'm angry. But what can I do? It's out of my hands."

"Look, I just have a few questions. It won't take too long—"

"I'm really busy right now, Jessica," she said. "Friends and fans have been calling since the interview to offer their condolences. I really need their support right now."

"What now? Are you still planning to go to the Cayman Islands like you said in the interview?"

She frowned. "The Cayman Islands? Uh, no, I'm not heading there. All I know is that I can't stay in Milan any longer. My time here is up, and I have to move on with my life."

"So you'll walk away from fashion? Just like that?"

She huffed. "What else would you have me do, Jessica? If I continue, the Crimson Caper will come after me again." She looked over her shoulder into the room and then back at me. "I really must go, Jessica. *Ciao*."

As the door slammed in our faces, I sighed. "So much for my questions."

"Shall we get going, Miss Prince?" Larry asked, checking his watch. "It's almost noon."

I nodded, knocking on Uncle Henry's door. "Uncle Henry? Are you coming with us to the police station? A certain... acquaintance is getting what he deserves."

"No, Jess. Too upset right now," he said from inside. "But good luck—and be safe."

I turned to Larry, Bruce, and Ben, shaking my head. "I hate seeing Uncle Henry like this. He really loves Carla and only wants the best for her. But she won't listen. She really *is* a stubborn woman—and that's coming from another stubborn girl."

"But she listened to the Crimson Caper all right," Ben muttered. "She let them destroy her life *and* her career. And we couldn't stop them. Man, this sucks."

I tapped my chin. "I might know how to catch the Crimson Caper, Ben. Maybe. It's a total long shot, but we have to get to the police station first."

"We're not going to like what you have planned, right?" Ben asked, sighing.

"Probably not, but it could work if I'm right. I just have to make sure of a few things first."

———

When we arrived at the police station, it was quieter than usual. No doubt the police officers knew about the inspector's plan to trap Salvatore so they made sure to clear out.

"You made it, *Signorina*," the inspector said, walking over to me. "He's almost here."

"Salvatore, right?"

He nodded. "Correct. *Signore* LaDoux and *Signora* Simpson are waiting outside to greet him. He's on his way right now, they said."

"What did they tell him to get him here?"

"They mentioned I was looking to get involved with the drug trade," he replied. "They even gave Salvatore money on my behalf as a down payment—money I look forward to confiscating."

"And Salvatore believed that?" Ben asked. "For a gangster, he's gullible."

The inspector shook his head, chuckling. "No, *Signore* —he *was* skeptical as I knew he would be. I had my officers stage a photo of me selling drugs to convince him. He was more than happy to have a member of the *polizia* on his team. He believes he's coming here to recruit me."

"And he's okay with walking into a police department on his own? As a mobster?" Ben asked. "Isn't that stupid?"

"He believes he's invincible. He's not aware of the evidence we have—or how *Signore* LaDoux double-crossed him. His cockiness will be his downfall."

"Inspector Esposito?" An officer approached. "His car just arrived. It's time."

"That's good. *Signorina* Prince, please take your friends and stay behind the main desk," the inspector said. "Wouldn't want him to run before I have a chance to arrest him."

I nodded, guiding Ben, Bruce, and Larry behind the desk. A few minutes later, Sasha and Lance walked through the front doors. They gave the inspector a little nod before Bruno Salvatore walked in after them with his security guards.

"Inspector Esposito," Salvatore said, bowing his head. "Nice to see you."

"And you, *Signore* Salvatore," the inspector replied, "but I'd much prefer you behind bars."

Salvatore chuckled. "On what charges, Inspector? I haven't done anything."

"You came here to proposition me and my officers. To have us join your drug organization," the inspector said. "Don't pretend this is an innocent visit, *Signore*."

"You can't prove anything, Inspector," Salvatore said, shrugging. "And it would be embarrassing for you to try."

"You must be mistaken, *Signore*," the inspector replied, pulling out a hard drive from his pocket. "I have all the evidence I need—files of your drug sales, buyers and sellers, and audio of you confirming your operation."

Salvatore glared at Sasha and Lance. "What's he talking about?"

"Ever since your proposition, I've been working with Interpol to bust you," Sasha replied. "And I think I have enough evidence to do just that. Should've been more careful, Salvatore. Or did you think we'd never have the guts to turn you in?"

Lance crossed his arms, nodding. "Time to pay for your crimes, *Monsieur* Salvatore. Nobody gets away with blackmailing Lance LaDoux. We aren't afraid of you anymore."

"And what about you, *Signore* LaDoux?" Salvatore asked. "You enjoyed working with me, didn't you? You had no problem taking your cut—even hoarding money for yourself."

Lance shook his head. "The lying words of a desperate man, Inspector. You can't listen to him."

"*Signore* LaDoux and *Signora* Simpson are innocent," the inspector replied. "They proved that by working undercover. And no jury would believe a mobster like yourself."

"I'm not going to prison. Not like this," Salvatore snarled, turning to his guards. "*Mio Dio*, don't just stand there. Do something!"

As his security guards removed their guns, a swarm of police officers with their weapons high surrounded them. The security guards lowered their firearms and Salvatore scoffed.

"It's over, *Signore* Salvatore," the inspector said, handcuffing him. "After years of extortion and selling narcotics, your own foolishness and hubris has ruined you."

"You can't trust LaDoux, Inspector," Salvatore said as they escorted him and his guards to the cells. "He's no saint!"

After he was gone, Lance shook his head. "Thugs like him will say anything to exonerate themselves. Pathetic."

"What will you do now, Mister LaDoux?" I asked. "You're still poor, aren't you?"

He sighed, nodding. "*Oui,* but I'll find a way. I always do. No need to worry about me, *Mademoiselle* Prince."

"In the meantime, my officers will search his properties to confiscate any drugs and money we find," the inspector said. "*Grazie* for your help, everyone."

"*Oui*, Inspector—it was no problem."

Sasha nodded. "Yeah, it's just good to have him off our backs. And we saved a lot of fashion designers in the process. Who knows what other industries he would've infiltrated next? We did the whole world a favor."

"Indeed. And if you don't need me any longer," Lance began, "I must meet with an old friend. *Au revoir.*"

"I should go, too," Sasha said. "I need a long bubble bath before I leave for New York—without a gangster to stop me this time."

"Will you get back into modeling now?" I asked.

She shrugged. "Maybe. Although, I did enjoy working undercover. And by the way, I saw the interview Carla gave. It's a sad day for the fashion industry—especially with the Crimson Caper still out there. But at least Salvatore's dealt with. See you around."

After she and Lance left, the inspector grinned. "We did it, *Signorina* Prince. We caught a mobster *and* the Crimson Caper."

I frowned. "We did?"

He nodded. "Indeed. Bruno Salvatore *is* the Crimson Caper."

"Why do you think that?"

"It's obvious, isn't it? You explained his motive to me," the inspector replied. "He wanted Carla to work for him, so he decided to ruin her career—draining her money and destroying her reputation. We know he propositioned her many times. When most of the attacks took place, Salvatore was missing, wasn't he? Perfect opportunity. Salvatore would get to be her hero—and in return, she'd be forced to help him with his illegal operations."

I shook my head, sighing. "No, Inspector. I wish it was Salvatore, but you're wrong. He had nothing to do with the sabotage. I guarantee you won't find any evidence of the Crimson Caper when you search his house."

It was the inspector's turn to frown. "Do you know something I don't, *Signorina*?"

I nodded, pulling out a napkin from my purse. I scribbled down an address with instructions and handed it to Inspector Esposito. "Yeah, and I don't have time to explain. Just come to this address and hide in the shadows, okay? If they see you, they might not admit it."

"Jess? What's going on?" Ben asked.

"Take Larry and Bruce and go with the inspector. I need to confront the Crimson Capers alone," I replied. "We need to hurry, though. They're getting away right now."

"Crimson Capers? Plural, *Signorina*?" the inspector asked.

"Yeah, plural. You once thought the Crimson Caper might be my uncle and an accomplice, so a team shouldn't be a surprise to you. Oh, and one more thing," I said. "Stop by and pick up Vincent, Antonio, and Enrique. But do it fast, okay? I'll text Uncle Henry and have him meet you at the location, too. I just hope he won't be too mad at me for running off again. But maybe he'll get over it when I solve this case."

"*Signorina* Prince, what is going on—"

I ignored him, rushing out the door. "Just follow the note and my instructions, Inspector. I'll explain everything soon!"

As I caught a cab outside of the police station, I gave the driver the address and told him to step on it. While he sped through the traffic, I called Uncle Henry on his cell phone.

"Hello, Jess," he said, picking up the phone. He still sounded a little sad. "Did everything work out at the police station? You still safe?"

"I am. And yeah, we busted Salvatore. He's going to jail for good," I replied. "But it's not why I called you. I texted you an address. You need to meet me there. When you find Inspector Esposito, he'll show you where to go. I gave him instructions too. Did you see the text yet?"

"Yes, I see it. But why the airport? We still have a day left of March Break. You aren't suggesting we leave early, are you? Jess, are you up to something again? Something I won't approve of?"

I sighed. "Maybe. It's not about March Break—and we're not leaving yet. Trust me, okay? Get down here as fast as you can. It has to do with Carla. She's in trouble."

I knew that would convince him. Before he could argue or question me, I hung up. I searched the online airport itinerary on my phone, looking for one flight in particular. The only flight listed.

Which would lead me to a direct confrontation with the Crimson Capers.

My heart pounded as the taxi pulled up to the airport. I flung a bunch of Euros at the driver, then he grinned and thanked me. When I'm nervous, I spend a lot of money. It helps to calm me down—but unfortunately, it didn't this time.

I rushed over to the front desk, relieved to find the secretary spoke English well. "Has flight eighty-seven left for the Cayman Islands yet?"

She brought it up on her computer, shaking her head. "No, *Signorina*—not yet. It's set for take-off in ten minutes."

I laughed nervously, doing my best dumb blonde impression. "Well, you see, I like, totally lost my ticket. I'm supposed to be on that flight. I can't wait to get a nice tan!"

She frowned. "Then I can't help you. No ticket, no flight. I'm terribly sorry."

"Oh, wait!" I replied, slapping my forehead. "I might've given my ticket to my friend, Lance LaDoux. Or maybe it was Carla Valentine. These things slip my mind sometimes. They *are* on the itinerary, right?"

"Friends, you say?"

"We're very close. I just spent the last week with them. We're supposed to continue our vacation, but as I said...."

She gave me a skeptical look. "I'm sorry, but I really can't divulge any information. For safety reasons. I'm sure you understand, *sí*?"

"Look, my name's Jessica Prince. I'm Henry Prince's niece," I replied. "Have you heard of him?"

She thought for a moment. "He's an American billionaire, isn't he? Wasn't he considered a suspect in the Crimson Caper investigation?"

"A total misunderstanding," I replied, twirling my hair. "He'll be *really* mad if I miss this flight. He booked it as a special treat for me, you know. Anyway, he's good friends with your Inspector Esposito. You know, the one investigating the Crimson Caper case? If I complain to him that you didn't let me on the flight, well, I'd hate for you to get in trouble. With the inspector *or* my uncle."

She sighed. "I do really need this job. It isn't easy being a single mother. But I can't get you another ticket. It's sold-out. The people you're looking for are both booked for the flight. *Signore* LaDoux purchased every seat under his name and informed us *Signora* Valentine would accompany him. But he didn't mention you, and if you don't have your ticket, *Signorina*, then there's nothing I can do."

"I'm guessing Lance and Carla already boarded, waiting for it to take-off right now?" I asked, and she nodded. "Just ask them to meet me by the gate. They'll have my ticket and then we can leave together."

"Oh, I don't know, *Signorina*. I really don't want to get in trouble with the airline...."

"Don't worry, I won't tell anyone. Like I said, once Carla and Lance see me, everything will be cleared up." I reached into my purse then pulled out a wad of Euros. "And there's a generous tip involved if you help me out."

Her eyes lit up as I fanned the money. "Maybe I can make an exception. But...this is still criminal. If the airline found out, I'd lose my job. How will I take care of my family then?"

"My uncle would make sure you were well-compensated. Look, Carla and Lance are up to something. I have reason to believe they know more about the Crimson Caper. So, if you help me, everyone will be so focused on that case that they won't remember what you did."

She sighed. "Very well. As long as you don't tell anyone about me. Come—right this way."

After giving her the money, I followed her through the crowd to the closed gate to flight 87. The secretary spoke with a security guard standing nearby, gesturing at me as they spoke in Italian. I gave a little wave and flipped my hair like a stereotypical dumb blonde.

The security guard picked up a walkie-talkie and spoke into it. The secretary walked over to me, nodding. "Your friends are on their way, *Signorina* Prince. But please be quick, all right? The flight's set to take-off soon. And I don't want to get in trouble."

"No problem. This totally won't take long," I replied. "But when they come, can you give us some privacy? I need to discuss something with them."

"That's not what we discussed."

I withdrew another handful of money.

"But seeing as your uncle is Henry Prince... okay, I can make it happen." She took the cash. The guard held out his hand, then she shared half. "But as I said, be quick, *per favore*."

I smiled, sweetly. "Thank you so much! You're like, the best person ever."

The secretary lady and the security guard left, leaving me in silence. I tapped my heel nervously on the tile floor, preparing my speech. A few minutes later, Carla and Lance came out of the hallway behind the long gate. As I suspected, they carried several suitcases with them, suggesting they had left in a rush.

"Jessica? What are you doing here? How did you get past security?" Carla asked, approaching me. "When the security guard radioed, I thought it was something serious."

"It *is* serious. I didn't realize you were leaving so soon," I replied. "You weren't going to say goodbye to me? What about Uncle Henry?"

She sighed. "I told you, Jessica—I need to move on. There's no point staying in Milan. I don't feel safe with the Crimson Caper around."

"So you're going to the Cayman Islands with Lance." I shook my head. "Give it up, Carla. I know everything."

"What do you mean, *Mademoiselle* Prince?" Lance asked, furrowing his eyebrows.

Before I could speak, Carla interrupted me. "It doesn't matter, Lance. If we stay here and chat, we'll miss our flight. Sorry, Jessica, but we need to go. *Ciao*."

As they walked through the gate, I followed them,

closing the door behind me. I'd have to be quick. The secretary and the security guard would return, and I was sure they'd realize I lied to them about having a ticket.

The hallway led to the other side of the tarmac where airplanes waited to take-off. Carla and Lance, with their suitcases in tow, rushed to the closest one. I assumed it was Flight 87 because no one else sat onboard.

"Carla, wait!" I said, chasing after her. "You can't leave yet!"

"Jessica, you can't be here," she replied, turning around. "You're going to get in trouble. You don't even have a ticket."

"I'm not going away until we talk—and I'm not letting you board that plane, either."

Lance sighed. "*Oui*? Then what do you want to talk about, *Mademoiselle* Prince?"

"Let's start with how Carla's the Crimson Caper," I replied, "and how you and Antonio are her accomplices."

Twenty-Nine

DISRUPTED GETAWAY

Lance scoffed. "*Mon Dieu, mademoiselle*! That's quite an accusation."

"Yeah, I know," I replied, crossing my arms, "and I wouldn't say it if I wasn't sure."

"Oh? Then answer this question, Jessica," Carla began. "Why would I sabotage my own fashion show?"

"Ben made me realize it, actually. He noticed how you loved the public eye. You gave interviews, waved to the people, took phone calls from friends offering their support. I remember hearing a phone call on the answering machine at your house. The journalist said he was calling you back, which meant *you* asked him for an interview—not the other way around. You also called Vincent's boss at the paper, telling him about the park incident. You went out of your way to get the media involved. It made you feel good, didn't it? Special?"

Carla shrugged. "So I like attention. I needed it for my fashion to be successful. That doesn't make me the Crimson Caper, Jessica."

"But you're wrong, Carla. It does," I replied. "Because that was your motive. It was a cry for attention—a way to get fame and respect in the fashion world. Being an up-and-comer is hard, and you needed an edge. You wanted more of a fanbase. More fame than just selling clothes online. By sabotaging yourself at your first runway show, you guaranteed sympathy and support from the world."

"Fashion's my one true love, Jessica. Why would I force myself to give it up?"

"You're giving it up for *now*—escaping to the Cayman Islands with Lance while it all blows over," I replied. "But you'll be back one day, and I'm betting the Crimson Caper won't be a problem then. You let it slip on TV you thought the Cayman Islands were a nice vacation spot. When you denied you said it to me, that's how I knew the truth."

"And how do I fit into all of this, *mademoiselle*?" Lance asked. "I can assure you, I am *not* the Crimson Caper."

"You're right—you can't be the Crimson Caper. With your cane and old age, you'd never be able to. But you *did* play a role in all this, whether you wore the crimson outfit or not. When Salvatore said you weren't innocent, I realized it," I replied. "Carla asked you to steal a chunk of Salvatore's drug money which would solve your financial problems—all the while he took the fall for you two. It gave Carla time to escape the Crimson Caper fiasco, and she could plan her comeback. The police would see you as the victim, Lance—and no one would believe a mobster when he accused you. Salvatore's involvement was good timing, and you took advantage of it."

Lance scoffed. "Ridiculous, *mademoiselle. Oui*, I've struggled financially in the past, but I'm above theft."

"Then if you didn't steal some drug money, how did you afford to buy every ticket on an airplane?" I asked. "The secretary told me. I'm guessing it was the only flight available and you wanted to be alone to revel in your victory. And you weren't aware of it, but Sasha and I followed you to the bank with that duffel bag. I saw you make a deposit then transfer the money to an offshore bank account in the Cayman Islands. It wasn't a coincidence it was right before you helped the inspector convict Salvatore. You knew the police would confiscate his drug money, so you needed to steal some first. Not too much to make it look suspicious, but enough for a new life."

Lance didn't reply.

"I only met Lance a few days ago," Carla said. "How could we have planned all this?"

"You didn't—not initially," I replied. "In the beginning, you were only working with Antonio. But when Lance told you about Salvatore's drug trade—forced to by Salvatore himself—you saw an opportunity to make off with thousands. It's why Lance kept wanting to get you alone—and he probably did, sometime before the dinner party. That was why you wanted his money so bad. You knew it came from a thug."

"I'd hate to burst your bubble, Jessica," Carla began, "but it isn't possible for me to be the Crimson Caper. Think back to my second fashion show. I wasn't the one who threw the paint on Josephine. There were witnesses. And I was there the other times when the Crimson Caper attacked, too. I can't be in two places at once."

"That's where Antonio comes in. He was your accomplice—trying to make you look innocent. Inspector Esposito suggested the possibility of two Crimson Capers," I replied. "Antonio was so in love with you that he went along with it. But there were some problems down the road, weren't there? Arguments?"

Carla crossed her arms. "Like what, Jessica?"

"Well, for starters," I began, pulling out my notepad, "Antonio set the fashion palace on fire—accidentally getting trapped inside—and framed Uncle Henry for it. He left the trench coat and threatening note behind so the inspector would know it was the Crimson Caper's fault. It's easy to tell Antonio hates my uncle. I'd guess he's jealous of your past relationship, right? Antonio saw him as a threat? He probably stole the matches from Vincent's apartment to do it. He *was* staying there at the time."

Carla scoffed. "I'd never frame Henry for anything. I still care for him, Jessica. And I wouldn't stand by while an accomplice framed him, either."

"Oh, I believe that," I replied. "I bet you and Antonio argued over who to frame for the Crimson Caper's sabotage. At first, you accused Vincent, but Antonio didn't want his brother to go to jail. Before that, you tried to make it look like Sasha by placing your scarf in her drawer, then later had Tony leave the lipstick threat at the hospital."

"*Mio Dio*, Jessica, this is absurd—"

"You tried to make it look like Josephine by having her design your outfits for you, then you broke into her room to scare her off. You even used Lance's lipstick to write the notes—with his help, of course—trying to make everyone look guilty. Finally, when Antonio was arrested at the hospital, you called Inspector Esposito as the Crimson Caper to protect him. You wanted to throw off the police as much as possible—anything to shift the blame. It's why you swore Antonio was innocent the whole time."

She glared at me but didn't protest. I figured I should continue.

"So Antonio went ahead and framed Uncle Henry, probably taking his fingerprints off those teacups we drank at your house. Antonio snuck in, remember? Only I bet he didn't have to. He was probably already there with you, talking about your next move, and hid when we showed up. He smashed the window to make it look like he broke in," I replied. "When Uncle Henry was arrested, you were genuinely shocked. You had to do something to fix the mess your ex-husband created."

Carla rolled her eyes. "And you have a theory for that, I'm assuming?"

I nodded. "Totally. You decided to dress up like the Crimson Caper and drive into the Markets, using Vincent's car to frame him. You probably went over to Vincent's apartment when he wasn't there, and Antonio let you in—unaware you were stealing his brother's car keys. Then you returned and secretly put them back. You wanted to make Uncle Henry look innocent while he was behind bars—the same thing you did for Antonio. You had the perfect opportunity, too. You refused to come with me and Ben that day, staying at the hotel for an alibi. When I got back, I noticed you had a burn mark on your hand. You claimed it was from the tea—but I think it was from handling the firecrackers. I'm thinking you accidentally burned yourself. Ouchie."

"This is all an elaborate story, Jessica," Carla said. "You've been reading too many mystery novels. You have no real proof."

I pointed at my notepad. "Oh, I think Inspector Esposito will agree with me. When your first fashion show was sabotaged, you disappeared. Josephine thought you went missing, but little did she know what you had planned. When you returned, it was a panic attack, you said. It gave you time for me to see you in the red trench coat and for you to manipulate the light system. When the lights went out, you put up the threatening banner. Red's your favorite color, after all—and you wanted to draw attention to the Crimson Caper. It'd attract the media for sure. Every time you disappeared, something bad happened."

"And? Is that it?"

"No. At the hospital, you said you called to check on Josephine. But while you were on the phone, I overheard you speaking in Italian," I replied. "I talked to Josephine after that. She said she doesn't know a word of Italian. When Ben turned on the subtitles for your TV interview, I remembered. I bet you were talking to Antonio on the phone all those times instead, probably planning more sabotage."

Carla was silent for a minute. "That hardly proves anything, Jessica."

"You and I met in the park that night, while you were dressed as the Crimson Caper. As we spoke, you called Josephine 'Josie.' From everyone I've talked to, you're the only one who used that nickname. It proved the Crimson Caper knew her personally," I replied. "And you tried to frame her again, telling me she wasn't as innocent as I thought. All to cover your tracks. Lance decided to show up, pretending to come from a failed drug deal, just to throw us off again. Playing games with us was your favorite part, right?"

Carla didn't say anything. I knew I was on a roll.

"And the red paint incident," I continued. "That was Antonio again, wasn't it? It's why I found drops of red paint near his seat in the crowd. I bet when the inspector takes a sample of his hair, it'll match the one left on the paint can. He accidentally left it there when he poured the paint over Josephine to cause a scene again. *And* he stole the clothes backstage and left that threatening note in your workshop. You told me he had a key, remember?"

Carla laughed. "You're insane. This must be a joke."

"I wish it were," I replied. "You see, little things you did started to add up. All your little mistakes. I wanted to give you the benefit of the doubt, but I couldn't ignore the evidence. And as my friend Madison said, sometimes the person least likely to commit the crime is guilty. You tried to get away with it, but you made too many mistakes."

Carla didn't say anything. She blinked, knowing I'd caught her.

"Since the final outfit set of the Crimson Caper wasn't necessary, I think I know where it is," I said, stepping forward. "Mind if I take a look through your suitcase, Carla?"

"No!" Carla replied, looking back at Lance and then me again. "*Mio Dio*, it wasn't supposed to be like this, Jessica. What started out as a simple way to get people to notice me was ruined by Antonio. He took it too far with the arson. He even put oil on the runway, despite my protests. Sasha could've been killed. I told him I didn't want anything violent or dangerous."

"But he didn't listen to you, right?"

Carla nodded, lowering her eyes. "Indeed. He was a fool in love—and it let me take advantage of him. When he framed Henry, I realized he was crazy and unpredictable. I wanted nothing more to do with him. But I couldn't turn him in or I'd implicate myself."

"Is that why he's not invited to your private getaway?"

Carla laughed. "Do you think I'd ever want an imbecile like him? I tried that once, and it didn't end well. But he *was* a big help with the sabotage, and I couldn't have done it without him. He knows nothing of our escape—and I won't let him see a dime of Salvatore's money. Now, how did you even find us, Jessica?"

"It was simple. I did a search on flights leaving Milan to the Cayman Islands," I replied. "There was only one in town —a commercial flight right at this airport. But you won't be making your flight, Carla. Inspector Esposito will be here soon. You can tell him everything you told me. It's the right thing to do, you know."

Lance reached into his pocket then pulled out a pistol. It looked like the same kind Salvatore and his thugs used. "I'm afraid not, *mademoiselle*. As I stole Salvatore's money, I borrowed one of his spare firearms for protection. I paid off a security guard to let it pass undetected through customs. He really needed the money—something about his mother undergoing cancer treatments. Good thinking, *oui*?"

I stared down at the gun. "Hmm. What about Manuel, your butler? Is he involved?"

Lance shook his head. "He knew about Salvatore, but I forced him to stay quiet—threatened him to. I paid his salary with Salvatore's money. But he knows nothing about the Crimson Caper—you're the only one who does. And in a few minutes, you won't be able to tell anyone, *mademoiselle*."

I looked back at Carla. "Will you really let him kill me, Carla? My death will hurt Uncle Henry. Don't you love him?"

She sighed. "I do, Jessica—but I have no choice. I can't go to jail. If I do, everyone will know the truth. My reputation will be ruined, and I'll never be able to return to fashion like I planned."

"I think you ruined your reputation yourself when you planned the Crimson Caper," I muttered. "Don't do this, Lance. Neither of you are murderers."

"*Oui, mademoiselle*," Lance began. "We're not murderers, but we *are* opportunists. If killing you means we keep our freedom, it's a worthy trade, don't you think?"

As Lance lifted the gun, I closed my eyes. I thought about Uncle Henry, Ben, Madison, Tiffany, and how I'd never see them again.

"Stop right there, *Signore* LaDoux!" Inspector Esposito cried behind me. "Put down the gun, *per favore*."

I opened my eyes and spun around. The inspector, with several officers by his side, had his weapon pointed at Lance.

Behind him, the concerned security guard and secretary I had lied to earlier stood there.

Perfect timing.

Lance lowered his gun, cursing in French. I took a deep breath while my heart raced. When I saw Uncle Henry and Ben, they rushed over to embrace me.

"Jess, we were so worried," Uncle Henry said, kissing my forehead. "A second later and Lance would've shot you."

"Yeah, not cool. Almost gave me a heart attack," Ben said. "But did you find the Crimson Capers?"

I nodded. "Carla and Antonio are the Crimson Capers. Lance stole millions from Salvatore's drug trade, and the two of them were planning to escape to the Cayman Islands together. Speaking of Antonio, did you bring him and the others, Inspector?"

"I'm right here, *Signorina* Prince," Antonio said, glaring at Carla and Lance. "Was this your plan, *amore*? To make me do your dirty work and then leave me in the dust?"

Carla sighed. "Tony, I can explain—"

"Jeez. I thought by helping you, you'd care about me again," Antonio said, shaking his head. "*Mio Dio*, I *am* a fool."

"I tried to warn you, brother," Vincent muttered. "You never listen."

"Carla doesn't care about anyone but herself," Uncle Henry said, glaring at her. "Isn't that right, Carla?"

She took a step forward, tears welling in her eyes. "I do love you, Henry. Believe that, *per favore*."

"I don't believe a word out of your mouth. Take her away, Inspector," Uncle Henry spat. "I can't look at her anymore."

"One last thing," I said. "Was I right before? Were you trying to taunt me by leaving clues I'd recognize? All the writing was in English, and you asked specifically for me in the park."

Carla scoffed. "That's true. You were always so nosy—so inquisitive. I wanted to scare you so you'd stop looking for the Crimson Caper, but you never did. I never thought you'd be the one to discover the truth. An annoying little girl."

I nodded. "People always underestimate teenagers. We notice more than adults think—and this time, it cost you everything."

Uncle Henry shook his head. "Goodbye, Carla. May you get what you deserve in prison."

The officers handcuffed Carla, Antonio, and Lance, dragging them back to the gate. As Carla left, she cried over her shoulder, begging for Uncle Henry to help her. He didn't glance her way at all. If I weren't so angry, I would've pitied her.

"They'll explain everything to you, Inspector—and my notes will help build your case," I said, handing him my notepad. "I wish it didn't end this way. I liked Carla and her fashion. I truly wanted to help her. For my uncle's sake, too. I had no idea she was the Crimson Caper all along until I really thought about it and it started to make sense."

"No one would've guessed," Uncle Henry said, sighing. "Not even me, and I knew the woman for a long time. She had us all fooled. You can't blame yourself, Jess."

"Your uncle is right. *Grazie, Signorina* Prince," the inspector said, taking my notepad. "If it weren't for you, I would've sent Salvatore to jail for the wrong crime. At least his drug operation will end, but it appears I have some things to learn from you, don't I?"

I shook my head. "Not true, Inspector. If anything, I was the one who was trying to keep up with *you*."

"I'd say you both helped each other. You made a good

team—despite my objections." Uncle Henry checked his watch. "Well, we still have a few hours in Milan before March Break is over. How about we go out for a proper meal now that this Crimson Caper business is over? You're welcome to join, Inspector."

"I think I will," Inspector Esposito said. "I know a great place not far from here."

I nodded. "Sounds great. I'm craving some authentic pizza. Solving a mystery really works up an appetite, you know."

Uncle Henry chuckled. "Oh, Jess. Never change."

Epilogue

MILAN TO WILLOWBROOK

After a lovely meal at a proper Italian restaurant—the first one we had in Milan—I said goodbye to the inspector. He told me he looked forward to me returning to Milan one day, and if I ever had a problem, I could call him for help. Despite living across the ocean. I thought it was pretty cool as I'd never had an inspector as a friend before. I had learned so much from him.

And maybe he had learned something from me. I hoped so, at least.

I visited the doctor once more who said my concussion had healed up nicely. Then we prepared to head home. Uncle Henry offered Sasha and Josephine a flight back to New York City on the Lady Luck—a slight detour from heading straight home to Willowbrook. They tried to refuse but Uncle Henry wouldn't take no for an answer. An hour later, Larry drove us all to the airport and we boarded my uncle's private jet.

"I can't believe Carla was the Crimson Caper this whole time," Josephine said. "And right under my nose, too. But do you know the upside?"

"I didn't think there was an upside," I replied, frowning.

She beamed. "Well, I was offered a job in New York City. Vogue heard I was Carla's assistant and felt bad for what I'd been through. They're really looking forward to working with me. Maybe one day, if I learn a lot from them, I'll even get to design my own fashion line. Can you believe that? Vogue!"

"I'm happy for you, Josephine. You deserve it," Sasha said. "But I think I'm going to pursue a career in law enforcement. The high stress of the fashion industry turned me into a brat... and a smoker. But don't worry—I'm kicking the habit. I've got a Nicotine patch under my shirt. And busting Salvatore was just too much fun. I should've realized something was up with Lance, though."

I shook my head. "He fooled us all, Sasha—Carla and Antonio did, too. The inspector told me their list of arrests is a mile long, and they're implicated in even more ongoing investigations. Sabotage, arson, lying to the police, theft. They're all going to jail for a long time."

"So is Bruno Salvatore. Heard his trial takes place later this week. He's not getting away this time, the inspector told me," Sasha replied. "And Enrique and Vincent are doing much better with Carla gone. Enrique's putting on his own fashion show—without Salvatore forcing him to work with him this time. Vincent's popular in the journalism world after interviewing the Crimson Caper herself, I heard."

"I guess everything worked out—except for the guilty ones," Josephine said. "Did you ever get an update on that evidence, like the hair on the paint can? Still can't believe that happened to me. It took several showers to wash it all off. Gross."

I nodded. "The hair strand matched Antonio—and oil was found in his apartment, used on the runway. The last Crimson Caper costume *was* in Carla's suitcase, just like I thought. I wish I'd been wrong about them, though. For my uncle's sake."

As the airplane ascended, I noticed Uncle Henry sitting alone by the window. I excused myself and walked over, taking a seat beside him. He looked up and gave me a small smile. I could always tell when something was bothering him.

"Hey. How are you doing?" I asked.

He shrugged, gazing out the window at the city below. "I loved Carla once—a part of me still does. I can't believe she'd do something so terrible. And she lied to my face so easily at the same time. She also put you, my only niece, in trouble more times than I can count on one hand."

"Yeah. I know you're hurt, but Carla will get what she deserves. The inspector will make sure of it." I placed my hand on his shoulder. "And don't worry. You'll find someone else who won't lie to you—someone much better. Trust me."

"I hope so," he muttered. "But I think I'm taking a break from relationships. When we get home, it's back to business."

Ben walked over, glancing out the window. "Man, there goes Milan. And to think we barely saw it!"

I nodded. "It *does* feel like we spent the whole week looking for the Crimson Caper."

"That's because we did, Jess—thanks to you," Ben replied. "But if you hadn't taken an interest in the case, Carla, Antonio, and Lance never would've gotten caught. A part of me wishes I didn't have to leave, though."

I frowned. "Why? Don't you miss home?"

He nodded. "Oh, sure I do. But don't you remember what my dad said? How I was able to go to Milan, but I'd be grounded when I got back? Gotta face my punishment. So don't solve any mysteries without me while I'm on house arrest, okay?"

I laughed. "I'll try, but they seem to follow me around. I can't wait to get home and tell Mads and Tiff I solved my first case. They'll be so proud!"

As I slunk down in my seat, preparing for the long flight, I pulled out the latest Julia Joy novel. Just as I opened the first page, excited for another thrilling read, I heard Ben chuckling.

"What?" I asked, looking up at him.

"You're reading more mystery? Aren't you sick of it yet?"

I smiled. "Me? Never."

THE END

THANK YOU FOR READING

Did you enjoy this book?

We invite you to leave a review at the website of your choice, such as Goodreads, Amazon, Barnes & Noble, etc.

DID YOU KNOW THAT LEAVING A REVIEW...

- Helps other readers find books they may enjoy.
- Gives you a chance to let your voice be heard.
- Gives authors recognition for their hard work.
- Doesn't have to be long. A sentence or two about why you liked the book will do.

About the Author

Dana Gricken is an author from Ottawa, Ontario, Canada. From self-publishing her first series in 2018, she's gone on to sign book deals with Fire and Ice Young Adult, Melange Books, Oliver-Heber Books, and Evernight Teen.

Please stay tuned for announcements on new books! In the meantime, if you've read and enjoyed her work, please don't hesitate to reach out to Dana on Twitter and Instagram—both @DanaGricken or her official website.

In her spare time, she enjoys watching Star Trek with her cats, reading, cooking, spreading kindness online, educating about mental health struggles, and playing video games. She hopes her books bring joy to people and wants to write over a hundred novels in her lifetime.

danagricken.com

facebook.com/dana.gricken.7

x.com/DanaGricken

instagram.com/danagricken

Also by Dana Gricken

WITH FIRE & ICE YOUNG ADULT BOOKS

Jessica Prince Mysteries

Jessica Prince and the Crimson Caper

Kingdom of V Trilogy

Kingdom of V

The Astrid Legacy

Coming of Age

The Soulless Trilogy

The Dark Queen

The Dark Evolution

Dark Cage

Novels

Chatter

www.ingramcontent.com/pod-product-compliance
Lightning Source LLC
LaVergne TN
LVHW090550110826
845146LV00001B/85

* 9 7 9 8 8 8 6 5 3 4 7 8 8 *